DORR TOWNSHIP LIBRARY (DOR)
3 1341 00060 3283
W9-AFR-293

Falling Awake

Falling Awake

JAYNE ANN KRENTZ

THORNDIKE
WINDSOR
PARAGON

This Large Print edition is published by Thorndike Press®, Waterville, Maine USA and by BBC Audiobooks, Ltd, Bath, England.

Published in 2005 in the U.S. by arrangement with G. P. Putnam's Sons, a division of Penguin Group (USA) Inc.

Published in 2005 in the U.K. by arrangement with Judy Piatkus (Publishers) Ltd.

U.S. Hardcover 0-7862-6641-4 (Basic)
U.K. Hardcover 1-4056-1102-2 (Windsor Large Print)
U.K. Softcover 1-4056-2089-7 (Paragon Large Print)

The text of this Large Print edition is unabridged.
Other aspects of the book may vary from the original edition.

Set in 16 pt. Plantin by Minnie B. Raven.

Printed in the United States on permanent paper.

British Library Cataloguing-in-Publication Data available

Library of Congress Cataloging-in-Publication Data

Krentz, Jayne Ann.
Falling awake / Jayne Ann Krentz.
p. cm.
ISBN 0-7862-6641-4 (lg. print : hc : alk. paper)
1. Dreams — Fiction. 2. Sleep — Research — Fiction.
3. Undercover operations — Fiction. 4. Large type books.
I. Title.
PS3561.R44F35 2004b
813′.54—dc22 2004057992

For Louisa Edwards, with thanks for the title. Yep, you were definitely cut out for a career in publishing!

DREAM ANALYSIS NUMBER: 2-10

Prepared for: Client #2
Rank of Dreamer: Level 5 on the Belvedere Lucid Dream Scale
Analyst: I. Wright, Research Assistant, Belvedere Center for Sleep Research

ANALYSIS AND INTERPRETATION

The elements and symbols indicative of extreme violence and sexual perversion in this dream are so exaggerated and so bizarre that they point to the conclusion that the individual perpetrating the acts is in the grip of a chaotic bloodlust. It is, however, the opinion of this analyst that such a conclusion would be a mistake. On the contrary, it is likely that the perpetrator may have deliberately staged his crimes with the goal of ensuring that investigators will view them as the creations of a deranged mind.

This analyst suggests that the key to unlocking the hidden message of this dream is the red scarf that the dreamer saw when he opened the closet door. Lacking additional context, this is as far as it is possible to take the analysis.

Submitted by: I. Wright

PS: This analyst cannot help but notice that the dreamer (Client #2) again reports the excessive and disorienting noise of the roller coaster in the gateway dream. This is the third such dream in which that occurs. It indicates that the dreamer is still experiencing a considerable degree of physical pain. Although Client #2 is clearly capable of controlling this discomfort while in the Level 5 lucid dream state, it is, at the very least, a serious distraction.

It is assumed that Client #2 consulted a doctor as this analyst advised in postscripts to the first two of these "loud" dreams and did not receive much help. Additional steps to help manage the pain and discomfort should be taken immediately.

This analyst suggests that the dreamer make an appointment with an acupuncturist.

DREAM ANALYSIS NUMBER: 2-11

Prepared for: Client #2
Rank of Dreamer: Level 5 on the Belvedere Lucid Dream Scale
Analyst: I. Wright, Research Assistant, Belvedere Center for Sleep Research.

ANALYSIS AND INTERPRETATION

The repetition of the color aqua blue is the most significant aspect of this dream report. All of these blue elements (the hammer, computer, photograph and mirror) have at least two things in common: (1) each is an object that is not customarily aqua blue in color, and (2) each is an object that does not appear to belong to the setting in which it was found. It is no doubt for these reasons that Client #2 has identified them with an odd color while in the Level 5 lucid dream state.

It is strongly suggested that these items be reexamined in light of this analysis.

More detailed context would, as always, be *greatly appreciated* by this analyst as it would allow for a more complete interpretation.

Submitted by: I. Wright

PS: This analyst is pleased to note that the extreme roller coaster noise of the earlier gateway dreams has receded in this dream report. She hopes this means that the acupuncture was successful and that the dreamer is no longer experiencing as much physical pain as was previously indicated.

It is also assumed that Client #2 is continuing to follow the steps this analyst recommended at the outset of this consulting relationship. In this analyst's experience, these measures help mitigate the traumatic effects of violent and bizarre Level 5 dreams: (1) Eat a primarily vegetarian diet (some fish is allowed but the client should definitely avoid red meat). (2) Do not watch violent films (old-fashioned 1930s-style screwball comedies are strongly suggested). (3) Do not read serial killer and other such graphically violent novels. They are obviously much too similar to your Level 5 dreams and will tend to reinforce the violent imagery. Romance novels are highly recommended instead.

1

A funeral always made for a bad day. Knowing that it was probably his screwup that had put Katherine Ralston into the ground made things a whole lot worse for Ellis Cutler that afternoon.

He was supposed to be able to predict the actions of his quarry. Everyone who had ever worked with him said he was a major dream talent. Hell, he was a legend back at Frey-Salter Inc., or at least he had been until a few months ago, when the rumors started up.

But in spite of his track record, the grim truth was that it had never even occurred to him that Vincent Scargill might kill Katherine.

"May God in his infinite mercy grant to Katherine's family and friends the serenity and peace of mind that can only come from the sure and certain knowledge that their loved one is at last in a safe harbor . . ."

Katherine had been murdered in her apartment in Raleigh, North Carolina, but her relatives had brought her body home to this small town in Indiana to bury. It was ten o'clock in the morning, but the muggy heat of a Midwestern summer day was building fast. The sky was heavy and leaden. Wind stirred the old oaks that stood sentinel in the cemetery. Ellis could hear thunder in the distance.

He kept apart from the crowd of mourners, occupying his own private space. The others were all strangers to him. He had met Katherine on only a handful of occasions. She had been hired after he officially resigned from his position at Frey-Salter to *pursue other interests,* as Jack Lawson put it. He still freelanced for Lawson, however, and he allowed himself to be dragged back half a dozen times a year to conduct seminars with the new recruits. Katherine had attended a couple of his workshops. He recalled her as an attractive, vivacious blonde.

Lawson had told him she was not only a Level Five dreamer but also a whiz with computers. Lawson loved high-tech gadgets but had no aptitude for dealing with them. He had been delighted with Katherine's skill.

Ellis felt like a vulture standing at Katherine's graveside. The malevolent cloud cover made the wraparound, obsidian-tinted sunglasses he wore unnecessary, but he did not remove them. Force of habit. He had discovered a long time ago that dark glasses were one more way of keeping a safe distance between himself and other people.

The solemn service did not last long. When the final prayers had been spoken, Ellis turned and started back toward his rental car. There was nothing more he could do here.

"Did you know her?"

The voice came from behind and a few yards off. Ellis halted and looked back over his shoulder. A young man who appeared to be in his early twenties was approaching swiftly across the wet grass. There was a churning intensity in the long, quick strides. He had Katherine's blue eyes and lean, dramatic features. Katherine's personnel file had mentioned a twin brother.

"We were colleagues," Ellis said. He searched for something that might sound appropriate and came up empty. "I'm sorry."

"Dave Ralston." Dave halted in front of him, bitter disappointment tightening his face and narrowing his eyes. "I thought maybe you were a cop."

"What made you think that?"

"You look like one." Dave shrugged, impatient and intense. "Also, you're not from around here. No one recognized you." He hesitated. "I've heard that the police often attend the funeral when there's been a murder. Some theory about the killer showing up in the crowd."

Ellis shook his head once. "I'm sorry," he said again.

"You said you worked with my sister?"

"I'm affiliated with Frey-Salter, the firm where she was employed in North Carolina. My name is Ellis Cutler."

Recognition and suspicion quickened in Dave's expression. "Katherine mentioned you. Said you used to work as some kind of special analyst at Frey-Salter but that you'd left to become an outside consultant. She said you were practically a legend."

"She exaggerated."

Dave stared hard at the cream-colored, generic-looking Ford parked under an oak. "That yours?"

"A rental. Picked it up at the airport."

Dave's mouth twisted in frustration. Ellis's intuition told him that the young man had been busily memorizing the license plate until he discovered the car was a rental.

"You probably heard that the cops think

my sister was murdered because she interrupted a burglary in her apartment."

"Yes," Ellis said.

He hadn't just heard the theory, he'd read every word of the investigating officer's report, probing for anything that might give him a lead in his own quest. He'd also looked at the photos of the victim. He hoped Dave hadn't seen those. Katherine had been shot at close range.

"My parents and the others are buying that story." Dave glanced briefly over his shoulder at the small group of people walking slowly away from the grave. "But I'm not. Not for a minute."

Ellis nodded, saying nothing.

"Do you know what I think, Mr. Cutler?"

"No."

Dave's hands tightened into fists at his sides. "I'm almost positive that Katherine was killed because of her connection to Frey-Salter."

Lawson was not going to like this, Ellis thought. The last thing the director wanted was to draw attention to his private fiefdom. After all, Frey-Salter Inc., was a carefully constructed corporate front for the highly classified government agency that Jack Lawson ruled.

"Why would anyone want to kill Katherine?" Ellis asked, keeping his voice as neutral as possible.

"I'm not sure," Dave admitted, his face stony. "But I think it might have been because she discovered something going on there that she wasn't supposed to know. She said that Frey-Salter was real big on confidentiality. Lot of secrecy involved. When she took the job she had to sign papers promising not to discuss sensitive information with anyone outside the firm."

Something about the way Dave's gaze shifted briefly and then quickly refocused in an intent stare told Ellis that he probably knew a lot more about his sister's work than he should have. But if there was a problem in that direction, it was Lawson's concern, he thought. He had his own issues.

"Signing a confidentiality statement is a common requirement in companies that conduct high-stakes research," Ellis said mildly. "Corporate espionage is a major problem."

"I know." Dave hunched his shoulders. Anger vibrated through him in visible waves. "I'm wondering if maybe Katherine uncovered something like that going on."

"Corporate espionage?"

"Right. Maybe someone killed her to keep her quiet."

Just what he needed, Ellis thought, a distraught brother who had come up with a conspiracy theory to explain his sister's murder.

"Frey-Salter does sleep and dream research," Ellis reminded him, trying to sound calm and authoritative. "There's not a lot of motive for murder in that field."

Dave took a step back, suspicion gathering in his eyes. "Why should I trust you to tell me the truth? You work for Frey-Salter."

"Outside consultant."

"What's the difference? You're still loyal to them. They're paying your salary."

"Only a portion of it," Ellis said. "I've got a day job now."

"If you hardly knew Katherine, why are you here?" Dave flexed his hands. "Maybe you're the one who killed her. Maybe that theory about the murderer showing up at the funeral is for real."

This was not going well.

"I didn't kill her, Dave."

"Someone did, and I don't think it was a random burglar. One of these days I'll find out who murdered my sister. When I do, I'm going to make sure he pays."

"Let the cops handle this. It's their job."

"Bullshit. They're useless." Dave whipped around and walked swiftly away across the cemetery.

Ellis exhaled slowly and crossed the grass to where he had parked the rental. He peeled off the hand-tailored charcoal gray jacket, sucking in a sharp breath when the casual movement sent a jolt of pain through his right shoulder. One of these days he would learn, he thought. The wound had healed and he was getting stronger. The visits to the acupuncturist had helped, much to his surprise. But some things would never again be the same. It was lucky he hadn't been passionate about golf or tennis before Scargill almost succeeded in killing him because he sure wasn't going to play either sport in the future.

He put the jacket in the backseat and got behind the wheel. But he did not start the engine immediately. Instead, he sat for a long time, watching the last of the mourners disperse. You never knew. Maybe there was something to that old theory about the killer showing up at the funeral.

If Vincent Scargill had come to bear witness to his crime, however, he succeeded in keeping himself out of sight. Not an easy thing to do in a small town in Indiana.

When there was no one left except the two men with the shovels, Ellis fired up the engine and drove toward the road that would take him back to the airport in Indianapolis. The news of Katherine's death had caught up with him while he was engaged in a series of business meetings in the San Francisco Bay area. He had barely made it to the funeral.

The storm struck twenty minutes later. It unleashed a full barrage of the spectacular special effects that make storms in that part of the country famous. The torrential rain cut visibility down to a bare minimum. Ellis didn't mind the wall of water. He could have driven the complicated maze of roads and state highways that led back to Indianapolis blindfolded. He had driven them once to get to the cemetery and once was all he needed when it came to learning a route. The part of him that intuitively picked up on patterns and registered them in his memory was equally adept at navigating.

Lightning lit up the ominous sky. Thunder cracked. The rain continued, deluging the fields of soybeans and corn that stretched for miles on either side of the highway. The rear wheels of passing cars sent up great plumes of water.

He felt the rush of adrenaline, wonder and awe that he always experienced when the elements went wild. He savored powerful storms the way he savored driving his Maserati, the way, once upon a time, he had savored roller coasters.

The raw, exhilarating passion of the thunderstorm made him think of Tango Dancer, the mysterious lady who sometimes walked through his dreams. He wondered what it would be like to have her sitting in the passenger seat beside him right now. Did she get a kick out of storms? His intuition, or maybe it was his overheated imagination, told him she did but he had no way of knowing for sure.

He wondered what she was doing at that moment out in sunny California. Although she had appeared in his fantasies more times than he could count during the past few months, he had never met her in person. That situation was supposed to have changed by now. He'd made plans. But Vincent Scargill had put those plans on hold.

Reluctantly he pulled his thoughts away from Tango Dancer and contemplated his next move in what his former boss and sometimes client Jack Lawson referred to as his *obsession* with Vincent Scargill. He would go to Raleigh, he decided, and check out the apartment where Katherine's body had been found. Maybe the cops had overlooked some small clue that would point him in a direction that would lead to Scargill.

Unfortunately, there was one real big problem with his personal theory concerning the identity of the man who had murdered Katherine Ralston. It was the reason he had not told Dave Ralston that he thought he knew the name of his sister's killer.

Vincent Scargill was dead.

Dave Ralston sat in his car, parked out of sight on a side road and watched Ellis Cutler drive away into the oncoming storm. Katherine's description of the Frey-Salter legend haunted him. *He's supposed to be the best agent Lawson ever had, but Cutler makes me nervous. You can't tell what he's thinking or feeling. It's as if he's always standing just outside the circle. He watches, but he doesn't join in the game, if you know what I mean. He's the walking definition of a loner.*

Loners were dangerous, Dave thought.

They went their own way and played by their own rules. Maybe this one had committed murder. Or maybe Ellis Cutler was pursuing some secret agenda on behalf of the mysterious Jack Lawson. Either way, Cutler was a for-real, genuine lead, the first one he'd been able to find. He had a name and the number of the rental car. This evening after the crowd of mourners left his parents' house, he would power up his computer and see what he could do with the information he possessed.

He was good with computers, just as Katherine had been good with them. It was one of the many talents they had had in common.

He put the car in gear and drove away from the cemetery without looking back at Katherine's grave. He knew he would not be able to return here to say farewell properly until he found the person who had ended his twin's life.

He had to get some justice for Katherine, he mused, not for her sake but for his own. They had shared that special closeness that only twins can know. She would be a part of him for the rest of his life. He would not be able to live with her memory if he failed to avenge her.

The shrinks had a word for it. *Closure.*

★ ★ ★

The following morning Ellis flashed his Mapstone Investigations ID at the manager of the apartment house on the outskirts of Raleigh where Katherine had lived and asked to borrow the key.

"Place hasn't been cleaned yet," the manager warned.

"No problem," Ellis said.

He let himself into the apartment, closed the door and took a moment to steep himself in the gloomy shadows. He was intensely conscious, as he always was on such occasions, of the respect owed to the memory of the dead.

After a moment, he walked slowly through the apartment, examining every detail closely, storing up the images to be examined later in his dreams.

The blood that had soaked the beige carpet had dried to a terrible, all-too-familiar shade of muddy brown. The killer had toppled the bookcase, emptied drawers and yanked pictures off the walls, no doubt in an attempt to create the impression of a wild, frantic burglary.

When he finished the unpleasant tour he returned to the living room and stood for a while near the patch of dried blood.

That was when he noticed the one object

that did not look as if it belonged in the apartment. The crime scene tape had come down. The police had obviously not considered the item to be evidence. He picked it up and tucked it under his arm.

At the door he paused one last time, allowing the dark, haunting atmosphere to flow over and around him.

I'll find him, Katherine, he vowed.

2

Belvedere Center for Sleep Research, near Los Angeles, California

"I had this really weird dream last night," Ken Payne said from the doorway of Isabel Wright's tiny office.

"Sorry, Ken, I don't have time to talk about your dream right now." Isabel picked up a stack of computer printouts that was only a little higher than Mount Rushmore. She started toward her desk. "I've got an appointment with the new director in a few minutes."

"This will only take a minute." Ken lowered his voice and checked the hallway furtively. "In the dream I'm driving a car toward an intersection and I know I have to brake or there will be a crash but I can't take my foot off the accelerator."

"Ken, please . . ." The toe of her shoe struck the heap of dream logs she had been forced to pile on the floor because every other surface in the cramped room was covered with books, journals and notebooks.

She staggered under the impact. The stack of printouts in her arms wobbled ominously, affecting her balance. She felt herself start to topple to the side.

"Oh, damn."

"Here, let me take those." Ken moved out of the doorway and deftly plucked the printouts from her hands.

"Thank you." Relieved of her burden, she grabbed the back of her desk chair and managed to steady herself

Sphinx, Martin Belvedere's large, ill-tempered tortoiseshell cat, glared from behind the steel grid door of his carrying cage. Isabel knew that excessive human commotion irritated him. Actually, there were a lot of things that irritated Sphinx. He was not in a good mood in the first place because life had changed drastically for him a few days earlier, when Martin Belvedere had dropped dead from a heart attack. Now he was fuming because she had stuffed him into the carrier.

Ken peered around the stack of reports, searching the cluttered office. "Where do you want me to put them?"

She pushed several annoying tendrils of hair out of her eyes, mentally cursing Mr.

Nicholas, her new hairstylist.

Mr. Nicholas was only the latest in a long series of stylists who had promised her the sun, moon and stars. More to the point, he had practically guaranteed that the new cut he had created for her, a style that curled just above her shoulders and framed her face with airy wisps of hair in various lengths, would give her instant sex appeal. The sucker had lied through his perfect white teeth. Her social life had not taken a great leap forward since the last trip to the salon. It had, in fact, slid backward a few notches.

But deep down she knew that, even as she mentally heaped recrimination upon his handsome head, she could not really blame Mr. Nicholas. She had no one to blame for her wretched social life but herself

For as long as she could remember, the only thing men wanted to do to her or with her was tell her their dreams.

Not that she was interested in dating Ken Payne, she thought. He was a cheerful, good-natured sort, always ready with a smile and a funny story; the kind of friend you could call when you needed someone to help you move. He had no doubt been the class clown back in elementary school.

But he was in love with a woman named Susan. Isabel knew that the only thing stopping him from asking his girlfriend to marry him was his recurring dream.

She motioned toward the corner of her desk. "You can set the printouts there."

"You sure? What about those old dream logs?"

"Just put the printouts on top of them, please."

"Okay." Ken cautiously set the stack down. He took a step back, eyeing the unstable-looking result with a dubious expression. "What the hell happened in here, anyway? Place looks like a cyclone hit it. Your office is always a little chaotic but this clutter is a lot worse than usual."

"The new Dr. Belvedere ordered all of his father's papers cleared out of the executive office this morning when he took charge. The janitors were told to take everything to the trash bin out back. I barely managed to catch them in time to rescue this stuff. Five minutes later and I would have had to dig it all out of the garbage."

Ken grimaced and looked at Sphinx. "So, you not only wind up saving the old man's cat from the pound, you also salvaged thirty or forty years' worth of Belvedere's crazy private research. You're too soft-hearted, Isabel."

Sphinx flattened his ears. Isabel stiffened and pushed her new, black-framed glasses up on her nose. In addition to spending a fortune on hairstylists in the past few months, she had also invested heavily in expensive, fashionable optical wear in an attempt to find a *look*.

The exotic, elegantly sculpted frames had been designed in Italy. The salesperson in the optical shop had assured her that they made a statement and brought out the green-gold color of her eyes but she had serious doubts. She had a nasty feeling that another trip to the optician's shop was on the horizon.

That was what came of finally obtaining a professional-level position with an excellent salary and benefits, she thought. The exhilaration of having a stable income at last had enabled her to splurge on a variety of long-delayed indulgences. Her former career as an operator on the Psychic Dreamer Hotline had not stretched to high-end salons and Italian spectacles.

The new clothes and fashion accessories were the least of her major purchases in the past year. The really big investment had been the furniture, all of which had come from Europe and all of which was currently still in the original packing crates and sitting in a rented storage locker because she had not yet found the Dream House.

She frowned at Ken. "Just because no one would publish Dr. B.'s research does not mean that his theories were crazy. Oh, I know what the staff said about him behind his back but you and the others should keep in mind that Dr. B. was your employer and he paid all of us very generous salaries."

Ken winced. "You're right. I suppose it would be more polite to call his theories 'out of the mainstream.' Anyhow, like I was saying, in my dream I'm in my car, heading toward the intersection. I can see another car, a red one, entering the intersection from the street on the left. I know that if I don't stop, I'm going to smash right into the other vehicle. I can see people inside the other car. A woman and a kid. I want to yell at them to stop but I can't —"

"But you know they can't hear you and you can't get your foot off the accelerator and there will be a terrible disaster if you don't find a way to stop the car," Isabel concluded, opening a drawer to remove her new designer shoulder bag. "We've been over this a dozen times, Ken. You know what's going on as well as I do."

Ken exhaled heavily and seemed to slump in on himself. The happy-go-lucky facade disintegrated. He rubbed his face in a weary gesture.

"The heart thing?" he said.

"Yes." She straightened and met his eyes. Her own heart sank when she saw the veiled fear that lurked in his gaze. "The heart thing."

"Yeah, sure." He tried for a wry smile. "I knew that. Hey, I'm an expert on sleep, right? Dr. Kenneth Payne, neuropsychologist and fellow here at the Belvedere Center for Sleep Research. I know an anxiety dream when I see one."

She walked toward him and came to a halt a step away. "I can only give you the same advice today that I gave you the first time you and I talked about the car dreams. Make the appointment with the doctor, Ken."

"I know, I know."

"You're a doctor, yourself. What would you tell one of your patients if he was in your shoes?"

"My doctorate is in psychology, not medicine."

"All the more reason you should realize that you can't postpone this any longer.

Make the appointment with the cardiologist. Give him your family medical history. Tell him that your father and your grandfather both dropped dead from heart attacks in their late forties. Get a thorough physical workup."

"What if it turns out I've got the same genetic heart defect that killed my dad and granddad?"

"They died decades ago. You're living in a different time and place. There are new therapies and treatments available for all kinds of heart problems these days. You know that as well as I do."

"And if it can't be fixed?"

She touched his shoulder. "The dreams aren't going to stop until you know whether or not you inherited the genetic problem. That little kid you see in the car in the intersection? The one whose face you can't quite make out? That's the son you may or may not have someday; the one you're afraid to have because you think you might pass along whatever it is that is killing the men in your family."

His face tightened. "You're right. I know it. I've got to act. Susan is starting to get restless. I can feel it. Last night she asked me if there was something I wasn't telling her."

"There *is* something you aren't telling her. You're afraid to tell her because you think it might scare her off."

"What woman in her right mind would want to risk starting a family with a man who has a serious genetic defect?"

"Make the appointment. Find out whether or not you've got the defect. And if it turns out you do have it, find out if there is anything that can be done to fix it."

"Okay, okay. I'll make the call."

She went back to her desk, found the phone beneath a jumble of papers and picked up the receiver. "Make it now."

Ken looked at the phone with the expression of a man who has just been invited to pick up a deadly snake. Then he glanced at his watch. "I'm a little busy this morning. Maybe after my next meeting."

"Make the call now, Ken, or don't ever darken my doorway to ask for an analysis of any of your dreams again." She held the receiver out to him, striving to sound as forceful and determined as possible. "I won't listen to another one if you don't call the doctor this minute. I mean it."

He looked surprised by her tone but he must have sensed that she was serious. Slowly he took the phone from her with one hand. With his other hand, he removed a small notebook from the pocket of his white lab coat.

She looked at the notebook. "The doctor's phone number?"

"Yeah." His mouth twisted sheepishly. "I wrote it down, just like you told me last week."

Relief lightened her spirits. "That was a good first step. Congratulations. Now, make the call."

"Yes, ma'am." He punched the number out with deliberate, methodical movements of one finger.

Satisfied that this time he was going to go through with the call to the doctor, Isabel went quickly toward the door. "I'll check back with you after my meeting with the new Dr. Belvedere."

"That reminds me, did you hear the latest rumors making the rounds this morning?"

She paused and looked back at him. Ken had finished punching out the number and was now sitting in her chair. He reached for the teapot on the table behind the desk. People did things like that when they came into her office, she reflected. They had no professional respect for the work she performed here at the center but they felt quite free to make themselves at home while they drank her expensive green tea and told her about the dream they'd had the previous night.

"What rumors?" she asked.

"Word is that Randy, the Boy Wonder, is convinced that he can turn the center into a hot acquisition target that will attract one of the big pharmaceutical companies."

She had heard enough about the new director to know that "Randy, the Boy Wonder" was the nickname the staff had bestowed upon Dr. Randolph G. Belvedere, the old man's sole heir.

"The gossip just started this morning," Ken continued. Then he broke off abruptly. He put down the teapot. "Yes, this is Dr. Kenneth Payne," he said very formally into the phone. His eyes locked with Isabel's. "I want to make an appointment with Dr. Richardson."

Isabel flashed him an approving smile, gave him a thumbs-up and hurried off down the corridor.

The interior of the Belvedere Center for Sleep Research was a maze of white hallways and stairwells that connected three floors of offices and labs. She had a lengthy hike ahead of her because the small Department of Dream Analysis where she worked was located on the third floor in a wing of the building. Dr. B.'s old office was on the same floor but in another wing.

She glanced at her watch again and stifled a groan. She was going to be late. Not the best way to start things off with a new boss.

She rounded the first corner, her lab coat flapping wildly in her wake, and nearly collided with the good-looking man emerging from a stairwell.

"What's the rush, Izzy?" Ian Jarrow asked, chuckling.

"Late for a meeting with the new director." She did not pause. "See you later."

"Hey, you did something to your hair, didn't you?" His eyes crinkled very nicely when he smiled.

"Yes."

"It's cute." He reached out as she went past, evidently intending to snag some of the wispy tendrils. "I like it."

"Thanks." She dodged his hand and hurried away, out of reach.

Aaargh. Cute. That did it. The style definitely had to go. Mr. Nicholas had promised to make her look sexy, not cute. Cute was for little girls and poodles.

Well, at least Ian had actually noticed her new cut, she thought, trying for a positive spin. That was better than having him not notice any change at all. But it was too late to make any difference in their relationship. They had stopped dating a month ago, right after Ian took her out to dinner and gently explained that he considered her a good friend, someone he could really talk to, almost a *sister.* He added that he hoped the fact that they would no longer be seeing each other privately wouldn't affect their friendship.

She could have written the script for him. All of her relationships ended in a similar, disturbingly mundane fashion. Men started out wanting to tell her their dreams, proceeded to ask her for advice and ended up regarding her as a good friend; the sister they never had.

If one more man told her he thought of her as a sister, she would be sorely tempted to strangle him with his tie.

The worst part was that now, at thirty-three, she was pretty sure she was on borrowed time. By forty, the line about thinking of her as a sister would probably metamorphose into *you're like an aunt to me.*

Just once it would be interesting to have a man look at her and see a warning sign: CAUTION, DANGEROUS CURVES AHEAD.

And know that he would keep on coming, regardless, like the exciting, mysterious man she fantasized about in her dreams.

Maybe she should try something a little more radical in the fashion line, she mused. Maybe it was time to purchase a pair of stiletto heels and a leather bustier. She had a sudden vision of herself striding the halls of the Belvedere Center for Sleep Research dressed as a dominatrix.

Ahead in the hallway, the door of the ladies' room opened. A tall, striking woman garbed in a hand-tailored lab coat stepped out.

"Isabel."

"Hello, Dr. Netley."

Amelia Netley's stellar résumé listed a number of glowing degrees and achievements in the field of sleep research. But it was her red hair, cool blue eyes and long, elegant legs that kept everyone buzzing. Isabel thought of her as a sort of modern-day Boadicea. Like the ancient queen of the Iceni who led the famous rebellion against the Romans in the British Isles, there was something regal and dedicated about her.

A number of betting pools had been formed to pick the name of the lucky man she would deign to date first but Isabel had a feeling that Amelia would keep everyone guessing for a while.

"Is something wrong?" Amelia asked, auburn brows drawing together in concern. "Why are you in such a hurry?"

"Got a meeting with the new director."

"Really? That seems strange."

Amelia had not been intentionally rude, Isabel decided. It was just that her people skills were somewhat deficient. It was not an uncommon problem among members of the research staff.

"Why do you say that?" Isabel asked politely.

Amelia's fine brows puckered a bit. "I heard that he has scheduled a meeting with each of the various department heads today. You're only a research assistant."

Isabel resisted the urge to grind her back teeth. She admired Amelia in some ways. She had even toyed with the idea of using her as a role model. Lately she had begun to wonder how she herself would look with red hair. But there was no getting around the fact that Amelia occasionally exhibited a certain lack of tact.

That did not make her unique on the center's staff Isabel reminded herself. No one except Dr. B. had ever taken the tiny Department of Dream Analysis seriously and that meant that no one had ever taken her own position as the center's one-and-only dream analyst seriously.

She summoned what she hoped was a cool, confident smile. "Shortly before he died, Dr. B. made it clear that he intended to appoint me head of the Department of Dream Analysis. Now that he's gone, I'm really the only one qualified to take the position."

Amelia's eyes widened faintly. Then, somewhat to Isabel's surprise, she nodded crisply, as if the thought had not occurred to her prior to this moment but now that it had, it made perfect sense.

"That's true, isn't it?" she said, her expression brightening. "Good luck to you."

"Thanks." Isabel turned to rush off down the hall.

"By the way," Amelia said, "I mentioned to Dr. Belvedere that you were the person who found his father's body."

Isabel paused again. "Did you?"

"Yes. Just thought I'd warn you in case he brings up the subject."

"Thanks."

"Finding the old man dead at his desk must have been a terrible shock for you."

"It was. Now, if you'll excuse me —"

"Certainly." Amelia actually winked.

"I'll look forward to seeing your name on the next list of department heads."

Absurdly pleased by this small show of collegial acceptance, Isabel inclined her head and tried to appear modest.

"I hope so."

She turned the corner and walked swiftly toward her destination. Visions of her future flashed before her eyes. The promotion to department head would not only elevate her status at the center, it would mean a hefty increase in salary. She did the calculations and concluded that if she was careful, the raise would enable her to pay off her credit card debt ahead of schedule. In a few months, she might even be able to start looking for the Dream House. She was tired of living in apartments. She longed for a home of her own.

She stopped thinking about her potentially rosy future when she drew closer to the door of the office. A wistful sensation went through her, a mixture of sadness and regret. She was going to miss Martin Belvedere. The old man had been irascible, short-tempered, self-absorbed and secretive. But he had recognized her unusual abilities and gave her the first serious, professional post she'd ever held in the field of dream research. She would be forever grateful to him for rescuing her from the Psychic Dreamer Hotline.

Belvedere had possessed a number of unsociable traits but there was no doubt about his commitment to dream research.

In recent years Martin Belvedere had developed an obsession with a phenomenon he claimed to have discovered in a small number of dreamers. He had created the term "Level Five lucid dreaming" to describe it. In his opinion it was a highly developed form of what was commonly referred to as *lucid dreaming*, the experience of knowing that you are dreaming while you are actually in a dream and the ability to exert some control over the dreamscape.

Lucid dreaming had been written about and discussed for centuries from the time of Aristotle on down to the present. The phenomenon had been studied off and on in modern laboratory settings but little progress had been made toward understanding the lucid dreaming state. Many scientific researchers had abandoned the effort altogether in favor of conducting research on sleep phenomena that could be recorded and analyzed by their instruments. They preferred to examine changes in brain waves, blood pressure and heartbeat. They talked of REM and NREM sleep and published papers that were heavily weighted with statistics, charts and graphs.

But Martin Belvedere had gone much further than other researchers. He had taken a bold leap into the unknown and theorized that some people could achieve a very advanced state of the lucid dream experience. He claimed that in what he called a Level Five state, certain individuals could access their powers of intuition, insight, creativity and unconscious observations in ways that enabled them to see what they could not in the waking state. Belvedere was convinced that extreme dreaming was essentially a form of self-hypnosis that had the potential to allow the dreamer to tap into the deep rivers of human intuition and awareness.

He had even ventured to say that extreme lucid dreaming was as close to a truly psychic experience as human beings could achieve.

From the day two decades earlier when he had first used the word "psychic" in front of an audience of professional sleep and dream researchers, Martin Belvedere had instantly become a pariah among his colleagues.

A few weeks ago, in a rare moment of personal revelation over a cup of tea, Belvedere had confided to Isabel how hurt and angry he had been when he realized that his friends and colleagues had gone to great lengths to distance themselves from him after the ill-fated conference. Rivals and competitors, of which there was no lack, pounced upon his allusion to a possible paranormal aspect of dreaming as proof that Belvedere had wandered across the border that separated scientific study from New Age mysticism.

In the last twenty years of his life, Belvedere had been considered eccentric at best and completely bonkers at worst by those in the field. But the remnants of the outstanding reputation he had established decades earlier had, nevertheless, clung to him like a worn and badly stained lab coat. His early, groundbreaking investigations into the biological and physiological changes that occur during sleep and in the dream state had assured him a place in the textbooks. It had also enabled him to establish the Belvedere Center for Sleep Research.

The center was located near Los Angeles in one of the untold number of industrial parks that littered the landscape of Southern California. There were two small colleges nearby, both of which provided a steady source of paid research subjects for the various sleep studies conducted in the center's labs. Students responded well to the idea of earning money while they slept.

Most of the professional staff at the center was engaged in conducting research into a variety of serious sleep disorders such as insomnia, sleep apnea and narcolepsy. The projects were commissioned and funded by various pharmaceutical companies and sleep disorder foundations.

But in the year she had been working alongside Dr. Martin Belvedere, Isabel had discovered his great secret: He had set up the center as an elaborate, respectable cover that enabled him to pursue his own, private research into extreme dreaming.

Extreme lucid dreaming was a valuable talent, Belvedere had maintained, and one that could be cultivated in certain adept individuals and used in a variety of fields, but only if the talent could be properly understood and controlled.

Everyone knew that the human brain was very good at tuning out most of the sensory stimulation that impacted it twenty-four hours a day, year in and year out. In fact, the ability to exert a high degree of selectivity over what sensory input would be utilized and what would be ignored was the only way the brain could make sense of the dazzling, overwhelming chaos that was reality, the only way it could stay sane. Total awareness would drive the mind mad.

Belvedere had believed that extreme lucid dreamers were held to the same limitations of sensory selectivity and focus that governed everyone else but that they had an additional gift: They could shift or alter that focus while in the extreme lucid dream state. Furthermore, extreme lucid dreamers — those he labeled Level Fives — could not only perform that feat to a very high degree, they could do it at will.

The possibilities were intriguing, Belvedere claimed. After all, a person who could selectively alter the way he or she looked at the world while in a dream trance would be able to discern things that would go unnoticed or unheeded while in the waking state.

He had believed that those born with the talent no doubt used it, either consciously or unconsciously. He suspected that artists who were extreme dreamers envisioned alternate views of reality and preserved them in paint and stone and other media for those who would not otherwise experience them. Mystics and philosophers used their extreme dreams for metaphysical exploration. Scientists endowed with the talent utilized it to find new ways to tackle research problems. Investigators who could drop into an extreme dream at will made use of the skill to pick up clues at crime scenes that others missed.

It had been Belvedere's goal to promote the study of extreme dreaming so that individuals who possessed an aptitude for it could be trained to use it more efficiently and to greater effect.

Extreme dreaming was not without a few problems, however, one of which was that a Level Five dream, for all its power and potential, was, nevertheless, a type of dream. And the dreaming mind often used symbols and elements that were difficult to interpret in the waking state. Some were relatively easy to analyze but others were bizarre and often baffling.

That was where she came in, Isabel thought. She was a Level Five dreamer who could analyze the most obscure images that popped up in extreme dreams.

At the entrance to the director's office, she paused to take a deep breath, straighten her lab coat and push her glasses higher on her nose. *Look professional. Look like you know what you're doing.*

She entered the small outer office. Sandra Johnson was obviously relieved to see her.

Sandra had served as Martin Belvedere's secretary since the founding of the center. She was a large, solidly built woman with a helmet of gray curls. Her uniform varied little from day to day. It consisted of an amply cut big shirt that she always wore outside a pair of black trousers, and several items of bright costume jewelry.

She and Sandra shared a bond of sorts. They had both been able to work with Martin Belvedere, and they were the only two people who had cried at his funeral. They also shared the dubious distinction of being the only two people from the center's staff who had attended the funeral.

"Oh, there you are, Isabel." Behind the lenses of her reading glasses, Sandra's eyes glinted with anxiety. "I was just about to have you paged." She glanced toward the closed door of the inner office and lowered her voice. "This is no time to keep the new Dr. Belvedere waiting. He is very tightly scheduled this morning."

"Sorry. Got held up." So much for starting off on the right foot. "Shall I just go on in?"

"No, no, I'll announce you." Sandra flattened both hands on the desktop and pushed her large, plump form out of the chair. "This Dr. Belvedere is a lot more formal than the other one."

"Too bad."

"Tell me about it. He doesn't even like the way I make coffee. I have been told that I have to stop at the coffee house across the street on my way into the office every morning to pick up a special double grande latte for him." She snorted gently. "The old man always said I made the best coffee he ever tasted."

She bustled out from behind the desk and knocked once on the door of the inner office.

A muffled voice instructed her to enter.

Sandra turned the knob and opened the door. "Isabel Wright to see you, sir."

"Send her in." The masculine voice was brusque.

Isabel braced herself. The last time she walked through that doorway, she encountered a dead man. Some images could never be erased. For the rest of her career at the center she would no doubt get flashbacks to that moment of shock and dread whenever she was summoned into this office.

"Please sit down, Ms. Wright." Randolph motioned toward one of the worn chairs on the opposite side of his desk.

"Thank you, sir." She sank down onto the edge of the chair, knees pressed tightly together, hands clasped in her lap. An uneasy sensation stole over her. There was something very ominous about the atmosphere in the room.

She glanced around, seeing the many changes that Randolph Belvedere had already made in the space that had been his father's domain for so many years. Sphinx's scratching post and food dish were gone. So was the mini-refrigerator where old Dr. B. kept a large stockpile of his favorite late-night snack, lemon-flavored yogurt.

She repressed a small shiver. The room now possessed a stark, sterile neatness that disturbed her on some deep level. The surface of the desk was frighteningly clear of clutter.

She quickly turned her attention back to Randolph. She had glimpsed him from afar on several occasions during the past few days, including at the funeral, but this was the first time she had seen him at close range. He had his father's imposing stature, gray eyes and fierce, hawk-like nose. That was where the resemblance ended.

Randolph was in his early forties, attractive in a stern, square-jawed, distinguished sort of way. He reminded Isabel of an anchor on one of the nightly news broadcasts. His hair was going gray and starting to recede at the temples.

He frowned as though not quite certain what to make of her. Then he sat forward with a solemn air and folded his hands together on top of his desk. "I have been going through my father's files. I must admit, I am confused about just what it is that you do here at the center, Ms. Wright."

"I understand," she said quickly. "Dr. Belvedere deliberately kept my job description vague. The clients who contracted with him for my services are very keen on confidentiality, you see."

"I noticed," Randolph said dryly. He unclasped his hands and opened the file folder. "There appear to be exactly two clients who routinely request your services, Ms. Wright. They are identified only by numbers. Client Number One and Client Number Two."

"Yes, sir. Dr. Belvedere did his best to honor their requests for anonymity." She cleared her throat.

Randolph's brow furrowed. "Mrs. Johnson informs me that there are no copies of the contracts my father signed with these two anonymous clients. She says that all of the business arrangements were handled verbally and that no written records exist."

"I'm sorry, I can't give you any information concerning the contracts," Isabel said. "I can only tell you that Dr. B., I mean Dr. Belvedere, took care of all the business issues relating to them personally."

"I see. Did you ever have any personal contact with either of these two clients?"

"No, sir." Mentally she crossed her fingers. Did dreaming about Client Number Two count as some sort of personal connection? What about attaching little tidbits of advice to the dream interpretations she wrote up for him? And then there was that glorious bouquet of orchids he had sent to her after she completed one particularly difficult report. Was that a form of personal contact? Probably not as far as Randolph was concerned, she decided. The bottom line here was that she had never met or spoken with either of the anonymous clients.

"You must admit that this arrangement between my father and these two clients was highly unusual, Ms. Wright."

"I don't understand, sir. Is there a problem with the anonymous clients?"

His jaw flexed. She finally sensed the anger that had been seething just beneath the surface of his distinguished facade and her spirits plummeted.

"Yes, Ms. Wright, there is a problem with both of them. I have no idea who these clients are. I can't locate any billing information. I can't even contact them to find out what the hell is going on because there are no phone numbers or e-mail addresses in the files for them."

She seized on that last statement. "I'm sure there must be e-mail addresses. Dr. Belvedere mentioned on several occasions that he corresponded with both clients that way."

"If that is the case, he managed to delete or destroy all of the correspondence on his office computer." Randolph's mouth twisted derisively. "Just another one of his little eccentricities, hmm?"

"I'm not sure what —"

"Come now, Ms. Wright. You worked with my father for several months. You must be aware that he was pathologically secretive and paranoid."

She suddenly understood the anger she had sensed a moment ago. Randolph Belvedere had father issues. No surprise there, she thought. Dr. B. had probably not been what anyone would call a great dad. All the old man had ever cared about was his research.

"Dr. Belvedere was very concerned with confidentiality, but in part that was because those two anonymous clients demanded it," she said warily.

"Tell me precisely what you did for these two clients," Randolph snapped.

"I performed a special kind of analysis for them on those occasions when the dreamers had difficulty interpreting the symbols and images that appeared in their dreams."

"I am aware that there are still some psychologists and psychiatrists who believe they can use the patient's dreams to help uncover repressed issues. But the field of clinical psychology has moved well beyond Freud and Jung in that regard. Very few properly trained therapists put a lot of stock in old-fashioned dream analysis these days. In any event, you do not appear to have been practicing therapy. You never even met your clients, did you?"

Okay, that had been a major problem, she thought, one she had complained about frequently to Dr. B. *I need context,* she had told him time and again. *I'm working in the dark.*

"I wasn't hired to do therapy," she said carefully.

"Just as well, since according to your personnel file, you don't even have a degree in psychology." He flipped open the folder on the desk. "It says here that you majored in history in college. It also appears that your previous job was at something called the Psychic Dreamer Hotline."

"You'd be amazed how much practical psychology you can pick up answering phones for the Psychic Dreamer Hotline. It was very educational." She was starting to get mad. "As I was about to say, Dr. Belvedere employed me to interpret the meaning of events and symbols that appeared in dream reports taken from a, uh, certain class of dreamers. You're probably aware that your father had a particular interest in what he termed Level Five lucid dreaming."

"I *knew* it." Randolph's voice was very tight. A dark flush rose in his cheeks. "He was still fiddling around with that psychic nonsense, wasn't he?"

She could feel the cold dampness of a trickle of perspiration under her arms. "I consider that an extremely narrow point of view, sir. In the last few years, your father devoted a great deal of his energy and expertise to the study of high-level lucid dreaming. He hired me to assist him in his research."

Probably best not to explain exactly *why* Dr. Belvedere had selected her to help him, she decided. The situation was bad enough as it was.

"The old fool never gave up, did he," Randolph said bitterly. "He was obsessed with his personal dream scale and that psychic dreaming crap."

"He did not consider it, uh, crap." She gripped the strap of her shoulder bag. "Dr. Belvedere was convinced that some people experience the phenomenon of lucid dreaming with a great deal more intensity and clarity than others. Most people have lucid dreams occasionally. On his scale they rank as Ones and Twos. A few have lucid dreams more frequently and with greater clarity — the Threes and Fours."

"And then we have the Belvedere Level Five lucid dreamer." Randolph's voice dripped with sarcasm. "The so-called psychic dreamer."

"Your father felt that it was a phenomenon that was worth serious study."

"Dreaming is dreaming, Ms. Wright,"

Randolph said flatly. "The consensus of most reputable modern research is that there is no scientific evidence to indicate that being aware of a dream or feeling in control of it is somehow a different or more special kind of dreaming. If anything, it merely indicates that the dreamer is probably not in a deep sleep at the time and is, therefore, more cognizant of what is going on in his own head."

"I'm sure you're aware that Dr. Belvedere believed there was more to the phenomenon, at least in some individuals," she said earnestly.

Randolph sighed and rubbed the bridge of his nose. "I was afraid of this."

"Afraid of what?"

"My father really did go completely wacko toward the end." He shook his head. "I suppose I can only be grateful that he died before he could completely tarnish his professional reputation by publishing any more of his crazy investigations into psychic dreaming."

A rush of anger momentarily blotted out her common sense and caution.

"That is an outrageous thing to say. It is obvious that the two of you did not have a good relationship. I'm sorry about that, but —"

"How d-dare you presume to analyze my relationship with my father?" Randolph was stuttering with rage now. "You have no credentials in the field of psychology, neuroscience or any other field that is even remotely connected to serious dream research. You have no business working at a respectable research facility of any kind."

"Sir, if you knew anything at all about your father, you must realize that, although he could be difficult, he was a brilliant man whose investigations into extreme dreaming will someday be validated by others."

She knew at once she had gone too far.

Randolph vibrated with so much tension that his hands shook. "My father was most certainly a capable researcher at one time. But he allowed his eccentricities to overwhelm his scientific training. I suspect that toward the end, he suffered from some sort of undiagnosed dementia."

"He was *not* demented." The only thing that kept her in her seat was the knowledge that losing her temper completely would provide Randolph with all the ammunition he needed to fire her on the spot.

To her surprise, Randolph smiled. It was not a nice smile, however. It was a thin, mean-spirited little grin of anticipation.

"Let's return to the subject of your position here at the center," he said. "Specifically, your lack of professional credentials and degrees."

"Dr. Belvedere felt that I had other qualities that made me useful."

"Yes, I know, Ms. Wright. But in case it has escaped your notice, I am now the director of the center, and, frankly, I don't have any use for you at all."

She thought about the large outstanding balances on her credit card statements and went ice cold.

"Currently the Belvedere Center for Sleep Research is considered to be a small, backwater lab in the world of sleep studies," Randolph continued. "Until now it has certainly not been a major player in the field. But I intend to change that. As of today, it will focus entirely on sleep research. There will be no more work done on my father's absurd dream theories. Do you understand, Ms. Wright?"

She thought about her beautiful new furniture sitting in the rented storage locker.

"You've made yourself very clear," she said quietly.

"We are going to ditch the woo-woo factor, Ms. Wright." Randolph was looking increasingly cheerful. "The Department of

Dream Analysis no longer exists. I am terminating your employment immediately."

She had nothing left to lose, she decided. "You're letting me go because closing the Department of Dream Analysis is the only way you can come up with to punish your father. Don't you think that's a little childish?"

"How dare you!" He straightened in his chair, righteous indignation blazing in his eyes. "I am p-p-protecting what is left of his reputation."

"Wonderful." She spread her hands. "Now you're rationalizing your actions by telling yourself you're doing this out of respect for your father. Give me a break. You're the one with the doctorate in psychology. You know as well as I do that's not going to work."

Randolph reddened. "I don't want to hear another word out of you, do you understand?"

She should stop talking right now, she thought, but she couldn't help herself. "You really ought to look into getting some counseling to help you deal with your father issues. They're not going to go away now that he's dead and you've got control of his company, you know. If anything, your obsession with proving yourself may get worse. That can lead to —"

"Shut up, Ms. Wright." He punched the intercom on his desk. "Mrs. Johnson, send someone from security to escort Ms. Wright out of the building."

There was a short, appalled silence from Mrs. Johnson's end.

"Yes, sir," she finally managed, sounding horrified.

Isabel got to her feet. "I'll go back to my office to collect my things."

"You will not move an inch," Randolph said flatly. "Your office is being cleared out as we speak. Your personal effects will be brought downstairs to the parking lot and handed over to you."

"What?"

Randolph gave her a triumphant smile. "By the way, I was informed that you intercepted the janitors who were ordered to destroy my father's research this morning. I have remedied the situation."

She stopped at the door and whirled around. "What are you talking about?"

"All of the papers and computer files in your office are being destroyed as we speak."

"You can't do that." Another thought struck her as she yanked open the door. *"Sphinx."*

"Come back here, Ms. Wright." Randolph leaped to his feet. "You are not to return to your office. You will be escorted from here directly to your car."

She ignored him to rush past Mrs. Johnson's desk. The secretary lowered the phone, her expression distraught.

Randolph thundered after Isabel. "I order you to return to this office and wait for security."

"You just fired me. I don't take orders from you anymore."

She flew along the corridor. Office doors opened as she went past. People came to stand in doorways, faces alight with curiosity and astonishment.

By the time she reached the wing where her office was located, she was breathless. At the end of the hall she saw a small knot of people in the hall outside her door. Ken barred the entrance, both arms extended to grasp the door frame on either side.

"Nobody comes in here until Isabel gets back," he roared.

Isabel recognized the three people confronting him. One of them, Gavin Hardy, was from the center's IT department. Gavin was the guy you called when the computers went down or the lab equipment malfunctioned. He was in his mid-thirties, thin, twitchy and very hyper. The only time he was ever still was when he was engrossed in a software problem. He was dressed in a pair of voluminous cargo pants and a tee shirt emblazoned with the logo of one of the mega casino-resorts in Las Vegas. Gavin's big goal in life was to devise the perfect system for beating the house at blackjack.

The second man at her door was Bruce Hopton, the head of the center's small security team. He was accompanied by one of his staff. Bruce was nearing retirement. The white shirt he wore was stretched to the breaking point across his ever-expanding belly. Security was not a major problem at the center. Most of the time Bruce and his people devoted themselves to making sure employees parked in their assigned slots, escorting the female nightshift workers out to their cars and performing the perfunctory employee background checks.

None of the three men looked happy to be where he was.

"Sorry about this, Isabel," Bruce muttered. "Belvedere himself gave us our orders."

Ken looked at Isabel.

"What the hell's going on?" he demanded. "These guys say they've been told to destroy all the files in your office and on your computer."

"It's true. Belvedere just fired me."

"That sonofabitch." Ken glared at Gavin and Bruce.

Gavin held up both hands in a defensive gesture. "Hey, don't blame us."

"Yeah," Bruce mumbled. "We feel just as bad about this as you do, Ms. Wright."

"I doubt it," she said. "I'm out of a job."

"I'm real sorry about that," Bruce said. "We're sure gonna miss you around here."

The regret in his face was sincere. She could not take her anger and frustration out on him. "Thanks, Bruce. If you don't mind, I have to get Sphinx."

Bruce nervously checked the hallway behind her. "I'm not supposed to let you back inside, Isabel."

"I'm here for the cat," she said evenly.

He hesitated briefly and then squared his shoulders. "Go ahead and get the carrier. I'll take the heat if Belvedere objects."

"Thanks, Bruce."

"Forget it. Least I can do after what you did for my grandson a few months ago."

Isabel moved into the office.

Ken stood aside. "Are you okay?"

"Yes, I'm fine."

"Sphinx is a little upset."

"I can tell."

Sphinx was crouched in his cage, ears plastered against his skull, eyes narrowed, fangs bared.

"It's okay, Sphinx. Calm down, sweetie." She hoisted the carrier. "We're going home."

"Belvedere can't fire you like this," Ken growled.

"Yes, he can, actually." She glanced at her cluttered desk and then determinedly turned away from the sight of all the work that was about to be destroyed. She had done her best to salvage Martin Belvedere's research, but she had failed. There was nothing more she could do. She had her own problems and they were big ones.

"Where is she?" Randolph called heatedly outside in the hall. "My instructions were clear, Hopton. Ms. Wright was not supposed to be allowed back into her office."

"She's picking up the cat," Bruce said quietly. "Figured you'd want him out of here."

"Cat? What cat?" Randolph appeared in the doorway, his anchorman features as tight and drawn as if he'd just been told that the network had decided not to renew his contract. "Damnit, that's my father's cat, isn't it? What's it doing here? I told Mrs. Johnson this morning that the creature was to be sent to the pound."

"Don't worry, Dr. Belvedere." Isabel walked toward the door, holding the carrier in both arms. "We're leaving. The best thing you can do is get out of my way. You're going to look awfully foolish if you decide to fight me over this cat. If I get really annoyed, I might open the door of this carrier."

Sphinx hissed at Randolph.

Belvedere got out of the way.

Hours later she sat at the table in the kitchen of her small apartment glumly regarding the array of bank and credit card statements. The windows were open, allowing the warm air of the early summer afternoon to circulate through the small space. She couldn't see the smog when she looked out across the pool and gardens toward the other apartments, but she could taste it in the back of her throat.

She had considered turning on the air conditioner but thought better of it after a short review of the state of her finances. A dollar saved on the electricity bill was a dollar that could go toward the payments on her precious furniture.

"We've got a big problem, Sphinx. I've made all the cuts I can. I'll cancel the gym membership and drop the insurance on the furniture first thing in the morning, but that's not going to be enough to bail us out. There's only one answer."

The cat ignored her. He was on the floor in the corner, hunched over a saucer of cat food. He tended to be extremely focused at mealtime.

"Given your expensive tastes in cat food and my outstanding credit card debt, we have no choice," she informed him. "The folks at the Psychic Dreamer Hotline are very nice and I could probably get my old job back, but, to be honest, it doesn't pay well enough to keep us in the style to which we have become accustomed. Got to think of the furniture. If I don't make the payments we'll find a repo man at our door one of these days."

Sphinx finished the last of his meal and padded across the floor to where she sat. When he reached her he heaved his bulk up onto her lap, hunkered down and closed his eyes. The sound of his rusty, rumbling purr hummed in the quiet kitchen.

She stroked him, taking a curious comfort in his weight and warmth. She liked animals in general but had never considered herself a cat person. When she thought about getting a pet for company, she usually thought in terms of a dog.

Sphinx was not what anyone would call cute or cuddly. But there was no getting around the fact that during the past year, the two of them had become colleagues of a sort. It had been Sphinx who alerted her to the fact that Martin Belvedere was dead.

She had spent that fateful night in her office, as she often did when working on a rushed dream analysis for one of the anonymous clients. Belvedere, an insomniac who usually spent his nights at the center, had wandered down the hall sometime around midnight to chat with her about the case before she went into her dream state. Everything had seemed so *normal,* she thought, or at least as normal as things got in her new career. Belvedere brought a container of lemon yogurt with him when he came to her office, just as he always did when he visited at that hour. He ate a portion of the yogurt while they discussed her latest project. Then he left with his unfinished snack to return to his office.

Shortly before two in the morning some

small sound awakened her. It brought her out of a disturbing dream full of symbols of blood and death, typical of the sort she interpreted for Clients One and Two.

She was still somewhat disoriented when she opened the door and found Sphinx pacing back and forth in the hallway. His agitated behavior was so unusual she knew at once that something was wrong. She picked him up and carried him back to Belvedere's office, where she discovered the director slumped over his desk.

That kind of experience invoked a bond, she told herself. She wasn't sure how Sphinx felt about her but she knew there was no way she could have let him go to the pound.

"Looks like I'm going to have to do what I swore I'd never do."

Sphinx gave no indication that he was in any way concerned with their financial future.

"It must be nice to be so Zen," she muttered.

Sphinx's purr got louder.

She reached for the phone and slowly, reluctantly, punched out the familiar number. While she waited for an answer, she thought about the two anonymous clients of the Belvedere Center for Sleep Research. Their consulting requests were erratic and unpredictable. Sometimes weeks passed between assignments. She wondered how long it would be before either of them learned that her services were no longer available.

Most of all she wondered if Client Number Two, otherwise known as Dream Man, would miss her when he discovered that she was gone.

3

Frey-Salter, Inc., Research Triangle Park, North Carolina

"You're still worrying about Ellis, aren't you?" Beth asked.

"Yeah. He's not getting any better. Worse, in fact." Jack Lawson absently registered the familiar squeak in the government-issue desk chair when he leaned back to plant his heels on the aged government-issue desk.

The squeak had come with the chair. Both had been new some thirty-odd years ago, when he was assigned to establish Frey-Salter, Inc., the corporate front that concealed his small, very secret government agency and its highly classified dream research program.

Frey-Salter was located in the Research Triangle Park of North Carolina, an area conveniently situated in the heart of a triangle formed by Raleigh, Durham and Chapel Hill. The park was home to a heavy concentration of cutting-edge pharmaceutical and high-tech enterprises. Frey-Salter went unnoticed among the large assortment of companies and businesses that operated there.

It wasn't only the chair that had been new three decades ago, he thought. He himself had been new back then. Young and eager and ambitious. He had also been madly in love with Beth Mapstone, the woman on the other end of the phone connection.

A lot of things had changed in the past three decades. The chair was getting old and so was he. His youthful zeal had taken on a cynical edge, although he still believed passionately in the importance of his work. He was no longer ambitious, either. He had built his empire. His goal now was to hang onto it until retirement and then see to it that the program passed into good hands.

Technology had changed a lot over the years, too. He was proud of the way he had adapted. The fancy, high-tech phone he was using today with its specially designed scrambling and encryption software was a far cry from the telephone that had come with the desk thirty years ago.

But one thing had not changed. He was still in love with Beth. Nothing could ever alter that. She had been his partner right from the start. He could still recall their first meeting at Frey-Salter's pistol range as though it were yesterday. Her hair was cinched back in a cute ponytail and she wore a pair of jeans that fit her so tightly he wondered if she'd used a shrink-wrap machine to put them on that morning. She outshot him by a country mile. He knew he was in love before they reeled in the paper targets.

"His fixation with the notion that Vincent Scargill is still alive has turned into some sort of obsession," he said. "It started with the incident at the survivalists' compound. Some kind of post-traumatic stress syndrome maybe. Hell, he damn near died that day."

"I know," Beth said quietly.

"Whatever it is, I don't like what's happening to Ellis." Lawson picked up a tiny hammer and struck the first of several small, gleaming, stainless steel balls suspended in a row on his desk toy. The first ball struck the next one in line, which clanged into a third. The effect rippled down the line of balls and then reversed. He always found the *ping-ping-ping* sound soothing. "I ordered him to talk to one of the shrinks here at Frey-Salter."

"Did he do it?"

"No. You know he doesn't take orders well. Never did. Always been a lone wolf."

"He needs a distraction," Beth said, sounding thoughtful. "Something to take his mind off Vincent Scargill."

"I've been thinking the same thing." Jack watched the silver balls bounce gently off one another. "Got an idea. A situation has developed out in California. Belvedere collapsed and died a few days ago. Heart attack."

Beth sighed. "I'm sorry to hear that. Belvedere was a strange duck and not exactly Mr. Personality, but his lucid dream research work was far ahead of the curve. Too bad it went unrecognized in his lifetime."

"Tell me about it. Anyhow, as it stands now, Belvedere's son, Randolph, has taken over the Center for Sleep Research."

"Don't worry, even if he discovers that there is an anonymous Client Number One, he won't be able to trace you or Frey-Salter. I made sure of that when I set up the e-mail contact system between you and Belvedere."

"I'm not worried about Randolph locating me," he said impatiently. "The problem is that one of his first official acts was to fire Isabel Wright."

"Damn. Not good. You'd better not lose her, Jack. You need her."

"Hell, I know that. Seems to me the best way to handle this now that Belvedere is gone is to bring her back here to Frey-Salter and tuck her away in a nice, quiet little office."

"Makes sense. You'll have better control over her that way."

"So here's the plan." Jack drank some coffee. "I'm going to send Ellis to bring her in. You said he needs a distraction, right? Let him play recruiting agent."

"Good idea. Just might work, too. I've had a feeling for a while now that he's rather intrigued by her. In fact, if this thing with Scargill hadn't blown up, literally, a few months ago, I've got a hunch Ellis would have looked up Isabel Wright on his own by now."

Jack smiled, pleased with himself for having impressed her. "Maybe I've got some heretofore undiscovered matchmaking talent."

The instant the words were out of his mouth, he cringed, mentally kicking himself. That had been a stupid thing to say under the circumstances.

"You're good, Jack," Beth said coolly.

"But when it comes to figuring out relationships, you're as dumb as a brick."

He rocked back and forth in the squeaky chair a couple of times, gathering his nerve. "Are you ever gonna forgive me, Beth?"

"I still can't believe you slept with that woman," she muttered.

"I still can't believe you actually went to a lawyer to see about a divorce. Give me a break, Beth, you've never pushed it that far before. I thought you had left me for real that time. I was a basket case. I was cracking up inside. I was vulnerable."

There was a short pause.

"Vulnerable?" Beth repeated, sounding as if she had never heard the word before. "You?"

"I read one of those advice books for people who are involved in failed relationships. It said that people are vulnerable when a mate walks out. They're inclined to do dumb things."

"You actually bought a book about relationships?"

"I didn't know what else to do. I was desperate." He banged the first ball on the desk toy so hard the steel spheres crashed into one another. "Look, Beth, I didn't know there was a rule against sleeping with someone else once your wife has gone to a lawyer. That sounded like the end to me. Thought we had split up for good. I wasn't thinking straight."

"You thought it was okay to have an affair with Maureen Sage just because I'd consulted a lawyer?"

"Like I said, I thought it was really the end for us that time. I was trying to drown my sorrows with Maureen, so to speak. It was a mistake, okay?"

Beth fell silent. He dared to hope.

"Go call Ellis," she said finally. "I've got a full schedule this morning. I'll talk to you later."

She ended the connection.

He sat there for a while, glumly gazing through the window that separated his office from the main lab and work areas. On the other side of the glass two agents were meeting with a couple of white-coated members of the research staff. Elsewhere people were busy at their computers. There was an air of purposeful activity about the place. Important work was being done. Crimes were being solved. Lives were being saved. Cutting-edge science was happening.

His empire, Jack thought. And he had built it with Beth's help. If he didn't get her back, the rest of it would cease to be important.

He hit the phone memory code that would connect him with Ellis.

4

San Diego, California

"We've got a very big problem," Jack Lawson announced from the other end of the phone. "Martin Belvedere dropped dead of a heart attack several days ago. His son has taken over the Center for Sleep Research. One of his first official acts was to fire Isabel Wright. She's gone."

The news hit Ellis with the shock of a small earthquake. Okay, he thought, get a grip here. This isn't the end of life on earth as we know it. But it was a hell of a jolt.

Tango Dancer was gone. He cradled the phone between ear and shoulder and set the frying pan down on the stove with such force that the two frozen soy sausages he had been about to cook bounced a couple of times from the impact.

"Everything okay there?" Lawson asked with casual concern. "Sounded like something fell on that end."

"Just put a pan on the stove." He was careful not to allow any indication of his reaction to the news show in his voice. Lawson was already worried enough about his mental state as it was. "It's lunchtime out here in California, remember?"

"Yeah, sure," Lawson said vaguely. "Forgot."

Lawson was fifty-seven, wiry and compact, with a completely bald head, a gravelly voice and the haggard, drawn features associated with lifelong smokers and marathon runners, although he did not smoke and never moved any faster than absolutely necessary. Ellis thought about him sitting in his cluttered office deep in the bowels of Frey-Salter, several time zones away in North Carolina.

"That's because you have no life outside Frey-Salter," Ellis said. Ignoring the soy sausages, he leaned against the counter and looked at the photo he had attached to the door of the refrigerator. "Time is meaningless to you."

Lawson snorted. "Time is everything to me. That's why I'm calling you. I want you to find Isabel Wright and bring her into Frey-Salter. I've been thinking about this for a while but there was no reason to rush into such a move. Things were working just fine the way they were. But with old man Belvedere gone —"

"Hang on, let's start at the beginning. Belvedere's dead?"

"Yeah. Several days ago."

"And you just found out?"

"Haven't had any reason to contact him for a couple of weeks." There was a shrug in Lawson's voice.

"Neither have I. Been busy with a new start-up project." And with his ongoing research into an old problem, but he sure wasn't going to mention that bit. He didn't need any more of Lawson's well-meant but really annoying lectures on the dangers of obsessing over the Vincent Scargill issue.

"As I was saying, the old man's son, Randolph Belvedere, took over as director of the center the day after he buried his father," Lawson continued.

"Didn't know Belvedere had a son."

"Beth looked into it. Turns out Belvedere and Randolph were what folks like to call 'estranged' for years. But the son was the old man's only heir. He got everything, including the center."

Beth Mapstone would know, Ellis thought. She owned Mapstone Investigations, a quasi-private security firm with affiliates in several states.

Beth was not only Lawson's wife, she was his partner in every sense of the word.

The pair had enjoyed, or endured, depending on your point of view, an on-again, off-again relationship for over thirty years. At the moment, they were off-again. But when it came to their professional relationship, they were always a team.

The formal relationship between Mapstone Investigations and Frey-Salter was officially that of corporate security firm and corporate client. In reality, however, Mapstone served as both an investigative arm for Lawson's secret agency and a convenient cover for his agents.

"What does Randolph Belvedere think of his father's theories of Level Five dreaming?" Ellis asked.

"Thinks they're pure crap, of course. He's into sleep research, though. Got big plans for the center. Needless to say, none of those plans involve Isabel Wright."

"But you have plans for her."

"I do, indeed," Lawson said fervently. "I want her right here where I can keep an eye on her."

"What did you mean when you said she was gone?"

"Gave notice to the manager of the apartment complex where she was living out there in LA, packed up her belongings and took off."

"I assume this phone call is not because you can't locate Isabel Wright."

"Hell, no. Beth found her right away. That's not the problem. The problem is convincing her to come back here to Raleigh to work at Frey-Salter. I don't want to take a chance on losing her to some other outfit."

"That's where I come in, I take it?"

"I'm counting on you to sell her on the idea of working directly for me."

"Why would I want to do that?"

"That hurts, Ellis. That cuts real deep. Our association may have started out on a business footing, but I like to think that we did the macho male bonding thing after you came to work for me."

"Was that what you call it? Felt more like me working my ass off in your lab every night while you conducted your Frankenstein experiments."

"What are you complaining about? All you had to do was go to sleep."

There had been a little more to it than that, Ellis reflected. He had not exactly slept his way through Jack Lawson's experiments, he had *dreamed* his way through them. And those dreams had not been sweet. He usually awoke from them in a state of physical and mental exhaustion. It sometimes took days to recover. The really bad ones still took that long.

He had been in the middle of his sophomore year in college when Jack found him. On the point of dropping out of school because the budding business analyst part of him was reluctant to take on any more student loans, he volunteered for a sleep research experiment.

He had not been keen on the idea of being hooked up to a lot of electrodes while he slept but he told himself that the money was good and he needed the cash. Deep down, however, he knew that was not the real reason he had decided to offer himself up as a research subject. The truth was that the extreme dreams had become increasingly disturbing. It had gotten to the point where he avoided going to bed, dosing himself with caffeine and other stuff to stay awake. But sooner or later he always crashed, and when he finally went under, the dreams were waiting for him.

The chronic sleep deprivation, combined with the unsettling effects of the surreal, ultra-vivid dreams, had left him too edgy to study. If he hadn't dropped out, he would surely have flunked out.

What he had not known was that Lawson's tiny, secretive government agency paid for the experiments using Frey-Salter as its guise. The sleep research conducted on the campus where Ellis was attending college was one of many such projects that Lawson had commissioned. Lawson was looking for people like Ellis.

Forty-eight hours after the results of the sleep research project were on Lawson's desk, Lawson himself was at Ellis's door, a dazzling contract in his hand. But it was not the promise of a lucrative job offer, tantalizing as it was, that swept Ellis off his feet; it was Lawson's reassuring conviction that, whatever it was that happened when Ellis dreamed, he was not going crazy.

Lawson had tossed out a second lure as well. He gave Ellis the chance to join a small, clandestine organization that was doing exciting work. For a nineteen-year-old who had been orphaned at twelve and who had spent his teenage years bouncing from one foster-care home to another, the offer was irresistible. For the first time in a very long while, he felt that he belonged somewhere.

Looking back, Ellis thought, it was probably no big surprise that Lawson had become a sort of father figure to him.

"You know, I'm going to miss the old man," Lawson said, sounding unusually wistful. "Martin Belvedere could be a pain in the ass but he was brilliant and he knew how to keep secrets." There was a short, meaningful pause. "At least, I think he knew how to keep 'em."

"You're worried that he might have said too much about you and your agency to Isabel Wright, aren't you?"

A rhythmic series of small squeaks and squeals sounded on the other end of the line. Ellis could almost see Lawson leaning back in his government-issue chair, swiveling slowly from side to side while he talked into the phone.

"It's a possibility I can't afford to ignore," Lawson admitted. "Let's face it, she worked closely with Belvedere for the better part of a year and she's obviously damn smart. Got to assume she picked up a few clues."

"I don't think you need to panic here. You're very good at keeping Frey-Salter in the shadows. Ms. Wright could not have learned much and even if she did make a few insightful guesses, what harm could she do?"

"Problem is, with Martin Belvedere gone, the situation has gotten real murky. I need to get Isabel Wright back under control and I need to do it as fast as possible. I can't afford to lose her. Also, I need to know if she's told anyone about the kind of work she did while she worked for Belvedere. Might be necessary to do some damage control."

Ellis gave a short, harsh laugh. "What are you afraid of, Lawson? Think Isabel Wright might take her suspicions to the media?"

"It could complicate things for me."

"Not a chance. The only news outlets that would pay attention to such an off-the-wall story are the supermarket tabloids. I can see the headlines at the check-out counter now: 'Secret Government Agency Tracks Killers in Dreams.' "

"I've got my funding to protect," Lawson growled. "I don't need that kind of publicity. You know how much heat the CIA and the FBI take whenever some enterprising reporter discovers yet again that they occasionally use psychics. Hell, they had to shut down the remote viewing project at Stanford back in the nineties because of the embarrassing press. Duke University closed its parapsychology research lab for similar reasons."

"The government has a long and extremely lurid history of financing psychic research," Ellis reminded him. "It's no secret."

"Yeah, but it isn't always fashionable. In the current funding climate, I can guarantee you that if certain people in Congress find out what's really going on here at Frey-Salter, they'll start screaming about how I'm wasting taxpayer dollars and I'll end up with serious budget problems."

"I've got great faith in your ability to secure funding. You've been doing it for over two decades. You're a survivor, Lawson."

"So are you," Lawson shot back a little too smoothly. "And the bottom line here is that we both need Isabel Wright."

"Yeah, I know. You don't have to remind me."

"I'll make this job worth your while, like I always do. Easy money, pal. All you have to do is track her down, feel out the situation to see if she's talked to anyone and then convince her to come work here at Frey-Salter. How hard can it be?"

"What makes you think she'll want to work for you?"

"Not a lot of openings for fired Level Five dream analysts," Lawson said. "Hell, most people don't even know there is such a thing. She's thirty-three, never been married and, according to Beth, hasn't dated seriously in months. All indications are that she's a meek, lonely, nervous little spinster who lives for her work. Martin Belvedere once told me that she often spent her nights sleeping on a cot in her office. She's probably anxious as hell now that she no longer has a nice little office to call her own."

Ellis did not take his eyes off the photo. "A meek, lonely, nervous little spinster, huh?"

"You don't sound convinced."

"She might be meek. She might be lonely. She might be a spinster. But whatever else she is, I seriously doubt that she's the nervous type."

"What makes you say that?"

"Hell, Lawson, given the kinds of dreams you and I have asked her to decode this past year, she must have nerves of steel."

There was a short pause on the other end. Somewhere in the midst of the long silence, Ellis became aware of an unpleasant, burning smell.

The soy sausages. He had neglected to turn off the burner.

"Damn." Straightening suddenly, he seized a towel, wrapped it around the handle of the frying pan and whipped the singed phony sausages off the stove. Smoke wafted across the kitchen. Alarmed that it would set off the detector, he opened a window.

"Everything okay there?" Lawson asked.

"I just burned lunch."

"You still sticking to that mostly vegetarian diet you started a while back?"

"Yeah."

"Don't see how you can stand all that healthy green stuff. Doesn't seem natural, you know?"

"You get used to it after a while." Sort of. He still wasn't sure how he felt about the fake sausages.

"A man's gotta have protein. How can you survive without the basic nutrients in good barbeque?"

"I still eat a little fish. Could we get back to the subject of Isabel Wright?"

"I was about to say that I've had a lot more experience with the research-oriented personality type than you have. Trust me, that kind can deal with stuff that would make a hardened agent shudder as long as they only have to look at it in a lab setting. Put them in the field and they fall apart, sure, but they're happy as Santa's little elves when they're surrounded by their computers and their instruments."

Jack Lawson was right ninety-nine percent of the time when it came to judging other people, Ellis reflected. It was one of the things that made Lawson so good at his job.

But one percent of the time he was wrong. When Lawson did make mistakes, they tended to be big ones.

Ellis was pretty sure that Lawson was wrong about Isabel Wright. He had picked up enough telltale hints and nuances to know that when she decoded his dreams, she didn't do it from some safe, detached academic place. He did not think she was immune to the violence embedded in the really bad dreams he sent to her to analyze.

"What if Isabel Wright doesn't want to work for you?" Ellis asked. "Got a fallback plan?"

"Don't need one. You're going to convince her that Frey-Salter would be a terrific career move. Tell her about the medical benefits."

Absently Ellis rolled his right shoulder, trying to ease the dull ache. He'd already had two operations on it and the orthopedic surgeon was talking enthusiastically about eventually doing a complete joint replacement. The doctors had assured him that there was a high probability that arthritis would set in a couple of decades earlier than normal because of the damage done by the bullet.

"Forget it, Lawson, you don't want me to go into the details of Frey-Salter's fabulous medical benefits. My viewpoint on that subject is a little skewed, due to the fact that I nearly got killed working for you."

"So push the retirement plan, instead. I don't care what you have to promise her to convince her to come into Frey-Salter. Just don't let her get away. I can't afford to lose her." Jack gave it a beat before adding, "Neither can you."

He couldn't argue with that. "Got to admit, she's a business asset for me."

She was a lot more than that, but damned if he would admit it to Lawson. He was having a hard enough time acknowledging the truth to himself.

"All right, I'll see what I can do," he said. "But no guarantees. Got a new address for her?"

"Beth faxed it to me a few minutes ago. Hang on a second. It's here somewhere." The sound of papers and files being pushed around on top of a desk filled the phone line for a time before Lawson spoke again. "Here we go. Town called Roxanna Beach, somewhere on the coast out there in California."

"I've heard of it. Never been there. Somewhere north of L.A., I think."

"She's got some family there. Sister and a brother-in-law. Beth says she's renting a house. Here's the address. Ready?"

Ellis reached for a pen and a pad of paper. "Yeah."

"Number Seventeen Sea Breeze Lane."

"Got it."

"Get moving on this, Ellis. As things stand, Isabel Wright is a loose cannon. I want her back under control as soon as possible."

Ellis tossed the pen aside. "Uh-huh."

"Call me after you find her."

"Right."

He hung up the phone, folded his arms and contemplated the photo on the refrigerator.

It was a picture of a slender woman dressed in a white lab coat. She had excellent shoulders and a proud, determined way of holding herself. She also had an interesting, intelligent face with big, mysterious eyes veiled by a pair of black-framed glasses. Her dark hair was pulled straight back into an elegantly severe twist that called attention to the delicacy of the nape of her neck.

In the photo she was smiling joyously, almost glowing, as she examined a vase of orchids that sat in the middle of her desk. He had no trouble at all imagining the passion hidden behind the lab coat and the glasses.

Definitely not a meek, nervous little spinster, he thought.

Tango Dancer.

5

The auditorium was filled to capacity. Isabel sat in the third to the last row, notebook and pen on the small desk that extended from the arm of the plush, theater-style seat. She was watching the speaker onstage, concentrating so she would not miss anything Tamsyn Strickland said, when she felt a whispery, atavistic thrill stir the hair on the nape of her neck.

Following an instinct that was probably as old as the species, she turned her head to look back over her shoulder to see who or what was closing in on her.

A man had entered the dimly lit chamber. He stood in the shadows behind the last row of seats. It was difficult to make him out clearly because of the low level of illumination but she could see from the way he stood that he was not interested in what was going on at the front of the room. Instead he took off a pair of dark sunglasses and examined the group of seminar attendees the way a large hunting cat studies the crowd gathered at the watering hole. Selecting his prey.

His gaze locked with hers. That was when she knew he had been looking for her.

Adrenaline splashed through her veins. She could have sworn that she heard energy crackling in the room. She was amazed that there was no flash of lightning.

What was going on here? Alarmed, oddly excited and somewhat dazed, she turned quickly around in her seat and forced herself to pay attention to the lecture.

Onstage Tamsyn Strickland, pointer in hand, launched into her closing remarks.

"Tapping into your personal creative potential is the focus of the Kyler Method," Tamsyn declared. Exuberance bubbled up through her words. "That is the skill that we will teach you, and believe me, you will learn it well. What's more, you will see the positive effects of the method at work in your personal life within the first twenty-four hours."

The audience was riveted. No surprise there, Isabel thought. Tamsyn was a charismatic speaker. She believed wholeheartedly in the Kyler Method, and when she was onstage, she could make the audience believe in it, too.

She was in her early thirties, attractive, divorced and zealously committed to her new career as an instructor here at Kyler, Inc. Tamsyn had found her calling in motivational lecturing.

Isabel gave it a few minutes and then, unable to resist, risked another glance over her shoulder to see if the stranger was still standing in the shadows at the back of the room.

He was there, all right. And still watching her. He inclined his head in a small gesture that signaled his recognition and let her know that he was waiting for her.

Isabel caught her breath and turned around again, very quickly. She had never seen him before in her life. She was positive of that. No woman would ever forget a man like that. How could he possibly know who she was?

"This is only an orientation session." Tamsyn paused at the front of the stage and spread her hands in a graceful rising motion. "The hard work comes later, in the seminars and workshops that you will attend over the course of the next five days. But I promise you that when you walk out of this room today you will know that your journey has begun. You will learn how to organize, manage and control your life in a way that will increase your personal satisfaction and prosperity. You will learn how to tap into your own creative potential. Your life will never be the same."

Tamsyn gave the audience one last megawatt smile and, with an actor's sense of timing, vanished from the stage through a gold velvet curtain.

The room exploded into applause. The spectacular art-glass chandelier that had been designed especially for the expensively decorated auditorium brightened gradually. The warm light that radiated through the translucent abstract sculpture revealed the room's paneled walls and rich, plush carpeting.

The massive chandelier was typical of the over-the-top design features that were incorporated into all the public spaces and classrooms at the headquarters of Kyler, Inc. Isabel knew that her brother-in-law, Farrell Kyler, president and CEO of the motivational seminar company, had spared no expense when he commissioned the architect and designer to construct the campus.

The crowd thinned out quickly. She realized that she was the last person still sitting in a seat. She could not delay this any longer.

She picked up her notebook and pen and

dropped them into her shoulder bag. Very deliberately she adjusted her glasses on her nose and slowly rose to her feet.

Maybe he would be gone by the time she got to the entrance of the auditorium.

Maybe the sun would not rise tomorrow.

She made her way to the end of the row of seats without looking toward the door. But when she reached the aisle, she had no choice but to look straight ahead.

He was waiting, one shoulder propped against the wall, arms folded, watching her come toward him. He wore a dark blue shirt that was open at the collar, the cuffs rolled up on strong forearms. The shirt was paired with charcoal gray trousers. Both had the close fit and elegant, masculine drape that only came with hand tailoring.

She was acutely aware of her own attire, which consisted of a Kyler red jacket, complete with a little crest on the left breast, and a pair of Kyler tan trousers. She was a walking ad for the Kyler Method.

When she was a few steps away he straightened and lowered his arms. Technically, he was not exactly blocking the exit, she thought. But it certainly appeared that way.

"Isabel Wright?"

She took a deep, steadying breath. His

voice was as interesting as sin and, in the wrong hands, probably twice as dangerous.

"Yes." She gave him the Desperately Professional Smile she had tried to perfect at the Center for Sleep Research. "Have we met?"

His answering smile was not much more than a faint curve of his hard mouth but there was an intimate, knowing quality to it that sent a frisson of excitement along every nerve ending in her body.

"Ellis Cutler," he said. "I believe you knew me as Client Number Two when you were associated with the Belvedere Center for Sleep Research."

Dream Man.

The world stopped for a couple of seconds. So did her breathing. This was Dream Man.

She managed to hold out her hand. "How do you do?"

Ellis's fingers closed around hers, firm and strong. She sensed the power in him but she also knew that it was under cool and complete control. Just like in his dreams, she thought.

"Sorry to show up here unannounced," he said. "Took me a while to track you down after we found out you'd left the center."

"We?"

He raised his brows. "Client Number One was also interested in locating you."

"I see."

"I'd like to talk to you. Can I buy you a cup of coffee?"

It was all very polite and innocuous. He was even trying to quietly reassure her by offering to have the conversation in a public venue. Nevertheless, she had a hunch that he would not politely and innocuously disappear if she refused to speak with him.

"Certainly." She tightened her grip on the shoulder bag and kept the Desperately Professional Smile in place. "There's a café outside on the terrace. It has a nice view of the beach."

"Sounds good." He took his sunglasses out of his pocket and put them on.

They made their way through the high-ceilinged lobby. The large space was lightly crowded with a sprinkling of late arrivals checking in for the week-long series of seminars. Isabel could feel a few curious glances coming from the staff at the reception desk. She ignored them. They were, she was quite sure, aimed at her companion, not her. Ellis Cutler appeared to be oblivious to the attention they were drawing but she was pretty sure he was aware of everything that was going on around them.

"Got to say I was a little surprised to find you here." Ellis leaned around her to open one of the heavy glass doors. "Never pictured you as the type to sign up for a course of motivational seminars. Always had the feeling that you were already very motivated."

She stepped out onto the long, wide terrace that fronted the sleek, modern facade of the seminar wing. "The Kyler Method is not just about developing a positive, motivated attitude," she said crisply. "It is also about tapping the creative side of your nature. It's about exploring options, seeing things in a different light, opening up your personal horizons."

"That sounds like a direct quote."

"Page one of *The Kyler Method: Ten Steps to Reinventing Yourself*."

"By Farrell Kyler, your brother-in-law. The book spent five months on the major best-seller lists."

"I see you've done your research on me," she said coolly.

"You've been analyzing my dream reports for a year, Isabel. You probably know me well enough by now to realize that I always do my research."

It was a simple statement of fact but it sent another small thrill of alarm through her. He was acknowledging that there was a strong, personal connection between them.

"Yes," she murmured.

All of her senses felt sharp and acute. She was intensely aware of the brisk breeze off the bay and the warmth of the summer sun. The sea was an electric blue mirror that dazzled her eyes.

She led the way to the far end of the terrace, where several tables shaded with colorful umbrellas had been set outside. There were only a handful of people in the vicinity. They sipped frothy espresso-based drinks or drank expensive water from bottles that bore labels printed in a variety of foreign languages.

Ellis indicated a table situated some distance from the others, offering a measure of privacy. The low, muted roar of the surf at the foot of the bluff provided a level of white noise that made it possible to talk without being overheard.

Isabel sat down in the shade cast by the red-and-tan umbrella. Ellis took the seat across from her.

A waiter dressed in a signature Kyler red polo shirt, tan shorts and high-end running shoes hurried over to take their orders.

Isabel smiled at him. "Green tea, please."

"You got it." The waiter looked expectantly at Ellis.

"The same," Ellis said.

If the waiter thought green tea was a wimpy drink for a man, he was too smart to reveal it. He dutifully noted the order on his pad and hastened off toward the glass doors of the café.

Ellis looked at Isabel. She could feel the intensity of his gaze right through the heat shield of his midnight dark glasses.

Pay attention, she warned herself. *You've been inside his dreams. You know how clever and subtle he can be, even when he's in the middle of a nightmare. Keep it cool. Keep your distance.*

"How are you feeling?" she asked on impulse.

So much for keeping her distance.

Something about his absolute stillness told her she had caught him off guard. He recovered almost instantly.

"Much better, thank you," he said in a mockingly grave tone. "Haven't had red meat in months. Taking my vitamins. Drinking plenty of green tea. Renting classic screwball romantic comedies. Haven't actually gone out and bought a romance novel yet, but I'll get around to it. Been a little busy lately."

His obvious amusement disconcerted her. She blushed and hastily sat back in her chair. "What can I do for you, Mr. Cutler?"

"Make it Ellis."

"Okay, Ellis." She waited.

"I understand you've left your job at the Belvedere Center for Sleep Research."

"I was fired."

He showed his teeth in a brief, soft laugh. "I'm not exactly a student of the Kyler Method but the next time the subject comes up, I suggest you put a more positive spin on why you left."

"How can you be positive about getting fired?"

"Try saying that you resigned to pursue other interests."

She pursed her lips, considering the phrase closely. "Resigned to pursue other interests. It does have a more positive ring, doesn't it? Thanks."

"You're welcome. Usually I charge a lot of money for advice like that."

"You do?"

Before she could question him further,

the waiter returned with a steaming pot and two ceramic cups. He set the tea things down and departed.

"I'm here to offer you another job," Ellis said in a surprisingly offhanded fashion. "Good pay. Good benefits. Guaranteed retirement plan."

Excitement swept through her. She tried not to let it show. "Working for you?"

"No. I would continue to contract for your services but you would be employed by another research lab. The situation would be similar to the one you had at the center."

He sounded almost bored, as if he were going through the motions, as if her decision was a matter of complete disinterest to him.

"I see." She thought about that for a moment and then decided to play a couple of her own cards. "Would this other lab by any chance be my former Client Number One? An unnamed government agency engaged in Level Five dream research?"

Ellis's brows climbed. "I take it you obviously know a lot more about your private clients than Martin Belvedere led us to believe."

He sounded impressed but not surprised, she thought, and certainly not alarmed. She got the distinct impression that he had already guessed that she knew a certain amount about her anonymous clients.

Her confidence rose. She picked up the teapot. He watched her fill his cup and then her own as if the small ritual fascinated him.

"After doing several dozen Level Five dream analyses it would be hard not to know something about my clients," she said, setting down the pot.

"I thought so." He made himself more comfortable in the chair, turning slightly to study some wet-suited surfers who were paddling out across the bay. "I told Lawson —"

"Lawson?"

"Jack Lawson. He's the director of Frey-Salter, Inc. Anonymous Client Number One to you."

"Ah."

"I told him that I would deliver his offer of a job. I've completed my assignment."

"No offense, but you didn't do much of a sales job," she said dryly.

He smiled his cool, edgy smile and picked up his cup. "Just said I'd make his offer for him. Didn't say I'd try to talk you into going to work at Frey-Salter."

"Just as well." She picked up the small cup with both hands, holding it between her fingertips. "Because I'll let you in on a little secret, Ellis. I've been doing a lot of thinking since Belvedere let me go. I've decided that I don't want to go back into a lab setting."

He continued to concentrate on the surfers. "I know that the kind of Level Five dreams Lawson and I asked you to interpret were . . ." He hesitated and took a swallow of tea. "Disturbing."

"True. But it wasn't the dreams that disturbed me the most. It was the way both of you withheld information from me."

That statement got his attention. He turned his head to look at her. "What do you mean? I can't speak for Lawson, but I made my dream reports as complete as possible."

"Oh, sure, you both gave me narratives of the dreams, but you didn't give me any *context*. I was never told anything about what was going on in the lives of the dreamers and even less about the subjects of the dreams."

His jaw tightened. "You must have figured out enough about the subjects to realize that they were extremely unpleasant."

"Of course. But that just made it all the

more frustrating." She spread her hands. "Because I never got any feedback on the results, either. Do you have any idea just how maddening it was to work that way?"

He looked blank. "Feedback?"

"I'm not stupid, Ellis. I may have been stuck in an office on the third floor at the Belvedere Center for Sleep Research for the past year, but it doesn't take a genius to figure out what you and the lab rats were doing."

"Lab rats?"

She ignored that. "You and Lawson's people are trying to use extreme dreams as investigative tools to solve crimes, aren't you?"

Ellis stretched out his legs and stacked his ankles, one on top of the other. She got the impression that he was doing some fast thinking, deciding how much to tell her.

"In a sense," he said cautiously.

"In a sense, my left toe. That is exactly what you're doing. Well, I did what I was hired to do to the best of my ability this past year. But not once during that time did either of you ever have the common courtesy to inform me of the results of any of the investigations I worked on with you. When I think of all the rush jobs, all the nights I spent on a cot in my office analyzing dreams because you had to have the answers as soon as possible, I could just spit."

He contemplated her for a long moment, comprehension building slowly in his expression.

"Well, hell," he said softly.

"Time and again, I asked Dr. B. to request the results of those cases. Time and again he told me that my requests were denied."

Ellis exhaled deeply. "Sorry about that. Lawson is real big on confidentiality. The requests I got from Belvedere all involved special cases that I handled for Lawson. The files were classified. You know how it is when you're dealing with government types. They aren't happy unless everything, including the instructions for operating the office vending machines, is stamped TOP SECRET."

"All I wanted was some closure on a few of the really bad cases. Was that too much to ask?"

"No."

"I didn't even have enough context to identify the most likely news stories on the Internet."

"Most of them weren't big enough stories to hit the major papers. Even if you had found some of them, all you would have learned was that local law enforcement officials had made arrests. Lawson keeps a very low profile. He never has any direct contact with the cops."

"So how does he get the cases that he assigns to you and the others?" she asked, eager for every scrap of information.

Again Ellis paused, evidently turning things over in his mind before deciding what to tell her. Then he shrugged.

"As far as outsiders are concerned, the cases are handled by a private investigation firm named Mapstone Investigations. The owner of the firm is very close to Lawson."

"A friend?"

"His wife. They've been together for about thirty years. They argue a lot but even when they're mad at each other, they still work together. Lawson trusts Beth Mapstone more than he trusts anyone else in the world."

"Including you?"

He picked up the small teacup. "Including me."

"I see." She drummed her fingers on the table. "Do you know how I work, Ellis?"

"Belvedere said that, essentially, you study a dream report and then you create a Level Five lucid dream of your own that incorporates the details of the subject's dream. You then analyze the subject's dream using your own extreme dreaming capabilities." He paused. "In other words, you walk through other people's dreams."

"Close enough. Now, given your personal, no doubt extensive experience with high-level lucid dreams, can you use a little imagination and figure out what never knowing the outcomes did to my own personal dreams? Did it ever occur to you that the lack of closure might give me a few Level Five nightmares?"

Grim understanding followed by something that looked a lot like genuine remorse drew his face into a stark mask.

"Shit."

She cleared her throat. "Yes."

"I figured analyzing the dreams wasn't pleasant, but it never occurred to me that they might affect your own, personal dreamscapes. Belvedere sure as hell never said anything about that. I guess I just assumed that you took a detached, academic approach to the process."

"I have a very vivid imagination, Ellis. Goes with the territory. Fragments of those nightmares hung around for weeks sometimes. And I had no context and no closure to help me get rid of them."

"Trust me, if I had been free to do so, I would have been happy to fill you in on the results of my cases. But Lawson wouldn't allow it."

"In my opinion Lawson is a control freak."

His mouth curved slightly. "You may be right."

"And since you are willing to work for him on his terms, I have to wonder about you, too."

He put down his cup, frowning. "You think I'm a control freak?"

She raised her chin and prepared to play what Gavin Hardy would have called her really big card.

"It doesn't matter what I think of you personally," she said smoothly. "What matters is that, as I mentioned, I have been doing a lot of thinking about my future in recent days and I have made a decision."

"I'm listening."

"I am tired of being used like a convenient piece of office equipment. From now on, if you or Lawson or anyone else wishes to utilize my extreme dream analysis services, you will have to contract with me directly. Furthermore, you will have to meet my requirements. Naturally I will guarantee client confidentiality. But I will also demand more context and feedback on each case."

He took a swallow of tea and looked fascinated. "Oh, man. Lawson is gonna be real upset about this."

"Then he can find himself another Level Five analyst." She held her breath, aware that she was risking everything with the move.

"You're the only one he's been able to identify," Ellis said. "Believe me, he's looked. Until you came along, he had to handle all the analyses and interpretations in-house, and there were a lot of mistakes made. Some of the symbols and metaphors in Level Five dreams are beyond weird."

Satisfaction made her almost giddy. She had been right, after all. Lawson didn't have anywhere else to turn. He needed her. So did Ellis Cutler.

She sat back in her chair and crossed her legs. "As I said, you and Lawson are quite welcome to sign a contract with me."

"Oh, man," he said again, almost under his breath. "This is going to be fun."

"I fail to see anything that is the least bit amusing about this situation," she snapped. "This is business." Committed now, she plunged recklessly ahead. "If I discover that a client fabricates any of the information concerning context or the final resolution of the various cases submitted to me with the intention of deceiving me or with the expectation of shutting me up, said client will no longer be eligible for my services."

"Understood."

"You think I'm joking?"

"No, Ms. Wright." His mouth jerked upward at the corner. "I can see that you are damn serious. You'll get no argument from me but I don't think Lawson is going to go for this new arrangement."

"If he doesn't like my terms, he is free to search for another analyst."

Ellis whistled softly. "You play hardball, Isabel Wright."

Gratified by that statement, she uncrossed her legs and got to her feet. "I've been taking lessons from some experts for the past year, namely you and Lawson. As I said, I've been doing a lot of thinking in recent days. I won't go back to working in the dark."

He tilted his head slightly, angling his gaze to watch her through the dark glasses. "In addition to freelancing for Lawson, I'm a business consultant, specifically a venture capitalist. I look at a lot of business plans. Speaking professionally, I feel obliged to point out a couple of negatives in yours."

She gripped the strap of her purse. "What negatives?"

"It's true that there are not a lot of people who can do what you do. But it is equally true that there also isn't a lot of demand for your services."

"I'm aware of that."

"You had a grand total of exactly two clients while you were at the center, right?"

"Right," she said, a little uneasy now that she could see where he was going with this.

"If Lawson doesn't agree to your contract terms, that will leave you with only one viable client. Me. Problem is, I get my special cases directly from Lawson, so if he doesn't want you involved, I won't be able to use your services."

She swallowed. "I understand."

"Think you can make a living without Lawson and his cases?"

"I don't know." She forced another Desperately Professional Smile. "Lucky for me I've got my new day job."

That made him go still again. "What's that?"

"I'm not here at Kyler to take a course of motivational seminars, Ellis. I'm going to work here."

"You're joking," he said, voice very flat and sure.

"Nope. I'm taking the instructors' course. On Monday I will begin teaching a series of seminars titled 'Tapping into the Creative Potential of Your Dreams.' "

He smiled. The smile stretched into a disbelieving grin. "Are you serious?"

"I am very, very serious. I need a steady paycheck while I get started in my new Level Five dream consulting career. My brother-in-law, Farrell Kyler, has kindly offered me gainful employment. I have accepted that offer."

Actually, she had thrown herself on Farrell's mercy and begged for the job but she saw no reason to go into the sordid details with Ellis. It was probably not a good idea to let a potential client know that you had financial problems.

Ellis was still smiling. "Teaching a motivational class on creative dreaming? I don't believe it. Everyone knows this motivational seminar stuff is a racket."

"No, not everyone knows that," she said, spacing each word very precisely. "A lot of people take the power of positive thinking quite seriously and with good reason. Motivational seminars work for people who are motivated enough to make them work."

"There's something a little circular about that reasoning."

His amused disdain infuriated her.

"You know what most folks would call a man who gets paid by a secret government agency to solve crimes in his dreams?" she asked very sweetly.

"A sharp con artist with a really good racket?"

"You got it. I don't think you're in any position to call my brother-in-law's business a scam, do you?"

"Point taken."

She inclined her head a fraction of an inch. "Let me know if you decide you want to become a Wright Dream Analysis client."

He smiled again, very slowly and very deliberately. It did odd things to her insides.

"Don't worry, Isabel. I'll get back to you."

6

Tango Dancer.

She had turned out to be exactly as he had imagined. Sexy, smoldering, mysterious, fascinating. Just the way she appeared in his dreams. Maybe it was those green-and-gold dreaming eyes.

He needed to report to Lawson. He also needed to do some thinking. He could feel everything in his carefully ordered world starting to shift and change. It was like being in the middle of a Level Five dream that had taken an unpredictable turn.

He'd had a plan when he moved back to California eight months ago, a plan that definitely involved Isabel Wright. But it did not include this shattering reaction to Isabel in the flesh.

Ellis walked out of the lobby of Kyler, Inc., got into the Maserati and drove a couple of miles beyond the Roxanna Beach city limits to the abandoned amusement park. He had discovered the fenced and gated collection of aging thrill rides, funhouses and concession stands the day before, when he turned off the main highway to take the old road into town. Amusement parks never failed to resonate with something deep inside him.

Roxanna Beach Amusement World was situated on a bluff above an empty stretch of windswept beach. It was a relic of a bygone era. There had been a time when small boardwalks and amusement parks with their roller coasters, Ferris wheels and carousels were common features along the California coast. But few had survived into the twenty-first century. The huge theme parks had come to dominate the thrill market.

He halted the Maserati in the empty parking lot, got out and walked across the cracked pavement to get a closer look at the skeleton of the roller coaster. He stood there for a long time, listening to the surf pounding the beach and tasting the salt-laden air.

The memories of his first roller coaster ride stirred the way they always did when he saw one of the scream machines. It had been a blustery spring day. He had to stand on his toes to make it past the sign that specified how tall a kid had to be to ride the coaster. His father bought the tickets, much against his mother's wishes.

She watched anxiously, afraid that Ellis was much too young for such a major thrill ride.

"It will give him nightmares," she said in low tones to Ellis's father.

"No it won't, he's a big boy. Besides, I'll be right there beside him. He can handle it. Isn't that right, son?"

"Sure, Dad. I'll be okay. I'm not scared."

He insisted on sitting in the front car. When the safety bar was lowered into place he felt a thrill unlike any other. He could still feel that first lurch and hear the ominous *clank-clank-clank* of the chain lift as it carried the train of cars to the top of the first hill. He could also hear his father's warning.

"There's no going back now."

He had loved every second of that wild ride. Ellis threaded his fingers through the chain links, remembering. The feeling of being scared witless while knowing all along that he was perfectly safe because he was strapped into his seat and his dad was right there with him was the most exhilarating experience he'd ever known.

Later the three of them had eaten cotton candy and popcorn and played some games in the arcade. He went home stuffed and happy. Contrary to his mother's fears, he did not have any nightmares. In fact, he entertained himself for quite a while reliving the exciting ride in one of the startlingly clear story dreams he was just beginning to learn how to create.

That first ride had set the pattern for all future Cutler family vacations. He and his father researched roller coasters from one end of the country to the other, selecting the most exotic and most exciting scream machines, and then planned trips around them. They became experts on the subject.

Together they savored the differences between the classic woodies and the elaborate steel roller coasters. They compared the amount of "airtime" — those glorious moments when you came up out of the seat and floated — delivered by the various machines. They discussed and charted the nuances of twister designs with their shrieking, high-speed turns and the out-and-backs with their steep hills and valleys.

And then, one afternoon when he was twelve years old, he was called out of class to face a small room full of very serious adults. They told him that both of his parents had been shot dead by a madman who walked into the restaurant where they were eating lunch and randomly murdered seven people before turning the gun on himself.

That night he spent what proved to be the first of many nights in the home of strangers.

The only roller coasters he rode these days were in his dreams.

He turned away from the silent relics, took the phone out of his pocket and punched in the number.

"How did it go?" Lawson demanded without preamble.

"Not quite the way you hoped it would. She's willing to continue consulting for you and me but she doesn't want to go to work at Frey-Salter. She's setting herself up in business."

"The hell she is." Lawson was clearly stunned. "She's just a naive little dreamer who's been stashed away in a small office at a low-rent lab for the past year. Before that she bounced around between one downwardly mobile job and another. The closest she ever got to a professional career was working for some phony psychic hotline operation. What does she know about operating a consulting business?"

"Looks like we're going to find out," Ellis said.

"Forget it. Out of the question. I told you, I want her brought into Frey-Salter. Can't have her running around out there on her own."

"She's not interested in your offer. By the way, she's figured out that she was consulting for some secret government research facility that is experimenting with extreme dreamers."

"Martin Belvedere told her about me and my agency? That SOB. He swore to me he never said a word —"

"She worked it out on her own. She's smart, Lawson. And she's a Level Five herself, remember."

"Huh. Think she's talked to anyone about what she knows?"

"No. She is well aware of how important confidentiality is to you and she's interested in having you as a client. She won't go to the media with her story."

"What's her objection to coming back here to work?"

"Seems she didn't like having all of her requests for case briefings ignored or declined. She wanted more of what she calls 'context.' She also wanted to know the results of the investigations."

"Those cases were confidential." Lawson's voice rose. "She had no need to know."

"Look at the situation from her point of view. She got all of the questions but she never got any of the answers. She said it was frustrating. Said she needs closure."

"Closure? Sounds like some kind of pop-psych babble."

"Most of the dream reports we asked her to look at were pretty bad," Ellis reminded him. "She said the anxiety of never knowing the outcomes gave her nightmares."

"She's a Level Five. She's supposed to be able to deal with a few bad dreams."

"You know what? I think she's right about you, Lawson. You are a control freak."

"Maybe so, but I'm a control freak with a serious budget. Without me, Isabel Wright will have a real short client list. Does she get that part?"

Ellis smiled to himself. "Yes, but she doesn't seem to be worried about it. Got herself a day job to tide her over until her consulting business kicks in."

"What kind of day job? Don't tell me she's gone back to answering phones at the Psychic Dreamer Hotline."

"No. She's training to be an instructor in her brother-in-law's motivational seminar business."

"*What?*"

"You heard me."

"That's crazy," Lawson bellowed. "Why would she want to do something like that when she could be back here working at Frey-Salter?"

"Gee. I don't know. It's curious, isn't it? Maybe it's got something to do with not being cooped up in a tiny, windowless office and not having to take orders from a control freak who only tells you what he thinks you need to know."

"I'm glad you're finding this so damned amusing, Cutler. Because I'm not. Listen up. I hired you to bring her in. Stop messing around out there and do your job."

"You want my advice?"

"No."

"Well, you're going to get it," Ellis said. "Deal with her the way you did with Martin Belvedere. Pay her well. She'll respect your demands for confidentiality."

"I don't want another independent. I want Isabel Wright working here at Frey-Salter where I can, uh —"

"Control her?" Ellis offered.

"Where I can keep an eye on her," Lawson amended.

"Forget it. Not going to happen."

"You sound a little too damn cheerful about all this," Lawson muttered suspiciously. "What are you up to?"

Ellis opened the door of the Maserati and got behind the wheel.

"I've been thinking that I need to broaden my perspective and maybe take a more positive approach to life," he said. "Maybe I'll sign up for a course of motivational seminars."

"I don't believe I'm hearing this."

"Isabel's going to be teaching a class called 'Tapping into the Creative Potential of Your Dreams.' Who knows? Maybe I'll pick up a few pointers."

He ended the call before Lawson could finish sputtering.

7

Vincent Scargill dreamed . . .

He stands on the high cliff, poised for the dive into the vast blue depths of the sea. He will plunge down beneath the cool, shimmering surface, counting each breath he takes underwater until he reaches the sparkling clear place where the currents carry the dream images.

But as he watches from the top of the cliff, a great wave rises out of the ocean. It is huge, a vast wall of water that dwarfs the cliff top where he stands. He knows it will crash over him, crushing him, drowning him, making it impossible for him to dive into the clear currents below.

As the tsunami bears down upon him he sees that the waters have turned blood red . . .

"Vincent, wake up." The firm voice summoned him from the dreamscape. "Wake up, Vincent."

He tried to resist, reluctant to abandon the attempt to dive into the dreamscape. It was his only hope of escaping this place that had become his prison.

But in the end, he had no choice. The voice had broken through the fragile barrier that separated a high-level lucid dream from wakefulness. Once pierced, there was no going back through the veil. He would have to reconstruct another dream and that was not easy to do these days.

He had made progress since the terrible morning when he nearly died in the explosion at the cabin, but not nearly enough. The head injury had healed within a few weeks but the damage that had been done to his dreaming capability was far more extensive than either he or his companion had realized. He could no longer access the gateway dream, the one that took him into the extreme dreaming state.

He opened his eyes. His companion was bending over him, watching him closely.

"Are you all right?"

"No." He sat up on the edge of the sofa and glanced at the clock. It was nearly midnight. He had spent two hours trying to get into the dream state. "All I get is that damned red tsunami. Maybe if I took a higher dose I could get past it."

"Perhaps, but we must be very, very careful. An overdose might destroy your Level Five capability altogether. Too much might kill you."

Rage surged through him. He shoved himself to his feet and went to stand at the window. "This is all Cutler's fault. He did this to me."

"I know, Vincent. Trust me, we will find a way to enable you to dream again."

He brooded on the strip of palm trees that lined the avenue below the condo window. He had spent a large portion of the past few months in this place and he hated it.

He had few memories of those first weeks following the explosion. His dreams had been blurred and fragmented. Eventually they began to clear, however, and he believed that he was regaining his Level Five ability. In an effort to speed up the process, his companion began giving him increasingly large injections from their small supply of CZ-149, the experimental dream-enhancing drug produced back at Frey-Salter. But the stuff was not helping much. If anything, the tsunami was growing larger and more violently crimson with each dose.

A few weeks ago, desperate, he had slipped out of the condo while his companion was gone and contacted Martin Belvedere personally. He knew he could trust the old man to keep quiet. All Belvedere cared about was his research, and Vincent knew he could offer him an interesting case study.

He met with Belvedere in a small café near the Center for Sleep Research. The location had been Belvedere's choice. They sat together in a cheap vinyl booth drinking bad coffee while he gave the old man his recent dream reports and told him about the head trauma that had impacted his Level Five abilities.

Belvedere made copious notes and then he took the information back to his office to study. They met again two days later at the same café. But all the old man had been able to tell him was that the giant red wave was a "blocking" image that prevented him from accessing the gateway dream. Hell, he had already figured that much out for himself.

"I can't take this any longer." He gripped the windowsill so tightly all the blood was squeezed out of his knuckles. "That damned tsunami dream is making me crazy."

His companion tapped the tip of the pen against the desktop. "There is one other approach we can try. I just learned about it this evening. That's why I woke you."

He turned swiftly. "What approach?"

"In the past couple of months Frey-Salter has come up with a new version of CZ-149. They're calling it Variant A. My informant says it doesn't appear to have the side effects that the earlier version of the drug has. I'm told that the initial tests have gone very well."

"Get it."

"That's the problem. I almost didn't tell you about it because, to be honest, I don't know how to get it. There is only a very limited supply at the moment. Most of it is under tight security at Frey-Salter. Lawson gave the rest to the agent who is field-testing it for him."

He went cold. "Which agent?"

"Ellis Cutler."

"Bastard. *Bastard.*"

There was a dull thud. Pain crashed through his fist. He looked down and realized he had just struck the wall beside the window with such force that he had knocked a hole in it. Bits of painted wallboard lay on the carpet at his feet. There was blood on his hand.

Rage as red and fierce as the tsunami of his dreams washed over him. He looked at his companion through the crimson mist.

"Where is Cutler?"

"A place called Roxanna Beach."

He started toward the door.

"Vincent, wait. You can't risk exposing yourself. Lawson thinks you're dead. If he gets even a hint that you're still alive, he will hunt you down. He has the resources to do it. You know that. You won't stand a chance."

He stopped at the door. Some of the red tide ebbed from his brain. He was shaking and sweating now. He rubbed his temples, trying to think.

"I have to get the new drug," he said.

"I understand. But first we need a plan."

8

Randolph stared at the tall, thin man standing in front of the desk, so stunned by the news that the high-priced, forensic accountant had just delivered that he could not immediately react. Webber had to be wrong.

"Th-that's impossible," Randolph finally got out. He was horrified to hear himself stutter. Whenever the old childhood speech problem returned, it was a sure sign that he was under enormous pressure.

Amelia Netley said nothing but her fine jaw clenched more tightly. She continued to stalk back and forth in front of the windows as she had been doing for the past few minutes, her arms folded beneath her elegant breasts.

"I'm afraid it's a fact, Dr. Belvedere." Webber tapped the file against his palm and looked grim. "It took a lot of time and some very creative work to follow the money trail, but there's no doubt in my mind that what I just told you is the truth. I can see this comes as something of a surprise."

"Surprise? It's a frigging bombshell. Give me that file."

Webber handed it to him. "It's an extremely sophisticated financial setup. I had to dig deep to understand it."

"My father was not at all sophisticated when it came to business." Randolph slapped open the file. "He couldn't have done this himself."

Webber nodded thoughtfully. "Then it must have been the clients who went to such extraordinary lengths to conceal the payments."

"But why would they want to hide the fact that they were contracting with the center? It makes no sense."

"I don't know. I can tell you that one of them is a fairly small player. But the other, Client Number One, has obviously dropped some big bucks into the center over the course of the past several years. As you can see, the amounts got even larger in the last twelve months."

Randolph stared at the figures on the page in front of him. "Forty-seven percent of the total operating budget of the center has been coming from Client Number One for two decades?"

"The figure shot up to fifty-seven percent of the total income this past year."

Webber leaned over the desk to point to another row of figures. "You will notice that Client Number Two came on board about a year ago. He doesn't do anywhere near the same volume of business as the other one, but he is definitely a significant account."

"This is unbelievable," Randolph whispered. "B-between the two of them, these two anonymous clients accounted for over s-sixty percent of the center's gross receipts for the past year."

"Right. The rest of the income appears to come from a mix of small grants from some nutritional supplement manufacturers, sleep research foundations and a couple of small-time inventors who hired Belvedere to test various types of sleep aids."

"Th-th-this is a disaster." Randolph sagged into his chair. "Over sixty percent of the center's funding is coming from two unknown sources. It doesn't make any sense. What services was my father providing to them?"

Webber cleared his throat. "I'm still working on that. The records are all very vague. But as far as this past year goes, I did discover that the bulk of the billing for both accounts appears to have been connected to one particular department here at the center."

Randolph's stomach knotted. "Which one?"

"The Department of Dream Analysis."

Amelia's jaw clenched.

A great sense of impending doom settled on Randolph. He could almost hear Amelia saying *I told you so.* He made a fist with one hand to stop the tremor.

"Isabel Wright," he muttered. "I c-can't believe it. Who would pay that kind of money for some silly psychic dream analysis?"

Webber raised one scrawny shoulder in a mild shrug. "The pharmaceutical companies are rolling in cash. Maybe a couple of them decided to spend some of it on dream research. It might explain the secrecy. They've got a lot at stake when it comes to protecting their proprietary R and D data."

Randolph shook his head. "No sane, sensible corporation that has to show its shareholders a p-profit would throw several million dollars at a low-profile research facility like the Belvedere Center for Sleep Research just to fund investigations into my father's ridiculous psychic dream theories."

Webber pursed his lips and canted his head an inch or so to one side. "I suppose one or both of the anonymous clients might be wealthy eccentrics or religious cults with a thing about dreams."

"I told you there was something strange going on with the funding here, Randolph." Amelia stopped in front of the window, her brittle tension clear in every line of her body. "And I told you that it probably had something to do with your father's personal research interests. I also told you that meant that the extremely healthy cash flow was very likely connected to that ridiculous Department of Dream Analysis. Didn't I tell you that?"

He knew she was angry but he was, nevertheless, taken aback by the impatience and raw fury he saw in her face. They had been lovers for weeks. In the bedroom Amelia was far and away the most inventive woman he had ever met. But in the days following Isabel Wright's departure from the center, she had shown another side of her nature.

When he had refused to believe that Isabel Wright and the Department of Dream Analysis might be important to the long-term financial future of the center, she had insisted on bringing in a forensic accountant to take a deep look into the center's books.

"I d-don't understand," he said, utterly bewildered.

She crossed the office and stopped in front of his desk.

"Try to stay focused here, Randolph," she said. "I've been telling you for the past few days that it is absolutely critical that you persuade Isabel Wright to return to the center before those two accounts, whoever they are, realize she is gone. Now do you understand why?"

He pulled himself together and tried to concentrate. "How did you know that my father was doing so much business through that little department?"

"I kept my eyes open." She threw up her hands, exasperated. "I paid attention. I did the math. It was obvious to anyone who cared to look that there was no way Martin Belvedere could possibly have made the overhead and paid the excellent salaries here at the center with the funding he got for the routine sleep research projects. I knew there had to be some other source. Given your father's eccentricities, I concluded that other source was probably linked to Isabel Wright's dream analysis work."

He felt cornered. "What the hell am I supposed to do?"

Amelia planted her hands on the desk. "Exactly what I told you to do. Call her. Tell her that you made a mistake and you want her to come back to her old job. Tell her that you will make her dream come true."

He went blank. "What dream?"

"Promise her that you will appoint her head of the Department of Dream Analysis." Amelia looked knowing. "That's what she wants more than anything else. Don't worry, once she's back here, I'll take charge of that department. She can have her fancy title, but I'll control her and the interaction with those two well-heeled clients."

"I need to think for a m-minute." Mostly he needed to clear his brain of the panic that was nibbling at the edges. He should have known that his father would find a way to ruin everything for him, even from beyond the grave.

A few seconds of silence ticked past. Webber and Amelia waited, their impatience obvious.

He took a deep breath and reached toward the intercom. "First, I'll get the word out to the staff that Wright's departure was the result of a misunderstanding that has been cleared up. I'll have Mrs. Johnson let it be known that Isabel will be resuming her responsibilities immediately after she returns from a well-earned vacation."

Webber nodded wisely. "That may help put a stop to the office gossip."

"It shouldn't be that hard to talk her into returning to her old job," Amelia added quickly. She looked relieved. "According to her personnel file the only other work she's qualified for is answering phones at a psychic hotline. She'll be desperate by now. Make your offer a good one and she'll come flying back."

"Let's just hope that the two anonymous clients haven't found out that she's gone," Webber muttered darkly.

Randolph shuddered and punched the intercom. "Mrs. Johnson, has anyone called this office to inquire about Isabel Wright recently?"

"Why, yes, as a matter of fact there was one call. I explained that Isabel was no longer working here."

Webber and Amelia exchanged worried glances.

Oh, shit. Randolph told himself to stay calm. "Did the caller identify himself, Mrs. Johnson?"

"It was a woman, sir. I believe she said

she was with a credit card company."

Randolph allowed himself to take another deep breath. Out of the corner of his eye he saw Webber and Amelia relax slightly. If Isabel Wright had financial problems, that would make it all the easier to convince her to return.

"From now on, you will refer any and all questions c-concerning Ms. Wright directly to me. Is that clear?"

"Yes, sir."

"There has been a serious m-misunderstanding, Mrs. Johnson. Isabel Wright was not fired. She is on vacation and will soon return to her position here at the center. Please make certain that everyone else on the staff is aware of that."

"Yes, sir." Sandra Johnson's voice brightened. "If you don't mind my saying so, I'm delighted to hear that. I know a lot of other people will feel the same way. Isabel was very well liked around here."

"Yes, I got that impression." Randolph cut the intercom connection. He looked at Webber. "All right, that's all I can do in the way of damage control for now. The next step is to find Wright and let her know that she still has a job. I'll get her c-contact address and phone number from HR and call her personally."

"As soon as she knows you want her back, she'll realize that she's in the driver's seat," Webber warned. "She'd be a fool not to try to negotiate an increase in salary."

"She can have whatever she wants, including caviar pizza delivered every day for lunch so long as she comes back," Amelia snapped. "We're talking about a potential bankruptcy here, in case no one else has noticed."

"Trust me, I've n-noticed," Randolph said.

The anger was so thick in his throat he was about to choke. Damned if he would let the old man do this to him, he thought. The center was the only thing of value he'd ever gotten from his father. The bastard never had any time for him when he was growing up, never showed any signs of approval no matter how hard he tried to please him. Martin Belvedere had cared only about his dream research.

"The s-sonofabitch set me up for failure," he said, reaching for the phone. "But I'm not going to let him s-screw me over this time."

9

"Who was that man I saw you having coffee with yesterday?" Leila asked.

Startled, Isabel laughed.

Leila frowned. "What's so funny?"

"Nothing really." Isabel closed the Kyler Method instructor's manual she had been studying. "I just realized that it's been quite a while since anyone asked me that kind of question."

Leila's brows rose. "What kind is that?"

"One that makes it sound like I might actually have a social life."

They were sitting in Leila's office. All of the Kyler executive suites were first class, Isabel reflected, just like everything else involved in the business, but her sister's position as vice president ensured a particularly fabulous view. The darkly tinted, floor-to-ceiling windows looked directly out over the bay.

The elegant space was decorated in rich, warm neutrals with accents of black and Kyler red. The furnishings were expensive, modern pieces imported from Italy. Leila had overseen the interior design of every building at the Kyler headquarters. She had excellent taste.

But then, that was Leila through and through, Isabel thought. Her younger sister was not only extremely attractive, with her delicate features and excellent figure, she had a natural flair for style. Her hair was streaked with subtle blond highlights and cut into a fashionable bob. Her close-fitting cream-colored silk blouse and camel trousers sent a message of good breeding and refinement.

They were only two years apart, Isabel reflected, but they had always been opposites in many ways. Leila had played the role of the overachieving good girl, the one who made their fiercely competitive, highly successful executive father proud and pleased their socially ambitious mother.

From time to time Isabel had tried to warn Leila that her efforts were for naught. It had been clear to her early on that nothing either of them did was going to hold their parents' marriage together, but Leila kept on trying to do just that by being Miss Perfect.

Even after their parents had divorced and remarried, Leila continued to be the good daughter. She was the one who brought home the long strings of A's on her report cards, signed up for endless after-school activities in order to make herself look good to potential college acceptance committees, got elected to the student council and dated the kind of boys who were voted most likely to succeed. She attended an excellent college, established herself as a successful interior designer and topped off her list of accomplishments by marrying Farrell Kyler, a fast-rising executive in their father's corporation.

Isabel was well aware that she, on the other hand, had been a major disappointment. She loved her parents and as a child had wanted to please them. But as she grew older, the mysteries of her rapidly developing capacity to dream extreme dreams fascinated and consumed her. She needed answers but no one she talked to even understood her questions.

She had been labeled an "overly imaginative child inclined to daydream," a diagnostic understatement if ever there was one, and had spent a lot of time chatting with some very nice people in the counseling profession who tried to get her to participate in more school activities.

But the long line of therapists failed to draw her away from the consuming strangeness of her dream world. Her life, until she met Martin Belvedere, had been a lonely journey of exploration, self-discovery and low-wage jobs.

"I saw you with him out on the terrace in front of the café," Leila explained. "He didn't seem to be your usual type."

That gave her pause. "You really think I have a usual type?"

"Brian Phillips, Jason Strong and Larry Higgins, for starters."

"Huh. I see what you mean."

The three were among the handful of men she had dated in recent years. All followed the familiar pattern: a roller-coaster ride that started out with a lot of enthusiastic conversations about their dreams, followed by steep plunges into boredom.

"Well, if it makes you feel any better," she continued, "Ellis Cutler is not a hot date. If I'm lucky, however, he may turn out to be a client."

"You mean he's thinking about signing up for your new seminar here at Kyler?"

"No." She spread her fingers on the cushions and dug her nails slightly into the soft leather, bracing herself. "I did some dream analysis work for him while I was at the center. He's thinking of contracting with me for some more of the same."

Leila grimaced. Isabel pretended not to notice. She was used to that look on the faces of her relatives whenever the subject of her career path arose.

"You're serious about trying to establish yourself as a freelance dream consultant?" Leila asked.

Her tone implied that she had moved beyond her initial reaction of acute disapproval and was now resigned to the inevitable.

That was progress of a sort, Isabel thought, applying the positive thinking techniques she was studying in the Kyler Method manual.

"Yes," she said, going for upbeat and optimistic, "but it could take time to build up a client list. That's why I'm very grateful to you and Farrell for giving me a chance to work as an instructor here for a while."

"You're family," Leila said flatly. "Can't have you out begging on the streets."

"I don't know that I would have ended up on the streets," Isabel said, trying not to let her irritation show. Leila meant well, after all. "If push had come to shove, I could have gone back to my old job."

"Answering phones for that psychic hotline operation? Don't be ridiculous. Mom and Dad were horrified when they found out what you were doing there."

"It was a living."

"It was an embarrassment." Leila sighed. "By the way, have you told Mom and Dad that you got fired?"

"No." Isabel slouched deeper into the sleek leather sofa. "I learned a long time ago that it's best if I don't give them too much information until I've settled into a new job. It just upsets them."

"I suppose there's no need to e-mail them the bad news."

"Look on the bright side. They'll be giddy with relief when they find out I'm going to work for you and Farrell for a while."

"Yes, but they're not going to be so thrilled when they find out you're planning to set yourself up as some sort of psychic dream consultant."

"We've been through this a million times, Leila. I've told you over and over again that I do not consider myself to be psychic."

"You've worked for at least two so-called professional psychics, to my knowledge."

"You know, some folks would say that giving seminars designed to teach people how to tap into the creative potential of their dreams is not a whole lot different from doing psychic dream consulting."

"That's ridiculous," Leila said instantly, outraged. "The Kyler Method is a proven technique that can be applied to any aspect of one's daily life. There's no reason it won't work with dreams."

"If you really feel that way," Isabel said quietly, "would you mind telling me why Farrell doesn't want me here?"

Leila froze. "Of course he wants you here. Why do you say he doesn't?"

"Call it a wild hunch but every time I run into him in the hall he seems to be looking for a way to avoid me. I get the impression that it wasn't his idea to offer me this job."

Leila's mouth tightened. "It will work out."

"Damn. I knew it. I was afraid of this."

"Afraid of what?"

"You convinced him that he had to give me a job because I'm family, didn't you?"

"For the past year, Tamsyn and I have been encouraging Farrell to add new courses to the syllabus. Kyler, Inc., must stay competitive. Classes in dreams are trendy. They'll pull a new market."

Her sister's strange mood sent a trickle of unease through Isabel. "In other words, Farrell did not want to bring me on board as a new instructor. You and Tamsyn pressured him into it, didn't you? No wonder he isn't acting real happy to see me."

"I wouldn't worry about Farrell, if I were you." Leila abruptly rose to her feet. "It certainly isn't your fault if he isn't happy. As far as I can tell, nothing pleases him these days."

Isabel was shocked by the bitter edge on her sister's words. "Leila, what's wrong?"

For a moment she thought she was not going to get an answer. Then she saw the glint of tears in Leila's eyes. She leaped off the sofa and hurried around behind the desk to hug her tightly.

"Tell me," she whispered.

Leila said nothing. But the tears spilled down her cheeks.

Isabel rocked her gently. "Tell me, please. I can't stand not knowing what's making you so unhappy."

"Oh, Isabel, I'm afraid that Farrell may be turning into a carbon copy of Dad."

"What?"

"It's true." Leila yanked a couple of tissues from the box on the desk and blotted her eyes. "It used to be Farrell and me. We were a team. But now it seems to be Farrell and the business. That was the way it always was with Dad, remember? The only thing he cared about was the next big deal." Leila sniffed into the tissue. "And the next beautiful young wife, of course."

"Leila, you aren't trying to tell me that Farrell has gotten involved with another woman, because I wouldn't believe it. Not for a moment."

"No, of course not." Leila grabbed another tissue. "Farrell is too honest to cheat on me. But he's consumed by the business these days. He's always talking about new directions and goals for Kyler. He spends half the night in his office going over marketing and expansion plans. He even postponed our vacation to Hawaii. Do you know how many dinners I've eaten alone in the past month?"

"Leila, hold on here —"

"Farrell is absolutely obsessed." Leila sighed. "Just like Dad."

"Whoa, stop right there." Isabel released her, took a step back and waved her arms to get her sister's attention. "As I recall, and my memory is quite clear on this point, Farrell has always been passionate about his business."

Leila shook her head. "Not the way he is lately. He used to *practice* the Kyler Method. He always claimed that the hallmark of a good executive was the ability to delegate. He was conscientious about keeping a balance in his life. Until a few months ago, we both left the office at a reasonable hour. We took weekends off. Went to Hawaii a couple of times a year. But lately, Farrell seems driven to devote all of his energy to Kyler, Inc. The company is all he cares about, as far as I can tell."

"I don't know what to say. I always thought you and Farrell had the perfect marriage."

"No relationship is perfect." Leila turned away. "But I am very good at projecting the right image, aren't I?"

"Leila?"

"That's what I do, isn't it? Pretend that everything is perfect. I've been doing it all my life. Talk about positive thinking. I was doing the Kyler Method before it was even a gleam in Farrell's eye. I'm the original Pollyanna."

Isabel patted her shoulder. "Have you tried talking to Farrell?"

"Of course. But he always finds a way to avoid the subject. He keeps saying that he just needs a little time. I'm feeling trapped. I'm not sleeping well and when I do sleep, I have the most disturbing dreams about —" She broke off, grimacing. "Never mind."

"Hey, it's okay to go there with me. Dreams are my thing, remember?"

"No offense, but I don't need you to tell me that I'm having anxiety dreams. Who wouldn't in my situation?"

"Sometimes it helps to talk about them," Isabel said. "It can clarify issues."

"The dreams are about children, Isabel." Leila tossed the used tissue into the trash. "I don't think there's any clarification needed. I intended to be pregnant by now. You know that. I even drew up plans for the nursery."

"I know how much you've always wanted to be a mother. I thought Farrell was big on having a family, too."

"He said we should put it off until Kyler, Inc., was established on a firm footing. And I agreed. But things are going well now and he's still making excuses. He says the business needs his undivided attention. Remember how Dad always used to say that whenever he couldn't make it to a school play or go on vacation with us?"

"Farrell is not Dad," Isabel said.

"I keep telling myself that, but I'm starting to feel so *alone,* the way Mom must have felt when she realized her marriage was falling apart."

"You're not alone," Isabel said quietly.

"I'm here. Don't ever forget that."

Leila managed a watery smile. "Thanks. You know, I'm sorry you lost your job at the Belvedere Center for Sleep Research but I'm really glad you're in town for a while."

"Trust me, I'm glad to be here, too." She glanced at her watch. "Got to run. My next class starts in three minutes. Kyler Method instructors are never late. Sets a bad example."

"Isabel, about this Ellis Cutler. What, exactly, do you know about him?"

"Well, he told me that he's a venture capitalist. Advises startup companies and finds investors to finance them. You could call him a business consultant, I suppose."

Leila frowned. "A business consultant? And he wants to hire you to analyze his dreams?"

"Go figure, huh?"

10

He was waiting for her when she emerged from the seminar room that afternoon. She didn't see him immediately because she was the last one to leave, but she could feel him. It was like coming too close to an electric fence. Little shocks pulsed through her.

He was wearing his dark glasses indoors again. She wondered if he wore them to bed and immediately got a sexy vision of him walking toward her across a bedroom wearing nothing but a pair of sunglasses. She felt herself turn violently warm.

"What are you doing here?" she asked, trying not to look excited.

"I told you I'd get back to you."

"Oh, right." *He's a potential client. Smile, for heaven's sake.* She smiled. "Have you decided if you want to contract with Wright Dream Analysis?"

"Uh-huh. Mind if we discuss the details of the contract over dinner?"

She went blank. "Dinner?"

"In a restaurant. You know, where you

order the food off a menu and people serve it to you?"

"Oh, dinner." *Not a date,* she told herself. *He's asking you out for a business dinner. Huge, massive difference.* "Sorry, it's been a long day."

"I see."

She glanced around to make certain that none of her fellow instructor trainees was within earshot and then lowered her voice. "Don't tell anyone I said this, but, frankly, four hours of positive energy and creative, strategic thinking has a numbing effect on the brain. At least it does on mine."

"All the more reason to take the evening off and relax."

"I think you're right. I'll take you up on your offer of dinner. Thanks."

"It's a deal. When do you get out of here?" he asked.

"I've got one more class and then I'm done for the day."

He grinned at her pained expression. "Good luck in getting through another hour of positive thinking."

She straightened her shoulders. "A Kyler Method instructor finds a positive way to deal with every bump in the road. Problems are opportunities in disguise."

"Is that a fact? Could have fooled me.

It's been my experience that problems are usually just problems."

She gave him a sunny smile. "Shows how much you know."

"Isabel." Tamsyn spoke from midway down the hall. "There you are. Farrell and I have been looking for you."

Isabel turned.

Farrell was in his late thirties. He had an athletic frame and he was handsome in a rugged, clean-cut, western sort of way. But Isabel did not think that most people, male or female, noticed his looks, one way or another. It was Farrell's dynamic personality that pulled you into his force field. He had charisma, loads of it. He never forgot names and faces and he could make conversation with anyone, regardless of age or background.

Isabel had once mentioned to Leila that Farrell would have done very well in politics. Her sister had laughed. *Farrell is too ethical for the political arena,* she had said with loving pride. *He couldn't handle the sausage-making parts, the backroom deals and the compromises.*

Tamsyn looked as vital and attractive offstage as she did when she stood in the carefully directed lights at the front of the auditorium. She practically vibrated with enthusiasm. Her Kyler jacket was carefully tailored to discreetly exhibit the curves and cleavage created by the expensive breast implants she had invested in following her divorce two years ago.

Tamsyn turned the full force of her high-energy smile on Ellis. Isabel sensed her intense curiosity.

"Hello," Tamsyn said warmly. "I don't believe we've met."

"Farrell, Tamsyn, this is Ellis Cutler," Isabel murmured. "Ellis, this is Tamsyn Strickland, an instructor here at Kyler, Inc., and my brother-in-law, Farrell Kyler, the founder of the Kyler Method."

Everyone shook hands and said the polite words.

"Are you attending this week's seminar series, Ellis?" Farrell asked.

His eyes tightened a bit at the corners as he studied Ellis. Only someone who knew him well would have detected the faint signs of wariness, Isabel thought. Farrell was not sure what to make of Ellis. He was being cautious.

"No, I'm here to see Isabel," Ellis said.

"Really?" Tamsyn's curiosity level had clearly gone up another notch. "Are you a friend of hers?"

"New client," Isabel said quickly. "I'm

starting up a private consulting business."

Farrell winced. "The psychic dream thing?"

"Not exactly," Isabel said evenly.

But, as usual, the correction went unnoticed.

Tamsyn rolled her eyes good-naturedly. "I'm amazed. I would never have guessed that you would be the type of man who would go in for the woo-woo thing, Ellis."

"I am not a psychic," Isabel said forcefully. No one paid any attention.

"Some people are fascinated with orchids and others have a thing for golf," Ellis said. "Personally, I've always been interested in dreams."

"So, dreams are a hobby for you?" Tamsyn asked.

Ellis smiled slightly. Light glinted ominously off the lenses of his dark glasses. "You could say that."

Farrell studied him. "I assume Isabel has told you that she's going to be teaching a course in dreams for us here at Kyler?"

"She mentioned it, yes," Ellis said.

"I have to admit, I was somewhat reluctant at first. I'm concerned that a course on dreams might send the wrong message. We're not about the New Age thing here at Kyler. But Tamsyn and my wife have convinced me that it will be a popular class."

"We certainly won't be taking a psychic or mystical approach to the course," Tamsyn assured everyone. "We've made that clear to Isabel. Farrell and I want the class taught according to the same guidelines that apply to all the other Kyler Method seminars. The idea is to teach students to use dreams to inspire the creative process. Right, Isabel?"

"Right," Isabel murmured.

"Isabel will teach the class using proven creativity-enhancing techniques such as free association and journaling," Tamsyn continued.

"Good to know there won't be any of the woo-woo stuff," Ellis said politely.

Tamsyn glanced at her watch. "Farrell, we've got that appointment with Dan and Gary in five minutes. We'd better be on our way."

"Yes." Farrell put out his hand again. "See you around, Cutler."

"Oh, yeah." Ellis gripped his hand and shook briefly. "As long as Isabel is here in Roxanna Beach, you will definitely be seeing me around."

Farrell's jaw tightened in what might have been disapproval but he merely nodded once and turned to walk away.

"Goodbye, Ellis." Tamsyn gave him another high-voltage smile. "You might want to think about signing up for Isabel's dream class."

"I'll consider it," he said.

Isabel watched the pair walk away along the carpeted hall. "Don't get me wrong, I'm grateful to them for this job but I sure hope I get my dream consulting business up and running real quick. I'm not sure I'm cut out for a long-term career as a Kyler Method instructor."

"What was your first clue?"

"I don't think I look good in this blazer."

11

Isabel changed her clothes three times before settling on a classic little black dinner dress. According to her fashionable mother, one could never go wrong with a little black dress. Jennifer Wright had made mistakes when it came to the men in her life, but never when it came to the clothes. Unfortunately, Isabel thought, unlike Leila, she had not gotten her parent's fashion genes.

She studied her image with a critical eye. With its deep cowl neckline and three-quarter-length sleeves, the dress appeared to achieve a nice balance between casual and elegant. The asymmetrical skirt added a touch of fashion flair.

"What do you think, Sphinx?"

Sphinx, ensconced in the center of the bed, opened his eyes at the sound of his name. He showed no interest in the dress.

"Thanks. I'll take that as unqualified approval."

She reached for a pair of gold earrings, threaded them through the tiny holes in her earlobes and then took another look at herself in the mirror. The skirt of the dress was cut quite high on one side. Was that fashion flair or just tacky? What note was she trying to strike here, anyway? Ellis was a client, not a date. Maybe a sober business suit would have been a better choice.

But this was Dream Man. All he had ever seen her wearing to date was that dumb Kyler blazer. She just could not bring herself to drag out a dull business suit.

She glanced at the clock. He was due in five minutes. There was no time to try a fourth outfit. This dress was going to have to work.

She heard a low, muted rumble. At first she thought it was Sphinx, cranking up his heavy purr. Then she realized it was a car engine.

"This is it, Sphinx. My big night with Dream Man."

Sphinx twitched his ears.

Out in the street, the low rumble of the big engine stopped.

Adrenaline perked through Isabel's veins. She stepped into the strappy high heels and checked the sleek knot at the nape of her neck. Another pang of uncertainty fluttered in her stomach. Was the overall effect too severe?

The knock on the front door told her that time had run out. She took a deep breath, squared her shoulders and walked out of the bedroom. Sphinx rose, stretched, yawned and followed. She heard a heavy thud behind her when he landed on the floor.

"We may want to talk about cutting back on your chow, Sphinx. There is a fine line between statuesque and plump."

The six large packing cartons she had found waiting for her on her doorstep when she got home that afternoon littered the route to the front door. She had managed to drag them inside but they were too heavy for her to lift or stack. It occurred to her that the clutter would not make a good impression on a prospective client. If there was one thing she had learned from watching Leila and Farrell over the past few years, it was that in business, image was everything.

Damn. Maybe she should have offered to meet Ellis at the restaurant.

Another knock sounded on the door. This one was a bit more forceful. There was no turning back now.

She smiled her best entrepreneurial smile and opened the door. The brisk, snapping breeze hit her carefully arranged hair with the force of a small hurricane.

"Good grief." She reached up with both hands to anchor the loosened tendrils that whipped wildly around her face. So much for the businesswoman image. "I didn't realize it was blowing so hard out here."

"Storm coming in off the ocean," Ellis said. He watched her from the other side of the ever-present dark glasses.

"Yes, I got that impression." She stepped back into the hall. "Come on in while I do something with this hair."

She checked her image in the hall mirror and made a face. The style was ruined. Reaching up, she removed the clip that had anchored the chignon. Her hair tumbled down around her shoulders.

"It looks good that way," Ellis said quietly, watching her in the mirror.

She hesitated and then, on a whim, shrugged. "Okay, I'll leave it down."

She turned, taking in the sight of him standing in her private space. He looked good, she thought. Actually, he looked great. He wore a pair of close-fitting black trousers, a silver gray shirt with an open collar and an elegantly cut, slightly slouchy jacket woven in shades of gray and black.

Sphinx approached slowly, tail held high.

He surveyed Ellis with the air of one predator sizing up another.

Ellis crouched and politely held out his fingers. "Didn't know you had a cat."

"He was Dr. Belvedere's cat. Randolph didn't want him and neither did anyone else at the center."

"So you took him?"

"It was either me or the pound." She picked up her purse. "What could I do?"

He gave her an oddly thoughtful look. "You could have let him go to the pound."

"Not an option." She smiled wryly. "Sphinx and I were colleagues at the center for a year. I couldn't let them take him away."

Sphinx sniffed Ellis's fingers. Apparently satisfied with the show of respect, he turned and padded off toward the kitchen and his food dish.

Ellis rose and surveyed the cartons and boxes. "Looks like you haven't had time to unpack."

"Those aren't mine." She hesitated, frowning a little. "Well, I suppose they are now, given that they were addressed to me. They were delivered this afternoon."

"What's inside?"

"According to the letter that accompanied them, about thirty years' worth of Dr.

Martin Belvedere's personal dream research. Evidently he religiously sent copies of his work on extreme dreams to his lawyer to hold for publication after his death. Kind of ironic, actually, because the first thing his son, Randolph, did after he took over the center was destroy all of his father's research. Guess he didn't know that Dr. B. had a backup plan."

"Sounds like the old man knew his son pretty well."

"Yes. A sad situation. They were estranged for years. Randolph still has a lot of unresolved father issues."

"Why did you get all of Belvedere's papers?"

She exhaled deeply. "According to the lawyer's letter, Dr. B. trusted me to see to it that his theories were not lost or destroyed. Belvedere yearned for validation and vindication, even if he had to get it after his death."

"And he stuck you with the job of making sure he was not forgotten in the field of dream research."

"Yep."

"What are you going to do with those cartons?"

Glumly she surveyed the large boxes. "Rent another storage locker, I suppose."

"That's going to cost you over time."

"I sort of figured that out for myself."

"But you're going to take care of them, just like you're taking care of the cat, aren't you?"

"I owe Dr. B. a great deal. If it hadn't been for him I'd probably still be answering phones at the Psychic Dreamer Hotline."

He smiled. "Something tells me that sooner or later you would have escaped the hotline. Ready to go?"

"Yes."

He opened the door and looked at her as she went past him out into the blustery evening. She could feel the electricity crackling in the air in advance of the storm.

"Want me to put the top down?" he asked.

Surprised, she glanced at the sleek vehicle sitting in front of the house. Delight and anticipation welled up inside her.

"Oh, yes," she whispered. "That would be lovely."

He smiled again, as if he had already guessed her answer and was pleased with it.

The drive along the bluffs into town was

the most exhilarating experience Isabel could remember in a long, long time, maybe the most exhilarating thing she had ever done in her entire life, she reflected.

Ellis handled the sleek, sexy sports car exactly as she had suspected he would: with absolute control and intuitive competence. His reflexes were perfectly in sync with the powerful engine and precision steering.

The heavy clouds were closing in fast, blotting out the last of the sunlight. It would be a while before the rain struck but the steel-colored waters churned and boiled in anticipation.

She felt a little high, she realized. It was as if she were channeling some of the atmospheric energy.

Ellis glanced at her. "You like storms?"

"I *love* storms."

He smiled his mysterious smile.

The wind howled around the Maserati. Isabel could feel her hair lashing around her face. She laughed.

"Talk about a really great flying dream," she said.

"You ever actually have one of those?"

"I have them all the time." She turned her head to look at him through her wild hair. "What about you?"

"Oh, yeah." His hands flexed slightly on the wheel. He did not take his attention off the road. "And you're right. This sure feels like one hell of a flying dream."

Half an hour later, inside the restaurant, he took off his dark glasses, slipped them into the pocket in the lining of his jacket and looked at Isabel across the table.

He knew all about dangerous thrill rides, he thought. He took psychic risks in his dreams, physical risks working for Lawson and huge financial risks as a venture capitalist. But he also knew how to protect himself from the really hazardous stuff in life. He had learned that lesson at the age of twelve. When it came to intimate relationships of any kind, he had always been very careful to play it safe. If you never loved, you never had to mourn a loss.

Tonight he was on the verge of tossing a lifetime of caution out the window. There was no doubt in his mind that sitting across from Isabel was far and away the most reckless thing he had ever done.

If he had any sense, he would turn around and walk away right now, he told himself. But he knew he wasn't going to do that. He was already on the roller coaster and it was too late to get off. He could feel the anticipation and the promise of the rush.

She was all Tango Dancer tonight, he thought. Her dark hair gleamed in the low, intimate lights. The sexy curves of her shoulders, outlined by the snug-fitting material of her black dress, were even more seductive in person than they had been in the photo on his refrigerator. He had to work hard not to just sit there and stare at her. He wanted to absorb every detail, from her fascinating eyes to the warmth of her voice and the subtle scent of her body.

The rain had struck just as he pulled into the restaurant parking lot. He barely got the top up on the Maserati in time to protect the leather upholstery. Then he and Isabel made a mad dash for the shelter of the entrance.

For some reason they both found the situation hilarious. They were still laughing, as if they shared some secret, cosmic joke, when they reached the hostess's podium.

The sense of intimacy was spellbinding. He wished he could take Isabel down onto the beach and make love to her in the sand with the wind and the waves crashing around them. Something in her eyes told him that she would have gone with him.

It was as if one of his own extreme

dreams had become real. Except that in his Level Five dreams he never had to make dinner-table conversation.

"Did anyone at the Belvedere Center for Sleep Research ever figure out just what you and the old man were doing?" he asked after the waiter had delivered an appetizer of chilled shellfish.

"No." Isabel's copper nails sparkled as she squeezed a wedge of lemon over the cold mussels, clams and oysters. "The rest of the staff just wrote off the Department of Dream Analysis as another example of Dr. Belvedere's eccentric nature. Everyone knew he had some really strange theories, of course, but they pretended not to notice because he brought in the funding that paid their salaries."

He helped himself to one of the mussels. "Did they consider you eccentric, too?"

She wrinkled her nose. "I think they viewed me more as the office mascot. No one took me seriously. As far as the staff was concerned, I was only there because Dr. Belvedere wanted a personal assistant to help him organize his private research. He owned the place so he got to do what he wanted."

"That attitude must have been hard to take at times."

"It could be annoying occasionally." She picked up a tiny fork and pried one of the clams out of the shell. "But for the most part my position at the center was what you might call a dream job for me."

"How so?"

"Thanks to Dr. Belvedere, I learned I wasn't the only person in the world who experienced what he called Level Five dreams. It was —" she hesitated — "reassuring to know that there were others like me out there, somewhere."

"I know what you mean."

"In addition, I got to actually use my abilities. It was frustrating at times because, as I told you, I never got context or feedback, but it was also the most satisfying work I've ever done."

"Like I said, Lawson has found some other Level Five dreamers, but he still hasn't turned up anyone else who can do what you do," he said.

Her eyes widened a little behind the lenses of her glasses. "How does he find extreme dreamers?"

"He funds sleep research projects at various places around the country. The researchers and the subjects all think he's doing neuroimaging studies. And he is, in his own devious fashion. But what he's really looking for in the data are the brain wave patterns that indicate an ability to go into a Level Five dream."

"Has he discovered a lot of Fives?"

"No, only a handful."

"What does he do when he finds one?"

"Most of the people he has located have wound up working for him at Frey-Salter."

She gave him a strange, wistful smile. "I don't want to go to work in Lawson's agency, but I must admit, there is one aspect of the job he's offering that does tempt me."

"What's that?"

"Being able to meet and talk to other people who are Level Fives."

It took him a beat to get the message. When he did, he was floored. "You've never even *talked* to another Level Five?"

She popped another mussel out of its shell and put it between her lips. "You're my first."

He stared at her, so suddenly and so violently aroused he was profoundly grateful for the low-hanging tablecloth. His mind went blank. He watched the faint, sexy movement of her throat as she swallowed the mussel and frantically tried to remember what they had been talking about.

"When did you first start experiencing

the really intense stuff?" he managed.

"I've always done some lucid dreaming but things really picked up during my last two years in high school."

"Same with me. I can remember having lucid dreams when I was a kid but they got stronger and clearer in high school."

She nodded. "It makes sense it would happen that way if you subscribe to the new theory that dreaming is a function of cognitive development."

"Meaning the brain gets better at dreaming as it develops?"

"Sure. Just as it gets better at logic and reasoning. In fact, a lot of the experts who buy into the cognitive development theory believe that dreaming is really just another form of thinking, but a rather passive version of it. The reason that we don't recall most of our dreams is because we don't usually pay much attention to them due to the fact that, duh, we're asleep."

"I've heard Lawson talk about that theory."

"Dreaming might be very similar to the kind of zoning out you do when you get into a car and drive a familiar route that you've driven a hundred times before." She smiled. "You know how it feels when you get out of the car at the other end with no sharp, clear memory of the drive itself?"

He looked at her. "No."

She frowned. "You've never had that experience?"

"I like to drive," he said simply. "I pay attention."

She made a face. "Exceptions to every rule, I guess. As I was saying, it's a reasonable theory."

He smiled a little. "But it comes from the same experts who don't believe there's any such thing as a Level Five lucid dream, right?"

She laughed. "Right. But I give them credit for trying to conduct a scientific study of dreams. For years a lot of good researchers wouldn't even touch the field because it was seen as very soft science at best."

"They feared that any investigation would prove to be a slippery slope that started with fuzzy psychology and went straight downhill into the pits of psychic phenomena and mysticism."

She shrugged. "You can understand the problem. How do you objectively study something that can't be seen or measured? Furthermore, you're completely at the mercy of your research subjects. They can tell you anything they want about their dreams and you can't prove it or disprove it."

"True." He ate the last oyster. "Did you ever talk to anyone about your extreme dreams?"

She was amused. "Well, let's see, I believe I mentioned them to a guidance counselor in high school. I was wondering if there were any special career opportunities for people like me. She concluded that I was on drugs and called my parents. A couple of years later I talked to a doctor. He suggested that my intense dreaming was a side effect of medication. When I told him I wasn't taking any meds, he decided that I probably needed some."

"I know the feeling. I talked to a couple of doctors my first year in college. Got the same diagnosis. They advised me to lay off the drugs. After that, I stopped mentioning the dreams to people. But a year later, I met up with Lawson."

She gave him a sympathetic look. "And you were so grateful to discover that someone actually understood your dream experience that you would have worked for him for free, if necessary, right?"

"I was grateful," he said dryly. "But not that grateful. Let's just say that we negotiated a deal."

"Is Lawson a Five?"

"No, but he's probably a solid Four on Belvedere's scale. High enough to sense the possibilities and certainly curious enough to try to figure out how to make a Five useful."

The waiter returned to remove the empty appetizer dish. When he was gone, Isabel sat forward and lowered her voice.

"Lawson ran some experiments with drugs to see if he could enhance dreaming, didn't he?"

"How did you know that?"

"I got some really bizarre Level Five dreams from him several months ago. I could tell there was something off. I asked Dr. B. if the subjects were on drugs. He said he wouldn't be surprised."

"It was a short-lived experiment," he admitted. "Lawson didn't pursue it because the results were unpredictable. The stuff was something called CZ-149. It was originally developed as a drug designed to enhance dreaming but it had some unpleasant side effects."

"What kind of side effects?"

"In regular subjects it produced a kind of hypnotic trance. In Level Fives the results were extreme dreams that were so real the subjects could not distinguish them from waking life. It made them highly suggestible."

Her brows snapped together in a disapproving frown. "I hope you didn't let him experiment on you."

"Not a chance. I'm too old for that kind of thing." He tore off a chunk of crusty sourdough and dipped it into the little bowl of olive oil. "I leave the experiments to Lawson's new recruits. They're young and eager."

She gave a mock shudder of relief. "I'm very glad to hear you didn't fool around with that CZ-149."

"How did you find Belvedere?" he asked.

"He found me." Her eyes sparkled with laughter. "He called the Psychic Dreamer Hotline one night when I was on duty. Turned out he called it every few months just to see if, by chance, they had accidentally managed to hire a Level Five. Naturally I thought he was just another kook at first. But we talked. One thing led to another. We met. He tested me and then offered me a position at the center. I grabbed the opportunity."

The waiter returned to set down the entrees.

"Belvedere wasn't a Five, was he?" Ellis asked.

"No, like your friend Lawson, I suspect he was a strong Four. But he developed the lucid dream scale and postulated that it probably went as high as five."

"So, in all the time you worked for Belvedere he never brought another Level Five into the center?"

"Not while I was there." She hesitated. "But he said something once or twice that made me think he had located another extreme dreamer a few months before I arrived. I got the impression that the person was a male. Later I worked it out that he had probably referred him to Client Number One."

A cold chill settled in his gut. "Scargill."

Had to be, he thought. Lawson had brought Vincent Scargill into Frey-Salter a little over a year ago. He had said something about Belvedere having come across him online.

Isabel paused, fork in midair, and gave him a politely inquiring look. "I beg your pardon?"

"I think the name of the dreamer was Vincent Scargill," he said aloud.

"Did you work with him?"

"Not exactly."

"Is he still with Lawson's operation?"

"He's dead. Or so they say."

She lowered the fork. "What are you talking about?"

"It's a long story." He picked up his knife. "It is also one of Lawson's biggest secrets. He'd have my head on a platter if he knew I'd even mentioned Scargill to you. Do me a favor, pretend you never heard the name, okay?"

"Okay. But I have to tell you that when I found out I'd missed having the chance to work with another Level Five because Dr. B. had turned him over to another lab, I got a little depressed for a while. Martin Belvedere treated me well enough in his own way but he was always off in his own world. There was no one else I could talk to about my work. It was rather lonely at times."

Ellis looked at her and felt the blood turn to ice in his veins. She had come that close, he thought, to having a killer as a colleague.

He sent up a silent message of gratitude to the spirit of Dr. Martin Belvedere. It had very likely been nothing more than chance that had caused the old man to send Scargill to Frey-Salter rather than bring him into the center. Or maybe the old man had had some qualms about Scargill. Whatever, it had been a near thing. The world of high-level dreamers was a very small realm.

12

The fast-moving winds had blown themselves out by the time Ellis bundled Isabel back into the Maserati two hours later. Rain continued to fall in a soft, steady pattern that transformed the lights of Roxanna Beach's boutique commercial district into colorful jewels.

He drove the six-block strip of restaurants and shops, trying to think of a way to delay the inevitable. He did not want to take Isabel home but he sure as hell could not invite her back to his room at the Seacrest Inn. That would be way too tacky on a first date.

First date. There, he'd finally admitted it to himself. He had been thinking of this evening as a date since the moment he decided to ask Isabel to have dinner with him.

"What made you decide to leave Lawson's agency?" Isabel asked.

He considered his answer while he turned a corner and drove onto the road that would take them back to her place.

"I was with Lawson full-time for over ten years but it was what you might call an accidental career. I still think of it as a sort of sideline. My real interest has always been in business and investing. My father founded a software company that was very successful. Guess it's in my blood."

"What do you like about the business world?"

He thought about it for a moment. It was a question he had never asked himself.

"I get a rush out of playing for high stakes," he said slowly. "I like to use my dreaming talent to spot patterns and trends in the economy. I like catching the wave before anyone else even knows it's there."

"But you still work for Lawson."

"Like I said, it's a sideline."

"Why do you do it?"

"The money's good," he said carelessly.

She watched him from the shadow. "You don't do it for the money."

"No?"

"I think you do it because hunting bad guys in your dreams is your way of doing the right thing. It's your contribution to society. You help make the world a little safer."

Damn. She thought he was some sort of

hero. He could feel himself turning a dull red. He was very grateful for the pool of darkness that filled the small space inside the Maserati.

"Don't get the wrong idea here," he said. "I work for Lawson a few times a year because I owe the guy and because I can always use additional investment cash."

"Those are not the only reasons you do what you do," she said quietly. "Don't forget, I've read a lot of your dream reports."

Her absolute certainty shook him.

"You're the one who pointed out earlier this evening that people can tell you anything they want about their dreams and you have no way of proving that they're lying," he reminded her.

She smiled a little. "If you had lied to me consistently in your dream narratives, I would have sensed it. Tell me, how did your family react when you took the job with Lawson?"

"I lost my parents when I was twelve." He kept his voice completely neutral, the way he always did when he talked about the past. "They were victims of some crazy who had a bad case of workplace rage. My folks were in the wrong place at the wrong time."

"Ellis." She turned abruptly in the seat to look at him. "What happened? Who raised you?"

"The State of California."

"Foster homes?"

"Yeah."

"My God. Talk about a nightmare."

Out of the corner of his eye he saw her start to reach out as though to touch him. Her pity was the very last thing he wanted.

"They weren't all bad," he said, putting a lot of ice into the words because he wanted her to get the message. "Some were better than others. In any case, I was only in the system for three years. No worse than being sent away to boarding school."

"Oh, sure. Just like boarding school. Give me a break." She paused. "How come you were only in the system for three years?"

"I left the last home when I turned fifteen."

"You ran away? How did you survive on your own at that age?"

The anxiety in her voice almost made him laugh. "How do you think I survived? I went into business for myself. I told you I've always had a knack for turning a profit."

She cleared her throat. "What kind of business could you get into at that age?" She paused. "Or shouldn't I ask?"

"Well, I gave considerable thought to entering the illegal substances market," he said, keeping his tone mockingly serious. "But I guess I've always been a strategic thinker when it comes to business. I took a good, hard look at the profit-risk ratio and decided that the long-term prospects in that particular field were not very good."

"Come to think of it, you don't see a lot of successful drug dealers over the age of thirty, do you?" she murmured. "They're either dead or in jail. Then, too, I suppose the competition is rather fierce."

"The competition is only part of the problem. Maintaining a core market share is very difficult. Your best customers tend to die on you."

"Okay, so you were too smart to sell drugs on the street." She leaned her head back against the seat. "How *did* you make a living?"

"Online."

She sucked in her breath in startled surprise and then laughed. "Of course. Should have thought of that."

"I started out buying and selling for other people. Took a commission on each trade. Then I moved on to buying some products in bulk and reselling them at my own website."

"You really are a born entrepreneur."

"I continued to dabble a bit in high school and managed to graduate. Decided to try college. In my second year, I signed up as a research subject in one of Lawson's sleep studies, and the rest is history."

"You know," she said after a while, "your decision to become a venture capitalist is as appropriate as the work you do for Lawson."

"How's that?"

"You're a major dreamer, right? By making it possible for other people to start up their companies, you're helping them to pursue the great American Dream."

He laughed. "You know, you may be cut out for the motivational seminar field, after all. You sure know how to put a positive spin on things."

She folded her arms. "Do you use your Level Five dreaming capabilities in your venture capital work?"

"Frequently. The process is very similar to the dreaming I do for Lawson. I look for patterns and clues. The difference is that when it comes to the business dreaming I'm working with the financial markets and the personalities of the entrepreneurs and investors who are involved. I generally have a fair amount of information in those situations so I don't require so much help with interpretation. That's why I haven't sent you any of those dream narratives to analyze."

He saw the turnoff for Sea Breeze Lane coming up on the left and reluctantly slowed for it. The temptation to keep going into the night was almost overwhelming. Maybe, if he drove fast enough and hard enough, they could outrun the dawn.

"Something wrong?" Isabel asked.

"No." *Yes. I don't want to leave you tonight.*

But he made the turn and drove slowly along the street of weathered beach cottages until he came to the one with the yellow porch light.

He parked in front of the rented house and pocketed the keys. Would she ask him to come inside for tea or a nightcap?

"Sorry, I don't have an umbrella," he said.

"It's not raining that hard," she said.

He unbuckled his seat belt and got out. Ignoring the light rain that dampened his hair, he tugged off his jacket and went around to the passenger side.

When Isabel popped out of the front seat, the slanted hem of her sexy little black dress rode up high on her leg, giving him a discreet glimpse of thigh.

His blood beat more heavily in his veins. He could feel the rising swell of his erection.

Don't get excited, Cutler. It was probably just an accident. Short skirts, low-slung cars, hell, these things happened. It was one of the reasons automobile designers engineered vehicles like this one.

But what if she was deliberately flirting with him? He sure didn't want to misread the signals here.

He draped his jacket over her shoulders. Just doing the gentlemanly thing, he assured himself, trying to protect the lady's dress from the inclement weather.

"Run," he advised. He didn't know if he was telling her to flee from the rain or from him.

"I won't melt," she promised.

Lucky you, he thought. *I just damn well might.*

Together they raced up the steps. Isabel reached into her purse for her key. He sensed her hesitating.

Invite me inside. Just say the magic words.

"It was a lovely evening. Thank you, Ellis."

"My pleasure." He took the key from her hand and inserted it into the lock. "You know, we never did talk contracts."

She looked at him, baffled. "Contracts?"

"I'm sure you have one for me to sign," he said easily. He opened the door. "If you'll give me a copy of your standard contract, I'll go over it tonight. We can talk about any problem areas in the morning."

"I don't actually have a standard contract yet." She moved into the doorway and looked at him with a worried expression. "I haven't really had time to think about setting up the legal side of my business. What with moving and training for my new job at Kyler, things have been rather chaotic for the past few days."

"No problem. We can talk about the formalities tomorrow."

He sensed her hesitating again, as though considering the risks of diving off a high board. At that moment Sphinx appeared, padding into the small hall to greet them.

Isabel glanced down at the cat and then looked up quickly, resolve gleaming in her eyes.

"Would you like a cup of tea before you

drive back to the inn?" she asked.

Anticipation flashed through him, as if he had just climbed aboard the front seat of the roller coaster. Unknown thrills awaited.

"Sounds good," he said, managing, just barely, to keep it polite and casual.

He moved through the doorway before she could change her mind. She stepped back, set her purse on the hall table and started to move off in the direction of the kitchen.

He reached out to retrieve his jacket. "I'll take that for you."

She froze when he touched her shoulder. So did he. Beneath the thin knit fabric of her dress he could feel the heat of her skin and the soft, lushly rounded curve of her shoulder.

"Beautiful," he whispered.

For what had to be the longest moment of his life, they stood, unmoving, in the close confines of the tiny foyer. He did not take his hand off the sensual curve of her shoulder. He wasn't sure he could.

She turned her head slightly and looked at his fingers. She contemplated them for a few seconds and then she met his eyes and smiled just a little.

The invitation was unmistakable and irresistible. Gently he slid her glasses off her nose and set them on the hall table next to her purse. She blinked, as though he had removed a veil.

Very deliberately he eased his jacket off her shoulders and dropped it beside the glasses.

He wasn't really undressing her, he thought, but somehow it felt as if that was what he was doing.

He rested his hands lightly on either side of her throat and traced the outline of her delicate jaw with his thumbs. When he toyed with her gold earrings she flattened her palms lightly on the front of his shirt.

"I've never had much luck with romantic relationships," she said very seriously. "So this is probably not a good idea, especially since we're going to be working together on a professional basis."

"I've never been real good at the relationship thing, either." He threaded his fingers through her hair. "What do you say we don't jinx this by telling ourselves that this has to be the start of a long-term situation?"

A wistful look came and went on her expressive face. With obvious reluctance, she moved her hands away from his chest and curled them around his wrists.

"I'm not interested in a one-night stand," she said very gently but very firmly.

Nice going, you idiot. Now she thinks you're just looking for a quick roll in the hay.

"Neither am I." He pulled her closer. "So what do you say we take this nice and slow? We go for a good night kiss. Nothing more. No commitments. No promises. No problems tomorrow if one of us decides not to mix business and pleasure."

Something that might have been relief mingled with regret and amusement lit her expression.

"What do you call an arrangement like that?" she asked.

"A free pass to a thrill ride." He stroked her lower lip with one finger. It trembled at his touch and everything inside him clenched with need. "Good for one night and one night only."

"All right."

He covered her mouth with his before she could change her mind. The plan was to make the kiss slow, seductive and non-threatening. The last thing he wanted to do was screw up big time with Tango Dancer.

He sensed the caution in her but he could also feel her eagerness and curiosity. The knowledge that she was attracted to him sent a highly charged rush of energy through him. Whatever was going on here, it was working in both directions.

He deepened the kiss. She responded with a soft, urgent little sound that just had to be the most erotic thing he had ever heard in his entire life. Her arms wound around his neck.

He drank his fill and was still thirsty. He managed to drag his mouth away from hers long enough to kiss her smooth throat. She shivered, gave a small gasp and dug her fingertips into his shoulders.

The tantalizing scent of her body and the faint, herbal fragrance of her hair were addictive. Sliding his palms down the length of her back, he savored the warm, sleek curves of her body through the clingy material of her dress. A vision of how she would look and feel naked in a bed made him groan aloud.

She stiffened. "Ellis?"

"It's okay." He slipped the gold earrings slowly, carefully out of her ears. "I have a vivid imagination where you're concerned, that's all. I've spent a lot of time during the past few months wondering what it would be like to hold you like this."

"You've thought about us kissing?" she whispered, blushing furiously.

"Yes."

"Oh, my." She buried her face against his shoulder. "I suppose it's only natural that we would be curious about each other."

He caught her chin on his forefinger and urged her to look at him. "Are you telling me that you've imagined this moment, too?"

Her cheeks were flushed and her eyes were fever-bright. "I've spent a lot of nights working on your dreams, Ellis Cutler. Naturally I was curious."

He studied her intently. "Are you equally curious about all of your dream clients?"

"No. Not the way I was about you. I wanted to know if the real you would be anything like the you I imagined when I worked on your dreams."

"Come to any conclusions?"

She framed his face with her hands and brushed her lips lightly across his. "Yes. You are exactly as I knew you would be."

He looked into her incredible eyes and wondered if he would ever be able to pull himself free of the spell she was weaving around him.

"You and I know better than most people that dreams can't be trusted," he made himself say.

"There is truth in dreams. You just have

to know how to look for it." She raised her brows, amused. "That's why you hire me, remember?"

He told himself it would be a huge mistake to take what was happening between them seriously. Isabel's elevated interest in him had a lot to do with the fact that he was a Level Five, just as she was. She had admitted that she longed to meet someone else who dreamed the way she did. It was probably inevitable that she would allow herself to be intrigued, perhaps even a bit enthralled, by the first man she met who knew what it meant to go into an extreme dream state.

He kissed her again, wrapping her close. She melted into him.

The roller coaster was moving faster now, heading into a dangerous turn.

But he suddenly realized he did not want to be an experiment for her. He did not want to be used as an experience meant to satisfy her curiosity about what it would be like to have sex with another Level Five.

Reluctantly he raised his head and eased her away from him.

"I think I'd better leave now." He kissed the tip of her nose. "Tomorrow we'll talk about contracts that will protect you."

An enigmatic expression veiled her eyes.

She stepped back and coolly clasped her hands behind her back.

"Protect me from who?" she asked softly. "You?"

"A lady who can do what you do shouldn't take chances with strangers." He picked up his jacket, hooked it over his shoulder and opened the door. "Good night, Isabel."

She trailed after him, watching him cross the porch and go down the steps. Sphinx made another appearance. She reached down and scooped him up in her arms. The big cat's purr was loud in the night.

"Ellis?"

He paused on the last step and looked at her. She was a sultry silhouette framed by the low light of the foyer lamp.

"Yeah?" He waited, wondering what he would do if she invited him back inside. He knew he wouldn't have the will to walk out a second time that night.

She rubbed the place behind one of Sphinx's ears. "Drive carefully."

"I'll do that," he said. "Lock your door."

She obeyed without protest. He waited until he heard the sound of the dead bolt sliding home before he walked to the Maserati and got behind the wheel.

He drove away from the welcoming glow

of Isabel's porch light, keenly aware of the empty seat beside him. He thought about the unfamiliar kind of need that the kiss had unleashed inside him. Taking Isabel to bed a few times wasn't going to fix this problem. This was more than sex, and that meant it was very dangerous. He could control his dreams, but he had learned that real life was a crapshoot.

Tonight's free pass was the only one Tango Dancer was going to get. He couldn't afford to give her another. It would cost him too much.

13

Isabel dreamed . . .

She reclines on an elegantly curved Regency-style sofa covered in dark blue velvet and trimmed with gold tassels. The only lamp in the lavishly decorated room illuminates the place where she waits for Dream Man. Her nightgown is made of pale candlelight-colored satin. It is cut very short. The hem barely covers the swell of her buttocks. The neckline plunges between her breasts.

A door opens and Dream Man enters the room. She cannot see him clearly yet but she knows it is him. She has invited him into her dreams on a regular basis for several months now. The routine is familiar

She senses that there is something different about him tonight, however. It bothers her that she cannot immediately comprehend what it is.

Then it comes to her. She does not

know what he will be wearing this evening

This is not how it is supposed to be.

On every other night she has always known how he will be dressed. These are her own private, erotic Level Five fantasies. She controls every aspect of them.

In the past she has always taken great care to set the stage before slipping into one of these extreme dreams. She has always taken the time to dress the man of her dreams in some glamorous, romantic style: a highwayman's dashing cloak and mask, perhaps, or early-nineteenth-century breeches, jacket, polished boots and an intricately tied cravat. When she was in the mood for an after-the-ball scenario, she usually opted for a formal tuxedo, pleated white shirt and bow tie.

But she cannot remember what she specified for this evening. She cannot even recall making the decision to have him come to her tonight.

A strange panic ruffles her nerves.

Dream Man walks toward her through the shadows. Her pulse beats more quickly. He has not yet touched *her but already she can feel the heavy pull of desire deep in her body.*

Alarm bells sound. She knows that she should pay attention to the warning. The fact that she does not know how her midnight lover will be dressed tonight is important.

The alarm bells are louder now, more insistent.

Dream Man comes closer. There is a strange inevitability about this whole thing that is really starting to worry her. Maybe she should end the performance now. She tries to rise from the sofa but she cannot move.

He is approaching swiftly. One more stride will bring him into the pale pool of light that spills across the sofa.

At last she catches a glimpse of his face and sees how he is dressed. Shock reverberates through her. Now she knows for certain that she is not in control of this dream . . .

She surfed into full wakefulness on the crest of an adrenaline wave.

She sat straight up in bed, trembling. Perspiration dampened her cotton nightgown. She was breathing much too quickly and she was intensely aware of her own pulse.

Sphinx loomed over her, his broad head silhouetted against the pale glow of the night-light in the hall. She could see the glitter of his eyes.

"I'm okay." She realized he was somewhat agitated and raised her hand to stroke him reassuringly.

The phone beside the bed rang, jarring her. She recognized the sound as the alarm bell she had heard in the dream. Swallowing hard, she reached past Sphinx to grab the receiver. Without her glasses, she was forced to squint a little to read the large, glowing green numbers on the face of the clock. Twelve thirty-seven.

Her first worried thought was that the voice on the other end of the line would likely be Leila's reporting an emergency in the family.

"Hello?" She realized that she sounded hoarse and anxious.

"Isabel?" Her name came out slurred. *Ishabel.*

Definitely not Leila. The voice was familiar but she was still disoriented from the unplanned dream. She could hear very loud rock music in the background.

"It's me, Gavin Hardy. Your old buddy

from IT at the Belvedere Center." Gavin raised his voice to be heard above the music. "You haven't forgotten me already, have you?"

"I don't understand." She pulled her disordered senses together with an effort and swung her legs over the side of the bed. "What on earth are you calling about at this hour of the night? Where are you?"

"Right here in Roxanna Beach," Gavin said. "I'm sitting in a bar across the street from the motel where I'm staying."

"Have you been drinking?"

"Had a few beers. I needed to do something to kill the time while I waited for you to answer your damn phone. Where've you been all evening?"

"I went out to dinner and turned off my phone."

"So that was it. Tried to call you every fifteen minutes from about seven o'clock on until ten or so. I started to wonder if maybe I had the wrong number. Finally gave up and came over here to get something to eat before trying again. Man, am I glad to hear your voice."

"Are you all right?"

"I'm swell now that I've finally got ahold of you."

"You're not driving, are you?"

He snorted. "That's the Isabel we all knew back at the center. Just can't help worrying about folks and handing out the good advice, can you? Relax, like I said, the bar is right across the street from the motel. I walked over. I'm not driving so I won't run down any of the fine, upstanding citizens of Roxanna Beach on my way back to the room."

"What are you doing here?"

"Came to see you." This time the *see* came out *shee*. "Got a little present for you." He lowered his voice. "But I'm afraid I gotta charge you for it. Sorry about that. If I could afford to give it to you for free, I'd do it. Believe me. You're a real sweetheart, Isabel."

"I'm changing my ways," she warned.

"Nah. You couldn't do that."

"Gavin, try to stay on topic here. Why did you come all this way to see me and why are you calling at such a late hour?"

The music swelled into a driving crescendo, blotting out some of Gavin's words.

". . . on my way to Vegas. Problem is, I owe some people there some money. My new blackjack system didn't work quite the way I thought it would last time I was in town."

"I can hardly hear you."

". . . like I was saying, I've tweaked the program a bit and I'm pretty sure it will fly this time. But I gotta pay off my old gambling debts before they'll let me back into any of the big games, see?"

"No. I don't. What do your gambling debts have to do with me?"

"I need to raise some cash," Gavin said loudly. "That's why I'm calling you. I've got something to sell that I think you might find valuable. You're my only hope, 'cause I sure don't know anyone else who wants this information."

"What information?"

"Contact numbers for old man Belvedere's three special anonymous clients." Gavin was almost shouting now.

"Are you serious?"

"Serious as a heart attack. Figured since you were the one who did most of the work for those accounts, you might want to get in touch and tell 'em you're, like, you know, freelance now."

"Wait, did you say that there were *three* anonymous clients?"

"Yep."

"I only worked for two clients. I never knew there was a third."

"Neither did I and I thought I knew all

of the old man's secrets. What happened was, right after he tossed you out on your ear, Randolph Belvedere told me to destroy all the files on his old man's office computer. Took me a while to get to it on account of the bastard was giving orders like crazy for the first few days after he took over. I had to, like, prioritize, you know?"

"Go on," she said.

"Also, I was sort of busy fine-tuning my blackjack system. So I kind of put Dr. B.'s computer aside. I mean, what was the rush, huh? The guy's dead. Anyhow, I finally got around to taking a look at the files he had stored on his hard drive a couple of days ago. For kicks I went through them. They were all password-protected so it took me a while."

"What did you find?"

"Most of them were just research notes about his extreme dream theories. But one of those files had a different password. A real tricky code. Made me curious, you know?"

"That's where you found the e-mail addresses for the three clients?"

"You got it. The old man had a few secrets he kept from you and me both. I tried tracing the three but they're all locked and scrambled a dozen different ways. Whoever they are, those three clients don't want anyone tracking them down. Looks like real expert work. Maybe if I had time I could untangle them but maybe not. Thing is, they aren't much good to me, anyway. What would I do with those clients? Also, I'm sort of in a hurry to try out the new version of my system in Vegas. So I decided to see if you were interested in the addresses."

"Let me get this straight. You want to sell those e-mail addresses to me?"

"I'm real sorry about that part, Isabel. Honest. But I need the cash, see, and I just don't know anyone else who might pay a few bucks for these addresses." His voice vibrated with tension. "Are they worth anything at all to you?"

"I'm afraid I'm having a cash flow problem myself at the moment, Gavin. My bank account is hovering around zero and my credit cards are maxed out."

"Even a few hundred bucks would help," Gavin assured her. "I could go to one of the little casinos way off the Strip where they don't know me and turn it into a stake that I could use to get into a big game."

"I could come up with maybe two hundred bucks cash."

"Oh, shit. Is that all? I'm pretty desperate, Isabel."

She tried to think. "I know one of those three clients personally. He might be interested in talking to you."

"Hey, if he's still big on keeping secrets, maybe I could do a deal with him, you know?"

"What kind of a deal?"

"Gotta think here. Maybe he'd like to know who the other two clients are or something. Or maybe he'd be willing to pay me not to sell his address to the other two."

"No offense, Gavin, but that sounds a lot like blackmail."

"Nah, it's just business."

It was not exactly business as usual, she thought, and Ellis probably wasn't going to like it. But she had a hunch that he would want to discuss the situation with Gavin.

"Okay, I'll call him and then call you back," she said. "Where are you staying?"

"Motel out on the old highway. The Breakers. I'm in number eight. I'm heading back there now. Give me a call after you talk to your client and we'll make arrangements. I'd better give you my cell phone number because I doubt if the manager's office is still open to handle calls.

The place is sort of a dive, you know? Got a pen?"

"Just a sec." She fumbled with her glasses and then picked up the pen on the bedside table. "Okay, go."

He rattled off a number. "Call me back as soon as you can, okay?"

"I'll try."

"Thanks, Isabel." Gavin's voice almost throbbed with heartfelt relief. "You don't know how much this means to me."

The phone clicked in her ear.

She sat on the edge of the bed, absently petting Sphinx for a moment while she pondered developments.

Then she bent down and dug the Roxanna Beach phone book out of the drawer in the bedside table. She found the number for the Seacrest Inn and dialed it quickly.

While she waited for him to answer, she thought about why the dream she'd had earlier disturbed her so deeply.

It wasn't the fact that Ellis was Dream Man. Heck, she already knew that. She had made the decision to install unknown Client Number Two in the role months ago. The only thing that had changed this week was that she now had a face to go with everything else that she knew about him.

No, the real problem was Midnight Man's attire tonight. In that single glimpse she'd managed to get before Gavin's call woke her she had realized that Dream Man had not come to her in any of the usual, rakish sartorial guises she had designed for him on previous visits.

Tonight he had been garbed, instead, in a pair of black trousers, silver gray, open-collar shirt and a well-tailored jacket woven in shades of gray and black. It was the outfit Ellis had worn that evening.

She tried to tell herself there was nothing to worry about. It was just a dream, for heaven's sake. But she was lying to herself and she knew it.

Because the truth was that tonight's dream had not been one she had orchestrated for herself as a pleasant, erotic interlude to be enjoyed on her terms in a safe, controlled state of extreme lucid dreaming. This evening's show had been unplanned, unpremeditated and unpredictable. Her dreaming mind had come up with it all by itself after she had fallen sound asleep.

No need to be afraid, she assured herself at least not yet. But she should probably be real worried.

14

It was still raining when he left the bar. He hunched deeper into his windbreaker the one with the logo of his favorite casino on the back, yanked his billed cap lower over his eyes, stuck his hands into his pockets and tromped across the gravel parking lot.

The stretch of old highway that separated the bar from his motel was poorly lit. There were no streetlights or signals. The only illumination came from the neon signs above the bar and the one that announced the motel. There were no crosswalks or sidewalks, either, but who cared? There was hardly any traffic.

The crunch of footsteps on gravel behind him startled him out of his reverie.

"*What?*" He spun around and then had to grab hold of the fender of a pickup truck because he was a little unsteady on his feet.

His first panicked thought was that the casino had sent collectors after him. Cold sweat broke out on his forehead.

A figure moved out of the shadows.

"Hello, Gavin."

Not a casino enforcer. The relief was so great he nearly crumpled.

"What the hell?" He pulled himself together. "What are you doing here?"

"You were assigned to wipe the files off Martin Belvedere's hard drive."

"So what? Just doing my job."

"I wondered if you found anything of interest."

This was getting a little weird. "You followed me to ask me that?"

"You can't blame me for being curious after the way you disappeared so suddenly today."

"I didn't disappear," Gavin muttered. "I just decided to take some time off."

"You told your colleagues that you were ill."

"So sue me. I got plenty of sick time coming."

"One of the people in your department overheard you making some calls before you left the center. He said it sounded like you were trying to locate Isabel Wright."

"We're friends, me and Isabel," he said. "Just thought I'd stop in and say hello while I'm in town, that's all."

"I didn't realize you and Isabel were that close."

"Look, I don't know what this is about,

but it's late and I'm planning to get up early."

"You did find something on Martin Belvedere's computer, didn't you? I thought so. It was the only explanation that made sense."

"I don't know what you're talking about. I was ordered to wipe that hard drive." He could feel himself starting to sweat again. "I didn't steal anything, if that's what you're trying to say."

"You misunderstand. I'm not accusing you of stealing company data. I just want to know what you found and why you came here to talk to Isabel Wright. There must be some connection. Otherwise it doesn't make sense for you to go out of your way to stop off in Roxanna Beach. It's not exactly on the road to Las Vegas, is it?"

"My reasons for being here are none of your business. This is personal."

"I'm willing to pay for whatever information you found, Gavin."

Excitement swamped his growing unease. "Yeah? Well, hell, why didn't you say that in the first place? What kind of money are we talking?"

"First tell me what you've got. Then I'll tell you what it's worth to me."

"E-mail contact information for old man

Belvedere's three anonymous accounts." He waited anxiously to see if that generated any interest.

"I'm impressed. I would very much like to have that information. I've got a few hundred in cash on me but if we can find an ATM I could make it an even thousand. I know that's not a lot but it's all I can come up with tonight. Unless you want to wait until the banks open tomorrow?"

Gavin calculated quickly. The bright lights of Las Vegas were calling. No reason he couldn't sell the information twice tonight, maybe double his profits. And no need for either client to know about the other.

This was one of those win-win situations.

"There's an ATM down the street at that gas station on the corner," he said. "I noticed it this afternoon when I filled up my car."

"Fine. I'll drive over and get the money. It would probably be best if we weren't seen together. Why don't you go back to your motel room? I'll meet you there in a few minutes."

"Suit yourself."

Las Vegas, here I come.

15

Ellis knew he was dreaming. There was nothing unusual about that. He was a Level Five lucid dreamer, after all. He even recognized this particular dreamscape. But there was something different about it tonight. . . .

He stands in the center of the circular room. The ceiling is transparent. He can see the night sky through it. High, gothic-style entrances to dozens of darkened halls ring the space.

Tango Dancer comes toward him from one of the many corridors. He wants to make love to her more than he has ever wanted anything in his adult life. But he is afraid that afterward she will walk away from him and vanish into one of the mysterious halls.

She glides into the circular room, smiling a feminine invitation that makes him ache with desire. She stops in the shadows. Raising one hand, she beckons him with a graceful curl of her fingertips.

He does not move. He knows that if he stays where he is she cannot see him clearly. It is better that way.

"Are you afraid of me?" she asks.

"No," he says. "I'm afraid of wanting you this much."

"Why?"

"I don't know," he lies.

"Yes you do. You think that I will leave you."

"Everyone leaves."

"Will you let that stop you from touching me?"

"No." But a great despair and anger well up inside him because he knows what will happen. She will demand more than he can risk giving her. She will want to see him, really see him. She will want to get very close and he cannot allow that. He has a rule about letting people get close. He put that rule in place a long time ago, when he was twelve.

She reaches out to him with both hands. "Come with me."

He starts toward her because, in spite of everything, he cannot resist her.

But when he gets close enough for

her to see his face, she turns and runs away, disappearing into one of the dark gothic passages . . .

The harsh jangle of the phone jarred him awake.

He sat up quickly, trying to ignore his erection and the tight, heavy sensation in the lower part of his body. The phone rang again.

He swung his legs out from under the covers, planted both feet on the floor and looked at the face of the radio alarm clock. Twelve fifty-three. It was the room phone. Not Lawson, then. Lawson always called him on his personal phone.

That left Isabel. At this hour? Adrenaline spiked. His pulse pounded.

He grabbed the phone. "This is Cutler."

"Ellis?" Isabel hesitated. "I'm sorry to disturb you. I know it's late, but —"

"What's wrong?" He cut in before she could get out another word.

"Well, I want to ask you a hypothetical question."

He glanced at the face of the bedside alarm clock again. "It's almost one o'clock in the morning so I'm going to assume that this question is more than hypothetical. What is it?"

"It's a little complicated."
"Isabel —"
"All right, here's the question. Do you think there are any serious laws against an honest citizen buying or selling e-mail addresses, at least one of which was created specifically for a government agency that doesn't officially exist?"

He made it to her front door in fifteen minutes flat. She was waiting on the porch. The yellow lamplight gleamed on the glossy black, calf-length raincoat she wore. Her hair was drawn up into a careless twist at the back of her head.

She flew down the front steps, the black coat flapping around her, and yanked open the passenger-side door. She slid into the seat beside him and glared at him through the lenses of her black-framed glasses.

"I'm warning you, Ellis, I won't let you threaten Gavin."

"Fasten your seat belt." He put the Maserati in gear and accelerated swiftly.

"Ellis, I mean it." She fumbled with the seat belt. "He's not a criminal. He's got a gambling addiction."

"Where is he?"

"The Breakers Motel." She shot him an uneasy look. "Just outside of town on the old highway. I tried to call him back on his personal phone a few minutes ago but he didn't answer. Gavin is having some financial problems with a casino. He sounded worried."

"Trust me, he's got a good reason to be worried."

"I told you, all he wants is some cash." She sat tensely in the seat, arms crossed beneath her breasts. "In hindsight, I can see that it was a mistake to call you tonight."

"No, your mistake was in refusing to tell me where Hardy is staying unless I agreed to pick you up and take you with me to confront him."

"I didn't care for your tone of voice when I told you what had happened."

"You didn't care for my tone of voice? I don't believe this. I was pissed when you wouldn't tell me where Hardy was staying. How the hell did you expect me to sound?"

"I couldn't let you confront him alone," she said firmly. "I was afraid you'd scare the daylights out of him."

"That would have been a good start."

He shifted gears. The Maserati leaped forward so fast the change in speed slammed both Isabel and him back into the seats. He was accustomed to it. Isabel was not but she said nothing. She did, however brace one hand against the dash and give him a quelling glare.

This was bad, he thought. They were in the midst of a major quarrel. Things had been going so well, too. They'd made it through a first date and a first kiss. And now he was blowing the whole thing because of his little obsession problem. At this rate she was going to conclude that he was a dangerous, unpredictable lunatic.

"Don't you think you might be overreacting?" she asked.

He downshifted for a curve. "No."

"For heaven's sake, they're just e-mail addresses." She spread her hands. "Two of which you already know."

"Let's get something clear, I'm not real worried about what Hardy does with my e-mail address or with Lawson's, either, for that matter. They're both so well secured that I doubt if there are more than half a dozen people on the face of the earth who could trace them back to their sources. In any event, once I tell Lawson what's going on, those addresses will cease to exist."

"Okay, so it's the third client you're concerned about," she said, amazingly calm.

"Yes." He changed gears again, wondering what was going through her mind.

Still bracing herself against the dash, she angled her head slightly to study his profile. "I'll admit I'm curious about the identity of Number Three, myself. The implication is that there is another Level Five dreamer out there somewhere who wants secrecy as badly as you and Lawson do."

"That's the implication, all right."

"I can understand a degree of interest on your part," she said patiently. "But would you mind telling me why you're freaking out about it?"

He considered how much to tell her. She already knew a great deal about Lawson's operation and if she was serious about contracting out her services to Lawson and him, she was going to learn a lot more.

Hell, she had a right to know.

"I am very, very wired about this third client because I think there is a possibility that he just might be the man I mentioned earlier at dinner, Vincent Scargill."

"Maybe you better tell me a little more about him."

"The only thing you need to know tonight is that Scargill is a Level Five killer."

"Oh, my God." Her voice went very soft as she absorbed the ramifications. "An extreme dreamer who is also a sociopath and a murderer would be —"

"Right. Your worst nightmare."

Isabel did not like the way she had been feeling since Gavin's call. "Jittery" was the only word she could come up with to describe the strange sensation. Sitting in the seat next to Ellis for the past few minutes had done nothing to elevate her mood. It was a lot like sharing a den with a hungry wolf. All traces of the warm, sensual promise that she had experienced in his arms earlier when he kissed her good night had vanished. In its place was a steady, ice-cold intensity that was disturbingly familiar. She had sensed it often enough in his dream reports.

The news that a person like Vincent Scargill existed and was at large had made things a whole lot worse.

She was about to start asking questions, lots of them, when she was distracted by a myriad of flashing lights.

The sputtering neon sign that marked the Breakers Motel and the one that spelled out the words BAR and LIVE MUSIC were directly opposite each other. But neither of them provided the eye-dazzling strobe effects that dominated the scene. Those came from the emergency and police vehicles that sat at angles on the edge of the road, blocking traffic.

A number of people, most in uniforms of one kind or another, were visible. A gurney was in the process of being loaded into the back of the ambulance. The victim's face and body were entirely covered.

"Accident," Ellis said tersely.

Isabel watched the doors of the ambulance close. A chill whispered through her. "A very bad one."

Ellis downshifted swiftly, slowing smoothly to a halt. A police officer, flashlight in hand, walked across the pavement to the Maserati. Ellis lowered the window.

"Sir, the road is closed for an investigation. Hit-and-run. You'll have to turn around."

"I'm headed for the motel," Ellis said.

"Okay." The officer stood back and waved him into the parking lot entrance.

Isabel could not take her eyes off the ambulance. "Ellis."

"Yeah?" He slipped the Maserati into a space close to room number eight.

"There are no lights on in Gavin's room," she whispered.

He glanced at her, frowning slightly as he shut down the engine. "Probably trying to keep a low profile."

"Maybe." She gripped the edge of the seat on either side of her knees, staring hard at the ambulance. "But he said he was going to walk back to his room from the bar. You don't think that . . ." She trailed off, not wanting to put her fears into words.

Ellis turned to look at the scene on the road.

"Damn," he said very softly. "Stay here."

This time she did as he ordered, mostly because she did not want to hear the news that she felt certain he would bring back.

Ellis got out of the car and walked through the rain to where the nearest cop stood directing traffic. There was a short conversation.

When he returned to the Maserati, he leaned down to speak to her through the open window. His expression was grim.

"It's Gavin Hardy, all right. Hit-and-run. He's dead. No witnesses. I told the cop that you knew Hardy because sooner or later it's going to come out."

She swallowed hard and looked past him. Two officers had detached themselves from the main group and were coming across the motel parking lot.

"I suppose those cops want to talk to us?" she said.

"Good guess.

"What do we tell them?"

"The truth. No more, no less. Hardy wanted to sell you some contact information for some of your former clients. You agreed to meet with him to discuss it. When you got here, you found the accident scene. That's all you know."

The cops were closer now, only a few strides away.

"What about the connection to Jack Lawson's operation?" she whispered urgently.

Ellis raised his brows in a politely quizzical expression. "Who's Jack Lawson?"

"What about your suspicion that one of the e-mail addresses belongs to that killer, Vincent Scargill?"

"Guess I forgot to mention one small fact. Vincent Scargill is dead."

16

The following afternoon Isabel sat with Tamsyn at one of the terrace tables outside the café at Kyler, Inc. The rain had stopped shortly before dawn, leaving a day that jarred and strained Isabel's exhausted senses to the point of pain. The sky was too blue. The sun was too bright. The surface of the bay glittered as though it had been sprinkled with shards of broken mirrors. And then there was Tamsyn, vivid and energetic as ever, her expensive centerfold cleavage on display in her carefully styled Kyler blazer.

It was all somewhat overwhelming after the long, depressing night, Isabel thought. A person could be expected to endure only so much bright stuff. In self-defense, she removed her regular glasses and reached into her purse for her prescription sunglasses. She positioned them firmly on her nose and immediately felt much better able to deal with Tamsyn and the over-bright day.

"I'm so sorry about your friend," Tamsyn said. "What a horrible thing that must have been for you, coming across the accident scene the way you did."

"He wasn't exactly a friend. He was a coworker at the center."

"If he was just an acquaintance, why did you feel you had to go visit him at one o'clock in the morning?"

Good question, Isabel thought.

"He said he was having financial troubles," she murmured. With an effort of will, she picked up a fork and stabbed a slice of the avocado on her plate. There were a lot of valuable nutrients in avocados. She was in desperate need of nutrients today. "I felt sorry for him."

"And Ellis Cutler went with you?" Tamsyn asked, her voice a little too smooth.

"He wasn't spending the night with me if that's what you're asking. He was asleep at the inn when I called him. I didn't want to go out to see Gavin Hardy alone at that hour."

"But you felt you could ask Cutler to accompany you?"

"We had dinner together earlier in the evening," Isabel said tensely. "We'd talked. I felt comfortable asking him, yes."

Tamsyn nodded but she did not look satisfied with the answer. "What are the cops saying about the accident?"

"Not much. No one saw the car that ran down poor Gavin. But they figure that the force of the impact caused a fair amount of damage to the vehicle. They're hoping for a tip, maybe from an auto repair shop. Meanwhile they've got nothing."

All things considered, the interview with the police had gone amazingly well. It was fascinating how far one could go with the truth and yet keep secrets if one wished to do so. In the end she and Ellis had been able to answer every question honestly without any references to a clandestine government agency or a dead man named Vincent Scargill.

Yes, I knew Gavin Hardy. Yes, he said he needed money to pay off his gambling debts. Yes, I said I'd be willing to meet with him to discuss the possibility of paying him for contact information regarding some former clients. No, I never got the addresses. Mr. Cutler? He's a business associate and a friend. I called him because I did not want to come out here alone in the middle of the night to meet Gavin. I'm sure you can understand. My job? I work at Kyler, Inc. . . .

Tamsyn crossed her legs and picked up her latte. "What's going on with you and Ellis Cutler, anyway?"

"I told you, he's a new client."

"With whom you had a date."

"Business dinner."

Tamsyn dismissed that with a wave of her hand. "One of the other instructors saw you two at a restaurant in town last night. She said it all looked very cozy."

Isabel put down her fork. "Why is everyone so concerned about my relationship with Ellis Cutler?"

"So it is a relationship?"

"Not the way you mean." She picked up her teacup. "Not yet. But say, for the sake of argument, that it turns into the kind of relationship you're talking about. What's the problem? I would have thought you'd be thrilled for me."

"It's obvious that he isn't your type. You can't blame me for being concerned."

"Why."

"Why, what?"

Isabel finished munching the avocado slice and swallowed. "Why does everyone say that Ellis isn't my type?"

Tamsyn frowned, evidently baffled by the question. "He just isn't, that's all. It's obvious."

"Not to me."

"Isabel, this is me, your good buddy Tamsyn, remember? I've known you since college. You're the one who warned me not to marry Dixson and you're the one who helped me get out of the marriage after I realized that you were right about him being abusive. I'm just trying to return the favor here."

"Don't worry, Ellis is not an abusive man."

"You're sure of that?"

"Positive." She reflected on the brief discussion she and Ellis had had concerning Vincent Scargill very late last night on the way home. He didn't go into any great detail, but he promised to tell her the whole story today. "He's got issues. Who doesn't? But being cruel is not among them. And you don't owe me any favors. In fact, I owe you for getting me this position here at Kyler."

"No, you don't."

"I most certainly do. In case you weren't aware of it, there are not a lot of career opportunities for folks in my line. Furthermore, I'm skating on thin ice, financially speaking. I needed this job very badly and you and Leila are the ones who talked Farrell into giving me a shot at it. So I owe you."

"The class on dreams will be hot. I'm sure of it." Concern darkened Tamsyn's expression. "What do you mean, you're on thin ice financially? Are we talking serious debt?"

"Sort of."

"I don't understand. I thought you were getting a decent salary at the Center for Sleep Research. Leila and Farrell kept saying that it was such a relief to know you were financially secure at last."

Isabel cleared her throat. "I made some investments."

"Please tell me you didn't do something stupid in the stock market."

"I'm not in the market."

"Did you buy a house?" Tamsyn looked relieved. "That's usually a good investment. I'm sure you'll be able to sell it."

"Not a house."

"Well, then?"

"If you don't mind, I'd rather not discuss it."

There was no way Tamsyn would understand about the furniture, she thought. Neither would Leila or Farrell or her parents. You didn't buy several thousand dollars' worth of furniture when you didn't have a house or an apartment in which to put it.

"All right, keep your big secret," Tamsyn said. "But I've got to tell you, you're just making me that much more nervous."

"Why?"

"For Pete's sake, you're involved with a guy who drives a Maserati."

"So?"

"So you have a long history of dating men who drive boring cars."

Isabel smiled in spite of herself. "You know, you're right. I never thought of it like that."

Tamsyn flattened her hands on the table. "Pay attention here. You are hanging out with a man who has no visible means of support, drives a very expensive car, wears hand-tailored shirts and is so eccentric he wants to pay you to analyze his dreams. Does any of this worry you?"

Isabel thought about that. "My life certainly has gotten a lot more exciting lately."

"This isn't a joke. Speaking as your friend, I think you should be very careful when it comes to dealing with Ellis Cutler."

Isabel thought about that, too. Then she picked up her fork and attacked her partially eaten salad with sudden enthusiasm.

"Too late," she said. "There's no going back."

17

"Hardy's death was no accident." Ellis lounged against the railing of the inn room's small balcony and watched the play of sunlight on the bay. "I'm almost certain."

Lawson pondered briefly on the other end of the phone connection. "Almost certain?"

"I don't have any proof But if we're talking coincidence here, it's a big one. What are the odds that he would get killed by a hit-and-run driver less than half an hour after he talked to Isabel?"

"Long, I'll grant you that much. Still, you said the guy was drunk, it was raining and the road was poorly lit."

"All true. But the timing stinks."

"I'm not going to argue with you on that point." Lawson fell silent for a couple of seconds. "You said Hardy owed money in Vegas?"

"Yes. But this isn't the way those folks usually do things."

"True. Not good business. Can't collect

if the guy is dead. But some people might feel there's value in making a point to other folks who owe money."

"Then they would have done something a little flashier. A hit-and-run on a lonely road late at night isn't going to get a lot of attention outside the town where it happened."

"All right, for the sake of keeping this conversation going for another five minutes, let's say that Hardy was murdered. What's your best guess?"

"Unknown Client Number Three," Ellis said.

"You're sure there was a third client?"

"That's what Hardy told Isabel. No reason for him to make up something like that."

"And this Number Three maintained the same level of secrecy that you and I had?"

"According to Hardy, the e-mail address was deeply encrypted."

"The old man never said a word about a third client," Lawson muttered. "And here I thought Belvedere and I were pals. Must have worked together for damn near twenty years. Hard to believe he was holding out on me."

"You know as well as I do that all Martin

Belvedere cared about was funding his research. If he kept silent about Client Number Three, it was probably because someone paid him enough to make it worth his while."

"Shit. Another agency. Has to be. No one else would have that kind of money to throw around."

"I thought I was supposed to be the one who leaped to conclusions," Ellis said.

"The difference between my conclusions and yours is that I've got several decades' worth of experience surviving in a government job to back me up. This is a cutthroat world. Everyone knows how hard it's been to make the CIA and the FBI talk to each other and neither will talk to local law enforcement. And that's just the tip of the iceberg when it comes to interagency communication problems. There's a lot of money and power at stake."

He'd heard all this before, Ellis thought. When Lawson got started on this particular rant it was very hard to stop him.

"Uh, Lawson, maybe we should —"

"I'm telling you, in my time I've seen government agencies spend more money and manpower trying to destroy a rival agency than they did on whatever project they were mandated to complete. Trust me, whoever he is, if he had enough money to buy Belvedere's silence and co-operation, he's got a taxpayer-based budget."

"Are you finished?" Ellis asked.

"I need to find out the identity of that third client," Lawson ground out. "He's out to get me. I can feel it."

There it was, Ellis thought suddenly, the opening he'd been waiting for.

"Sure, no problem," he said smoothly. "It so happens that I'm available for another contract. Standard rate. Deal?"

Lawson swore again and then heaved a resigned sigh. "Don't look now, but your mercenary side is showing."

"It's the side that pays for the good clothes and the nice car. Hell, what do you care how much I cost? Not like it's your money."

"You're a little too eager for this assignment," Lawson said, suspicious.

"I'm the best you've got available and you know it. I'm in place, I've got the background and I'm good."

"Don't try to con me, Cutler. I've worked in government a lot longer than you have. I know more about conning people than you'll ever learn."

"You want me to take this assignment or not?"

"I know where you're going with this and I don't like it."

"Yeah?"

"Two words. Vincent Scargill. Listen to me, Ellis, you're letting your crazy obsession with that bastard color everything you do. You won't be able to think, let alone dream clearly, if you don't step back from it."

"I'm not one of your agents anymore, Lawson. I don't take orders from you."

Lawson groaned. "What the hell was I thinking, sending you after Isabel Wright?"

"You were thinking that you could use her to distract me from looking for Vincent Scargill," Ellis said. "And it worked, at least for a while. But not any longer."

There was a short pause.

"How did she do when you two talked to the cops last night?" Lawson asked.

"Relax, you've got nothing to worry about. She acted like a real pro. Answered all the questions truthfully but she didn't give up anything that would have complicated your life."

"Glad to hear that," Lawson said, sounding genuinely relieved. "I was afraid I might have to do some damage control this morning."

"No."

"Well, that's one bit of good news, at least."

"That's one of the things I admire most about you, Lawson. You really know how to do the glass-half-full thing." Ellis straightened away from the railing. "Don't worry, I'll find out who that third client is for you."

"Listen up, Cutler. You can have the assignment. Hell, you're going to go looking for Number Three, anyway. But you're supposed to be a professional. Don't go doing anything stupid that will end up bringing down Frey-Salter. You need this place as much as all the other Level Fives need it."

"I'm aware of that."

That seemed to appease Lawson a little. "I'll talk to Beth and ask her to look into the circumstances surrounding Hardy's death," he said. "No sense in wasting your time on that front. She's got the resources to do it discreetly. And she's thorough."

"No argument there."

"Meanwhile, you concentrate on Isabel Wright. She may know more than she realizes or she may know someone else back at the center who can give you an angle on the identity of Client Number Three."

"True."

"Fine. Stick with Isabel Wright, then, and see what you can learn from her. She's the best lead we've got."

"You're trying to distract me again, Lawson. But it's okay. I happen to agree with you. Isabel is my best hope."

18

After Tamsyn left for a class, Isabel finished her salad and pushed the empty dishes out of the way. She opened the hefty instructor's manual to Lesson Six: "Empower Your Students."

She was making notes on teaching the importance of identifying and focusing on one's personal strong points and wondering how she could possibly connect that to creative dreaming when the light shifted in a subtle fashion.

She looked up and saw Ellis coming toward her across the terrace carrying paper cups emblazoned with the café's logo. He wore black trousers and a khaki shirt. A narrow leather belt rode low on his waist. As usual, his eyes were concealed behind a pair of sunglasses. She was rather pleased that she happened to have her own shades in place. Two could play the guess-what-I'm-really-thinking game, she decided.

"Get any sleep last night?" he asked, setting the cups down on the table.

"Not much." She pried the lid off her

cup and discovered green tea. Perfect. "What about you?"

"Couple hours, max." He pulled out a chair, sat down and snapped the lid off his cup. "Spent a lot of time thinking and then I called Lawson."

"Well?" She closed the manual very quickly and shoved it out of the way. Lawson and his mysterious agency were a lot more interesting than learning how to empower students. "What did he say?"

"He admits that Gavin Hardy's death may be more than an amazing case of coincidence in action, but he's skeptical. However he has his own agenda in this situation."

"And that is?"

"He desperately wants to learn the identity of Belvedere's anonymous third client. So desperate, in fact, that he just hired me to investigate that angle."

His cool, uninflected tone of voice made her curious. "That's just what you wanted, isn't it?"

"Sort of."

"What do you mean? You were planning to look into this mess anyway. Now you've got Lawson's backing and resources. Not to mention you'll get paid for your time."

"The thing is, the situation is what you

might call delicate."

The rock-solid line of his jaw worried her. "In what way?"

"Lawson thinks the third client is some honcho in another government agency that is engaged in the same type of Level Five dream research and is equally obsessed with secrecy."

She frowned slightly. "I've heard there can be communication problems and even major turf wars between various government agencies."

"After more than three decades in government work, Lawson is what you might call paranoid on the subject of his rivals, real or imagined."

"In other words, he's got his own theory about Client Number Three and it doesn't align with yours."

"He sure isn't going for the idea that Vincent Scargill is Number Three or that Scargill was the one who murdered Hardy."

She widened her hands. "So what if Lawson has his own theory about who killed poor Gavin? The bottom line is that he's agreed to let you investigate."

"Like I said, it's not quite that clear-cut." Ellis drank some tea and then lowered the cup with great care. "He told me to stick close to you because he thinks you're our best lead."

"Oh, wow." Excitement spiraled up inside her.

He watched from behind the dark glasses. "On that point, Lawson and I happen to agree."

"Oh, *wow.*" It was all she could do to stay in her seat and try to look professional. "I get to assist you with your investigation?"

He raised his brows. "You're a lead, not an assistant."

Her spirits plummeted. "Oh."

"But I would very much appreciate your cooperation," he added softly.

Be bold, she thought. This is your big chance. You're a freelance dreamer now with a skill set to sell. You're in a position to negotiate. *But what if he calls my bluff?*

Nothing ventured, nothing gained, etc., etc., she reminded herself. You're supposed to be a future Kyler Method instructor. Think positive.

"I could cooperate a lot more effectively if I were actively assisting you in your investigation," she said, going for super cool.

His expression tightened. "Isabel —"

"I'm serious, Ellis. I realize I haven't had any field experience, but I've got a lot of

Level Five dream experience. Also, I know more about the inner workings of the center than you do because I was inside it for a year. And when it comes to Dr. B., I've got more context than you could possibly have. I worked side by side with the man for months. Face it, you need me."

"There's a lot you don't know about this situation."

She spread her hands. "Okay, fine. So fill me in."

He looked at her for a long time, not speaking. She knew he was once again deliberating how much to tell her. The habit was becoming annoying.

Seconds stretched out into a full minute of silence.

Isabel sighed, sat back and held up her hand, palm out. "That's it, I've had enough of operating on a need-to-know basis, especially when I don't agree with you or Lawson on what I need to know. Either start treating me like an equal and a professional or find yourself another Level Five dream analyst who is sufficiently familiar with this case to help you conduct an investigation."

His brows rose above his dark glasses. "There is no one else I can substitute and you know it."

She smiled grimly. "Yep."

"You're playing hardball again, aren't you?"

She shrugged.

"Thought so. Getting pretty damn good at it, too." Ellis went quiet for another few seconds. "You handled yourself well with the cops last night," he said eventually.

She got the feeling that observation was important.

"Thank you," she murmured.

Another long moment slipped past. She realized she was holding her breath. And then Ellis inclined his head once, very deliberately, in acceptance of her terms.

"Right." He extended his legs and braced his elbows on the arms of the chair, fingertips pressed together. "You are now officially assisting me in this investigation."

She tried not to let her eagerness show. Composing herself she folded her arms on top of the closed manual and assumed a serious, attentive expression.

Ellis tapped his fingers together once. "I told you last night that Vincent Scargill is supposed to be dead."

"But you don't believe that."

"No."

She waited.

"The first thing you need to know about

this case is that Lawson and Beth think I've developed an unhealthy obsession," Ellis said neutrally. "They believe I'm suffering from some form of post-traumatic stress syndrome and that it has affected my Level Five dreaming capabilities in such a way that I've created a fantasy version of what really happened to Vincent Scargill."

"I'm listening."

He fixed his gaze on the bay. "You know how Scargill came to work at Frey-Salter."

"Dr. B. found him and sent him to Lawson."

"Scargill was twenty at the time." The corner of Ellis's mouth turned up slightly in a humorless smile. "He reminded me of myself at that age. Young and eager. Excited as hell to find someone who understood what he could do with his dreams. Downright thrilled to be working in a real-life super-secret government agency. Couldn't wait to prove himself."

"Go on."

"Scargill followed the usual training path at the agency. He did some assisting, practiced with mock cases and took the weapons and self-defense classes. He got his first big case a few months after he started. It was a kidnapping that was referred by one of the Mapstone Investigations affiliates. Scargill did a Level Five dream and solved it very quickly. The victim was rescued and the kidnappers were apprehended. As usual Beth's people got the credit. That's how it works."

"There's never any mention of Lawson's agency or the work his people do."

"No. But back at Frey-Salter, Scargill was definitely a rising star. Lawson was very, very pleased with him."

"And?"

"Scargill liked being a star. But on his next assignment, things didn't go so smoothly. No big surprise. He hadn't had much experience, after all. But he was furious when Lawson called me in to take over the investigation."

"I think I'm getting the picture here. Young, eager recruit doesn't like having his case turned over to the old pro."

"I prefer to use the term 'pro' without the qualifier," Ellis said dryly.

"Right. Sorry. Pro it is, not old pro."

"Thanks. I appreciate that. As it happened, neither Lawson nor I realized just how intense Scargill was when it came to showing the boss that he was the number-one dream hunter."

"Is that what Lawson calls his agents?"

"No. Lawson calls his agents *agents*.

Dream Hunter was Vincent Scargill's somewhat romanticized description of his job."

"Got it."

"About six months ago Lawson figured Scargill was ready for another case. He gave him a kidnapping. The situation was similar to the first one that Vincent had solved so spectacularly a few months earlier. Lawson had a theory that Scargill might have a special aptitude for that kind of crime."

"Do the agents specialize in certain kinds of crimes?" Isabel asked curiously

Ellis nodded. "Some of them do. They develop a feel for a type of criminal activity just as criminals develop a certain pattern and style in their crimes. In any event, Scargill did a dream and solved the case almost immediately. Lawson was impressed and gave him another assignment. Scargill came up with the answers overnight. He was on a roll. Within a three-month period he racked up half a dozen successes. He didn't even need any assistance when it came to analysis and interpretation."

She thought about that. "So I didn't see any of his dream reports?"

"No. Like I said, the guy seemed to be a natural."

"And you began to get suspicious?"

"It just seemed too good to be true," Ellis said. "When I heard about Scargill's track record, I told Lawson there was something wrong. He didn't want to believe me. He was convinced that Scargill had a unique type of talent."

"What did you do?"

"I went into an extreme dream and came up with a few leads. I checked them out on my own because I knew Lawson wasn't interested and I didn't want to alert Scargill."

"What did you find?" she asked, intensely curious.

"Information that indicated that Scargill had staged at least some of the crimes that he later pretended to solve."

"Oh, jeez." She swallowed. "Are we talking serious crimes?"

"Kidnappings and abductions. He seemed to specialize in them."

"You said he solved the crimes. I don't get it. If he was the perpetrator, who got the blame for committing the abductions?"

"That was the really clever part," Ellis said softly. "Because the cases were always successfully closed. Problem was, a pattern started to appear there, too. In the last four the bad guys all wound up dead. They all conveniently took their own lives before they could stand trial."

A cold feeling descended on her. "Scargill murdered innocent people and made it look as if they were the ones who committed the crimes?"

"That's just it, they weren't innocents. They actually did commit the crimes. What's more, they all had long-standing criminal records coupled with long-standing mental health problems. I think Scargill must have had some way of identifying the kind of people he could set up. Then he worked on them individually, taking advantage of their dangerous, unstable natures to prod them into the kidnappings."

She drew a deep breath, a little stunned. "And afterward, no one was surprised to learn that those people had gone off the rails. Probably not surprised by the suicides, either."

"It was a brilliant piece of game playing on Scargill's part."

"But didn't the law enforcement authorities see the same patterns that you did?"

"No," Ellis said, "because the cases were scattered all across the country. The police in Arizona had no reason to compare notes with the cops in Kentucky or California."

"What about Mapstone Investigations? You said Lawson always gets his cases from that source. Didn't someone there notice that something was wrong."

"Scargill was very good at setting the stages for his crimes. He loved to play computer games. I think that's where he got some of his ideas. There were patterns, of course. Hell, the patterns are always there if you know where to look for them. But he managed to keep them concealed for months."

"What happened?"

"There was one final kidnapping about three months ago," Ellis said. "It ended with me getting shot up and Scargill supposedly dying as the result of an explosion."

19

"So that's what happened to you," Isabel whispered tightly. "I *knew* you had been hurt. I could see it in your dreams. That loud roller coaster sound in your gateway. Did you take all those vitamins and mineral supplements I told you to get?"

The concern in her voice made him smile slightly. He had still not gotten beyond the novelty of having someone worry about his health and well-being.

"In the past three months I've spent a fortune in health food stores," he assured her.

"What about the acupuncture? Did it help?"

"Yes, although when I got a close look at all those little needles I almost walked out of the treatment room."

"I'm glad you went through with it." She pressed her lips together, evidently not entirely satisfied but willing to let it go for now. "Okay, tell me about that last case involving Scargill."

"The kidnapper was another typical

Scargill choice, a real nutcase. His name was McLean. He was one of those survivalist fanatics who was convinced that he had been appointed to found a new society based on a theory of government invented by him. His wife, Angela, had shown the good sense to divorce him. He was enraged when she left. I don't know how Scargill found him, but he was perfect. Probably didn't take much effort at all to talk McLean into kidnapping his ex."

"What did he do with her?"

"He took her to the remote mountain area where he and his idiot followers had a small compound. I heard about the case from a friend of mine who works at Mapstone Investigations. I knew right away that it was destined for Vincent Scargill. It had all of the earmarks."

"You decided to look into it yourself?"

"Yes. I didn't tell Lawson because I figured Scargill would find out."

"Did you dream?"

"No, I just did some old-fashioned detective work. McLean and his friends were not the sharpest knives in the drawer. They had bought so many guns and so much ammunition in such a short period of time that anyone could have followed their trail."

"So why didn't the cops follow it? Why did the case end up on Lawson's desk?"

"Because the ex-wife's relatives were afraid to go to the police," he explained. "I told you, Scargill staged every aspect of his little games very carefully. It appears that he always hired a woman to pose as a psychic right after the kidnappings occurred. The fake psychic would contact the families, telling them she'd had a vision. She always warned them that their only chance was to avoid the cops and call Mapstone Investigations, instead."

"How could he be sure Mapstone would refer the cases to Lawson's agency?"

"Scargill knew what Lawson looked for in a case. He made certain each of his kidnappings had some aspect about it that ensured that it wound up being referred to Frey-Salter."

"Sounds like Scargill is not only very smart, he learns fast."

Ellis tapped his fingers together again. "I think that was one of the reasons it took Lawson so long to realize he had a problem. He kept seeing Scargill as just another promising young recruit with real dream talent but no particular street smarts. He had a hard time comprehending that the bastard could outwit him. In fairness, though, I have to admit that Lawson was somewhat distracted at the time."

"By what?"

"He and Beth had had another one of their big blowups. It happens regularly. They've been married for years but they have a hard time living together. Probably because they're too damn much alike. They go along fine for months and then, wham, they have a flaming row. In the normal course of events, Beth moves out for a few weeks. Eventually they both cool down and go back to bed. But while they're apart, Lawson is not only more bad-tempered than usual, he doesn't always focus well."

"So the situation with Scargill occurred while Lawson was upset because of the problems in his marriage?"

"Yes," Ellis said. "And unfortunately the breakup was an unusually bad event this time. In fact Beth and Lawson are still living apart. But that's Lawson's fault. He made a very, very big mistake right after Beth moved out."

"Let me guess. He had an affair?"

Ellis raised his brows. "How did you know?"

She shrugged. "Seemed obvious from what you've already told me."

"Lawson was very depressed. He thought his marriage was really over for good this time around. He allowed himself to get drawn into an affair with one of the members of his staff. Word got back to Beth eventually, of course."

"Who was naturally enraged because Lawson broke one of the unwritten rules of their marriage."

"Hadn't thought about it in those terms," Ellis said reflectively, "but that pretty much sums up the situation. The net result was that Lawson was not paying as much attention to his job as he should have been for a couple of months and that's when Scargill went rogue."

Isabel whistled. "Good grief, I had no idea there was so much melodrama going on back there at Frey-Salter. But it's not all that surprising, is it? Lawson's agency may be a secret government organization but when you get down to the nitty-gritty, it's just another workplace environment where men and women are put together in close quarters under pressure. Bound to be some excitement."

"Trust me, the day Beth confronted Lawson with the affair, I heard the explosion all the way out here in California."

She looked fascinated. "You live here?"

"I have an apartment just outside of San Diego."

"Huh. I just assumed you lived back in the Raleigh-Durham area near the Research Triangle Park."

"I did for a long time," he said. "But about eight months ago I decided to move out here to California."

This was not the time to tell her that he'd made the move because he knew she lived in California and he wanted to feel closer to her. It had all been part of his grand plan to nudge his way gently into her life and see if he could make a place for himself. But that had been before Vincent Scargill.

"I see," she murmured.

He straightened a little in his chair, refocusing. "Getting back to Scargill, it turned out there was one major flaw in his game-playing routine. To maintain his pose as a hotshot agent, he had to wait until the case hit Lawson's desk before he could go into his big act. That generally didn't take too long, of course, especially with kidnappings. But in the McLean case, I was a couple of steps ahead of him."

"How did you manage that?"

"I've been doing this work for eighteen years," he said dryly. "There are some advantages to age and experience."

She smiled slightly. "Such as?"

"Such as having good connections with some of Beth's people. A couple of them owed me favors. Like I said, one of them alerted me to the McLean case because it fit the profile I had given him."

"What did you do?"

"I enlisted the help of two friends at Mapstone, guys I'd worked with in the past and knew I could trust. We located McLean's compound. In addition to McLean and his ex, there were a handful of other people on the scene. Future leaders of the new society. We created a major distraction for them."

"How?"

"Set fire to one of the outlying storage sheds. Most of the men rushed to put it out. When they were occupied, I went in, grabbed Angela McLean and got out."

"It was that easy?"

"There were a couple of complications." Namely the two guards who had been left behind, he reflected. But there was no need to go into unnecessary detail. "But no major problems."

"The wife must have been terrified."

He smiled, remembering. "Angela turned out to be a real trooper. Gutsy and smart. She realized right away that I was there to rescue her and she didn't panic. We made it out of the compound together. There was a lot of chaos and noise. People started shooting. I was still in the open at that point. That's when I took the bullet in my shoulder."

Out of the corner of his eye he noticed that her fingers trembled slightly but she just nodded.

"I went down but I managed to get back on my feet. Beth's people provided cover and half dragged me back to the SUV. We had just reached it when we heard the explosion. Later we found out that the ammo stored in one of the sheds had somehow ignited. Most of the members of McLean's group survived but McLean and one of his aides died."

"What about Vincent Scargill?"

Ellis watched the flash of light on the bay. "That's where it all gets murky. I spent the days immediately following the incident in a hospital. I was not in good shape. The local police and news media got involved, of course. And Beth and Lawson conducted their own private investigation. You know what they say about too many cooks spoiling the broth. I gather it was mass confusion, a classic snafu."

"Did Beth and Lawson find anything?"

"Sure," he muttered. "Among other things they found evidence that Scargill was there at the compound that day."

"What kind of evidence?"

"One of his shoes. There was a lot of blood on it. Got a hunch he's the one who fired the shot that hit me."

"But they didn't find Scargill?"

"No. However, a few days later Beth's people learned that a man answering the description of Vincent Scargill staggered into the emergency room of a mid-sized hospital about two hours from the McLean compound. He had suffered serious head trauma and was incoherent. He died that same day."

"What about the body?"

"That's the really interesting part," Ellis said softly. "There was a mix-up in the hospital morgue. The computer records later showed that the body of the man Beth and Lawson think was Vincent Scargill was mistakenly released to a local funeral home. The attendants thought they were picking up someone else. They had instructions to cremate."

She winced. "I think I know how this is going to end."

He nodded slowly. "By the time the

screwup was straightened out, the body that had been identified as Scargill was ashes. Scattered ashes, at that."

There was a long silence from the other side of the table. He waited it out with a sense of stoic resignation. There was nothing more he could do. He had no proof to offer her that he had not dreamed up the entire story.

"So, no body," Isabel said quietly.

"No body."

She nodded once, very crisply. "Okay, I can see why you're somewhat skeptical about the fate of Vincent Scargill."

Ellis peeled off his sunglasses with a slow, measured motion and looked at her. He felt as if he were standing in front of her stark naked.

"You can?" he said carefully.

"Definitely."

"In the three months since that explosion at the McLean compound there has been absolutely no indication at all that Vincent Scargill is still alive. Not unless you count the death of a woman named Katherine Ralston. Beth and Lawson don't count it because the police are convinced that she was the victim of a burglar she happened to surprise in her apartment."

"No convenient arrest in that case?"

He was impressed with the quick observation. "No. I have to admit that the Ralston murder doesn't fit Scargill's usual pattern."

"Why are Beth and Lawson so sure Scargill is dead?"

"DNA evidence from some blood that was taken at the hospital where the records showed he died. It was a match for Scargill. The emergency room admission records made it clear that his condition was extremely grave when he arrived and it was no surprise to any of the doctors who reviewed the records later that he didn't make it."

"Beth and Lawson do believe that he staged the McLean kidnapping, though, right?"

"Yes. But they think I'm experiencing some sort of post-traumatic stress and that I have become obsessed with the deluded belief that Scargill plotted the entire incident at the compound to get rid of me. My theory is that I was supposed to die that day, not Scargill, and that when the investigation was complete, it would appear that I was the one who had set up the kidnapping."

"But you lived," she said quietly. "And everything went wrong for Scargill." She reached up and removed her own dark glasses. Her dreamer's eyes were as bright and magnetic as the light on the bay. "Under the circumstances, I'd say you've got a right to be obsessed until proven otherwise."

He started to breathe again. "Thanks, I needed that."

"Hey, we extreme dreamers have to stick together."

She said the words easily, as if it was only natural that the two of them should be bound together somehow, just because they were Level Fives. Probably would have been happy to form an alliance with any other extreme dreamer. He reminded himself once again that maybe that was all that was going on here.

She had said it herself, yesterday, he thought. She'd been working in the dark for her entire life, never had a chance to meet or talk to another Level Five, let alone go to bed with one. She was curious. *Try to keep some perspective here.*

Nevertheless, in spite of all the caveats and warnings he gave himself, he couldn't resist the surge of need and desire that swept through him. *Nothing wrong with satisfying a lady's curiosity.*

"What do we do next?" she asked with

the boundless enthusiasm of the amateur sleuth. "I can't wait to get started."

He stifled a groan. Amateurs were always problematic. They made mistakes. They got carried away. They did things that could get them killed. Priority One here was to keep his daring little Tango Dancer safe.

"I'm thinking that there are a couple of places to start looking for answers," he said cautiously. "It might be useful if you called a few people back at the Center for Sleep Research and find out if there's any in-house gossip going around about Gavin Hardy. No one will think it strange if you ask some questions. After all, Gavin was on his way to see you when he was run down. Naturally you're concerned and curious."

"Okay, I can do that." She looked pensive. "I'll start with Ken Payne. I've been meaning to get in touch with him, anyway."

He wondered if Ken Payne was an old boyfriend. Sometimes it was better not to ask. "Fine."

"What else?"

He reflected for a moment, trying to come up with safe jobs for her. "Might be worth taking a look at those papers and notes that Belvedere's lawyer sent to you."

She made a face. "I think there's about three decades' worth of research in those boxes."

"We'll start with the most recent files and work back."

"Makes sense," she agreed. "We can start this evening." Her eager excitement was almost infectious. He had to remind himself that he was a jaded old pro with a dangerous obsession about a dead guy.

"Okay," he said.

She glanced at her watch. "I've got to run off to a class. Why don't you come to my place for dinner? I'll make my phone calls and we can start work on Belvedere's research together."

Nothing personal, he chanted silently. Nothing personal. Just dinner and some research files.

"Sounds like a plan," he said.

20

"Sphinx, the world as we know it has just shifted yet again beneath our feet," Isabel announced at five o'clock that afternoon. "I can tell for sure that, whatever else was going through Ellis's mind last night when he kissed me, he is definitely all business now."

Unfazed by this news, Sphinx heaved his bulk up onto the faded cushion of the chair in front of the window. He folded himself into a large, furry bundle and went into Zen mode.

"For the moment, at least, he is one hundred percent focused on finding Vincent Scargill." She set the heavy grocery bags down on the granite counter that divided the kitchen and living area. "Sadly, I'm afraid that having hot sex with me is no longer at the top of his to-do list."

Sphinx moved his tail restlessly. Maybe he was bored with the conversation. More likely the topic of human sex embarrassed him, she thought.

"The thing is, if I want to impress him, I've got to be just as cool and professional as he is." She removed the plum tomatoes from the grocery sack and set them on the counter. "I want him to take me seriously. No more batting my eyelashes and showing a lot of thigh. When a man is concentrating on catching a bad guy, he's not going to be interested in romance. That comes later. Maybe. I hope."

The throaty rumble of the Maserati's high-powered engine sounded outside in the street. Sphinx pricked his ears.

Isabel's pulse kicked into high gear. "Oh, my gosh, he's here already."

Hastily she yanked the remaining items — a log of goat cheese, two large bunches of fresh spinach and a package of frozen, uncooked puff pastry — out of the sack.

Sphinx bestirred himself to get down from the chair and amble toward the front hall. Obviously he had already learned to recognize the sound of Ellis's car.

"I'm not trying to impress him with my cooking," she assured the cat, pulling the bottle of hideously expensive California cabernet out of the sack. "A man on a mission isn't going to pay much attention to food. This is just simple fare. I would have made a tomato-and-goat-cheese tart and fixed a lovely spinach salad tonight regardless of whether or not I was expecting a man for dinner." She froze, assailed by a sudden wave of horrified doubt. "Oh, jeez, that's not real macho food, is it? What was I thinking? I should have bought some salmon and grilled it with asparagus and maybe some sourdough bread. I should have done *potatoes*. Men like potatoes. Oh, jeez, *I'm making a goat cheese tart*. This is a disaster, Sphinx."

The knock on the front door interrupted her in mid–panic attack. *Pull yourself together. You're a professional. You have got to be cool, woman.*

She made herself walk to the front door and fling it open. Sphinx padded outside to greet Ellis, who was coming up the steps with a briefcase that looked as Italian and as expensive as the Maserati.

He halted in front of her, politely quizzical. "Something wrong?"

Wrong? What could be wrong? The man of her dreams was standing right in front of her and she was in a state of sheer, unadulterated anxiety because she was going to fix a tomato-and-goat-cheese tart with puff pastry, for Pete's sake, instead of something manly like grilled salmon and potatoes.

"No, of course not," she said, pleased with the blithe, breezy way it came out.

"Come on in, I'll open the wine. We can talk about our plans while I fix dinner."

Maybe he would be so intent on his manhunt that he wouldn't notice the puff pastry.

Ellis set the briefcase down beside the chair in the small living room and took a quick look around while Isabel made herself busy in the kitchen. He hadn't had a chance to examine the place the night before and he was deeply curious.

The furnishings looked as if they had come with the house. The sofa, chairs, coffee table and lamps were all nondescript and well worn, veterans of a lot of years of summer rentals.

He was mildly surprised not to see more evidence of Isabel's personal style and tastes in the room. He had figured her for the kind of woman who would put her stamp on her environment. Why the bland backdrop? Probably hadn't had time to do any interior design.

The collection of volumes in the plank-and-glass block bookcase proved to be the exception to the generic feel of the place.

He glanced at a few of the titles and smiled. As he had expected, it was a mixed lot that ran the gamut from serious academic dream research to the bogus television psychic stuff. G. William Domhoff's *The Scientific Study of Dreams* sat side by side with a collection of Jung's essays on dreams and a popular book that purported to tell people how to interpret the symbols that appeared in their dreamscapes. Freud's groundbreaking work on the psychological analysis of dreams was juxtaposed with Stephen LaBerge's experimental reports on lucid dreaming. The legendary sleep studies conducted by Dement were wedged between copies of the elaborate Hall/Van de Castle dream coding system and a volume containing Patricia Garfield's theories on the same subject.

This was where Martin Belvedere had hoped to see his work shelved, he thought, right next to Freud, Jung, Domhoff, LaBerge and the others. He wondered if Isabel would someday make the old man's dream of respect and recognition come true. One thing was for sure. Belvedere had been right to entrust his papers to her. If anyone would take on the responsibility of getting him published posthumously, it was Isabel.

"Wine's ready," she announced cheerfully. "And I've got some hors d'oeuvres, if you're hungry."

"You don't have to call me twice."

He crossed the living area and took a seat on one of the high-backed swivel chairs at the counter. In spite of the seriousness of the situation and the knowledge that Isabel probably would have fixed dinner for anyone who showed up on her doorstep, he could not ignore the bone-deep satisfaction he was feeling. There was an inexplicable sense of rightness about this cozy domestic scene. It was as if some part of him were trying to tell him that this was where he belonged, what he had been waiting for all these years.

Or maybe the problem was simply that he could not remember the last time anyone had cooked dinner for him.

Isabel set a glass of wine and a small dish containing an assortment of olives, tiny strips of carrots and crunchy pale jicama, together with some cheese and crackers, in front of him.

"Here's to our future as dream analyst and client," she said cheerfully, raising her glass.

He was thinking of a much more intimate relationship but he figured this was not the time to mention it.

"To us," he said, wondering if she was so intent on having him as a client that she was no longer interested in having him as a lover.

The phone in the living room shrilled an irritating summons just as Isabel took a sip from her glass.

"Excuse me," she said.

Hastily she put the wine down and rounded the far end of the counter.

He swiveled on the chair, one heel hooked over the bottom rung, and watched her scoop up the phone.

"Hello?" she said. Surprise flashed across her face. "Dr. Belvedere. I wasn't expecting . . . Yes. Yes, thank you. I'm doing very well. Did you hear about poor Gavin Hardy? Yes, he was killed by a hit-and-run driver last night. It was tragic. . . . What's that? Oh, I see."

Ellis watched her closely, wariness gathering inside him. What the hell was this about?

"That's very nice of you, but I've made my decision," Isabel said politely. Her eyes met Ellis's. "I don't want to go back into a lab setting. . . . Yes, that's right, I'm going to open up a consulting business. . . . What?" She frowned and held the phone a short distance from her ear. "Sir, you're getting a bit loud."

Ellis could hear Belvedere shouting at

her all the way across the room. He couldn't make out the words, but there was no doubt about the tone. Belvedere was furious.

"No, I most certainly did not know that the contracts prohibited me from working with any of the three anonymous clients," Isabel said coldly. "As a matter of fact, I've never seen any contracts. If you've got proof of such a clause, I will, of course, want to show it to a lawyer. . . ." She paused again. "No, I'm sorry, sir, I don't have that information."

She broke off abruptly and then put the phone down very gently. "He hung up on me."

"Let me take a giant leap in the dark here," Ellis said. "Belvedere offered to let you return to your old job at the center."

"With a substantial increase in salary." She smiled. "I have to tell you, it felt very good to turn him down." She walked back into the kitchen and picked up her wineglass. "He sounded quite anxious. Evidently he has just discovered that anonymous Client Number One paid some hefty fees for my services."

"What did he say about Hardy's death?"

She frowned. "He had heard the news but he didn't seem the least bit interested.

All he cared about was getting me back to the center. When I declined his offer he got mad and demanded contact information for Clients One and Two."

"But not Three?"

"No." She paused and then shook her head decisively. "I got the impression he only knows about two anonymous clients."

"And when you didn't give him any information that would help him identify them, he threatened you with legal action if you lured Clients Number One and Two away from the center."

She looked smug. "Guess I'm a player now, huh?"

He raised his brows. "Oh, yeah."

Her expression turned uncertain. "He was bluffing when he said the two anonymous clients had signed contracts that made it impossible for me to do any consulting work for them outside the center, wasn't he?"

"Relax, neither Lawson nor I signed any contracts," he assured her. "Didn't want to leave a paper trail. You're free to consult with us." He considered briefly. "Sounds like Number Three didn't sign anything, either."

She picked up a knife and started to slice tomatoes. "Do you think the fact that

Randolph was so callous and unfeeling about what happened to Gavin Hardy means he might have had something to do with his death?"

"If he killed him without getting the information concerning the three mystery clients out of him first, he really screwed up, didn't he?" Ellis said.

"True. I'll call my friend Ken Payne after dinner and see what he has to say about the situation at the center. He's always a great one for in-house gossip." She turned toward the refrigerator and then paused, looking worried. "Do you have a problem with puff pastry?"

"Depends what you plan to do with it."

She looked anxious. "Cook it and serve it for dinner."

He smiled slowly. "If you make it, I will come."

21

She finally got ahold of Ken Payne at ten o'clock that evening. He sounded pleased to hear from her.

"Isabel, I've been meaning to call you but I've been kind of busy since you left. I kept that appointment with the cardiologist. The next thing I knew, I was headed into surgery."

"What was it?"

"Aortic aneurism. Disaster waiting to happen but a straightforward repair job if you find it in time. Had the operation on Monday. I'm home and doing great."

"Ken, I'm so relieved to hear that."

"They said the problem is often hereditary and that an aneurism is probably what killed my father and grandfather. It often goes undiagnosed because there are no symptoms until it ruptures, and then it's usually too late. The results look very much like a sudden heart attack so that's usually what goes down in the records as the cause of death."

"But you're okay, now?"

"Better than new they tell me. Susan is here with me." There was a short pause and then Ken came back. "She says thanks for everything. Needless to say, I second that. I really owe you, Isabel."

"I'm just relieved that everything worked out so well."

"What's going on with you? I haven't been back to the center since the operation but I've heard things are kind of chaotic there."

"Yes, I can imagine. Not my problem anymore, though — I'm starting a new job at my brother-in-law's company. It will pay the bills until I can get my consulting business up and running. Did you hear about Gavin Hardy?"

"Yeah, Jason called with the news this afternoon. What a shocker, huh? What was Hardy doing in your neck of the woods?"

She looked at Ellis, who was crouched in front of one of the six cartons containing Martin Belvedere's research papers. He was sorting the documents by date.

When they had opened the first box after dinner they were dismayed to discover that several decades' worth of notes, dream logs and unpublished journal manuscripts had been dumped haphazardly inside. Evidently, although the lawyers had dutifully saved everything Belvedere sent to them over the years, they had not felt any obligation to organize the mass of paperwork.

"Gavin was trying to put together a stake so he could go back to Las Vegas," she said carefully. "He offered to sell me some confidential client information he had discovered on Belvedere's computer, but he was killed before I could find out what it was."

"Confidential client data, huh? That sounds like something Hardy would try to peddle. He wasn't a bad sort, but he definitely had a gambling addiction."

"He lived for those trips to Vegas," she agreed. "Did Jason have any other office gossip from the center?"

"He mentioned that several people are dusting off their résumés. I'm thinking of doing the same. Word is that the funding has dropped off quite a bit since the old man died. There's even some question about whether or not Randolph will have to declare bankruptcy."

Isabel curled her legs under her and frowned at Ellis, who was listening to every word. "That sounds serious."

"That's about it, gossip-wise," Ken said. "Unless you're interested in the news that Randolph Belvedere and Amelia Netley are an item."

Isabel raised her brows. "No kidding? They managed to keep that quiet while I was there. Never had a clue."

"According to Sandra Johnson, they were seeing each other even before the old man died."

"Sandra would know. She sits right outside Belvedere's office and she doesn't miss a thing."

"There may be trouble in paradise, though. Sandra heard Amelia and Randolph arguing behind closed doors a couple of times after you left."

"Ken, you are a fountain of interesting office news, as usual."

They chatted for a few more minutes and then Isabel said goodbye and put down the phone.

Ellis stopped stacking papers, got to his feet and rotated his right arm in an absent, circular motion, loosening his shoulder. She saw the faint tightening at the corners of his eyes.

"Would you like some anti-inflammatories?" she asked, starting to rise from the sofa.

"I'm fine," he said tersely. "Did Payne have anything useful?"

"No, unfortunately. He's recovering from surgery so he hasn't been in his office since shortly after I left. The only gossip he had was the news that Randolph is sleeping with a member of the professional staff, Amelia Netley. Not very helpful, I'm afraid."

"Who's next on your list?"

She glanced down at the pad of paper on the table next to the phone. "Sandra Johnson. She was Martin Belvedere's secretary. Randolph inherited her."

She was reaching for the phone again when a muffled clatter followed by a soft thud sounded from the vicinity of the small laundry room off the kitchen.

Ellis spun around so quickly he was almost a blur. He dove for the briefcase and came up with a pistol in his hand.

Before Isabel could recover from her shock, he had hit the light switch on the wall, dousing all the living room lamps.

The space was plunged into darkness.

"Ellis —"

"Get down on the floor," he ordered, his voice dangerously soft.

"But —"

"Do it."

She sensed him moving toward the kitchen. It was all happening so fast she could scarcely understand it. Then she had a sudden, horrifying thought.

"Don't shoot, it's just Sphinx," she said quickly. "He's using the dog door in the laundry room. Please, don't hurt him."

There was a short silence. And then the light came on in the small space, spilling into the kitchen.

She saw Ellis silhouetted in the fluorescent glow, the gun alongside his leg, pointed toward the floor. He stood looking into the laundry room, his features stark and grim.

"You just had one hell of a close call, Sphinx," he said, his voice still frighteningly low and even.

Unconcerned with his brush with a messy death, Sphinx greeted Ellis with a few flicks of his tail and then padded to his food dish.

Isabel started to breathe again.

"Sorry," she said. "I forgot to mention the little dog door. Sphinx found it right after we moved in. He disappeared while I was unpacking. I thought he ran off. I was worried he wouldn't be able to find his way back but he came home a short time later, just as calm as you please."

For a couple of heartbeats, Ellis did not move. She was not sure he had even heard her. But just as she parted her lips to repeat her explanation of events, he turned, very slowly, as though reluctant to look at her.

"You're supposed to be on the floor," he said.

The ice in his words froze her to the spot.

"Ellis? What's wrong? I'm sorry you were startled." She was starting to get worried now. "Are you okay?"

His jaw was rigid and his eyes narrowed in a way that reminded her uncomfortably of Sphinx in a bad mood. She got the impression he was angry but whether he was mad at her or himself was not clear.

"Sorry," he said roughly. He stalked back into the living room and put the pistol inside the briefcase. Then he straightened and looked at her. "I've been a little jumpy for the past three months."

She cleared her throat. "Yes, I can see that."

"Didn't mean to scare you."

"You didn't scare me. I was concerned, that's all." She glanced at the briefcase. "Although I, uh, didn't realize that you were armed."

He didn't say anything, just stood there looking at her with an enigmatic expression.

She reminded herself that he had just responded to a perceived threat with a gun in his hand. There was probably a lot of adrenaline and testosterone still pumping through him. She needed to give him time to get himself under control.

"It's okay, Ellis." She made her voice as soothing as possible. "Why don't I fix you a nice cup of tea?"

He took a step toward her and stopped. "Next time I tell you to get down on the floor and stay there, you do it. Understood?"

She sighed. "You're really mad, aren't you?"

"I'm mad, all right. Last night someone you knew well got himself killed, remember?"

"I'm hardly likely to forget it."

"We aren't playing games here."

"I'm perfectly well aware of that." She felt her own temper start to flare. "You don't need to lecture me."

This discussion was turning into a full-blown quarrel, she thought. Why was that happening? Now that the small scare was past, they should both be relaxing, savoring the relief, maybe even joking about the incident.

But there was no amusement in Ellis. She could feel the edgy, battle-ready tension coming off him in dangerous waves of raw power. She wouldn't have been surprised if there had been a few sparks in the air.

"No," he said. "I don't want any tea."

She folded her arms tightly beneath her breasts. "Maybe a drink?"

"No." He ran his fingers through his hair. "You think I'm overreacting, don't you?"

"I think that, under the circumstances, your reaction is entirely reasonable."

"Lawson says my jumpiness is a side effect of my post-traumatic stress and my obsession with Scargill." Ellis scrubbed his face with one hand. "Maybe he knows what he's talking about. Maybe I have gone around the bend and just don't realize it."

"I don't believe that," she said quietly. "Not for a moment."

He lowered his hand and stared hard at her. "How can you be sure?"

She unfolded her arms and moved to stand directly in front of him, inches away. "I've walked through your dreams for the past year, Ellis Cutler. I would know if you were dangerously obsessed or deluded. I would also know if you were suffering from post-traumatic stress."

He exhaled slowly. "Yes. I think you of

all people would know the truth about me."

She smiled slightly. "Want that drink now?"

He shook his head, slowly, deliberately. Then he raised one hand and wrapped it lightly around the nape of her neck.

A rush of heat flashed through her, igniting her nerve endings all the way to her fingertips. She knew that her body's internal temperature-regulating mechanism had just gone on the fritz, because she was suddenly hot and cold all over.

"I dream about you," Ellis said. He spoke in the harshest of whispers, producing each word as though it were a chunk of ore that he'd been forced to dig from the farthest reaches of a deep, sunless cavern. "I dream about taking you to bed."

Her mouth went dry.

"You do?" She had to struggle to get the words out.

He searched her eyes. "I'm scaring you, aren't I? You're starting to wonder if maybe Lawson is right about me, after all."

"You're not scaring me."

"Didn't you just hear what I said? I *dream* about you. Some folks would call that a sign of an obsessive personality."

She touched the side of his face.

"Studies show that a significant percentage of dreams involve sexual content, and dreams about engaging in sex with strangers are quite common for both men and women."

"I don't dream about having sex with strangers. I dream about having sex with you." His eyes darkened. "And the dreams are all Level Five, extreme and very, very lucid. Do you have any idea how many cold showers I've taken in the past year?"

"Oh." She did not know what else to say. She was dazed and breathless.

His mouth twisted. "Now you're scared, aren't you?"

"No. Honest."

"You probably should be."

"You don't scare me, Ellis Cutler."

"Maybe not. But I think I'm scaring myself. I should go back to the inn." He took his hand away from her neck and started to turn toward the briefcase.

She was suddenly very cold.

"Ellis."

He stopped. The heat in his eyes burned away the chill.

"What is it?"

"I dream about you, too," she whispered starkly. "Level Five with all the trimmings."

He was very still. "You never saw me. Never knew what I looked like."

"In my dreams your face was always in shadow but I knew who you were. There was never any doubt." She smiled. "I knew enough about you to recognize you the other day when you walked into the auditorium at Kyler headquarters. Somehow you looked exactly like you were supposed to look."

He took a step toward her, not touching her but crowding all the air out of the space that separated them.

"I recognized you, too." Now he touched her, cradling her face in his warm, strong hands. "But I had an advantage."

"What was that?"

"After I started dreaming about you, I told Belvedere I wanted a photo of you. Gave him some tale about needing it for security reasons. Not that he cared one way or the other."

She went blank for an instant. Then a memory returned. Delight and wonder rose inside her.

"The gorgeous orchids," she whispered. "I remember Dr. B. taking a snapshot. He told me it was for his files." She broke off, her euphoric mood dropping like a stone when she got a sudden, bad flashback to all the failed hairstyles she had tried out in the past year. "I can't recall what phase I was in that day. What did my hair look like? Did it involve a lot of curls? Please don't tell me there were curls."

He smiled slowly. "No curls. Sounds interesting, though."

"I hope it wasn't my blond era, either. That was not a success."

He shook his head. "Your hair looked a lot like it does now. You had it pulled back into a knot at the back of your head."

"Oh, that's right, I was between experiments that week." She put her hand to her hair and winced. "This is my default mode. I call it the Desperately Professional Look."

"You don't look desperately professional when you wear your hair like this. You look like a sexy, sultry tango dancer."

"Really?" No one had ever described her as sexy, let alone as a sultry tango dancer. "I've never even taken tango lessons."

"Neither have I. But something tells me we could learn together."

"Oh, Ellis."

He used one hand to tilt her head back, baring her throat. She could have sworn that she could hear the first dramatic, mysterious chords of the bandoneón, the instrument forever associated with the most passionate dance in the world.

When Ellis kissed her shoulder she thought she would burst into flames. She shuddered and wrapped her arms around his neck, pressing herself into him.

His mouth found the delicate place just below her ear. He used his tongue and the edge of his teeth until she could not stop the delicious shivers that pulsed through her.

She drew the inside of her thigh upward alongside his leg, thrilling to the shudder that went through him and the powerful contours of muscle and bone beneath his skin.

By the time his mouth closed over hers, she was shaking with the intensity of the emotions pouring through her. Every nerve ending in her body was alive. The part of her that had been dreaming for so long was fully awake. No matter what happened, no matter where this moment led, she had to discover what awaited her in this bright, new dawn.

"Isabel." Ellis tightened his arms around her and crushed her against the length of his body. "I want you so much, I'm hurting tonight. I knew it would be like this."

She was stunningly aware of his fierce

arousal. There was nothing halfhearted or lukewarm about his passion. He had told her his dreams for nearly a year, but unlike the other men she had dated, he did not see her as a sympathetic friend or a big sister tonight. He saw her as a tango dancer, and in his arms she felt like one: daring, alluring, smoldering, gloriously, powerfully feminine.

At least once in a lifetime, everyone deserved the chance to make at least one dream come true.

She kissed him the way she had wanted to kiss him in her private midnight fantasies, deliberately trying to provoke and incite; experimenting, sampling, savoring.

Somehow her shirt had come undone. She didn't realize he had slipped the buttons until he was peeling the garment off her.

The emerald green fabric fell into a tropical pool at her feet.

Ellis traced the line of her shoulder with the edge of his thumb, as though mesmerized by the curves and angles there. Then he bent his head and kissed her just above her collarbone.

"You have the most beautiful shoulders," he whispered.

"I took out a gym membership last

year," she said before stopping to think. She blushed furiously. Great. That was a real sexy thing to say, she thought.

"It was worth every cent," he assured her gravely, and then he kissed her throat.

She wished she had known what was coming. She would have liked to have put on one of the sensual nightgowns she always wore when she dreamed about him. That was the problem with waking life. You couldn't predict it.

"Maybe Lawson's right." Ellis's voice was low and heavy with desire. "Maybe I am becoming obsessive. All I can think about right now is what it's going to feel like to be inside you."

She unfastened the buttons of his shirt and slid her hands under the edges so she could feel the sleek muscles of his chest. "That's okay, because that's all I can think about right now, too."

He removed her bra and cupped her breasts in the palms of his hand. When he brushed his thumb across one nipple she felt everything inside her tighten into a knot.

She managed to fumble his shirt off and then paused when she felt the unnaturally rough texture of the skin at the back of his right shoulder. Scars, she thought. Big ones. She was horrified in spite of the fact that she had known of the injury. He had come so close to death.

"This was where Scargill shot you, isn't it?" she whispered.

He hesitated. "Not real pretty, I'm afraid. The doctors said they could do some cosmetic surgery after it was healed but I never went back. I don't want to see the inside of a hospital again if I can avoid it."

She touched him as gently as possible. "It doesn't matter how it looks. I just don't want to hurt you."

"You won't." He raised his head. "But the damn shoulder doesn't work as well as it once did. That means I can't scoop you up in my arms and carry you off to the bedroom. I'd have to throw you over my good shoulder which seems a little tacky."

Laughter bubbled up inside her. "Guess what? I can walk."

"Lucky you," he muttered into her hair with great feeling. "I can barely stand up."

But he was obviously in better shape than he thought because he locked her close to his side and drew her down the hall. It took a while to get to their destination because every few steps he stopped and pinned her against the wall long enough to kiss her and remove another item of clothing. By the time they reached the shadows of her bedroom she had somehow managed to shed all of her clothes except for her panties.

She slid beneath the covers and waited for him. Ellis got rid of his own garments with efficient, impatient movements. He turned toward her and then stopped and just stood there, looking at her as if she weren't quite real. She realized that she was lying in a splash of moonlight.

"You are so lovely," he said.

She could not speak so she smiled tremulously and raised her arms to welcome him into her bed.

He said something low, husky and hungry-sounding when he lowered himself to her.

And then the world went away. All that mattered was the hot, damp passion of their lovemaking.

Ellis's kisses singed every part of her from head to toe. When he found the inside of her thigh she gasped and clutched at him. Burying her fingers in his hair, she twisted beneath him, feeling full and achy and frantic.

Her sexual experience had been limited — nonexistent altogether for the past year.

She had told herself that one of the reasons she found it easy to forgo intimacy was because she had never found any genuinely stirring pleasure in the act. Her private fantasy dreams had always been a great deal more satisfying.

But tonight she was swamped with sensations she had never experienced except in her dreams and even in those the feelings had never been so intense.

When she reached down to cup him in her palm, he groaned, rolled to cover her and rested his forehead on hers. She could have sworn he was shaking a little. His back was slick with perspiration.

He reached down between their bodies, found the part of her that was clenched tight and gently pried it open with his fingers. Her hips came up off the bed in response. With his hand he urged her toward the response that her body demanded.

When her release struck she was so overwhelmed and so undone she could not even cry out. She convulsed, sinking her nails into his back.

He was inside her before the shimmering ripples had subsided, sinking deep. The sudden pressure created by the heavy, rigid length of him caused her body to soar along the delicate border between exquisite pleasure and exquisite pain.

"Ellis."

He stopped at once, halfway inside her. When he raised his head to look down at her she could see his face etched in the moonlight. Highwayman, vampire, dashing rake; he was all of them, all of her midnight men.

"Are you okay?" he asked hoarsely.

"No. Yes."

She encircled him with her legs, tightening her thighs. He groaned and crushed her down into the bedding.

His climax tore through him.

She heard satisfaction, exultation and astonished pleasure in the husky, elemental, utterly male cry of release.

He came out of the bathroom some time later, got back into bed and wrapped her close. He put one hand behind his head and looked up at the ceiling.

"We should probably talk," he said.

Panic assailed her. Talking was dangerous. Talking was where things always went wrong. She did not want anything to spoil this perfect dream night.

"Not now." She drew her fingertips down his chest. "There's no need. Go to sleep."

"You're sure you don't want to talk?"

"Positive."

"Just as well, I'm not feeling real coherent at the moment," he said in a voice that was already thickening with sleep. He tightened his arm around her, pulling her closer to him. "Don't go anywhere, okay?"

An odd request, she thought.

"I'm not going anywhere," she promised softly.

That seemed to satisfy him. He relaxed immediately and she knew that he slept.

It was a while before she managed to drift off into slumber. A part of her resisted closing her eyes. She was afraid she would wake up in the morning and discover that it had all been a dream.

22

"I'm worried about Isabel," Leila announced. She put the day's edition of the *Roxanna Beach Courier* aside and reached for her glass of orange juice.

On the other side of the table, Farrell glanced up from the financial documents he was studying. She noticed that, in spite of his air of distraction and secretiveness these days, he was paying attention.

"Because she knew that guy who got run down out on the old highway or because of her connection to Ellis Cutler?" he asked.

"Both. But mostly because of Cutler."

She put down the orange juice glass without taking a sip, picked up a spoon and toyed with her cereal. Her appetite had disappeared in the last few weeks. She had lost five pounds. She told herself she was either dying of some dreadful, as yet undiagnosed disease or she was depressed because Farrell was getting ready to tell her that he wanted a divorce. She was not sure which news would be harder to take.

Farrell drank some coffee and briefly

considered. "Cutler is definitely not her usual type, is he?"

"No, and that's what's worrying me. All this talk of hiring Isabel as a freelance dream analyst is just plain weird. He doesn't appear to be some New Age type who would take the psychic thing seriously. He seems too tough and smart for that nonsense." She broke off, trying to find the words. "He looks dangerous, to tell you the truth. The whole situation strikes me as very strange."

Farrell did not bother to hide his amusement. "You have to admit that there's always been something a bit strange about your sister. Maybe it's a case of weirdness attracting weirdness."

The anger boiled up out of nowhere. "Isabel isn't weird, she's just different, that's all."

"Whoa." Farrell held up both hands, palms out. "I take it back. I was just trying to inject a little humor into the discussion. Sorry."

Leila took a deep, steadying breath. She and Farrell had always prided themselves on their ability to communicate. They rarely quarreled until the last few months. But lately it took very little provocation to make her snap at him.

"Isabel has always marched to a different drummer," Leila said wearily. "She's always had a fixation with dreams. But that does not make her a flake."

"I know. I apologize."

"I'm going to ask someone in HR to run a background check on Ellis Cutler. The kind we do on new hires. I want to at least be sure he doesn't have a criminal record."

Farrell shrugged and stuffed the financial papers into his briefcase. "Suit yourself. My guess is you won't find anything."

"Why do you say that?"

"Just a gut feeling. If Cutler has buried a few bodies along the way, he'll have made certain they are deep enough that no one can find them with a simple background check."

The spoon quivered in her hand. "Farrell, do you really think it's possible that he might have killed some people? Or are you just joking?"

Farrell actually hesitated a moment, head tilted slightly to the side, while he contemplated the question. She suddenly felt ill. Regardless of what was going on in their personal life, she trusted his judgment in such things. It did not bode well that he had to stop and think about the question.

"It's possible," he said finally. "But I

wouldn't worry about it, if I were you."

"For heaven's sake, why shouldn't I worry about it?"

His smile was wry. "Because if Cutler did get rid of some folks, there were no doubt very compelling reasons."

"How can you say such a thing."

"Give your sister some credit." He got to his feet and picked up his briefcase. "In spite of her eccentricities, Isabel is no fool when it comes to reading people. If she thinks Cutler is okay, he probably is okay."

"We can't depend on that. She's attracted to him. That means she may be ignoring the warning signs. Besides, if Cutler is as smart as you think he is, he could very well be deceiving her."

"My advice is not to get too worked up about this, honey." He came around the table and gave her a quick, absent kiss on the forehead. "Because from what I've seen of Ellis Cutler, there's not a damn thing you can do to keep him away from Isabel." He started toward the door. "See you at the office."

She crumpled the napkin in her lap. "You're in a big rush this morning."

"Got a meeting with the publicity staff at seven forty-five."

"I see."

He paused, frowning. "Are you all right?"

"Yes."

His mouth tightened. "You're still upset about that conversation we had last week, aren't you?"

"Stop calling it a conversation," she said tightly. "We aren't in one of your motivational workshops here, Farrell. There's no need to pretend that argument was an example of open communication. It was a quarrel, damnit. A bad one. And yes, I'm still upset about it."

Farrell flushed a dark red. The hand holding the briefcase became a white-knuckled fist. "I told you, I'm not ready yet to talk about children. Kyler, Inc., is in a very delicate growth phase. You've got to understand, Leila, I need to concentrate on the business."

"Farrell, please be honest. Is there something you're not telling me? Something I should know?"

He flushed and checked his watch again. "We'll have to talk about this some other time. I've got to get to work."

Anger, frustration and fear came together in a devil's brew of painful emotions that churned her insides. "You care more about the future of the business than you do about us. Why don't you just say it?"

"Because it's not true, damnit." Farrell's jaw locked. He checked his watch. "Look, I told you, I can't discuss this now. I've got a full day of meetings. Maybe we can do lunch at the café."

Lunch. Now he was giving her appointments, as if she were a client.

"I'm not sure I'm going to go in to work today," she said stiffly.

Farrell looked first baffled and then anxious. "Are you sick?"

"No. I just don't seem to have a lot of interest in your business today."

"It's not just my business. It's *our* business."

"Is that so?"

"You know it is."

"Well, I'm not so sure I want my half of your business anymore."

Farrell stood there, unmoving. A sense of uncertainty washed through her. She did not understand his expression. He should have looked outraged or uncomprehending. Instead, she could have sworn that what she saw in his eyes was pain and fear. But that didn't make any sense. Why should he be hurt or afraid? His dreams had all come true. Hers were the ones that had been put on hold indefinitely.

Farrell pulled himself together with a visible effort. "You're upset. We'll talk about this later."

"Why bother? You've already made your decision, haven't you?"

"I said, we'll discuss it later."

He swung around and strode quickly out of the room, clutching the briefcase.

She sat, trapped in a tangled skein of remorse and anger, until she heard the front door close behind him. What was happening to her? She loved Farrell. Until these past few weeks, she had believed that he loved her. The future had seemed so bright four years ago when they had married. But now it was all falling apart.

Silence echoed in the big house. The space around her felt utterly empty. She thought about all the times in her childhood when her father had phoned from some distant city to tell her he wouldn't be able to make it home in time for her recital. *It's okay, Dad,* she had lied. *I understand.*

It wasn't supposed to be this way, not with Farrell. There should have been babies by now. But the children she'd planned to have existed only in her dreams. She saw them almost every night.

Tears swam in her eyes. She put down the spoon and grabbed a handful of tissues.

23

Isabel ran for the door, aware that Ellis was watching her from his position at the counter.

She was in a mild frenzy because she had slept in late. There had barely been time to shower and dress. The downside was she had not had an opportunity to cook the elaborate breakfast she had planned to serve Ellis. The upside was there had been no time to have the conversation she was dreading.

She was halfway out the door, escape in sight, when Ellis stopped her in her tracks.

"When do you want to talk about last night?" he asked without any inflection.

All her tango dancing dreams flashed before her eyes. Gloom settled on her, weighing her down. She turned slowly, keys clutched in her fingers. He was going to tell her that he considered her a really good friend and a terrific dream analyst and, by the way, it was probably better not to mix business and pleasure.

"I've got classes all morning," she said,

cringing inwardly when she heard the brittle-bright note in her voice. "And you said you wanted to get started reading Belvedere's research papers."

He set the tea down on the counter, got to his feet and walked toward her.

"I thought women liked to talk about relationships," he said.

What was the point of delay? Putting it off wouldn't change anything. She'd had her one night with the man of her dreams. A lot of women never even got that.

She steeled herself "Okay, let's get this over with. Is this where you tell me that you'd like to be friends?"

"This isn't about our friendship. It's about last night."

"Do you think of me as a really swell pal?"

"I don't sleep with my pals."

"Do I remind you of a sympathetic aunt?"

"I don't have any aunts, sympathetic or otherwise. Isabel, I'm trying to talk about *last night*."

"You're sure you didn't wake up this morning and decide that maybe we should go back to a business relationship? Maybe have a couple of drinks together occasionally so you can tell me your dreams?"

"Am I missing something here?"

She held up a hand. "One last question. Do you think of me as your own personal advice columnist or fortune-teller?"

He did not answer that, at least not verbally. Instead, he took two strides forward, seized her shoulders and pulled her hard against his chest.

His mouth ravaged hers in a no-holds-barred kiss that stole her breath. The sensation was so intense she suddenly understood why a girl might faint at the prospect of a fate worse than death. But she was a tango dancer. Tango dancers did not faint. They danced. They seduced.

She managed to get one arm around his neck and returned the kiss with equal fervor.

When he released her a moment later, she was breathing again, but really, really fast.

"For the record," he said, "I do not see you as a pal, sympathetic aunt, advice columnist or fortune-teller. I see you as a lover. Is that clear now?"

"Clear." She swallowed and hastily adjusted her skewed glasses. "In that case, we can talk about last night. If you really want to, that is."

Ellis smiled slowly. "On second thought,

it can wait. You just answered a lot of my questions. Go to class. I'll see you later."

"Okay." She grabbed her purse, whirled and ran for the car.

He wasn't the only one who had just had some questions answered. Whatever else was going on here, Ellis definitely did not see her the way every other man in her life had seen her.

Shortly after ten that morning, Ellis's phone rang. He glanced at the code, winced and answered the call without any enthusiasm.

"What do you want, Lawson?"

"Wondered what the hell you were up to," Lawson growled. "Haven't heard from you in a while."

"Nice to know I'm missed." He put aside the unpublished paper that Martin Belvedere had no doubt hoped to see immortalized in one of the respectable journals of sleep and dream research and sank back into the chair.

"Makes me nervous when you don't check in while you're on an assignment. You know I like to be kept informed."

"You haven't heard from me because I haven't got anything to report," Ellis said patiently. "Anything new on your end?"

Sphinx, curled on the sofa on the other side of the coffee table, stirred, stretched and regarded him with an unblinking stare.

"No, damnit. I've had Beth's elves combing all the online dream research sites, looking for buried links to some other agency that might be using a phony public front to take in data. But so far, no luck."

Ellis could hear the annoying *ping, ping, ping* of Lawson's dumb desk toy on the other end of the line.

"Speaking of Beth," he said. "Did she turn up anything on the local hit-and-run investigation?"

"Talked to her a few minutes ago," Lawson replied. "She says the local cops haven't even found the damned car, let alone the driver. Hit-and-runs are tough to crack unless there's a tip. You know that."

"What about Belvedere's third mystery client?"

"Nothing there, either." Outrage rumbled in Lawson's words. "Whoever this guy is, he's as well hidden as I am. That's why I'm so damn sure he's fed, like me. Maybe CIA. They've fooled around with the psychic stuff often enough in the past. Remember that remote viewing program they ran for a while? It's not hard to imagine them getting involved in high-end dream research."

Ellis took his feet off the coffee table. "Interesting."

"What? That he might be CIA?"

"No, that he's as good as you are when it comes to hiding his tracks."

"Hell, everything I know I learned from Beth," Lawson said.

"And you taught it to me."

"So?"

"I wasn't the only one you taught, Lawson."

Lawson groaned. "You're back to Vincent Scargill, aren't you?"

"He was a fast learner. You said so yourself. In addition, he was good with computers. Remember those online games he was always playing? He knew more about the Internet than you and me put together. Probably even more than Beth does. The younger they are, the better they are with the newest technology. That's how it works. Just ask any parent."

"I know," Lawson said wearily,

Ellis heard the irritating *ping-ping-ping* again and resisted the urge to grind his teeth.

"How about you?" Lawson asked finally.

"What, exactly, are you doing out there in California?"

Ellis surveyed the mountains of old documents, notes and reports he had stacked and sorted by date around the living room. He had concluded that it would be best not to mention the six cartons of research files just yet. Once Lawson found out they existed, he wouldn't rest until he got his hands on them.

"I'm just doing some paperwork," Ellis said.

"Paperwork, huh?" Lawson sounded slightly relieved. "Call me if you get anything I can use."

"Sure."

Ellis ended the call, put the phone in his pocket and regarded Sphinx.

"I'm on the roller coaster," he told the cat, "and it's too late to get off."

It wasn't the great sex, he thought, although that had been very, very fine, indeed. Nevertheless, he was old enough to know that great sex was just that, great sex. It began and ended in the bedroom or some other convenient location.

Last night had been a whole lot more than great sex. Last night he had gone to bed with the woman who walked through his dreams.

24

Ian Jarrow looked around the terrace café, taking in the clusters of instructors in their Kyler red blazers, the eager students and the large manual that sat on the table beside Isabel. He shook his head, his derision clear.

"I can't believe you're going to work at a place like this," he said.

Isabel did her own quick sweep of her surroundings and was relieved to see there was no one sitting close enough to overhear the comment. That did not stop her from being annoyed by it, however. Farrell had worked hard to build Kyler, Inc. It had been his dream and he had made it real. No one had a right to knock someone else's dream.

"The Kyler Method is a very effective technique for a lot of people," she said sharply. "Just because you're not into motivational theory, don't assume that it doesn't have any value."

"Listen, no one is more motivated than I am today," Ian stated. "Why the hell do you think I got into my car this morning and drove all the way here to Roxanna Beach just to talk to you?"

"Funny you should ask." She took a bite out of her cucumber, dill and cheese sandwich. "I've been wondering about that."

She had found him waiting for her when she emerged from a seminar room a few minutes before noon. He was pacing the lobby, glancing at his watch.

Her first reaction was pleased surprise at seeing a familiar face. Then she noticed his anxious, impatient expression.

"I gather you talked to Randolph Belvedere last night," Ian said. "He offered to let you come back to your old job?"

"It was very nice of him," she said.

"Nice, hell, he's desperate to get you back. He called me right after he talked to you, gave me your new work address and more or less ordered me to come here today and convince you to go back to the center."

"I'm sorry, Ian," she said, trying to soften the blow. "I thought I made it clear to Randolph that I'm not coming back under any circumstances. I can't imagine why he thought you would be able to influence me."

He gave her a derisive look. "You know why he sent me after you. Obviously someone told him that we dated for a while and that we're still good friends. He's hoping you'll listen to me."

"I guess he misunderstood the nature of our relationship, hmm?"

She took another bite of her sandwich. It was delicious and she was surprisingly hungry. Probably the result of missing breakfast, she thought. The large, glistening dill pickle on the plate looked quite tasty, too.

Ian frowned, ignoring his ham sandwich, pickle and chips. "We are friends, Izzy."

"Oh, sure," she said quickly. "We're definitely friends. By the way, did you hear about Gavin Hardy?"

"The computer guy? Yes." Ian grimaced. "Word at the center is that he was killed in a hit-and-run accident somewhere near here."

"It's true."

"What was he doing in Roxanna Beach?"

"He came to see me. He was trying to put together a stake to take to Vegas."

"That's right, he was a gambler, wasn't he? Everyone said that he had a real problem."

"Evidently." She ate another bite of the sandwich.

"So." Ian looked around again. "What's

the big attraction for you here in Roxanna Beach?"

"A new job. A new career plan."

"You're really going to work for your brother-in-law?"

"Only until I get my consulting business going."

"What consulting business?"

"I'll be doing the same kind of thing I did for Martin Belvedere, except that I'm out on my own now."

"Why not come back and do it at the center?"

"Lots of reasons." She blushed and lowered her sandwich. "Also, if you must know, I'm sort of in a new relationship."

It felt good to say that out loud.

Ian looked baffled. "How can you be in a new relationship? You've only been here in Roxanna Beach a few days. You haven't had time to meet anyone."

She picked up the pickle, surveyed the broad, firm, rounded tip and took a dainty bite. "He's a client."

"Izzy, this is crazy."

"My life has changed somewhat since I left the center."

He scowled. "You're not acting like yourself. This isn't you."

"Got news for you, Ian, it is me."

"But you loved your old job. You were happy at the center. It's the right environment for you. By the way, did I tell you that Belvedere said that in addition to raising your salary, he'll let you have a full-time assistant if you return immediately?"

"That's nice," she said around another mouthful of pickle. "But I've decided that I'd rather be my own boss."

Ian narrowed his eyes. "It's this new guy you're seeing. He's the problem here, isn't he? What's he like?"

She smiled and raised the phallic-shaped pickle to her lips. "I'm told he's not my usual type."

"That sounds like a good reason to step back from the relationship and evaluate it," Ian said seriously.

"I have been evaluating it and I've come to some conclusions. I've decided that no one actually knows what my type is because I've been dating men who are *not* my type for so long that everyone just assumes that they actually *are* my type. See what I mean?"

"No."

"The problem I've had with relationships in the past is that, because men like you found it so easy to talk to me about the important things in their lives, because they were so ready to have serious, in-depth conversations, because they were so ready to share their deepest feelings, I told myself that the relationships must be good because we *communicated* so well. You know how much emphasis everyone puts on communication these days."

"Damnit, this isn't what I came here to talk about."

"Too bad, it's what I want to talk about."

Ian seemed fascinated in a horrified sort of way by the manner in which she was munching on the pickle. "What's this all about, Izzy? Did you finally get laid? That's it, isn't it? Your new client got you into bed. Well, congratulations to him. But if I were you, I wouldn't go making any long-term career plans based on a couple of orgasms."

It wasn't the crude words that jolted her, it was the pure male petulance, the *accusation* in his tone.

"It's not like you've got any right to be judgmental here, Ian," she shot back. "You're the one who took me out to dinner one evening and told me that you didn't think we had much of a future and that it would be a good thing for both of us to date other people. Remember?"

"It wasn't as if you wanted to climb all

over me, was it? Hell, every time I suggested we go away together or spend the night at my place, you came up with some weak excuse about having to work late at the office."

"You're blaming *me* for the fact that we broke up?"

"Why not? You're the one who put the physical and emotional distance between us, Izzy. You're the one who turned whatever we might have had together into a nice, safe, platonic friendship because that's the way you wanted it."

If he had whipped out a sorcerer's wand and used it to generate a lightning bolt, she could not have been more thunderstruck. As it was, she was so dazed by the burst of insight that she almost dropped the partially eaten pickle.

"Huh." She dug deeper, going for something more intellectual. "Huh."

Ian regarded her with a sullen air. "What's wrong? You've got a really weird expression on your face. Are you okay?"

"Yes." She gave him her brightest, warmest smile. "*Yes,* I am, thanks to you."

"What?"

She leaped to her feet, circled the table and gave him a big hug. He did not move. She released him quickly, went back to her chair and sat down. Enthusiasm bubbled through her.

"What the hell?" Ian mumbled.

"I can't tell you how much I appreciate this conversation, Ian. You have enlightened me."

Ian was looking increasingly uneasy. "What are you talking about?"

"That's it." She waved the pickle in a sweeping *voilà* gesture. "That's what I've been missing in my self-analysis."

"Uh, Izzy —"

"I thought I had it all figured out but I was lacking a piece of the puzzle. You just gave it to me. It's perfectly obvious now."

"It is?"

"You're absolutely right. I should have seen the pattern myself." She shook her head, amused at her own failure to grasp the big picture. "I guess it's one of those cases of being able to diagnose everyone but yourself."

"Pattern?" Ian repeated, wary now.

"It was my fault all along, every time." She aimed the pickle at Ian. "Thanks to your observation, it's clear to me that all of my previous attempts to construct healthy relationships with men have been doomed right from the start because I unconsciously squelched the possibility of romance and passion, to say nothing of love and commitment, in every instance from the outset."

Ian cleared his throat. His gaze darted to a point behind her right shoulder. "Yes, well —"

"I see now that I developed a pattern of deliberately encouraging men to talk to me about their problems." She nibbled on the pickle. Juice dripped. "That had the effect of making them instinctively switch gears."

"Uh." Ian glanced again from the pickle to the point beyond her shoulder and then he looked back at the pickle, riveted.

"You see, as soon as men started sharing their problems with me, they stopped seeing me as a potential lover and started viewing me as a buddy or a therapist. But that happened because I unconsciously manipulated that outcome early on in the relationships, long before another type of bond could be formed."

A hunted expression crossed Ian's face. He jerked his gaze off the pickle and stared at the space behind her chair. "Maybe we should discuss this some other time."

"Sorry, I need to talk about it now."

He put both hands on the table and

started to get to his feet. “I’d better be on my way —”

She motioned forcefully with the pickle. “This is important, Ian. Sit down. You owe me that much.”

Ian sat.

“Lord knows, I listened to enough of your problems while we were dating,” she reminded him. “The least you can do is listen to me tell you about my epiphany. You know how it is with epiphanies. When you have one, you can’t resist sharing it.”

“I didn’t come here to talk about us,” Ian said quite forcefully. He was looking more and more agitated. “We’re supposed to be discussing your return to the center.”

“Later.” More pickle juice dripped onto the table. She grabbed a napkin and dabbed the corner of her lips. “By the way, I’m not discussing our relationship. That’s finished, remember? This is all about me. As I was saying, it’s clear that I deliberately manipulated all of my relationships, including ours, in such a way that there was no hope of long-term success.”

Ian’s gaze was flickering wildly back and forth between the half-eaten pickle and the region behind her chair.

“I don’t really see the point,” he said.

"The point is that I was the one who made sure that things stayed in the safe zone. I was never in any real danger of falling in love. And deep down that's just the way I wanted it."

"That's very interesting," Ian said weakly. "But —"

"I know what you're about to say." She held the pickle straight up to stop him. "You're going to ask me *why* I wanted to play it safe. What motivated me to go out of my way to see to it that every relationship I ever had fizzled before it could grow into something deeper and more intimate."

"Uh —"

"The answer is obvious to me now, thanks to you."

"Well, hey, that's great." Ian shoved himself to his feet again. "Glad I could help. But I really did not come here to talk about your problems with relationships."

"Don't you want to hear why I've had those problems?"

"Not really." He was trying very hard not to look at either the pickle or the space behind her chair. "I've got to be on my way. Long drive back to the center."

"Don't rush off on account of me," Ellis said to Ian.

"Ellis." Isabel turned in her chair. She

smiled up at him. "I didn't know you were here. Meet Ian Jarrow. He and I were colleagues at the center. Ian, this is Ellis Cutler. He's my new client."

There was no need to add the fact that Ellis was also her new lover. She could see from Ian's nervous expression that he had already figured that out for himself.

"Jarrow." Light flashed ominously on the lenses of Ellis's dark glasses when he nodded at Ian.

"Cutler." Ian stepped back as if he were afraid Ellis might bite. "Nice to meet you," he said woodenly. "Izzy, I'll call you."

"Bye, Ian. Sorry for the wasted trip." She ate another bite of pickle. Juice squirted. "Tell everyone back at the center that I said hello."

"Sure." Ian turned and hurried away.

Isabel looked at Ellis. "What are you doing here?"

Ellis watched her finish the pickle. "I thought I'd take a break from going through those files and have lunch with you. But it looks like you've already eaten."

She examined the empty plate and the remains of the pickle. "No problem, I'm still hungry."

"I like a woman with a healthy appetite." He watched Ian vanish through the lobby doors. "Did Randolph Belvedere send him here to try to talk you into returning to the center?"

"Uh-huh." She licked pickle juice off her fingers. "I declined and then I started to tell him why all of my previous relationships, including the one I had with him, failed so miserably."

"Sounds like a real compelling topic of conversation."

"Apparently Ian didn't think so." She frowned at the lobby doors. There was no sign of Ian. "I think you scared him off, Ellis."

"Don't blame his speedy departure on me." Ellis lowered himself into the chair that Ian had just vacated. He pushed the plate of uneaten food aside and smiled at her. "It was your fault."

"Because I tried to talk to him about my failed relationships?"

"Doubt it. I think it had something to do with the way you ate that pickle."

They both looked at the plump, wet, round-headed pickle sitting on Ian's plate.

Isabel felt herself turn very pink. She cleared her throat.

"It does sort of resemble a —" She broke off.

Ellis nodded somberly. "Yes, it does,

doesn't it? And you ate every bite. A sight like that could make some guys nervous."

"But not you," she said, oddly satisfied by that knowledge.

25

Isabel's phone rang shortly after five o'clock that afternoon. She had just gotten out of her last class and her thoughts were on dinner. Food seemed to be playing a major role in her day, she reflected.

She took the call as she walked across the parking lot to her car.

"Hello?"

"Ms. Wright? This is Tom out at Roxanna Beach Self Storage."

Alarmed, she held the phone to her ear with one hand and fumbled for her keys with the other. "Is there a problem? I paid for the first two months' rent in cash, just as the manager insisted."

There was a slight pause on the other end of the line.

"I don't want to worry you, because I think everything is okay but I just went by your unit and noticed that the padlock is missing. Did you forget to replace it last time you were out here?"

"No, I most certainly did not. Are you sure it's my unit you're talking about?"

"Number G-fifteen. Says here on the form it's yours."

"Yes, that's mine."

"There's a lot of big furniture boxes inside. Doesn't look like anything's missing but —"

"There's something wrong here. I checked that padlock when I left. Look, I'm on my way. I'll be there in ten or fifteen minutes. Keep an eye on that unit until I get there, understand?"

"Sure, but like I said, I don't think there's anything missing. Probably you just forgot to lock up."

"I did *not* forget to lock up. See you in a few minutes."

She ended the call, dumped the manual and her notebook onto the passenger seat and got behind the wheel.

She shoved the key into the ignition and roared out of the parking lot. She punched in Ellis's number with one hand while she drove toward the old highway. He answered on the first ring.

"I have to stop by Roxanna Beach Self Storage on my way home," she said. "There's a problem with the lock on my unit."

"What kind of problem?"

"The attendant says it's missing. He thinks everything is okay but I know I locked up the last time I went out there. I'm sure of it."

"I'll meet you there," Ellis said.

"There's no need for you to drive all the way out there. The storage company is on this side of town. It will take you at least twenty minutes and I —"

"I'll see you there," he repeated.

He ended the call before she could argue further.

She drove to the sprawling rental locker facility on the outskirts of town and parked just inside the gates. There were two other vehicles in the lot, a battered pickup and an aged sedan.

She got out and walked swiftly across the graveled lot to the office.

There was no one behind the desk. A small sign announced that the attendant would be back in five minutes.

She was irritated by the delay until she recalled that she had more or less ordered the attendant to keep an eye on the storage unit until she arrived. She started briskly along the graveled path that led to locker G-15.

"Are you Ms. Wright?" A scrawny man with narrow features partially veiled by the brim of a gray cap waved at her from the space between two long storage buildings. He wore an ill-fitting gray work shirt bearing the logo of the Roxanna Beach Self Storage company. A small duffel bag dangled from one hand.

"Yes. You're Tom, I assume?"

"Yes, ma'am. Everything's okay."

"I want to see my unit for myself."

"I'm telling you, there's nothing wrong there."

"What about the padlock?"

"It was all a mistake. I got mixed up about the locker numbers, that's all."

"As long as I'm here, I'll double-check."

She went quickly past him, her low-heeled pumps crunching on the gravel.

"Suit yourself," Tom muttered. He slouched along in her wake.

"If any of my furniture is missing, I'm going to —"

She drew up short at the entrance to the locker. The garage-style door was closed but she could see that the heavy-duty padlock she had purchased was gone.

"Someone *did* break into my locker." She leaned down, seized the handle of the door and rolled it up. "If anything is missing, I swear, I will sue this company up one side and down the other."

When she got the door to shoulder height she couldn't stand the suspense any longer. She ducked underneath.

The large interior of the storage unit was drenched in shadows. But relief shot through her when she realized that she could make out the large shapes of the crates and cartons stacked inside.

She groped for the wall switch and flipped it.

The first thing she saw was a man's bare leg sticking out from behind the crate that held the sofa.

"There's someone in here," she shouted. "I think he's been injured."

She dropped her purse on the floor and hurried toward the fallen man. He was naked except for a pair of boxer shorts, grimy tee shirt and socks. There was a dark pool of blood on the floor behind his head. He groaned when she crouched down and touched him.

"Call nine-one-one," she shouted.

She was vaguely aware of Tom reaching into his duffel bag. But the object he removed was not a phone.

And quite suddenly she understood why the man on the floor was dressed in only his underwear. The thin man standing outside the locker was wearing his uniform.

She lurched back to her feet, horrified by the knowledge that she was trapped inside the locker. She was an easy target and there was nowhere to run. Belatedly, she scrambled behind the cover of the nearest crate but knew it would provide little in the way of protection from a bullet.

Before she had time to process the realization that she was going to die here with her precious furniture, she realized that the phony Tom was not pulling a trigger.

She could not see him now because of the crate but she heard the click of a lighter.

"Dear God," she whispered.

In the next instant an object hurtled into the storage unit. It slammed against the wall just above the crates at the rear of the space.

There was a muffled thud. Glass shattered. The sound was followed by an ominous *whoosh.*

Flames splashed on top of the stacked crates. A Molotov cocktail, she thought.

The metal door rumbled. She realized that Tom was yanking it downward. He intended to seal her and the injured attendant inside.

Panic drove her out from behind the crate. She no longer cared if the man had a gun. Better to die by a bullet than by fire.

She lurched forward, keenly aware of the swiftly narrowing strip of daylight. Smoke was filling the space with frightening speed.

The smoke detector installed in the roof

went off, adding an ear-piercing shriek to the chaos.

She dimly recalled that smoke was supposed to move upward. She went to her knees, crawling along the concrete. Her hand brushed against her purse. Instinctively she grabbed the strap.

The man outside had almost got the door closed. She flung herself headlong across the floor. There were only two or three inches of space between the bottom of the door and the concrete pad. Even if she managed to grasp the lower edge of the door before it hit the floor there was little likelihood she could force it up against the downward pressure that the creep outside was applying. He had gravity and raw male muscle on his side.

One inch of daylight left.

She was close enough to wedge her fingers into the space between door and pad now but if she did the descending door would crush her hand.

Unable to think of anything else, she shoved the doubled strap of her purse into the tiny space between the door and the pad. An instant later, most of the last of the daylight disappeared.

She heard the phony Tom fumbling with the padlock.

"Shit, shit, shit."

He was panicking and she understood why. He could not get the padlock in place because as long as the strap of her purse held the door partially open there was no way the hasp could align with the metal eye on the frame. In the noise and confusion, he probably did not realize that the door had not closed properly.

The fire alarm continued to screech. The flames flared at the rear of the unit. The smoke got thicker. She tore off her Kyler blazer and held it in front of her face, breathing through the fabric.

"Shit."

She heard the clang of metal on concrete and guessed that the man had given up and hurled the padlock aside in rage and frustration.

The next sounds she heard were running footsteps receding rapidly in the distance.

She could not afford to wait any longer. Struggling to her knees, she put both hands under the edge of the door frame and shoved upward with all her strength.

The door retracted quickly. Smoke billowed up and out. She saw no sign of the attacker. With luck he had not heard the soft rumble of the door above the squeal of the alarm.

She took a deep breath of relatively clean air and then ran back inside to where the unconscious man lay on the floor. She grabbed one wrist with both hands and tugged.

For a terrible second or two she was afraid she would not be able to drag him out of the unit. But the concrete provided a relatively slick surface. Once she got the man in motion, it was like hauling a heavy sled.

He mumbled and struggled, opening his eyes.

"Fire," she shouted. She had him almost to the door. "Got to get out."

He groaned and lurched to his knees. She got one of his arms over her shoulder and helped him stagger erect. She nearly crumpled under his weight but they made it to the safety of the graveled path. Nothing like adrenaline in a pinch, she thought. Another reason to be glad she had taken out that membership at the fitness club twelve months ago, she told herself. Her weight-training instructor would be proud.

Without warning Ellis appeared out of nowhere. "I've got him." He took hold of the injured man. "I called the cops. They're on the way." Sirens finally sounded in the distance.

She sucked in fresh air. "I have never been so glad to see anyone in my life."

"Looks like you had things under control." He lowered the attendant to a sitting position. "Like I told Lawson. Nerves of steel."

She started to ask him why he had said that to Lawson but broke off when she saw the limp form of the man who had tried to lock her and the attendant inside the burning unit.

"That's him," she said hoarsely. "The guy who tried to fry us. How did you know?"

"He was running out when I came running in. Didn't think it looked good. I asked him about you. He didn't even stop." Ellis shrugged. "So I decked him. Figured I could always apologize later."

"Don't worry," she said tightly. "You won't have to do that."

The sirens were closer now. But she knew they would not make it in time to save her very beautiful, very expensive, very uninsured furniture from the flames.

26

Ellis lounged on one of the kitchen counter chairs and watched the scene taking place in the living room. Leila, Farrell and Tamsyn formed a tight group around Isabel, who sat on the sofa with Sphinx huddled in her lap.

"I'm all right," Isabel assured them for the hundredth time. "Really. Not even singed. And so is that poor attendant. The real Tom."

Isabel's sister, brother-in-law and friend had burst through the front door only minutes after they received word of the events out at Roxanna Beach Self Storage. They had made it clear that they were there to provide comfort and support to Isabel and that Ellis was not part of the intimate circle. He had been neatly edged out of the picture within seconds of their arrival.

None of them knew and probably wouldn't have cared that his insides were colder than the far side of the moon and his mind was filled with screaming, waking nightmares of what had almost happened out at the storage facility.

He watched Isabel as she compulsively stroked Sphinx and explained what had happened. He was accustomed to being excluded. Hell, he had engineered his entire life so he could keep a safe distance from just this kind of situation, one saturated with emotion and intimacy. Better to stand just outside the zone. Better to maintain his status as an outsider.

But even as he told himself that this was the way he wanted it, he knew he was lying. It was too late to pretend that he could drive off into the sunset when this was all over.

"Thank God the attendant was not a huge man," Leila said, shuddering at the thought. "You might not have been able to haul him out of the unit."

Tamsyn shook her head. "I've heard it's absolutely amazing what you can do when the adrenaline kicks in."

Farrell looked grim. "Nevertheless, there are limits. That guy can thank his lucky stars that Isabel is in good shape."

It occurred to Ellis that none of the three had berated Isabel for taking the risk of going back into the burning locker to rescue the attendant. He studied their faces one by one and realized why. Each of them understood what Isabel had done because under similar circumstances, they would have attempted to do the same thing.

These were good people, he thought. They might not hold a high opinion of him, but he gave all of them a thumbs-up.

Tamsyn's attractive face tightened into an anxious frown. "What about the bastard who started the fire and tried to lock you and the attendant inside?"

"Thanks to Ellis, he's in jail," Isabel said. "The detective in charge of the investigation said he hasn't talked yet, but they're sure that he will eventually."

Farrell gave Ellis a considering look. Then he quietly detached himself from the group and walked to the counter.

"I want to have a word with you outside," he said in a low voice.

Ellis nodded and got to his feet. He had a hunch he knew what was coming.

They went out onto the front porch and stood at the railing for a while. Ellis put on his sunglasses.

"I want to know what the hell is going on here," Farrell said evenly. "My wife had a background check run on you this morning. Everything she found indicates that you're a legitimate businessman. But I'm not buying it."

"Yeah, I sort of got that impression."

Farrell turned to face him. "Isabel has never led what most people would call a normal life but she's never had the kind of problems she's had lately. I find myself looking for some reasonable explanation. But all I come up with is you."

"I know."

"Who are you, Ellis Cutler, and why are you hanging around Isabel?"

Ellis hesitated, but only for a few seconds. He had already made up his mind about how to deal with Farrell.

"Got a pen?" he asked mildly.

Farrell's hand automatically went to the gold pen in his pocket. "Why?"

"I'm going to give you a phone number. It's the private line of a woman named Beth Mapstone. She operates a large private investigation business that has affiliates in several states, including here in California. You can verify her identity and credentials. She'll answer your questions about me."

Farrell's brow furrowed. "Are you some kind of investigator?"

"Yes." He leaned against a post and folded his arms. "Used to do it full-time but now I'm freelance. Mostly I'm a venture capitalist these days."

Farrell slowly took his pen out of his pocket. "You're working on a case here in Roxanna Beach?"

"Yes."

"What's all this have to do with Isabel?"

"She's assisting me."

"Bullshit. Isabel doesn't know anything about investigative work."

"Got news for you. Isabel has been consulting for me and other Mapstone Investigation agents for the past year, although this is her first field job."

"Jesus, Mary and Joseph." Farrell rubbed his temples. "Not the dream analysis thing?"

"Afraid so."

Farrell did not bother to conceal his incredulity. "Are you telling me that there are serious criminal investigators out there using this Level Five lucid dreaming crap to solve crimes?"

"I know it's a little hard to believe —"

"I can believe some of it, all right," Farrell interrupted roughly. "But not all of it. I'm not a complete idiot, Cutler. I've got a background in the corporate world. I know enough to follow the money, and I can see that there's a lot of it tied up in this thing, starting with the center itself. I wondered how Martin Belvedere kept that place afloat. I never understood why he hired Isabel and paid her such a good salary when she's got zero credentials in the field of sleep research. Now you're telling me that you work for a criminal investigation firm that employs agents who use psychic dreaming as an investigative technique."

Ellis nodded. "Yeah."

Farrell glanced at the Maserati and then raked Ellis from head to toe, taking in the expensive dark green shirt, charcoal pants and leather shoes. "This firm pays its consultants enough money to enable them to drive high-end cars and wear hand-tailored shirts. Not the usual gumshoe attire, Cutler."

Ellis smiled. He was starting to like Farrell a lot.

"And this Mapstone Investigations operation uses Isabel to analyze its agents' dreams."

"You got it."

"Only one source I know of that would be likely to cough up enough money to finance a phony sleep research facility and pay people big bucks to solve crimes in their dreams," Farrell concluded dryly.

"What can I say?" Ellis unfolded his arms and widened his hands. "Your tax dollars at work."

Before Farrell could respond, Leila's voice rose from inside the house.

"No insurance?" she wailed. "What do you mean you don't have any insurance? There must have been thousands of dollars' worth of furniture stored in that locker."

"I had to make some cutbacks after I lost my job at the center," Isabel mumbled. "The gym membership, my insurance policy —"

"How could you do something so idiotic?" Leila demanded.

Ellis straightened away from the post, yanked open the front door and walked back into the house.

In the living room, Isabel was clutching Sphinx very tightly as she confronted Tamsyn and Leila. The cat had his ears flattened against his skull, annoyed with the fresh wave of commotion.

"I don't believe this," Tamsyn declared to anyone who would listen. "How could you be so foolish as to store a fortune in fine furniture in a self-storage locker and then drop your insurance?"

"I told you, I couldn't afford it."

Leila jumped to her feet. "Why on earth did you buy it in the first place?"

"Yes," Tamsyn demanded. "Why buy a

lot of expensive furniture when you don't have a house for it?"

Isabel said nothing. She just sat there looking stubborn.

Ellis had had enough. He moved, violating the zone of intimacy. He sat down beside Isabel and gathered her securely against his side.

"It was for her dream house," he said quietly. "Isn't that right, Isabel?"

"Yes," she whispered.

And then, for the first time since the events in the storage locker, she started to cry.

Ellis wrapped his hand around her head and pressed her face against his chest.

While Isabel wept, he watched Leila, Tamsyn and Farrell, challenging them silently to push him out of the zone. None of them moved.

An hour later, she had recovered her composure. She curled up on the sofa, Sphinx's solid, warm body cuddled against her leg, and drank the wine Ellis had poured.

"Thanks for getting rid of the others," she said wearily.

"You're welcome." Ellis spoke from the kitchen, where he was putting dinner together. "I was ready for a little privacy, myself."

"They mean well, but I've had about all the lectures on making poor financial decisions that I can take for one day."

Ellis dropped four slices of bread into the heated, buttered skillet. "Be fair. You gave them a hell of a scare today. They needed to blow off their shock and concern. The furniture and the lack of insurance were easy targets."

She was impressed. "That's very insightful of you."

"Not really." He slathered mustard on one side of each slice. "I'm probably just projecting. You scared the living daylights out of me today, too. I was ready to smash walls and yell, myself."

"But you didn't."

"Only because there are too many other things to worry about. Maybe I'll get around to it later, when this case is closed."

She turned the wineglass in her fingers, watching the play of light on the ruby red contents. "I guess I was a little obsessive about the furniture."

"Hey, you're talking to a guy who has been told that he has a tendency to obsess, himself. Personally, I don't see anything wrong with being obsessive. Not when it comes to something that's really important."

Isabel met his eyes across the room. "My furniture was very important to me. I bought it a few months ago. Walked into a furniture showroom one afternoon, saw the pieces and I just had to have them. I cleaned out my bank account to make the down payment and went into hock up to my eyebrows on my credit cards."

He dropped cheddar cheese onto the sizzling bread slices. "That accounts for your current cash-flow problems."

She frowned. "You were aware of my financial situation?"

"I'm in that line, remember?"

"Wait a second, are you telling me that you investigated my personal finances?"

"It was just part of a routine check," he assured her a little too smoothly.

"Hah. I don't believe that for a moment. More likely you and Lawson were worried that after I lost my job I might try to sell whatever I had learned about you and Lawson's little dream operation to the highest bidder."

"I didn't mention it to Lawson," he admitted. "I knew it might make him a trifle nervous."

"What about you?"

"Me? I wasn't worried at all." He glanced at her, smiling slightly. "But then, I know you a whole lot better than Lawson does."

She gave him a measuring look. "Are you telling me that it never crossed your mind that I might try to peddle some of your secrets in order to cover my debts?"

He shook his head, concentrating on the toasted cheese sandwiches. "Call me a naive, easily manipulated dupe, but I just couldn't see a woman who had advised me to read romance novels and stop eating red meat selling me out."

"Good thinking." She took a sip of wine and lowered the glass slowly. "How did you know?"

"About your dream house?" He reached for the spatula. "Not that hard to connect the dots."

"It doesn't exist outside my dreams," she said quietly. "But in my dreams I've designed and decorated every room. The furniture would have been perfect."

He slid the cheese sandwiches onto plates. "You'll get that house someday. And you'll find the right furniture for it."

"Think so?"

"Yes."

He picked up the plates with the toasted sandwiches on them and carried them into the living room.

She uncoiled her legs and sat forward. "That smells good."

"Glad to see your appetite is returning."

She picked up one of the sandwiches and took a large bite. "The mustard was a stroke of genius. Where did you learn how to make these?"

Shadows moved in his eyes. "My mother used to make them when I was a kid. I helped her sometimes. It's as close to serious cooking as I ever get."

She tore off a bite to feed to Sphinx. "You can make them for me and Sphinx anytime."

Ellis watched her eat the sandwich. The darkness receded from his expression.

"It's a deal," he said.

The phone rang just as they finished the last of the sandwiches. Ellis took the call. Isabel listened closely and understood that he was not happy with the news he was getting.

He finished speaking and ended the connection.

"That was Detective Conrad of the Roxanna Beach PD, the person assigned to investigate the fire."

"I gathered that much." She brushed crumbs from her fingers.

"The name of the guy they arrested at the scene is Albert Gibbs. His lawyer got him out on bail about fifteen minutes after they booked him. An hour ago he was found dead in his trailer. Overdose."

Her mouth went dry. "Oh, my God."

"He lived in a park about fifty miles from here." Ellis rested his forearms on his thighs. "Apparently he was so happy about getting out of jail that he went straight home and shot himself full of some extra strong junk."

She watched his face. "You're thinking that is rather a convenient conclusion, aren't you?"

"I'm thinking it sounds like Vincent Scargill from start to finish. He finds real losers, manipulates them into doing his dirty work and then he gets rid of them."

"What's Detective Conrad's theory?"

"He's looking for the neatest solution, naturally. Turns out Gibbs had a history of arson-for-hire. Did time for it about three years ago. The detective thinks he was hired to set the fire today but that your locker probably wasn't the intended target."

"So who does he think hired Gibbs?"

Ellis shrugged. "Presumably one of the other renters who probably wanted to get rid of some incriminating evidence stashed in one of the units. But between you and Tom, the plan fell apart. Tom noticed the missing lock and called you. One thing led to another. Gibbs panicked, knocked Tom unconscious and shoved him into your locker. Before he could get out of the yard, you were there, demanding to know what was going on. So he tried to get rid of you, too."

"Why does the detective think Gibbs just happened to pick my locker?"

"He's not sure but at the moment he's assuming that your locker just happened to be located near the one that Gibbs was hired to destroy. Gibbs probably figured that if the fire started in your space, it would look more like an accident and less like it had been set to damage evidence."

"Got it." She propped her ankles on the coffee table and went back to what had become her favorite hobby lately, petting Sphinx. "So much for Conrad's theories. Let's return to our own paranoid, sadly deluded view of this case. Why would Scargill tell Gibbs to target my furniture?"

"Damned if I know." Ellis frowned and

got to his feet. He went to stand looking out the window. "But I think it's clear that it was your furniture, not you. The only reason you were there at all was because Tom called you. Maybe it was a message to me."

"Scargill's way of letting you know that he might go after me if you don't back off?"

"Maybe."

"Hmm." She studied her toes. "Why not just kill me? Or you, for that matter?"

"Two words: Jack Lawson."

"Ah, yes. He is the eight-hundred-pound government Bigfoot in this thing, isn't he?"

"He's that, all right. As it stands now, Lawson thinks I've got some serious psychological issues. He believes that I'm cracking up slowly but surely because of what happened a few months ago and the way it affected my dreaming. At the moment, he's still convinced that Scargill is dead."

"But if he decides otherwise . . . ?"

Ellis closed the drapes and turned to look at her. "If you or I get killed in the course of this investigation, it's a sure bet that Lawson will decide that maybe I was right all along. He won't quit until he gets answers, and he's got the resources to rip

Scargill's cover, whatever it is, to shreds."

"I see." She swallowed. "Presumably Scargill knows this?"

"He does." Ellis turned back to the window. He braced one hand on the wooden frame. "You know, Albert Gibbs's death raises a question that's been bothering me for a while."

"What's that?"

"I've always wondered how Scargill finds all the losers he uses. And how he got so damn good at manipulating them. Hell, if he's still alive, he's only twenty-two years old. You don't learn tricks like that until you get some mileage under your belt."

She drummed her fingers on the sofa cushion, thinking about that. "I couldn't begin to guess how he locates them but as far as motivation goes, I imagine most of them would have been happy to do whatever he wanted if he paid them enough money."

"Not necessarily. A guy like Gibbs, who needed cash for dope, maybe. But not some of the others. Not McLean, the demented fool who kidnapped his ex-wife and hauled her off to his compound in the mountains. A couple of the other kidnappers didn't strike me as being particularly interested in money, either. They were too lost in their own delusional worlds to pay much attention to mundane things like cash. None of them demanded ransoms. All of them had other motives for the abductions."

She tilted her head back against the cushion. "Where are you going with this, Ellis?"

"Maybe I've been missing something in the profiles of the people he uses. I need to look at those guys from another angle."

"What other angle?"

"The way I do potential investors and start-up entrepreneurs before I decide whether or not to fund their projects. I need to find out if there are any connections that I've overlooked."

He swung around and went to his briefcase. She watched him take out a small computer.

"While you're doing that, I'll take a look at some of Belvedere's research reports." She sat forward and scooped up the nearest stack of papers. "I know how he worked. Maybe I'll spot something you missed."

"Good idea." He sat down at the counter and powered up the computer. "I'm getting that nasty feeling you get when you know you've missed something important in a Level Five dream."

27

An hour and a half later, Isabel closed the file she had been reading and tossed it onto the coffee table. Collapsing back against the sofa cushions, she removed her glasses and absently stroked Sphinx, who was a warm, heavy weight on her lap. The big cat purred contentedly.

"Some enterprising soul could probably make a fortune selling Belvedere's papers as a cure for insomnia," she announced. "I think he was so determined to be taken seriously that he deliberately wrote the dullest, most boring, most academic-sounding prose possible."

"That was my impression when I was reading those files earlier." Ellis studied the computer screen, looking impatient.

"Got anything?" she asked.

"Maybe. I told you all of these guys did time at various jails and prisons."

"Yes."

"Turns out that at least three of them spent some time in a place called the Brackleton Correctional Facility back in the Midwest. I'm checking to see if any of the others did stretches there, too. It's going to take a while."

"I thought you said Scargill used people who lived in various places around the country. They didn't all come from the same region or even the same state."

"That's true. But it's not unusual for overcrowded or underfunded prison systems in one state to ship prisoners off to another state to serve out their time." He punched a key. "It's possible these guys all went through the same facility."

"Would they have been there at the same time?"

"No." His mouth hardened. "That's the bad news. All of them did time in recent years but none of them did it at precisely the same time. I checked that out a few weeks ago. There's no way they would have been behind bars together, unfortunately. That would have been too easy. Still, if I can link them all to the same prison, I might be able to find other connections."

She studied the intense, focused lines of his body. It was getting late and he had made no mention of returning to the Seacrest Inn to sleep. Was he planning to spend the night here? If so, he had not mentioned it. She was pretty sure she would have remembered a comment like that.

Idly, she continued to pet Sphinx. "Is this how you always work?" she asked. "Fill your head with as much information as you can get about the crime and then go into a Level Five dream state to try to get some insights?"

"Yeah." He hit another key and then got to his feet, rotating his right shoulder in a familiar way. "Never figured out a more efficient method. What about you?"

"Same process. That's why it was so frustrating working with Dr. Belvedere's mystery clients." She made a face. "I could never get all the information I needed to give a really good interpretation. I had to wing it on several occasions."

"Your work is brilliant, even when you don't have a lot of context," Ellis said. "It's no wonder Lawson wants to bring you into Frey-Salter."

She smiled slightly. "Not going to happen. Think he'll sign a contract with me once he's convinced that I'm serious about going independent?"

Ellis was amused. "I don't think he's got any choice. You can name your own terms. My advice is to make him pay top dollar for your services. That's what Beth does."

She rubbed the spot directly behind Sphinx's ears. The cat purred louder and seemed to grow heavier and warmer on her lap. "I like the sound of that."

Ellis studied Sphinx. "Think cats dream?"

"Who knows? If you accept the traditional Freudian view that dreams are a form of wish-fulfillment, a way of living out the sort of fantasies that we repress when we're awake, it doesn't seem likely. After all, cats pretty much do what they want to do. They don't have a lot of problem with repressed fantasies."

"They do seem to act on their Inner Cat urges whenever they feel like it, don't they?"

She nodded, looking down at Sphinx. "The same thinking would apply to the classic Jungian theory, too. Jung held that dreams are a product of some collective unconsciousness featuring various archetypes and metaphors."

Ellis studied Sphinx. "Can't see a cat bothering with archetypes and metaphors."

"Then, of course, you've got your modern neuropsychologists. Some of them think animals do dream but others are convinced that dreaming is a cognitive function that develops as the brain grows and develops. They point to the fact that there's little evidence to suggest that babies dream, and they claim that the dreams of very young children are generally quite bland. They think that dreaming gets more intense and more coherent as children mature. That idea leads to the speculation that animal brains probably lack the cognitive capacity to dream." She stroked Sphinx. "At least in a way that we would recognize as true dreaming."

Ellis smiled. "Dreaming may be a human thing, huh?"

Sphinx flicked his tail in an annoyed fashion but he did not bother to open his eyes.

"Maybe." Isabel scratched Sphinx's back at the base of his tail. "Then you've got another group of neuropsychologists who are very big on the activation-synthesis theory. It holds that dreams are merely the result of random signals sent from the most primitive part of the brain stem during sleep. The brain is designed to organize whatever data it receives so, even in sleep, it tries to connect what are essentially dots of meaningless static into coherent images, no matter how strange or bizarre."

Ellis shook his head. "I'm not buying that theory."

She chuckled. “Me either.”

“So, bottom line here is that we still don’t know if animals dream.”

“Nope. More to the point, there’s a great deal that we don’t know yet about the nature of our own dreams.” She wrinkled her nose. “Take lucid dreamers, for example.”

“Funny you should say that.” Ellis reached out to turn down the lamp beside the sofa. “I was just thinking that there is one lucid dreamer that I would very much like to take right now.”

Energy shimmered invisibly in the room. Isabel caught her breath. Her hand stopped moving on Sphinx. The world seemed to go into slow motion, taking on an all-too-familiar dreamlike quality.

“I thought we were supposed to be working,” she managed.

“I think we both need a break.” Ellis lifted Sphinx off the sofa. “Take a walk, cat.”

Sphinx gave him an evil look, hoisted his tail into the air and stalked off toward the kitchen.

Isabel smiled, her insides warming under the heat in Ellis’s eyes.

He lowered himself onto the sofa beside her, removed her glasses and set them on top of the report she had been reading.

She blinked a couple of times, refocused and touched the side of his face.

He kissed her slowly, thoroughly, urging her to open her mouth for him. When she did, she felt the edge of his tongue gliding along her lower lip. With a soft little sigh, she gave herself up to the embrace, turning so that her breasts were comfortably crushed against his chest.

He tugged her pullover off over her head and unfastened her bra. She unbuttoned his shirt with fingers that had started to shake.

Ellis fell backward onto the cushions, taking her with him. He kept one foot on the floor and raised his other knee. She wound up draped along the length of his body, cradled between his thighs. Somehow her clothes melted away.

"Tell me your dreams," Ellis said against her throat. "The ones where we make love."

She could hardly breathe. "What do you want to know?"

He slid his hand down the length of her spine and squeezed her derriere. "I want to know what I do to you in your dreams."

She was suddenly on fire from head to toe and it wasn't from passion. She had never been so embarrassed in her entire life. *He wanted her to tell him the details of her erotic fantasies.* She had a feeling he was not talking about the costumes she scripted for him.

"Tell me," he coaxed, fingertips sliding up and down her spine.

A series of vivid dream fragments flashed through her brain. Words failed her. She couldn't talk about any of those things out loud.

"Do I touch you like this?" He traced the curve that divided the twin globes of her bottom.

She dropped her head onto his chest. "Ellis."

"Or like this?" His fingers moved lower. "You can just whisper the answer in my ear."

"Mmmph." There must be something she could say that would sound more seductive, more sophisticated, something a tango dancer would say, but she was rapidly losing the ability to think, let alone speak clearly.

"How about this?" He eased one finger slowly into her, probing gently.

"Ellis."

"I take it the answer is yes?"

She could feel the firm, solid shape of his erection through the fabric of his trousers. Reaching down she unzipped him carefully and took him into her hand. His breathing roughened perceptibly.

She put her lips to his ear. "Definitely a yes."

"Keep talking," he said in a voice that was starting to grow hoarse. "As you can see, I respond well to positive reinforcement."

"I noticed." She tightened her grip on him. "That feels good."

"How about this?"

"Yes."

"And this?"

"Oh my, yes."

And then she told him her dreams.

Some time later, he told her his.

28

Ellis emerged from the bathroom zipping his pants. He walked back into the living room where Isabel was still sprawled on the sofa, a chenille throw covering her hips.

She yawned, opened her eyes and studied him through half-lowered lashes. "Is it morning yet?"

"Not even close." He finished fastening his pants. "Eleven-ten."

"Just as well, because I'm exhausted."

"I'm not exactly ready for a marathon, myself." He reminded himself that he had work to do. But it was hard to resist the contented, relaxed sensation that had seeped into his bones. "Got to tell you, I thought my late-night fantasies involved some fancy gymnastics, but yours make mine look like a walk in the park."

"Hah." She gave him a smug smile and curled herself into a more comfortable position, pulling the chenille throw over her mostly nude body. "After trying out a few of yours, I don't think I could even take a walk in the park, at least not for another week or so."

He surveyed her from her elegantly arched feet to her tousled hair. She looked incredibly sexy lying there, still damp from their lovemaking. The scent of spent passion lingered in the atmosphere. He could feel himself stirring, growing hard again.

He reached down and patted her bare shoulder. "The good news is that we're both Level Fives. Between the two of us, we should be able to dream up plenty of interesting positions and techniques."

"You don't know the half of it," she agreed demurely. "I haven't even started dressing you yet."

He laughed. "You want me to get dressed before we do it again?"

"Wait until you see the wardrobe I've been working on for you."

"Wardrobe?" He was getting curious now.

"Never mind." She stood, tightened the throw around her breasts and kissed him lightly on the mouth before sauntering off toward the bathroom. "I'll explain everything when the time comes."

"Sure. Fine. I'm flexible." He enjoyed the sight of her hips swaying seductively as she sashayed into the hall. "Just as long as this wardrobe you have in mind doesn't involve any of those little leather thongs designed for the male anatomy or see-through briefs. I don't do leather or see-through stuff."

She gave him a look of sultry innocence and seductive promise. "Let's make it a surprise, shall we?"

She vanished into the hallway.

He smiled, recklessly allowing himself to savor this unfamiliar kind of intimacy. He should probably be worried about the sense of possessiveness that had taken root deep inside him but he didn't want to think about it now.

He crossed the room to the glowing computer screen and looked at the data that the highly specialized search program had collected while he was fooling around on the sofa with Isabel.

The name of the Brackleton Correctional Facility had popped up three more times. Excitement pulsed through him.

He heard the bathroom door open.

"Here we go," he said over his shoulder. "Gibbs, McLean and the others did time in the same prison. They weren't there together, but it can't be a coincidence that they're all linked to that place."

Isabel emerged from the hall tying the sash of her robe. "What does that tell you?"

"I don't know yet, but it's a connection and I've been needing one of those real bad." He slid onto the chair and started hitting the keys. "Damn well should have seen it sooner."

"What now?"

"I'm going to search for everything I can find that relates to Brackleton Correctional Facility and hope like hell I get something I can use."

She patted another yawn. "I'll finish the rest of Dr. B.'s recent files."

Half an hour later she picked up the next to the last folder in the stack. Sphinx, comfortably resettled on her lap, twitched his ears.

Inside the folder she found five legal-sized pages filled with Martin Belvedere's cramped, spidery handwriting. She flipped through them.

The phrase "head trauma" leaped off one of the pages.

"Ellis?"

"Yeah?" He did not look up from the screen.

"Didn't you tell me that when Vincent Scargill was admitted to that hospital emergency room shortly after the explosion he had severe head trauma?"

That got his attention. He swiveled around on the chair. “Yes. Why?”

She held up the paper she had just started to read. “I think these are rough notes for a case of impaired dreaming in a Level Five lucid dreamer who experienced severe head trauma.”

Ellis was off the chair and moving toward her before she finished speaking. “Any dates on those notes?”

She glanced through the five pages. “No. Maybe that’s why they were at the bottom of the pile.”

“You can probably translate Belvedere’s hieroglyphs a lot faster than I can. Read me some of it.”

“*. . . Subject reports that prior to his injury, he regularly experienced extremely lucid dreams. Following the trauma subject describes his dreams as fragmented, uncontrollable and very disturbing. Subject’s use of the word ‘uncontrollable’ suggests that he was accustomed to exerting a considerable degree of control over his dreamscapes before the accident. . . .*”

She scanned the next couple of sentences and paused.

“*. . . Subject requested a private consultation. He brought a series of five recent dream reports for review and analysis. . . .*”

“All right, we know the subject was

male," Ellis said, his voice low with anticipation. "If it's Scargill, it sounds like the injury he sustained in the explosion affected his extreme dreaming capability. He must have been desperate for help to contact Belvedere."

"Where else could he go? Besides, he had a personal connection with Belvedere, remember? Dr. B. was the one who first identified him and assessed his dream talent."

Ellis absently rubbed his injured shoulder and continued to prowl the room. "I take it Belvedere never called you in to consult on a head trauma case?"

"No. I would certainly have remembered something as unusual as that."

Ellis nodded. "Belvedere may have realized that Scargill was dangerous and wanted to keep you out of it."

"If he thought Scargill was a menace, why didn't he contact Lawson?"

"Martin Belvedere was a noted eccentric and damned secretive in his own right, remember? In addition, from what you've told me, all he cared about was his research. Scargill probably looked like a really interesting case study."

"Can't argue that point."

She went back to the notes, reading aloud.

". . . The series of dream reports suggests a consistent fear of being pursued and an inability to escape the pursuer. This is, of course, a common theme in many dreams, but there are some highly distinctive elements in this group. The image of the enormous red tsunami is particularly striking. . . ."

She halted in mid-sentence. "Wait, I remember the tsunami dream. Dr. B. showed me a portion of the narrative and asked if I had any theories about what it might mean."

Ellis stopped, facing her. He shoved his hands into the front pockets of his pants. "Well?"

"I asked for more context, naturally," she said very dryly. "Belvedere gave me almost nothing to work with although he allowed that the subject was an extreme dreamer who was having problems accessing the Level Five state. I assumed it was a narrative from someone in Client Number One's group."

"One of Lawson's people."

"Yes. I remember asking if it was possible it was a blocking image rather than a chase-and-pursuit dream. I suggested that the tsunami was an image the dreamer's sleeping mind had created to prevent him from getting into the Level Five state." She moved a hand. "But without more context, that was as far as I could go with the analysis."

"I'm betting that this guy with the head trauma is Scargill and that he's the third anonymous client," Ellis said. "It fits."

The computer beeped.

Ellis took two long strides to the counter and checked the screen. Satisfaction emanated from him in waves of fierce energy.

"Honey, you and I are on a roll tonight," he whispered.

She eased Sphinx's big head off her lap and jumped to her feet. "What did you find?"

"Each of the six men involved in the crimes Scargill orchestrated not only did time at Brackleton Correctional Facility, it says here that each one agreed to participate in an experimental project conducted at the facility in exchange for a promise of early release."

Isabel leaned closer to read the words on the glowing screen. "The project used a combination of behavior modification techniques and medication to teach the inmates ways of coping with the stress of the outside world after their release."

Ellis gripped the counter with one hand, his face hard and intent. "But there's nothing yet that connects Scargill with Brackleton or this prison therapy project."

Isabel hugged herself "Looks like the next step is to find out more about that special prison behavior modification project."

Fifteen minutes later Ellis gave up in disgust.

"Blank wall," he said. "The project was officially terminated due to lack of funding a year and a half ago. The rest of the records have vanished."

"They say nothing ever vanishes entirely once it's put on the Internet," Isabel stated.

"Maybe not, but it can sure disappear as far as I'm concerned. I know my limitations. I'm a damn good dreamer and a pretty fair venture capitalist, but I'm not a magician when it comes to the Internet. We need one of Beth's wizards, and that means I need Lawson to authorize the expense." He glanced at his watch. "It's three in the morning back in North Carolina. I'll call him in a few hours and fill him in on what's going on here."

"Are you sure he'll help?" She frowned. "I thought you said he was solidly against your investigation."

"He is, but he owes me a few favors,"

Ellis said evenly. "I'm going to call in a couple."

"Does this mean we get some sleep now?"

"It means *you* get some sleep." He wrapped one hand around her nape and kissed her. "I'm going to do some serious dreaming."

29

He went into the guest bedroom, closed the door and turned off the lights. It was always easiest to slide into his gateway dream in the dark. He had a hunch that was because he had developed the skill during the endless, lonely, very scary nights following the loss of his parents. In those days his rapidly developing lucid dreaming talent had offered a sanctuary. He had used it to create dreamscapes where he could forget his fears and loneliness for a while.

He sat down on the edge of the bed, took off his shoes and lay back against the pillows. For a few minutes he focused on all the various bits and pieces of information he had accumulated, trying to let go of all previous assumptions and conclusions. The whole point of looking at a case in an extreme dreamscape was to come at it from an entirely different angle. The dreaming mind was not bound by the same rules of logic that governed the waking mind.

Lawson was convinced that Level Five

dreaming was essentially a combination of a natural talent for self-hypnosis and lucid dreaming. Beth speculated that it was a form of active meditation. Martin Belvedere had concluded that it was a psychic talent.

Whatever the case, he had gotten very good at putting himself into a state of consciousness somewhere between the waking and sleeping worlds. It was a state in which he could manipulate and control the dreamscape and yet remain open to suggestions from his unconscious mind in a way that was not possible when he was fully awake.

When he was satisfied that he was ready, he closed his eyes and climbed aboard the roller coaster.

The cars lurch into motion, ascending the impossibly high lift hill slowly, inevitably, taking him up to the highest point on the track. He is the only passenger. The sound of the chain lift is a steady drumbeat in his head that takes him deeper into the dream state.

Clank, clank, clank . . .

The front of the train reaches the top. He is sitting in the first seat so he has a clear view of the dizzying drop below. For an instant he hovers there, looking down at the track that spirals away into the darkness.

The cars shoot over the top of the lift hill. The world falls away and he plunges into his own, private dream world.

Isabel curled up in a corner of the sofa, covered her bare feet with the hem of her robe and listened to the silence from the guest bedroom. She had turned off all the lights except for the one on the table beside her. A few minutes ago she had been feeling quite drowsy but now her brain was racing.

Sphinx emerged from the kitchen, padded across the living room and heaved his bulk up onto the sofa. He butted his head against her hand.

"Hi there, big guy," she whispered.

Sphinx sprawled on his side next to her and closed his eyes. She rubbed his ears. He switched on his internal engine, purring so heavily she could feel him vibrating.

"Our lives have certainly changed since Dr. B. died, haven't they? I'll bet you never imagined you'd lose that cushy setup you had at the center, did you? I guess I took it for granted, too. That's why I bought all that furniture and started looking for a house. Oh, well, that's the way it goes."

Sphinx twitched his ears but did not open his eyes.

She continued to pet him absently and thought about how he had awakened her the night Martin Belvedere died. For a time she let her mind drift, recalling the shock of opening the door of the office and finding the body.

Opening the door . . .

She reached up and turned off the one remaining lamp in the room. The bulbs in the porch fixtures still burned but the glow she could see through the cracks in the curtains had the eerie, luminous quality that occurred when light was reflected off mist. At some point during the last few hours fog had rolled in off the sea, enveloping them in a ghostly vapor.

She had opened the door of the office and found the body . . .

She contemplated that for a moment longer. Then, on impulse, she closed her eyes and summoned the carriage that she used to take her into her gateway dream.

She waits for it at the top of the steps as she always does. The long skirts of her gown and cloak drift lightly around her. It is midnight and the only lights are those in the windows of the empty mansion behind her.

She hears the vehicle before she sees it. The clatter of hooves and wheels on the paving stones grows louder, establishing a familiar rhythm.

The elegant, black-and-gilt equipage comes into view, a dark shape against the greater darkness of the night. There is no coachman but the horses know what to do.

The carriage halts in front of the mansion. She descends the steps, counting them off one by one. Fifty, forty-nine, forty-eight, forty-seven . . .

When she reaches the last step the door of the carriage opens. She steps inside. The door shuts. The vehicle sets off, carrying her into the dreamscape.

The cars slam down the incline, rocket through a steep, tight turn and rush toward the first scene. He tries to examine every detail, aware that his dreaming mind has fashioned the vision out of the images and data he had fed into it earlier. He has learned that in the dream world, incidents and objects are often weighted differently than they are in the waking realm. A small detail that meant nothing when he looked at it in the light of day can assume great significance here.

So he looks at the scene very closely as the cars fly past. He sees Lawson sitting at his big, government-issue desk, bald head gleaming in the light of the fluorescent lamps, reaching for the phone.

"I'll be with you in a minute," Lawson says. "Gotta call Beth."

The cars zoom past the image, whip through a loop-the-loop and careen toward another scene.

Lawson again. He is just hanging up the desk phone. "Beth says she checked the hospital computer records, herself. The body they mistakenly handed over to the funeral home was Scargill. She did a DNA match using some blood they took in the ER. Cause of death was severe head trauma. Looks like he caught some fallout from the explosion. . . ."

The cars sweep past the scene, round another swooping curve and drop straight down into a twisting stretch of track. Adrenaline slams through him.

The carriage turns down a narrow lane. Dark stone buildings loom on either side of the passage. There are lights in some of the windows. She catches glimpses of people moving about inside the rooms. One of them turns to look at her. She recognizes Gavin Hardy. He is wearing one of his favorite Las Vegas tee shirts.

She can see that he is seated at a card table. There is someone beside him, a familiar figure with a beaky nose, sharp blue eyes and a mane of unkempt white hair.

"Hi, Isabel." Gavin waves cheerfully. "I finally made it back to Vegas. Look who's here. The Old Man himself. But the SOB doesn't even see me. So what else is new, huh? He's got a good hand, though, and since he's not paying any attention, I think maybe I'll help myself to one of his cards."

The carriage rolls past the window. She looks into the next room and sees Martin Belvedere slumped over his desk. The door to his inner office is closed. As she watches it opens.

But it is Randolph who walks into the scene, not her. He smiles.

"Going to be some big changes at the center now that my father is gone," Randolph says. "No more lemon yogurt."

She continues to stare into the dream chamber and realizes she is peering into a seemingly bottomless well of night.

She hears the rattle of harness and the iron-shod hooves of the horses striking the paving stones. The carriage starts to roll forward. But just as the scene starts to slip away she sees a shadowy figure move in the hall behind Randolph. He is not alone at the scene of the crime. She leans forward, trying to get a clear picture of the other person but the darkness of the hall is too deep.

Somewhere in the distance her dream lover calls her name, shattering the trance.

"Isabel . . ."

She came out of the dream with a suddenness that evidently annoyed Sphinx. He lashed his tail.

"Ellis?" She sat up slowly, shaking off the

trancelike effects of the Level Five dream.

"Sorry, honey." Ellis moved in the shadows, reaching out to switch on one of the reading lamps. "Didn't realize you were asleep."

"It's okay." She swung her feet to the floor and pushed her hair back behind her ears. "I was dreaming."

"Yeah?" He watched her with dark curiosity. "Regular or extreme?"

"Extreme. Gavin Hardy and Martin Belvedere featured prominently. What about you? Any luck?"

"Yeah, but if I'm right, the problem is even bigger than I thought." He lowered himself into the wing-back chair. Controlled tension radiated from him. His eyes were sharp and cold. "I went into the dream to search for possible patterns involving Scargill and the men he used from that behavior modification program at the Brackleton Correctional Facility. But the images that kept recurring did not involve him or the prison."

"What did you see?"

"Lawson," Ellis said. "Sitting at his desk, his phone in his hand. He had either just talked to Beth or he was about to talk to her."

"Go on."

"He tells her everything. She's still his partner, even if they are having problems at the moment. He couldn't run his operation without her."

"Back up, you're going too fast for me."

Reflectively, Ellis massaged his right shoulder with his left hand. "If I'm right about Scargill faking his own death, he had one real big issue to worry about after he staged his grand finale."

"What?"

Ellis dropped his hand and shrugged. "He needed to know whether or not Lawson bought the story. To feel safe, Scargill had to find a way to keep tabs on what happened at Frey-Salter after he disappeared."

She let that sink in. The implications were unnerving.

"You think he has an accomplice in Lawson's operation?" she asked uneasily. "Someone who leaks information to him?"

"It's a possibility. He uses other people when he needs them, but he wouldn't want them to have too much information."

"So how do you think he arranged to figure out how his game plan was going down with Lawson?"

"I can't be positive, but I've got a feeling the message in my dream is that he did it the old-fashioned way. He bugged Lawson's fancy, high-tech, super-encrypted phone."

For an instant she was speechless. "But that means that every time you talked to Lawson —"

He nodded, his face hard. "And every time Lawson talked to Beth, Scargill may have been listening."

She folded her arms and thrust her hands inside the sleeves of her robe. "Was he good enough with computers to do that? What about opportunity? Could he have simply walked into Lawson's office and messed around with the phone?"

"To tell you the truth, I'm inclined to doubt that Scargill was that good. He was sure big on playing the online games but I never saw him take an interest in any of the serious software programs that Lawson uses for dream research and analyses. And Lawson sure as hell never mentioned anything about Scargill being a tech wizard."

"So?"

Ellis's mouth tightened. "So there was someone at Lawson's agency who was good enough to bug an encrypted phone, someone who would have had opportunity and who might have had motive."

"What motive?"

"Love."

Comprehension hit her in a shock wave. "Katherine Ralston."

"Yes. I think he used her to bug the phone for him after he faked his death. Hell, maybe he used her to change the morgue records at the hospital, too. Then he murdered her."

She shuddered. "You're right. This is a really big problem."

Ellis was silent for a beat. "There is one bit of good news in all this."

"What's that?"

"I've been careful about what I've said to Lawson on the phone in the past few days because I didn't want him to think that I had gone completely over the edge where Scargill was concerned. He doesn't know about my suspicions concerning the fire in your storage locker, and I haven't had a chance to tell him about the link to the behavior modification program at Brackleton."

"You did tell Lawson that you were suspicious about Gavin Hardy's death," she reminded him.

"Yes, but Lawson ordered me not to get involved, remember? He said he'd have Beth keep track of the police investigation and then he advised me that there was no hard evidence to indicate that Hardy's death was anything but a hit-and-run."

She took a deep breath. "Okay. Assuming Scargill does have a bug on Lawson's phone, all he knows for sure is that you're here in Roxanna Beach because Lawson asked you to recruit me for Frey-Salter."

"It's something, at least. One thing's for damn sure. I can't risk telling Lawson anything else about this situation until I can get him outside Frey-Salter. Same goes for Beth. Those two share everything."

"Except a bed, apparently."

"The current separation is only temporary. Sooner or later they'll get back together."

She rested a hand on Sphinx's broad head. "You said this particular separation has gone on much longer than usual because Beth discovered that Lawson had had an affair a few months ago."

"That's right. He broke the ground rules of their relationship."

She looked at him, careful to keep her expression as neutral as possible. "You sound like you don't subscribe to that set of rules."

"Hell, I couldn't handle a screwy relationship like that one in the first place, much less figure out the rules."

She smiled. "It does sound complicated.

You know this is going to seem a little far out, but just how mad was Beth when she found out that Lawson had the affair?"

"Real mad. Furious."

"Mad enough to want to try to exact some revenge?" she asked softly.

At first Ellis seemed bemused by the question, as though he did not understand it. Then she saw understanding dawn.

"You think Beth might have teamed up with Scargill to punish Lawson?" Ellis asked in a tone that suggested he wanted to be absolutely sure he had got it right.

"Just a thought."

Ellis turned that over silently for a respectable period of time and then shook his head. "No. Leaving aside their personal relationship, which has always seemed screwy to me, they need each other professionally. They have to work together, even when they're not sleeping together. It's been like that for over thirty years. Can't see it changing now. Besides, Beth definitely has a temper, but she's not vindictive. I can't see her going to such lengths to get even for Lawson's stupid fling."

"You know them. I don't."

He sat forward, fingers linked between his legs. "It's an interesting scenario, though. One that probably should have occurred to me but didn't. Good observation on your part."

She was pleased by the compliment. "Thanks. I know I've got a lot to learn about the investigative side of this business but I like to think I've picked up a few things working for you and Lawson this past year."

He smiled briefly. "Think you've got a talent for the profession?"

"I sure hope so. It pays so much better than the Psychic Dreamer Hotline or my brother-in-law." She huddled deeper into her robe. "Now it's my turn. Want to hear about my dream?"

He leaned back, hands gripping the arms of the chair. "Yes."

"I'll admit I haven't had any experience setting up clue-hunting dreams but I've walked through a lot of yours so I decided to give it a shot tonight. And there is one aspect of this case in which I probably have a lot more context than you do."

"Are you talking about Gavin Hardy?"

"No," she said. "Tonight I dreamed about Martin Belvedere."

Ellis waited.

Her hand stilled on Sphinx's head. "I think that he might have been murdered."

Ellis did not move for a few seconds. She

could see him processing the information and wondered if he would dismiss the conclusion out of hand.

"What makes you say that?" he asked simply.

"Two reasons. One of them is Sphinx."

He glanced at the cat. "Go on."

"The door to Belvedere's office was closed when I went to find him. But Sphinx was out in the hall."

Ellis looked thoughtful. "You said you found him at your door acting agitated."

"Right. Sphinx had free run of the place but he has a strong commitment to saving energy. His own."

"I did get the impression that he's not a great believer in unnecessary exercise."

"No, although he often made the trip into my wing to see me. I think he liked my windowsill in the afternoon because of the sunlight. But other than that, he stayed in Dr. B.'s inner office most of the time." She sighed. "I suspect that Belvedere cared more about Sphinx than he did about any human, including, apparently, his own son. The point is that I'm almost positive he would never have closed the door of his office if he knew that Sphinx was out of the room."

"Not even to have a private conversation with someone?"

She hesitated. "He might have done that but as soon as the person left, the door would have been opened."

"Unless he collapsed from a heart attack before he could get to the door."

"True. But there's another reason why I think he was killed. There was no yogurt carton in the trash can beside the desk."

"Why is that important?"

"He had come to my office earlier, around midnight, to talk about the dream report I was analyzing. He was carrying a carton of lemon yogurt. He had just started it. He loved lemon yogurt. But when I found him later, there was no empty carton in the trash can in his office. No spoon, either. It didn't register with me at the time because I was so shocked by his death. I was frantic, dialing the emergency numbers and trying to give CPR. But tonight the image of the empty trash can came back to me in the form of a bottomless well."

"What do you think happened to the yogurt container?"

She breathed deeply. "The message I took from my dream is that it's very possible someone injected the yogurt with the poison that killed Dr. B. and then returned later to remove the evidence."

They sat in silence for a while.

"Drugs," Ellis finally said softly.

"Yes." She shivered. "Dr. B. died of a heart attack. But there was no autopsy. What if someone used a drug to stop his heart? There are a number of meds that could do that if the wrong dosage is given, although the average person probably wouldn't know how to use them to commit murder."

"But we're not dealing with the average killer here." Ellis's mouth crooked downward. "Scargill could certainly have picked up not only some heavy-duty research meds but also a working knowledge of how to use them while he was at Frey-Salter."

She met his eyes. "In my dream I saw Belvedere slumped over his desk just the way I found him. The door opens. But it isn't me who walks into the room; it's Dr. Randolph Belvedere."

"A guy who would know a thing or two about sleeping potions," Ellis said softly.

She hesitated, thinking about the dream. "I think there was someone else with him but I couldn't get a clear picture."

"Your dreaming mind was probably trying to insert Scargill into the dreamscape because you know he's involved in this. But you don't know what he looks like so you couldn't get a clear picture."

"Okay, that makes sense." It didn't feel right though, she thought. She reminded herself that, while she had analyzed a lot of crime scene dreams, tonight was the first time she had engineered one for herself. She lacked experience in this end of the business. She shook off the uncertainties because there was nothing she could do about them now. "What happens next?"

"I'm going to pay a visit to the center tomorrow. Do a little looking around, ask some questions."

"Maybe I should go with you," she said eagerly. "I know my way around there."

"No, I want to go in without anyone knowing who I am or why I'm there. Besides, you've got your first official Kyler Method class tomorrow and the weekly reception for the seminar attendees in the evening, don't you?"

She groaned. "Forgot about both. I'd better not miss either or Farrell will really be ticked."

Ellis checked his watch. "I need some sleep. I'll go back to the inn, get some rest and leave first thing in the morning."

She took a deep breath. "You can sleep here if you like."

He smiled his slow, sexy smile. "I like."

30

Isabel insisted on fixing breakfast before he left the next morning. He ate it sitting at the kitchen counter, and savored every bite. It took him a while to understand why the scrambled eggs, rye toast and phony soy sausages tasted so good. Then it hit him that the best part of the meal was that Isabel was sharing it with him.

He wasn't accustomed to having breakfast with his dates, he reflected while he munched toast and watched Isabel feed Sphinx. Probably because long ago he had made it a rule never to spend the entire night with any of them. Hanging around for breakfast was a step he had not wanted to take. Too much like taking off his sunglasses, maybe. He had sensed that a woman would look at him differently in the morning light, maybe see the side of him that he preferred to keep safe in the shadows. Maybe he would look at her differently, too. Maybe he would be tempted to leave the safe zone.

But somewhere along the line he had already taken the leap in the dark with Isabel. He looked at her and wondered what she was thinking about this business of sharing breakfast together. One thing was for sure, this was not the time to ask.

"I'll drop you off at Kyler on my way out of town," he said. "I should be back this evening before the reception ends. I'll pick you up."

She paused in the act of pouring more tea. "But I won't have my car available. I'll need to come home and change for the event."

"Pack a bag." He forked up some eggs.

"Ellis —"

"Honey, I don't want to have to worry about you today, okay? I'll be a lot more comfortable if I know you're surrounded by people you know at Kyler while I'm out of town."

She looked first startled and then she grew thoughtful. "You told me yesterday that you didn't think I was in any real danger because if anything happens to me it would cause Lawson to reopen the inquiry into Scargill's death."

His stomach clenched but he kept his expression casual. "That's my working theory and I think it's solid. But I don't want to take any chances. With Beth and

Lawson out of the loop for now, I don't have any way of arranging protection for you until tomorrow or the next day at the earliest. I've got a feeling I can't let things sit that long. Promise me you'll stay at the Kyler offices until I return, all right?"

Her expression said she was not pleased, but she nodded. "Okay." She headed for the bedroom. "I'll get the things I'll need to change for the reception."

He reached out and caught her wrist when she went past him.

"Thanks," he said quietly.

Her eyes softened. "Promise me you'll be careful today."

Breakfast with a woman was not the only novelty he was experiencing with Isabel, he thought. Having someone worry about him like this was new, too.

"Promise," he said.

The fog that had rolled in during the night was still clinging to the old highway when they drove into town a short time later.

"I need to get some things from my room," he told Isabel. "The inn is on this side of town. I'll pick up my stuff and then take you to your office at Kyler."

"Sure."

The parking lot of the Seacrest Inn was almost empty. He stopped the Maserati in a space near the entrance, got out and reached back inside for his briefcase.

It struck him as he walked around the rear of the car that Isabel might have a few qualms about being seen with him at such an early hour. The implication that they had spent the night together at some location other than the inn would be fairly obvious to even the dimmest front desk clerk.

Before he could ask her if she wanted to wait outside, she had her door open and her seat belt unlatched. She did not look like she was at all worried about what the desk clerk would think, he noticed. That made him feel good for some reason. He took her arm. Together they walked into the lobby.

The clerk, whose name tag read "Jared," did give them an interested look when they came through the glass doors but he merely nodded politely at Isabel before he spoke.

"Good morning, Mr. Cutler," Jared said cheerfully. "Your business associate arrived late last night. I put him in the room across the hall from yours, as he requested."

Ellis felt Isabel's sudden tension. He squeezed her elbow lightly in silent warning.

"Thanks," he said to Jared. "Appreciate it."

"No problem," Jared said.

Ellis guided Isabel to the stairs. She waited until they were on the second floor before she asked any questions.

"What business associate?" She was definitely worried now.

"Not Scargill."

"How do you know?"

"Because he's too well trained to make the mistake of asking for me in person in a small hotel like this, let alone pretend that he's a business associate."

"One of those ex-prisoners he's been using?"

"I don't think so. If I'm right, this guy's another amateur, like you." He opened the briefcase and reached inside for the pistol. "But we old pros prefer not to take chances."

She looked at the gun with somber eyes but said nothing.

He released her arm. "Wait here until I make sure."

He walked to the door directly across from his own, stood just out of range of the peephole, the pistol alongside his leg, and rapped sharply.

"Room service," he declared.

He heard footsteps inside the room and knew that the occupant was attempting to get a look at him through the peephole. Then he heard the chain lock being released.

The door opened.

"But I didn't order —" Dave Ralston began. Then he got a good look at Ellis. His mouth fell open.

"Relax," Ellis said, moving into the room before Dave could recover from his shock. "It's complimentary."

Dave stared at the gun. Fear made his mouth tremble a little. But he faced Ellis with rage and defiance.

"Are you going to kill me the way you did my sister?" he asked.

"I hate questions like that." Ellis put the pistol back into the briefcase. "There's no good answer."

31

Isabel's first reaction was enormous relief. Ellis had been right, the man in the room was not Scargill or one of the ex-cons. Then she saw the anger and uncertainty in Dave Ralston's face and her heart went out to him.

"Ellis told me about Katherine," she said gently. "I'm so sorry, Dave."

He sat rigidly in the chair at the small desk. When she had entered the room a moment ago, she got the impression that he planned to stick with the name-rank-and-serial-number approach to the formalities. But the mention of his sister's name made him flinch. He stared hard at Ellis, who was lounging against the wall.

Ellis returned the stare from behind the impenetrable shield of his dark glasses.

"Yes, I know you suspect that Ellis might have killed Katherine." Isabel went to the small counter that held the in-room coffeemaker, picked up the glass pot and filled it from the faucet at the small wet bar. She did not feel like a cup of coffee. She disliked the stuff. But the tension level in the room needed to be reduced as rapidly as possible. In her experience nothing could achieve that goal as quickly as the serving of food or drink. "But I can assure you that he didn't do it."

"How do you know?" Dave burst out.

At least he had spoken to her. That was progress. "Because I know him very well. Far better than you do, certainly. Ellis is not the type who would kill in cold blood, especially not a woman."

"What makes you so sure?" Dave demanded.

She glanced at Ellis. He was making no attempt to get involved in the conversation. She got the impression that he was content to step back and let her deal with Dave. Just a couple of amateurs, in his view, she reflected. But, hey, everyone had to start somewhere, right?

She considered how to proceed while she got the coffee going.

"Ellis is an extreme dreamer," she said. "I assume you know what that means?"

Dave's eyes slid away from hers. "Katherine told me that they did a lot of weird dream research at Frey-Salter. All that Level Five profiling stuff."

"Ah." She flipped the switch on the machine.

"What's that supposed to mean?" Dave muttered.

"Nothing, just that I get the impression that your sister talked to you about her work."

"We were twins," Dave said quietly.

"I see, well, as I was saying, I also work for the same agency indirectly as a sort of consultant."

"Yeah?" Dave was clearly dubious. "What kind of consulting do you do?"

"I specialize in interpreting the dreams of people like Ellis here, who are very strong lucid dreamers. I probably interpreted some of your sister's dreams this past year, although none of the individuals from Frey-Salter were ever identified in the dream reports so I can't be certain of that."

"What are you?" Dave asked. "Some kind of shrink?"

"I do a lot of counseling," she said smoothly. "But the point here is that I've had a great deal of experience analyzing Ellis's dreams. That's why I feel that I know him well enough to assure you that if he had murdered someone in cold blood a few months ago, I would have sensed it in his dream reports."

"Bullshit." Dave made a disgusted

sound. "Why would he have told you about a dream that would have incriminated him?"

She listened to the *drip, drip, drip* of the brewing coffee.

"After you've analyzed a lot of Level Five dream reports from one person over a span of time, you can't help but pick up a good, working knowledge of his or her personality and character," she said.

"Yeah?" Dave gave Ellis another wary look. "What if he was real careful about what he included in his reports?"

"If Ellis had taken to doctoring his dream reports in order to scrub out any references to an act of cold-blooded violence, I would have sensed that something was wrong." She shrugged. "Granted, I might not have known precisely what he removed from the narratives, but I would almost certainly have realized that he was trying to disguise some aspect of the dream."

"You're that good?"

She smiled. "I'm a Level Five, too. Dave, listen to me. Ellis didn't kill your sister. He's trying to find the man who did."

Dave said nothing, but she could feel his certainty wavering.

The small coffeepot was full. She removed it from the burner and poured the contents into the two cups emblazoned with the logo of the Seacrest Inn.

"Let's try this from another angle," she suggested, walking across the room to hand one of the cups to Dave. "What makes you believe that it was Ellis who murdered Katherine?"

Dave reached out automatically to take the cup, but his hand was shaking so badly he nearly spilled the contents.

"I think maybe he killed her because she found out that he was stealing Frey-Salter secrets and selling them. Maybe he's the one who killed her lover, too."

There was a short, stunned silence. Isabel looked at Ellis, waiting for his denial. He said nothing. If possible, he looked even more bored.

Dealing with the male of the species sometimes required an astounding degree of patience, she thought. She more or less shoved the second cup of coffee into Ellis's hand. He frowned, but he took it.

"Ellis didn't kill either of them," she said.

"What did Katherine tell you about her lover?" Ellis asked.

"His name was Vincent Scargill," Dave said slowly.

Ellis nodded. "That fits."

Dave's expression tightened. "She said they had to keep the affair quiet because she was afraid she might get fired if Lawson found out about it. She said it was always the woman who lost her job when workplace relationships came out into the open. She had seen it happen at Frey-Salter when Lawson himself got involved with a member of his staff. When the affair ended, the woman was forced to transfer to another position in some other agency."

Ellis grimaced. "Have to admit, Katherine might have had a reason to be concerned after that incident, although I can't see Lawson firing any Level Five. He hasn't got enough of them as it is." He drank some coffee and slowly lowered the cup. "Here's what I think happened, Dave. I believe that Scargill faked his own death. Afterward, he contacted Katherine secretly and got her to bug Lawson's office phone. When that was done, he killed her to keep her quiet."

Dave's gaze switched back and forth between Isabel's and Ellis's face. Isabel sensed that he was finally starting to listen and process the information they were giving him.

"Why would Katherine take the risk of

bugging Lawson's phone?" Dave asked. "She worked for the guy and she liked her job."

"She liked her job but she loved Vincent Scargill," Ellis said. "My guess is that he probably gave her some story about being set up. Maybe told her that he needed proof that I was the bad guy so he could take it to Lawson. He asked her to help him."

Dave put the coffee cup down hard on the desk. "I'm not buying any of this yet. I need more proof that you're telling me the truth."

Ellis hesitated. "I found something in your sister's apartment. I want to show it to you."

He straightened and bent over the briefcase. Alarmed, Dave gripped the arms of his chair and started to get to his feet.

"It's all right," Isabel assured him. "He's not reaching for the pistol."

"What, then?" Dave did not take his eyes off the briefcase.

"This." Ellis removed a magazine from a manila envelope. "It was in Katherine's living room. Something about it seemed wrong at the time but I couldn't figure it out. All I knew was that it didn't fit into the scene. I tried a Level Five dream but that didn't help." He gave Isabel an ironic look. "Probably because I didn't have enough context. But it did reinforce my hunch that it was important."

"You stole that from her apartment?" Dave snatched the magazine out of Ellis's hand and flipped it over to look at it. For a few seconds he just stared at the photo on the cover with an uncomprehending expression.

Isabel looked over his shoulder and saw a picture of a cobra. "Ugh. Snake."

Dave's face became even more grim and desperate. Slowly he raised his eyes to look at Ellis. "Where, exactly, did you find this?"

Somewhat to Isabel's surprise, Ellis slipped off his dark glasses before replying.

"On the floor," Ellis said. "Very close to where Katherine was found. I think what bothered me was that this was the only issue of the magazine in the place. There's no subscription label so I assume she bought it at a newsstand. Was Katherine interested in nature and wildlife? I didn't see any other books or magazines on that subject in her place."

"Oh, shit," Dave whispered in a strangled voice. He could not seem to take his eyes off the cobra. He appeared to have been transfixed by the creature. "Oh, *shit.*"

Ellis watched him closely "Talk to me, Dave. Is it the magazine or the snake that interests you?"

"The cobra." Dave's stunned expression gradually transmuted into anger. "That was the symbol of his avatar."

"Explain," Ellis ordered.

Dave put the magazine on the desk very carefully, as though he feared the cobra might strike. "Katherine played one of those big, online fantasy world games, the kind that thousands of people can play at any given time. They call them massively multiplayer games."

"Go on," Ellis said.

"The one Katherine liked involves a world of towns and cities. The players have various powers and skills. They compete to rule the urban zones. Each player gets an avatar."

"An avatar is a computer-generated character in the game?" Isabel asked.

"Right." Dave did not look away from the cobra. "The players give their avatars whatever personality traits or quirks or temperaments they choose. They also select symbols or heralds for their banners and shields. You know, like the knights and nobles did in medieval times."

Isabel shuddered. "Talk about a setup that allows people to act out their repressed side."

"Yeah," Dave said. "It's supposed to be a game of strategy but a lot of the players go overboard. They really get into the life they create online. It's like an endless Level Five lucid dreamscape."

Isabel noticed Ellis's brows climbing at that comment but he kept silent.

"I've read about that syndrome," she said to Dave. "Some players don't play the game just to win, they play it to have a life. Through their avatars they form relationships with other players."

Dave swallowed visibly. "Sometimes people get really intense, all right. That's what happened to Katherine about three months ago."

"After Scargill's death," Ellis said quietly.

Dave nodded. "Yes. I tried to tell her that she was getting way too involved but she wouldn't listen. She had introduced Scargill to the game when they were dating, you see. It was one of the things they did together. I guess playing the game after his death was her way of hanging onto his memory. But one day a couple of weeks before she was killed —"

He broke off abruptly.

"What happened, Dave?" Isabel asked.

"She suddenly sounded a lot better. More like her old self. I thought she was coming out of her depression. I figured maybe she was seeing someone new."

Ellis's expression sharpened. "Did you ask her?"

"Sure." Dave looked at the photo of the cobra. "She said she wasn't seeing anyone new but that things were definitely looking up. She said she didn't want to talk about it on the phone but she promised to tell me everything the next time we got together." He exhaled slowly. "I never saw her again. Two weeks later she was dead."

Isabel touched his shoulder gently. For a moment no one spoke.

After a while Ellis reached out and took the magazine from Dave's grasp.

"Thank you," he said quietly. "You've confirmed some of my own conclusions and you've given me some useful information. Now I'll tell you what I know and what I think I know."

Dave's throat worked but Isabel could see that he had himself under control.

"I'm listening," he said.

"Technically speaking, some of what I'm going to tell you comes under the heading of classified information," Ellis said quietly. "At least as far as Lawson is concerned. But you already know a lot more than you're supposed to know about the work that's done at Frey-Salter so I'm not going to worry about it. In any event, you've got a right to be informed about what is going on."

"You mean, what *you* think is going on," Dave said.

Ellis's mouth curved faintly. "Yeah. What I think. Okay, here's how I see it."

He gave Dave a quick, concise summary of events. As far as Isabel could tell, he left nothing out.

"Everyone except me is satisfied that Scargill is dead," Ellis concluded. "They think I'm obsessed with a dead man. But my theory is that Scargill is still alive." He pointed at the cobra. "And you've just given me a little bit of proof that supports my version of events."

Dave sat down slowly, shaken. "I still don't understand why you think the magazine proves anything. Katherine probably bought it as a sort of keepsake because it represented something she shared with Scargill."

"That may be why she purchased it but I don't think that's why I found it where I did on the floor. It was located only a short distance from where she fell, Dave. I believe that she managed to grab it just before she was shot. The impact of the bullet probably caused her to drop it. That's why there's no blood on it."

"Wouldn't Scargill have noticed it and recognized his own game avatar?"

"The magazine was facedown when I found it," Ellis said softly. "My hunch is that Scargill never saw the cover."

Dave studied the magazine as if he were trying to read a half-forgotten language that could be deciphered if he just worked at it. "The police said the place had been vandalized as well as burglarized."

"If I'm right, Scargill tore up Katherine's apartment in order to simulate an out-of-control murder-robbery. He's a game player, remember. But now that we know the magazine had some personal meaning for her, what are the odds that Katherine would have been killed with it practically in her hands?"

Dave's eyes lit with understanding and savage pride. "She did her best in the last moments of her life to name her killer."

"I think so, yes," Ellis said.

Dave dropped his head into his hands. "She left the clue for me. She must have known that I was the only one who could make sense of it. I did eventually go to her apartment to help Mom and Dad pack up her things but by the time we got there the place had been cleaned."

"You mustn't feel bad, Dave." Isabel put her hand on his shoulder. "Even if you had seen the magazine immediately after the killing and understood its significance, it's highly doubtful that the police would have paid any attention to you."

"Because Scargill is officially dead and cremated," Ellis reminded him softly.

Dave raised his head, his face bleak. "This is crazy."

"No, it's not," Ellis said. "Not if you go with my theory that Scargill is still alive. Then everything else falls into place."

There was a long silence. Both men drank their coffee.

Ellis set down his empty cup. "How did you find me, Dave?"

Dave had gone back to staring at the picture of the cobra. He seemed distracted. "What?"

"How did you locate me?" Ellis repeated patiently. "I wasn't deliberately trying to hide but not very many people know that I'm here in Roxanna Beach."

"Oh, yeah, I see what you mean." Dave

shrugged. “I tracked you online. It wasn’t that hard. You may be some kind of hot-shot secret agent when you work for Frey-Salter but the rest of the time you maintain a legitimate business identity. You’ve got corporate credit cards, a driver’s license and a Maserati, for crying out loud. How hard could it be to find you? Especially since, like you said, you weren’t trying to hide.”

Ellis smiled, evidently satisfied. “Are you as good as Katherine was when it comes to computers?”

“Probably. Why?”

“Because I’ve hit the wall when it comes to online research and I can’t trust my usual sources. I need some help.”

“I’m still not completely sure you’re the good guy in this thing,” Dave muttered. He flicked a speculative glance at Isabel. “But I agree that finding that picture of the cobra in Katherine’s apartment does point toward Scargill.”

Ellis checked his watch. “I’m in a hurry here. Want to help me find your sister’s killer or not?”

“You know the answer to that,” Dave said.

32

Halfway through the first session of "Tapping into the Creative Potential of Your Dreams," Isabel knew she had a disaster on her hands. An atmosphere of restless boredom had enveloped the seminar room five minutes into her lecture. One man in the first row had gone to sleep. Most of the other attendees were glancing at their watches every few minutes. Tamsyn, observing from a seat at the back of the chamber, appeared increasingly concerned.

Okay, so I'm not cut out to be an instructor of the Kyler Method. Another career path down the drain. So what else is new?

The fact that half her mind was fully occupied in wondering what Ellis was doing was not helping her stay focused on the job at hand.

She glanced at the clock. Half an hour to go. She would have given anything to walk off the stage but she knew she had no choice but to plow ahead.

"People tend to recall only the dreams they have just before they awaken and very often not even those. But researchers are convinced that most of us dream actively all night long. You can prove this easily enough by waking people up at various points during the night and asking them about their dreams. Trust me, they'll tell you. Probably more than you really want to know."

No one laughed at the small joke.

A man seated in the third row raised his hand. She had noticed him earlier, in part because he was one of the few men in the room with a beard. His was closely cut, with a stylish flair that accented the handsome angles of his cheekbones and jawline. The other reason she had picked him out of the crowd was because he was one of the few people who seemed genuinely interested in her lecture.

"Yes?" she said brightly, so desperately grateful to him for showing some interest that she wanted to hop over the first two rows and kiss him on both cheeks. "You had a question, sir?"

"I was just wondering," he said in a low, resonant voice, "why we don't remember many of our dreams?"

"Theories vary but one that sounds reasonable to many researchers is that we simply aren't paying much attention while we sleep. We don't focus on a dream unless it happens to be particularly vivid or unless it contains a strong emotional element." She held up a notepad. "Which brings me to the first step in the process of tapping into the creative potential of your dreams." She paused for effect, as she had learned in her instructors' classes. "Take notes. Keep a pen and a pad of paper beside your bed. Or try a recorder. Whenever you wake up in the middle of the night, write down whatever you can recall of your dreams. Your goal is to create a dream log."

She waved the pointer with a flourish, trying to regain the attention of some people in the back row who were chatting among themselves. The tip of the wand moved across the top of the podium, sweeping her carefully arranged notes to the floor.

For a moment everyone in the room, including her, stared at the fallen note cards.

"Excuse me." She crouched and frantically gathered up the cards.

The murmur of conversation in the back row got louder.

She staggered erect and put the cards back on top of the podium. Gripping the edges of the stand she looked out at her audience, half of which was now engaged in low-voiced conversations. Someone's cell phone rang. Just to make matters worse, the person took the call.

I don't believe this, she thought. *It's just a really bad dream. Okay, maybe not as bad as a crime scene dream, but darn close.*

With an effort of will she gathered herself. Thirty minutes to go.

"Step two," she said through gritted teeth, "is to look through your dream log at the end of each week. You will be searching for recurring themes and ideas, but my advice is not to waste time on the more traditional interpretive approach, which relies on symbols. In the old days of dream research it was felt that every element in a dream actually meant something other than what it appeared to be. If you dreamed about a closed door you were experiencing a fear of change. If you dreamed about a mirror in which you cannot see your reflection you were worried about how others see you, and so forth."

The man with the neatly trimmed beard raised his hand. "What's wrong with taking that approach? I've always heard symbols are important in dreams."

In the back row, Tamsyn gave a tiny,

negative wave of her hand and shook her head. Not hard to interpret those symbols, Isabel thought. Tamsyn wanted her to leave the topic and get back to the discussion of dream logs.

But she couldn't ignore the one person in the class who was actually paying attention, she told herself. She smiled at the bearded man.

"The idea that our dreams contain critical symbols that must be interpreted is extremely ancient and comes down to us from a variety of cultures," she said quickly, trying to rush through the explanation. "It was strongly reinforced in the twentieth century by Jung and Freud and others who took a psychological approach to dream research."

Another hand went up. She pretended not to notice.

"It is extremely risky to put too much emphasis on symbols in dreams for the simple reason that there are as many interpretations of various symbols as there are people who try to interpret dreams," she continued. "While some analysts would see that closed door I just mentioned as a symbol of fear of change, others would interpret it as the rational barrier that stands between our civilized nature and our deepest, most primitive thoughts and repressed desires."

The woman who had just raised her hand spoke up loudly.

"But the door must mean something," she insisted.

Isabel spread her hands. "It could be just a door with no particular significance at all. Maybe one you noticed out of the corner of your eye earlier in the day when you walked down the street. That's the problem with dream symbols. If you attempt to use them to interpret the meaning of your dreams, I suggest that you do not rely on a dream encyclopedia or theories of universal archetypes. Instead, think of the objects and events in your dreams in terms of personal context."

In the back row, Tamsyn sagged in her chair, apparently resigned to disaster.

"What's context?" the bearded man demanded.

Isabel turned to him. "I am talking about what is going on with you in your own life. Are you facing a major career decision? If so, maybe that door does represent a fear of change or having to make a choice. But deal with the decision-making process while you are awake. Don't look to your dreams for solutions. A decision that appears rational and right in a dream is actually quite arbitrary and may be entirely wrong for the waking world. Dreaming and waking thought are two different states of mind, literally."

"I thought this class was supposed to be about tapping into our dreams to get creative answers," someone whined from the fifth row.

Another phone warbled. A man in the tenth row dove into his pocket to respond.

In the back, Tamsyn put her face in her hands.

Let me out of this nightmare, Isabel thought. But she knew there was no escape. She couldn't even tell herself that she would eventually wake up and discover it was all just a dream. She was trapped.

Ellis slipped the twenty-dollar bill across the counter. The plump, good-natured café owner made it disappear into the pocket of her apron. She had told him that he could call her Daisy.

"All I know is that the doc was real regular in his habits." Daisy leaned forward a little, providing a view of her generous cleavage. "He ate his dinner here, same as usual on that night. Had the special. On Thursday nights he always ordered the special. Turkey, mashed potatoes and gravy. It was his favorite."

"He didn't look ill?"

"Looked fine to me." Daisy shrugged well-upholstered shoulders. "But that's the way it is with a heart attack, ain't it? One minute you're fine. The next, you're a goner."

"Not always," Ellis said softly. "In a lot of cases there are prior symptoms. Nausea. Shortness of breath. Chest pain."

"If he was having any of those things, he didn't let on. Ate every bite. Doc had a good appetite. One of my best customers."

"Do you know where he went after he left here that evening?" Ellis asked, dutifully making a note on a pad of paper.

"Sure. Said he was headed straight back to his office at the center. That's where they found him, wasn't it? Dead at his desk?"

"Yes," Ellis said.

"Doc hardly ever went home. Had a real problem with insomnia, you know." Daisy tut-tutted. "Told me once he hadn't had a good night's sleep in forty years, poor man."

"I see." Ellis finished the bad coffee and got to his feet. He should have brought along some bags of green tea, he thought. Evidently he had become addicted to the stuff at some point during the past few months. "Thanks for the information."

Daisy squinted a little. "Mind if I ask why you wanted to know what Doc had to eat that night?"

"I'm retracing his movements on the day of his death."

"Yeah? How come?"

"Insurance investigation," Ellis said. "My boss wants me to be sure it wasn't suicide. Company doesn't pay out on suicides."

"Damned insurance companies. Always looking for a way to get out of paying." Daisy snorted. "I'll tell you one thing. Doc wouldn't have taken his own life. Leastways, not that night."

Ellis tried not to look too interested. "What makes you so sure?"

"He was real excited about something he was working on at the time."

"Did he talk about the project?"

"Not to me, he didn't. But he had a couple of meetings here with a tall guy who looked like he'd gone through a windshield sometime in the past few months. Had some bad scars on his face, right about here, you know?" She tapped her forehead and jaw. "Wore his hair sort of long and he looked like he was trying to grow a beard to hide the scars."

Ellis kept his expression polite and as casual as possible. "Any idea what they discussed at the meetings?"

"Nope. Sat over there in the corner booth and talked real quiet like. But I could tell they were both real intense and Doc was excited. If he was gonna commit suicide, you'd think he would have waited until after he finished his special project."

Ellis pocketed his notebook. "Sounds like a logical assumption."

After what seemed like an eternity, the class finally ended. Tamsyn made her way forward while the students surged toward the exits.

Isabel slumped against the podium. "You don't have to tell me, I know I was terrible."

"Not terrible," Tamsyn said, speaking very precisely. "It was a very *interesting* talk."

"One man in the front went to sleep. Everyone else looked like they were thinking about lunch or picking up their voice mail messages."

"Okay, there were some dry parts, but we can work on those."

"I appreciate your positive attitude, but

we might as well face facts here. I don't have your flair for this type of work. It was kind of you and Leila to talk Farrell into giving me the opportunity, but I think it's clear that I don't have what it takes to be a Kyler Method instructor."

"You can do it, Isabel," Tamsyn said, shifting into full Kyler Method mode. "Let's go over your presentation points before the next class."

"Thanks, but no thanks." Isabel gathered up her notes. "I'm going to talk to Farrell right now and let him know that I'm resigning. Something tells me that he'll be thrilled."

Randolph Belvedere felt as if he had just found out he might be holding a winning lottery ticket. He struggled not to let his desperate hope show on his face.

"Are you telling me that my father took out a large life insurance policy?" he asked, stacking his hands on the desk in what he thought looked like a calm, centered, controlled pose. The truth was, his fingers were shaking so badly he was afraid the dangerous looking insurance investigator might think he had a tremor.

The man seated on the other side of the desk had introduced himself as Charles

Ward. When Mrs. Johnson had shown him into the room a few minutes ago, Randolph's first thought was that Ward didn't look like an insurance company employee. His suit was expensive but it was cut along Euro-sleek lines, not the traditional, conservative, more boxy style favored by most American businessmen.

But it wasn't Ward's clothes that worried him, it was Ward himself. The suit might have come from Italy, but Ward looked like he came from the wrong side of the tracks.

"All I am allowed to say is that I am looking into the circumstances of Dr. Belvedere's death," Ward said, making it clear that he was not about to give out unauthorized information. "If my findings warrant further action, someone else will contact you to discuss the details of the policy."

"I see." Randolph pressed his right hand very tightly on top of his left. "Can you tell me whether or not the policy is a large one?"

"Let's just say that I'm expensive." Ward smiled enigmatically. "The company doesn't send me out to investigate a claim unless the policy is large enough to make it worthwhile to hire me.

"I understand." Randolph realized that his mouth had suddenly gone very dry. He had to swallow a couple of times before he could continue. "Well then, what is it you want to verify?"

"Cause of death."

Randolph's first reaction was bewilderment. "There's no question about that. My father died of a heart attack."

"I'm sure that's correct," Ward said easily. "But with so much money at stake, my company wants to be absolutely certain."

"What other possibility is there?"

"Suicide."

"Are you crazy?" Randolph was dumbstruck. "My father would never have taken his own life."

"Relatives often say that. It's amazing how few people see it coming."

Randolph shook his head once, absolutely certain. "My father lived for his research." He grimaced. "I'll be the first to admit that he was very much on the fringes of his field, but that doesn't change the fact that he believed in his work. He wouldn't have taken his own life."

"The center does sleep research," Ward pointed out calmly. "I'm assuming that means that your father would have had access to a variety of sleep medications, some of which are probably experimental, right?"

Randolph ground his back teeth. "I assure you, my father did not conduct experiments on himself."

"You probably knew him better than anyone else." Ward shrugged. "But my employer wants me to ask a few questions. I'm supposed to talk to some of the people who were working here the night he died. Just routine stuff. The sooner I file my report, the sooner the company pays off. Any objections?"

"Not at all. I'll make sure that my secretary alerts the staff. Feel free to talk to anyone you like. You'll soon find out that I'm telling you the truth. My father did *not* commit suicide."

Ward stood and picked up his briefcase. "Got a hunch you're right about that."

33

"Good news, Farrell, I think I'm going to make at least one of your dreams come true." Isabel closed the door of the inner office and sat down in one of the leather chairs. "I'm quitting."

Farrell looked up from the papers he had spread out on the desk, blank-faced with surprise. "Why?"

"Because I have no talent for this work. None whatsoever. I just came from my first lecture and I can tell you that it is a miracle that half the class managed to stay awake."

"I see." Farrell sat back, thoughtful now. "Leila won't be happy to hear this."

"Yeah, well, my family has never approved of my career choices, you know that."

"Probably because you've never actually had what anyone would call a real career."

"Enough about me," she said evenly. "Let's talk about you."

"Don't worry, you'll be paid for the time you put in as a trainee instructor."

"I'm not worried about my paycheck. Well, I am, of course, but that's another issue. At the moment I'm a lot more concerned about you and Leila. I told myself I should stay out of it." She sighed. "But I just can't seem to help myself. What's wrong?"

He stiffened. "What are you talking about?"

"Come on, Farrell, it's been clear to me from the start that you only hired me because Leila and Tamsyn put pressure on you."

His mouth thinned. "I admit I wasn't real keen on the idea of a creative dreaming seminar. Sounded a little too metaphysical and New Agey for the Kyler Method."

"There's more to it than that. You've been trying to avoid me ever since I got here. When we do come face to face you act like you have an appointment elsewhere. On top of that, my sister is very unhappy. What's going on, Farrell?"

"Keep your voice down." Farrell glanced toward the closed door. "I don't want Sheila to overhear you. We try to maintain a positive, businesslike image around here. The last thing I need is a major scene in my office."

"I've got news for you; if you don't tell me what's going on, you're going to get a full-blown family quarrel right here in your executive suite."

Farrell studied her speculatively for a few seconds. "You'd do it, wouldn't you?"

She straightened her shoulders. "Yes, I would."

"You're right, you know. This is none of your business."

"I love Leila and I care about you. We're family. What do you expect me to do?"

"Try to fix things, of course." He shoved himself up out of his chair and went to stand at the window. "That's what you do, isn't it? Give advice to other people?"

The bitterness in his words made her go very, very still.

"Farrell?" she prompted gently. "Are you seriously ill? Because if that's the case, you must know that Leila loves you and would want to be there for you, just as you would be there for her."

"I'm not ill."

"Thank God." She relaxed slightly. "But I don't understand. What else could possibly be so terrible that you would be afraid to talk it over with Leila?"

He stared glumly out the window at the elegant lines of the lobby of Kyler headquarters. "It's all coming apart, Isabel."

"What is coming apart?"

"Everything I've built during the last four years. That dream I had, the one you and Leila convinced me to make real, has become a nightmare."

She watched him uneasily. "Define 'nightmare.' "

"I'm overextended financially. I've got some big loan payments coming up in three months and I don't have the cash reserves to make them. Kyler, Inc. is headed straight into bankruptcy. I'm on a runaway train and I don't know how to stop it."

"Are you telling me that this is just a business problem?"

He swung around to stare at her. "*Just* a business problem?"

"I was afraid it was something really serious."

"For your information, this is about as serious as it gets. But I guess I can't expect you to see it that way, can I? You're the one member of the family who isn't interested in success, the one whose idea of investing is to buy thousands of dollars' worth of furniture, store it in a rental locker and drop the insurance, the one whose big, long-term goal is to set herself up as a psychic dream consultant. Sure, I can see why you wouldn't be overly concerned about a little thing like bankruptcy."

She cleared her throat. "I'm going to let that go for now because, well, because you're sort of right. But neither my current financial situation nor my career objectives are the issue here. And, no, I'm sorry, Farrell, but I don't think your business problems are anywhere near as serious as your marriage, and I can guarantee you that Leila will take the same point of view. Why haven't you told her you're in trouble?"

"Don't you understand? I'm supposed to be Mr. Perfect. The man her daddy approved of right from the start." He jabbed at his chest with his thumb. "I'm the guy who goes on television talk shows and tells people that if they follow my method they can become successful, just like me."

"You can't possibly believe that Leila only married you because you're a success and Dad gave his approval."

Farrell exhaled deeply. "I know that's not the sole reason she married me. But I'm also damn sure she wouldn't have looked twice at a guy who dug ditches for a living."

"That's not fair. She loves you, Farrell, and it's not because you're successful. It's because you're the person you are — a good man with some big dreams. Okay, so maybe some of the dreams aren't working out. So what? That doesn't change the important things."

"It's not that simple, Isabel."

She pushed herself to her feet. "Listen up, brother-in-law. My sister is sinking into a deep depression because she thinks Kyler, Inc., has become more important to you than having a family. Trust me, finding out that the reason you've been acting weird lately is because you've got financial problems is going to come as an enormous relief to her."

Farrell hesitated, desperation in every line of his body. "How do you know that?"

"I know my sister." She went to the door. "But try to remember that Leila has a few dreams of her own and that they all involve having a full-time husband who cares about his family. You might not be able to make every dream come true, but you have the power to make that one real, don't you?"

She went out into the hall and closed the door very quietly behind her.

34

Bruce Hopton dropped the heavy, leather-bound logbook onto the desk and flipped it open. "This is the sign-in sheet for the night the old man died. Need anything else?"

"One thing." Ellis set his briefcase on the floor and pulled out a notebook. "I'd like to talk to someone who can give me a little background on every member of the staff who worked that night."

Hopton rested his bulky frame against the edge of the counter, watching Ellis closely. "I've been head of security here at the center since day one. I know everybody."

"You'll do," Ellis said.

It took them fifteen minutes to go through the list of people who signed in and out on the night of Belvedere's death. As promised, Bruce recognized them all.

Halfway down the list, Ellis put his finger under Isabel's name.

"Ms. Wright often worked nights," Bruce said. "Sure miss her. She was a real nice lady." He paused. "You ever hear of a condition called sleep paralysis?"

"Yes." Ellis glanced up, curious about the change of topic. "It's a sensation some people get occasionally when they're transitioning from the dreaming state to the waking state. They suddenly feel paralyzed and they are because the brain hasn't yet switched off the mechanism that keeps them from moving around during a dream."

Bruce nodded, very serious. "Ms. Wright explained it. She said that mechanism is what protects the sleeper from fall- ing out of bed at night or worse. But occasionally the switch doesn't get turned off when it's supposed to and you wake up still frozen. You can't move. Can't speak. Whatever dream you're coming out of gets tangled up with the paralysis and you hallucinate. Very scary stuff."

Ellis wondered where this was going. "Some researchers think that sleep paralysis may explain the stories of alien abductions. People who report that kind of thing usually say they felt paralyzed. Other cultures have other metaphysical or supernatural explanations for the experience."

"My grandson was experiencing sleep paralysis once or twice a week," Hopton said soberly. "Had terrible hallucinations and nightmares. Got so the kid was terrified to even go into his bedroom. Tried to stay up all night just so he wouldn't fall asleep. His folks thought at first that he was just being difficult. Then they started to wonder if he had some kind of mental illness, you know?"

Ellis understood. He smiled slightly. "So you told Ms. Wright about your grandson's dreams and she explained what was going on."

"Yep. She talked to the kid. Reassured him that he was okay. She also gave my daughter and son-in-law the name of a doctor who was familiar with that kind of thing. Turned out the sleep paralysis was being triggered so frequently because of some medication that my grandson was taking. When they switched meds he stopped having the experiences." Bruce rubbed the back of his neck. "Don't know how long the poor kid would have gone on suffering if it hadn't been for Ms. Wright."

"I see." Isabel at work, Ellis thought. Fixing things. He moved his finger to the next name. "What about this person?"

"That's Dr. Rainey. She's been on the staff forever. Works in the sleep lab so she spends a lot of nights here, too." Bruce drew his busy brows together. "Huh."

"What?"

"That's funny. Thought Dr. Rainey was out of town for a couple of days that week. I remember she said something about going to visit her son and his wife in Mendocino. She must have got home early and decided to come in to work that night."

The familiar icy trickle of adrenaline slithered through Ellis.

"I'd like to talk to her as soon as possible," he said, keeping his voice very even.

"Sure. No problem. Belvedere said you could talk to anyone you want." Bruce glanced at the clock on the wall. "I saw her earlier today. She's probably upstairs in her office now."

Dr. Rainey was in her mid-sixties, short, stocky and impatient with the interruption.

"There must be some mistake," she snapped, glowering over the tops of her reading glasses. "I was out of town that night. Didn't get back until the following day. I remember what a shock it was to come back and hear that Martin had died."

Ellis opened the sign-in log. "Is that your signature, ma'am?"

Dr. Rainey scowled at the scrawled name. "No, it is not. My handwriting is bad, but it's not that bad." She removed her glasses and peered more closely at Ellis. "I don't understand. What is this all about?"

"I think someone signed in using your name that night," Ellis said.

"Why on earth would anyone do that?"

"Good question." He looked at Bruce. "How hard would it be for a person to sign in under someone else's name?"

Bruce did not look happy. "Not hard at all. Got someone on duty around the clock downstairs but the sign-in log just sits out on the counter. No one checks the names against the faces or bothers with ID unless the person signing in is a visitor or a new member of the staff."

"In other words, one member of the staff could sign in under someone else's name."

Bruce scratched his bald head and appeared even more comfortable. "Sure, guess that would be possible. As long as the guard recognized the person as a member of the staff there would be no reason to see what signature was actually written down on the log. I mean, you'd just assume it would be the right one. What would be the point of one employee signing in under another's name?"

Mass confusion and plausible deniability in the event anyone ever questioned who was in the building on the night of Belvedere's death, Ellis thought.

He walked out the front door of the center a short time later and got into the driver's seat of the Maserati. He left the door open and sat at an angle, one foot inside the car, the other on the ground.

It was almost two o'clock. He needed food. He also needed to talk to Isabel. Of the two basic necessities, Isabel was more important.

He took out his phone and called her number.

She answered on the first ring. "Hello?"

"Congratulations. You have just graduated from amateur sleuth to professional. You were right. It looks like someone probably did murder Dr. Martin Belvedere."

"Good grief." She sounded shocked, in spite of the fact that it was her idea in the first place. "What did you find out?"

"Among other things, I confirmed that Belvedere met with Scargill or someone matching Scargill's description on at least two occasions."

"Dr. B. mentioned two meetings in his notes," she said thoughtfully.

"In addition, it looks like a member of the professional staff signed in for the night shift on the night that Belvedere died. Whoever he was, he used another staff member's name."

"Wait a second. If it was a member of the staff, it had to be someone the guard recognized. That means it couldn't have been Scargill."

"True."

"Whose name did the person use?" she asked, curious.

"Dr. Elizabeth Rainey."

"Rainey? Whoever signed her name must be a woman, then." She hesitated. "Or maybe not. Those guards never check the signatures if they recognize you. A man could have signed Dr. Rainey's name."

"Either way, it still leaves us with the fact that it wasn't Scargill."

"You sound annoyed."

"Looks like he's using someone else again." He rested one arm on the wheel. "It complicates things."

"Well, I doubt that this new assistant, whoever he or she is, will turn out to be a former resident of the Brackleton Correctional Facility or a graduate of the behavior modification program they operated there."

He watched people coming and going across the parking lot. "What makes you so sure of that?"

"The center runs routine employment background checks. Granted, they are fairly superficial but I'm sure Hopton's people would have picked up on a conviction and prison time."

"Anyone who could change computerized hospital morgue records could probably change a prison record without too much trouble."

"Good point," she conceded. "Well, the upshot is that it looks like Dr. B. was probably murdered by a member of the center's staff, one who was in the building that night."

"Yes."

"And I was just down the hall," she whispered.

The self-recrimination in her words worried him. "Stop it. Don't even think of going there, Isabel. There was nothing you could have done."

She said nothing.

He wanted to reassure her, but he was far away and the feeling that time was running out was riding him hard.

He looked at the notes he had made. "At least I've got a list of suspects. That's a start."

"I just realized that, technically speaking, I'm on that list."

"We're not speaking technically," he said. "I seriously doubt that we'd be able to prove murder in any event, even if we exhumed the body."

"Because the drugs that were used probably wouldn't show up in a toxicology report?"

"Right. Those scans are very limited."

"What's your next stop?"

He checked his notes again. "I'm going to talk to the guard who was on duty that night. Dick Peterson. Know him?"

"Of course. I remember he was one of the people I called after I found the body. You're in luck. Dick knows everyone at the center and he's got an excellent visual memory."

He tapped the notebook against the steering wheel. "I'll let you know what he says. Everything okay on your end?"

"Well, no, to be honest. I handed in my resignation to Farrell this morning after my first and only class. I was a disaster."

"Don't worry about it, honey. Just increase your consulting fees. Lawson and I can afford it."

"Oh, sure, easy for you to say. I still don't have signed contracts with either of you. But that's not the really bad news."

"There's more?"

"Farrell told me that he's facing bankruptcy in three months," she said.

"Oh, man. That's gotta be tough to handle. It's obvious he's put his heart and soul into Kyler, Inc."

"Yes." She cleared her throat. "I've been sitting here thinking about his situation."

"Yeah?" He flipped through his notes, making a mental list of questions he wanted to ask the guard.

"Maybe you could help him."

"Help who?" He blanked for a few seconds. "You mean your brother-in-law?"

"That's what you do, isn't it? Consult for entrepreneurs and investors? Show them how to make their businesses profitable?"

"In my other life." He closed the notebook. "Look, Isabel, I'm a little busy at the moment."

"I know. But when this thing with Scargill is finished, maybe you could sort of consult for Farrell."

He had to smile. "You just can't stop trying to fix things, can you?"

"People tell me it's my most irritating characteristic."

"Lucky you've got a lot of other really interesting characteristics that more than compensate for your tendency to hand out free advice." He pulled his foot into the car, closed the door and fired up the engine. "See you in a few hours."

"Good. Drive carefully. The fog never did burn off completely today and the weather forecast is calling for more of it this evening."

Her concern had the customary warming effect on him. It was the same feeling he got when she told him to read romance novels, get acupuncture and lay off the red meat.

"You know, Isabel," he said, driving out of the parking lot. "When this is over we really are going to have to talk about our relationship."

"It's too late. I've already fallen in love with you."

She ended the connection before he could recover from the shock.

35

Farrell let himself into the front hall of the big house. He was sweating and his mind was still reeling. Ever since Isabel had left his office he had been trying to think about what to say to Leila. But nothing brilliant or even mildly intelligent surfaced from the maelstrom of emotions, fears and uncertainties that were seething in what was supposed to be his brain.

The house was very still. It occurred to him that he had not even realized that Leila had gone home early until he walked down the hall to her office and discovered she was not there.

That was not like Leila. She was always at headquarters in the afternoons on reception days. The special social events were important. They set a tone and encouraged interaction between attendees and instructors. It was Leila who handled all the arrangements, from supervising the caterers to selecting the flower arrangements. Later she would play hostess to his host.

But today she had gone home early. And he hadn't even been aware of the fact that she had left. For some reason that shook him almost as much as what Isabel had said earlier. Maybe he really had allowed himself to get sidetracked by the impending financial disaster.

He walked slowly through the elegantly tiled foyer and then crossed the glass-walled living room with its view of the foggy bay, listening for her in the deep silence.

"What are you doing here?" she asked from the kitchen doorway. "Is something wrong at the office?" Anxiety flared in her eyes. "Are you ill?"

He stared at her. She was dressed in a pretty, flowered robe and slippers. Her hair was damp from a recent shower.

"Kyler, Inc., is not more important to me than you are," he said, speaking the first coherent words he could string together. "How could you think that?"

Her eyes widened a little. Then she sighed. "I see you've been talking to Isabel."

He started toward her. "She came to my office today to tell me she is resigning as an instructor."

Leila winced. "She quit? So soon?"

"Yes." He stopped a short distance away, trying to read her eyes. "And then she told me that you think I care more about the company than I do about you."

Leila hugged herself very tightly. "You're spending so much time in your office. You're never home."

He rubbed his temples and decided he might as well finish what he had started. "Leila, Kyler, Inc., will probably be in bankruptcy court three months from now."

Stunned, she just looked at him. "Farrell."

"I screwed up big-time. We're going to lose everything. I saw it coming a few months ago and I've been working frantically to find a way out." He shoved his hands into his pockets. "But there is no way out."

"This is our business. We're partners. Why didn't you tell me we were in trouble?" She looked both furious and hurt.

"Because I was sure that when you realized that you married a failure you'd pack your bags and leave me," he admitted. "I was in denial, I guess. I was trying to put off that day as long as possible."

She lowered her arms, took two steps toward him and gripped the lapels of his shirt. "How could you possibly believe that I would leave you because of a business failure?"

He gripped her arms. "Sweetheart, I knew when I married you that you had certain expectations. You admire your father and he approved of me. You probably thought that I was like him in many ways. Hell, he figured the same thing. But I can guarantee you that he won't be feeling the same way about me three months from now."

"Listen to me, Farrell. I married you because I love you and because, even if you happened to be successful at the time, I sensed that, deep down, you were *not* like Dad."

That stopped him cold. "What are you talking about?"

"My father had affairs with other women throughout the time that he was married to my mother," she said very steadily. "He was never home. He missed every school play, every recital and several birthdays because he was too busy doing his big business deals or traveling to meet with politicians and lobbyists. We never took vacations with Dad. He's been married twice since the divorce, both times to women who are younger than I am. Do you really think I wanted to marry a man like that?"

The great weight that had been crushing him for the past several months lifted so suddenly he thought he might actually be able to fly.

"I didn't understand," he whispered, dazed.

"No, I can see that." She loosened her grip on his shirt and raised her fingertips to his face. "I suppose that's my fault for not making it clear. I just assumed you understood."

He pulled her close against him. "Maybe we should both sign up for one of those Kyler Method seminars on communication skills."

She smiled tremulously. "Oh, Farrell." She put her head on his shoulder. "I've been so scared. So desperate."

"So have I," he said into her hair. "But not any longer. I can handle anything if I know you're with me."

"Always."

They stood together for a long time. After a while Leila stirred in his arms.

"We should probably go back to the office," she said reluctantly. "This is reception evening, after all. There will be a million and one little details. There always are."

"Tamsyn and the others can handle them."

"But . . ."

He framed her face and smiled down into her eyes. "You and I have other priorities."

"Such as?"

"What do you say we get started on that family we plan to have?"

Joy lit up her face. "You're right. That sounds a lot more important than the weekly reception."

He picked her up in his arms and carried her down the hall to the bedroom.

36

The good-looking man with the neatly trimmed beard was waiting for her in the hall outside her small office.

"Ron Chapman." He gave her a friendly smile. "I'm enrolled in the seminar series this week. Just wanted to tell you how much I enjoyed your class on creative dreaming this morning."

Isabel's spirits, which had been at low ebb since the debacle, immediately skyrocketed. Nothing like a little positive feedback.

"Thank you. I'm afraid a lot of the students found it pretty dull."

"You could have fooled me. You sure know your subject."

"Well, I've worked in the field of dream research for some time," she said, trying to come across as both modest and authoritative. "But I must admit that teaching other people how to get creative inspiration from their dreams is a real challenge."

"You did great this morning. I'm looking forward to the next class." He checked his watch. "Uh-oh. Looks like I'm running late for the session on time management. Probably not a good sign, huh?"

She laughed. "Enjoy the class."

"I'm sure I will. See you at the reception this evening."

"I'll be there."

Tamsyn emerged from the ladies' room just as Ron went past on his way down the hall. She gave him one of her vivacious smiles.

"Mr. Chapman," she murmured.

He paused. "Please, call me Ron. I understand we're all on a first-name basis while we're here at Kyler headquarters."

"That's right." She indicated her name tag. "I'm Tamsyn. I'm on the staff."

"It's a pleasure, Tamsyn."

Isabel could almost see the sparks flickering between the pair. Instant attraction in action.

Tamsyn waited until Ron Chapman had disappeared around the corner. Then she winked at Isabel.

"Hmm," she said. "Nice. Very nice."

Isabel raised her brows. "I'll bet there's a rule against fraternizing with the seminar attendees."

"Sure." She rubbed her hands together. "But there isn't any rule about dating one of the students after he's finished the program. Don't you think he's attractive?"

"Who? Chapman? He seems nice enough."

Tamsyn glanced back down the hall, looking thoughtful. "Actually, I would have said he's your type. Sort of academic-looking, polite. Well mannered."

"That's it? You think he's my type because he comes across as intelligent and well mannered?"

Tamsyn made a face. "Okay, maybe he seems like your type because he's not intimidating."

"Aha, now we get to the real issue." Isabel peered at Tamsyn over the rims of her glasses. "I take it you find Ellis intimidating?"

"Well, yeah. Sort of." Tamsyn cleared her throat. "Interesting but intimidating."

"Now that's where you and I differ on the subject of Ellis Cutler," Isabel replied. "I find him very interesting but not at all intimidating."

Tamsyn arched her brows. "Give me a break. You don't think he's just a little scary?"

Isabel pondered that, lips pursed, for about three seconds. "In the right circumstances, I think Ellis could scare the daylights out of some people."

"But not you?"

"Not me."

"I give up." Tamsyn opened both hands in a what-can-I-do? gesture. "You've fallen for him, haven't you?"

"Yes. Before I even met him, as a matter of fact. You could say he's the man of my dreams."

Tamsyn nodded. "Yeah, I'm starting to get that impression. What can I say, except good luck." She glanced at her watch. "I've got to run. The caterers and the florist arrived a little while ago and no one knows where Leila and Farrell are. They've both disappeared. Someone's got to take charge."

Isabel laughed. "I can't think of anyone who can do that better than you."

Tamsyn hurried away, a bundle of sparkling energy and enthusiasm.

Isabel watched her go and wondered if anything would come of the attraction between Tamsyn and Ron Chapman.

Workplace romances are so highly volatile, she reflected, letting herself into her office. They are unpredictable, destabilizing and potentially painful. And here she was, breaking the rules, herself, by sleeping with her one and only client.

She propped herself on the corner of her desk and thought about the problem of workplace romances for a while. They were always high-risk affairs. People got hurt. People got mad.

Some people went looking for revenge.

37

An hour later Ellis thanked Dick Peterson for his assistance, climbed back into the Maserati and drove to a nearby park. Adrenaline snapped and crackled through him. He stopped, opened the door to get some fresh air and called Dave.

"Anything yet?" he asked.

"I finally found the information you wanted on that behavioral modification program at Brackleton," Dave announced. Pride and excitement hummed in his voice. "You were right. Looks like someone tried to delete all the records but that's pretty tough to do once the information goes online. The folks who ran this program did everything online for nearly a year until they shut down."

"Got a list of the names of the professionals involved?"

"Sure. There were only three primary researchers. I tracked them down to see where they are now."

"All gainfully employed?"

"Two of them are. They moved on to academic institutions. They're teaching classes in criminal behavior and sociology. The third person seems to have disappeared. I'm working on it."

"Don't waste any more time on the search," Ellis said evenly. "The third person took a new identity and now works at the Belvedere Center for Sleep Research."

"I assume that was not just a lucky guess?"

"No. It all fits together now. Took me this long to see it because I was a little obsessed, just like Lawson said. I focused on Scargill and figured he was using a few losers from that behavioral modification program when he needed muscle. Never occurred to me that he wasn't the one running things."

"He's still involved in this, though," Dave pointed out.

"Yes. But either way, he's not working alone. He's had a lot of help, right from the start."

Isabel turned away from the window of her small office, unable to shake off the certainty that had settled on her. She took out her phone and called Ellis's number. He answered on the first ring.

"I was just about to call you," he said in a cold, dangerous voice. "Where are you?"

"In my office." She frowned. "Why?"

"Get out of there. I don't want you to be alone, not even in your office. Go hang out in the lobby or the café, someplace where there are a lot of people around. I'm just leaving LA now. I'll be there in about two hours. A little less if the fog isn't bad."

A chill slithered down her spine. "Did you find Scargill?"

"No. I found out who's working with him, though."

"That's what I was calling about," she said quickly. "Remember I told you that in my dream there was someone standing behind Randolph Belvedere but I couldn't see a face? I think I know who the person is —"

The door of the office opened, interrupting her.

Amelia Netley walked into the room. She was dressed in an apron emblazoned with the logo of a local floral shop. Her red hair was bound up in a scarf

She had a gun in her hand.

"Hello, Isabel." Amelia smiled her very bright, very shallow smile. "I assume you're talking to Cutler? Give me the phone."

Isabel hesitated, so cold now she could barely feel the phone in her numb fingers.

"Give it to me." A strange look flashed in Amelia's eyes.

"Do what she says," Ellis said softly in Isabel's ear. "It's okay. Remember, she needs you."

Isabel tossed the phone to Amelia, who caught it quite deftly in her free hand. She did not take her attention off Isabel when she spoke to Ellis.

"Hello, Ellis. You remember me. You knew me as Dr. Maureen Sage when I worked at Frey-Salter. You'll never know what a shock it was to see you in the hallway at the center this morning. It was just dumb luck that I happened to spot you first and managed to avoid you. I realized at once, though, that I had no choice but to move very quickly."

There was a short, tense pause. Isabel could not hear what Ellis was saying to Amelia but she could see that Amelia did not like it.

"That's bullshit and you know it as well as I do," Amelia said, suddenly violently furious. "When this is over Lawson will be finished. Do you hear me? *Finished.*"

There was a freakish stillness following the outburst. No one moved. Isabel was pretty sure that, on the other end of the connection, Ellis was not saying a word.

In the next moment Amelia regained control just as quickly as she had lost it, her face smoothing back into an attractive facade that belied the gun in her hand.

Oh, boy, talk about mood swings, Isabel thought.

"Now then, if you want to keep your little dreamer alive," Amelia said, sounding calm and in control again, "you will do exactly what you're told. I know precisely where you are because before I left the center today I put a GPS bug on your precious Maserati. I am tracking every move of that car. I'm sure you could find the locator given enough time, but time is one of the things you no longer have, Cutler. Start driving back to Roxanna Beach. If you're not precisely where I tell you to be two hours from now, your irritating little dreamer will be dead five minutes later."

38

Ellis let the Maserati have its head when he reached the freeway. *This is it,* he thought. *Always wondered what my worst nightmare would be like. Now I know.*

He intended to use the same route back to Roxanna Beach that he had used earlier in the day to drive to the center. It was a mix of freeways and old roads designed to avoid the centers of towns and other congested areas.

He forced himself to concentrate on his driving and on making plans. Isabel would be safe at least until he got there. Amelia would not risk killing her until she was certain that he was in her control. He was just beginning to put together the pieces of the puzzle that would tell him why Amelia had risked snatching Isabel but the outline of the big picture was finally starting to take shape. Should have seen it three months ago.

He punched out Dave's number.

"What's happening?" Dave demanded.

"She's got Isabel."

"She kidnapped her right out of Kyler headquarters?" Dave was stunned.

"Amelia Netley, aka Maureen Sage, doesn't have any problem with taking a few risks."

"Why grab Isabel?"

"She says she'll release Isabel unharmed in exchange for me."

"You believe her?" Dave asked, incredulous.

"No. But that's another issue. I'll deal with it later. Right now I'm working on the fact that Amelia has given me a two-hour window to get to Roxanna Beach. That's just barely enough time to do it within the legal speed limit, assuming the fog isn't too bad."

"You're not going to worry a whole lot about the speed limit, are you?"

"There's a complication. She's got a GPS bug hidden somewhere on my car."

"Bad news. With one of those gadgets she can track you every inch of the way in real time right on her personal phone."

"I'm familiar with the technology," Ellis said dryly.

"Sorry. Just meant that making like a Formula One driver to buy yourself some time won't do you any good. She'll know if you get to Roxanna Beach ahead of schedule. Hell, she'll know where you are at any given moment. She'll know if you even stop to take a leak."

"Like I said, it's a complication."

"What about Scargill? Any sign of him?"

"Got a hunch he's doped to the gills on an experimental dream-enhancing drug called CZ-149."

"That rings a bell," Dave said. "I think Katherine may have mentioned it."

"It was developed at Frey-Salter under the direction of Dr. Maureen Sage, aka Amelia Netley. She's an expert on psychopharmaceutical drugs. The stuff was probably based on whatever formula she used on the inmates at Brackleton. Lawson okayed some tests on it but halted the experiments because of the side effects. Later he transferred Sage out of the agency. She's the woman he had the affair with. She was not a happy camper when she left. In hindsight, I think it's probably safe to say she was seriously pissed."

"What are the side effects of this CZ-149?" Dave asked in a subdued voice.

"I never tried it, personally. One of the first things I learned working for Lawson was never to volunteer for any of his damned experiments. But I heard that the CZ-149 makes it difficult for Level Five subjects to distinguish the boundaries between their dreams and waking reality."

"That could get a little wild."

"I'm told the confusion can last for hours. The stronger the dose, the longer it messes up your mind. Wouldn't be surprised if that's how Amelia is controlling Scargill. He may have been so desperate to regain his Level Five dreaming capability after he was injured that he's allowing her to inject him with the crap."

"What are you going to do? Call the cops?"

"I can't take the risk. Amelia would kill Isabel in a heartbeat if she thinks she's been double-crossed. But if I can get to Roxanna Beach ahead of schedule and without Amelia knowing that I'm in town, I might be able to do something before she realizes that I'm in the neighborhood. But I'm going to need your help."

"You don't need to ask twice. What do you want me to do?"

Ellis told him.

"Oh, man," Dave whispered, awestruck. "I get to drive the Maserati?"

39

"I know what your tsunami dream means," Isabel said quietly. She sat on the floor in the corner of the old, tumble-down concession stand, her knees curled under her, hands tied behind her back.

Amelia had forced her into the back of the florist's van at gunpoint. There had been no opportunity to shout for help or to attract attention because the van was parked in a little-used section of the parking lot behind the main building.

There had been an additional complication in the shape of a twitchy, mean, slightly crazy-looking little man in a black knit cap, black sweatshirt and black cargo pants. She assumed he was another graduate of the Brackleton Correctional Facility's experiment in behavior modification. His name was Yolland and he seemed to think he was on a mission to thwart the actions of an agent who worked for a global corporation that was intent on polluting the environment.

The fog had grown thicker and heavier

as evening approached. Yolland had driven the van cautiously along the winding road to the abandoned amusement park on the lonely bluffs outside Roxanna Beach.

Amelia had walked Isabel through the gate in the high, chain-link fence. Once inside the grounds Isabel was steered through the eerie, foggy shadows created by the rows of sagging, boarded-up concession booths, arcades and dark, looming thrill rides.

It was after five. The shutters closing the opening at the front of the stand had been partially pulled aside. There was enough gray, misty light left in the day to illuminate the shadowy interior. She could make out the faded image of a corn dog on the back wall.

A tall man in his early twenties with a thin, bearded face and haunted eyes had been waiting inside the concession stand. Vincent Scargill looked even more jittery and unstable than Yolland. Either that or he was feverish, Isabel thought. There was a film of sweat on his brow.

"I still say we don't need her," Scargill had muttered, wiping his forehead with his sleeve.

"She will ensure that Cutler remains cooperative." Amelia had checked the screen of her small phone where she was watching the progress of Ellis's car. "He's making good time. Should be here in another hour and a half. Keep an eye on Isabel. I'm going to make sure Yolland is in position. I also want to check on some of the other arrangements."

"What other arrangements?" Scargill had asked, blotting more perspiration off his brow. "It's supposed to be a simple trade. You said that as soon as Cutler hands over the new version of the CZ-149, we're out of here."

"Take it easy," Amelia soothed. "I'll handle the details. Just don't let our major asset get away while I'm gone. She's the only thing we have to trade for the meds."

"Okay, okay," Scargill muttered. He looked at Isabel with the eyes of a man fast approaching his limits. "She's not going anywhere."

The moment Amelia had left, Isabel tossed Scargill her one and only lure. *I can tell you the meaning of your dreams.*

Scargill paced back and forth in front of the arcade booth counter, a lean, lanky, hunched shadow in the darkened interior. He wasn't just ill, she realized. There was an air of despair and desperation about him. He reminded her of a junkie who had gone too long between fixes. He held a pistol loosely in one hand.

"What can you tell me about my tsunami dream?" he rasped in a hoarse voice.

"Do you know who I am?" she asked gently.

"Yeah, sure." He made an impatient motion with the gun. "The doc told me you were Belvedere's special Level Five dream analyst."

"That's right. Martin Belvedere showed a portion of your dream report to me. He wanted my take on it." She paused. "I'm sure Amelia must have told you that I'm an expert on extreme dreams."

"Some expert." His mouth twisted. "Are you the one who told Belvedere that the red tsunami is a blocking image? A symbol of my inability to access the Level Five state? Thanks for nothing. You think I couldn't figure out that much for myself? I know I'm blocked, damnit. I wanted Belvedere to tell me how to get past it. The CZ-149 isn't working."

"I keep telling people that I do my best work when I have context. I need to know something about the dreamer and the situation in order to provide the most accurate interpretation. But Dr. B. wouldn't tell me anything about you or the circumstances surrounding your dream." She broke off, making certain she had his full attention before adding, "Now, of course, I know a great deal more so I can do a better job. It would be helpful, though, to have a few additional details."

"What the hell do you need?" Scargill demanded, wiping more sweat off his face. "My social security number?"

"Can I assume that your gateway dream involves water?"

Scargill hesitated. He looked as if he were trying hard to focus on her face. Interested at last.

"Yeah," he admitted. "I usually dive down to get into it. But now all I see when I try to enter the dream is that damned red tsunami waiting to drown me if I even make an attempt to access a Level Five state."

"I understand that you suffered some sort of head injury and that it affected your dreaming."

He swore again, angry and frustrated. "My wound healed. Supposedly everything's back to normal inside my head. Why can't I dream the way I did before?"

"Stay with me here, I'm still gathering context. I got the feeling from what you said to Amelia that you think Ellis can provide you with a new and improved version of a dream-enhancing drug?"

"That's right." The pistol in his hand shook ominously.

"You do realize that Amelia is a liar and a killer," Isabel said very calmly. "You can't trust anything she says."

"That's not true. The doc is trying to help me."

"Actually, I suspect she's setting you up."

"Bullshit."

"She doesn't intend for any of us — you, Ellis, me or even Yolland — to survive the night."

"Shut up," Scargill hissed. "Stop talking about the doc. You don't know anything. She saved my life that day at the cabin."

"Only because she concocted a new plan to use you. That's what Amelia does, you see. She uses people to get what she wants."

"I told you to stop talking about her." Scargill resumed his restless pacing. "Tell me about my dream."

"I'm doing my best." She drew a deep breath and let it out slowly. "Still trying to pick up some context. Tell me, when you consulted with Martin Belvedere, did you inform him that you were getting regular doses of the CZ-149?"

"No."

"Well, that certainly explains why neither he nor I could get a handle on your tsunami dream."

Scargill turned and took a threatening step toward her, his desperation and fear palpable forces in the shadows. "Tell me about my dream, damnit."

"Okay."

The fog was so thick now that Amelia could no longer see the parking lot beyond the chain-link fence. The heavy, gray mist was eating up the daylight before the sun had even set. She hadn't counted on the weather being such a major issue tonight. But it wasn't like she'd had a lot of choice, she thought angrily. When she'd seen Ellis in the hallway outside Belvedere's office she knew she had to move and move quickly.

How had he put it together? she wondered for the hundredth time. She really would like to know if she made a mistake. She made it a point to learn from her mistakes. That was just good scientific procedure, and she was nothing if not an excellent scientist. Brilliant, actually. Her parents, both researchers in the field of genetics, had set out to create a perfect child. They had recognized her talents in her early childhood and made every effort to hone and shape them.

She had been sent to the most advanced schools and supplied with special tutors. Success and perfection were demanded at every turn and she tried her best to meet that demand, no matter what it cost her to do so. She sacrificed everything — toys, friends, romance — to achieve the goals her parents had ordained for her. After all, they had made it clear from the beginning that they could only love a perfect, successful child.

Eventually, of course, she had been forced to kill her mother and her father. There had been no choice, really. It turned out that no one could achieve absolute perfection every time. Inevitably, there were setbacks along the way. The day she graduated from college she decided she could no longer tolerate the cold disdain and disgust with which her mother and father met her occasional failures. So she got rid of them.

But even though they were long gone, she could still hear their cruel rebukes when things went wrong.

"Yolland?" She stopped near the gate.

"I'm ready for the bastards." His voice came from inside one of the ticket booths that faced the entrance. "They think they can destroy the environment and get away with it. But they're going to learn a lesson tonight, I promise you that much."

She stifled a groan of disgust. Her roster of ex-con subjects from the program at Brackleton was going to be short by one more name before this night was finished, and good riddance. Working with these guys was always problematic but they did have their uses. She reminded herself that it had been extremely fortunate that two of them, Albert Gibbs and Yolland, happened to live in the Los Angeles area and had been available to her on such short notice.

"You're a real hero, Yolland," she said. "Not many people would have the courage to do what you're doing. Are the fuses ready?"

"All set."

"Remember, wait for my signal."

"Got it."

"So why can't I get past that red tsunami?" Scargill asked, anguished.

"I don't think you're going to like hearing my analysis, but here it is," Isabel said gently. "I believe what I'm about to tell you is accurate because I've had some experience interpreting the dreams of a few of Lawson's people who tried CZ-149. That red tsunami that's blocking your gateway dream?"

"Yeah?"

"It's your dreaming mind letting you know that you can't access your gateway dream because of the poison flowing through your bloodstream. That's why the water is red, you see. It's the color of blood."

He stared at her, shaking more violently. "What poison? What are you saying?"

"The CZ-149. It doesn't enhance Level Five dreaming, it interferes with it. I'll bet that Amelia is giving you a fairly stiff dose on a regular basis to keep you from accessing your gateway dream."

"That makes no sense. Why would she do that?"

"So she can manipulate you more easily. From what I've heard, the drug has a hypnotic effect on Level Fives. It makes them highly vulnerable to suggestion and influence. If Amelia allows you to dream normally again — heck, if she even allows you to *think* clearly again — you would figure out that something is very wrong and start asking awkward questions. She can't afford to let that happen."

"That's not true. It can't be true. Why would she rescue me and then try to keep me from dreaming?"

"If I'm right, and I'm pretty sure I am, she's got two goals," Isabel said. "The first is to get control of her very own lab. She's accomplished that, more or less. The second is to destroy Lawson and his operation. Tonight she intends to use all of us — you, me, Ellis and even poor Yolland — to do that. What's more, she's going to make sure we're all dead by morning because she can't afford to leave any of us alive."

"You're wrong," Scargill snapped. "This is all about proving to Jack Lawson that Cutler has gone rogue. Lawson trusts that bastard. He won't listen to the facts. Cutler has convinced him that I was the one who went bad and kidnapped and killed a bunch of people. That's why I'm playing dead. I've got to stay out of sight until we get Cutler and the proof we need to show Lawson."

"She lied to you, Vincent. I told you, that's what she does. She lies. She is also very flexible." Isabel paused, gathering her thoughts, aware that she had only one chance to try to convince him. "Let me go back to the start. Amelia's first scheme involved seducing Lawson in an attempt to gain control over him and, through him, the Frey-Salter dream labs. That plan failed when Lawson ended their affair and transferred her to another agency."

"But —"

"Ever resourceful, Amelia promptly came up with Plan B. She decided to go after a privately owned sleep research lab and in essence, set herself up in competition with Lawson. But to be successful, she knew she would need at least a couple of Level Fives. They aren't easy to find, as you well know. So she set out to steal one from Lawson."

Scargill leaned heavily against the counter, clearly struggling to keep himself upright.

"That would be me?" he asked, his disbelief clear.

"Yes. She suckered you into thinking that you were solving all those kidnappings on your own and then she played on your pride and sense of competitiveness, feeding your ego. When the time was right, she was going to convince you to resign from Lawson's operation on the grounds that you were underappreciated."

"And then put me to work for her?" he concluded skeptically.

"Uh-huh. After she got kicked out of Lawson's agency, Amelia set her sights on gaining control of the Belvedere Center for Sleep Research. She knew enough about the facility to realize that if she got it, she would also get a second Level Five."

"You?"

"Yep. With the two of us, plus her own talents, she could give Lawson some major competition, maybe even bring him down. She could become the most important researcher in the field of extreme dreams. Who knows what she could accomplish? But there was a major problem."

"Cutler." Scargill breathed deeply and tried to straighten his trembling shoulders. "The doc said he was jealous of me."

"He wasn't jealous, but he also wasn't buying your brilliant dream sleuthing. Amelia knew he was suspicious, and after a year at Lawson's agency, she also knew that he wasn't going to give up and go away. She realized that she had to get rid of him before he discovered that she had orchestrated the kidnappings and murdered a few people in the process."

"No," Scargill muttered. "No, damnit."

"It wasn't going to be easy. She was well aware that Lawson and Ellis had been friends for a long time. If anything happened to Ellis, Lawson was sure to conduct an investigation. She decided to have Ellis die in the line of duty."

"If you're talking about that day at the survivalists' compound when everything went to hell . . ."

"She staged that whole event knowing that Ellis would recognize another suspicious kidnapping and try to intervene," Isabel said quickly. "She intended for him to die in a firefight with the people at the compound, even if she had to pull the trigger, herself. Who would know the difference afterward?"

Scargill was shivering more violently now. He huddled in on himself, gun clutched in his hand. "I don't understand. Damnit, I can't think. There's something wrong with me. I've got a splitting headache. *I can't even think straight.*"

"Things went wrong that day at the compound when the ammo shed exploded. Amelia tried to kill Ellis but failed. You, her only major asset at that point, were badly injured."

"The explosion," Scargill whispered. He rubbed his temples with one hand.

"Amelia grabbed you and got you to the hospital. Later she changed all the computer records to make it appear that you had died. Then she took you, along with plenty of stolen CZ-149 to control you, and split for California. There she seduced Randolph Belvedere and plotted his father's death."

"Stop it." Scargill raised the nose of the pistol. "I don't want to hear any more. You're trying to confuse me."

She had nothing to lose, Isabel thought. All she could do was keep talking and hope that some of what she was saying penetrated the haze that the CZ-149 had created in Scargill's brain.

"Amelia achieved her second goal, more or less. Through Randolph Belvedere, she got control of the Belvedere Center for Sleep Research," she said. "But things went wrong again when Randolph fired me. That's Amelia's big problem, you see. She's brilliant but she keeps miscalculating because she doesn't understand other people's motivations. She assumes everyone is driven by the same things that drive her, but she's wrong. I think that's probably making her crazy."

Scargill looked at her with a strange expression on his face. "Maybe you're the one who's crazy."

"Always a possibility, of course."

Amelia checked the screen of her phone.

The tiny moving dot that was the Maserati was slowing. Angrily, she hit the redial button.

"You'd better keep your speed up, Cutler. You've only got an hour and twenty minutes left. At the rate you're going now, you'll be late, and you know what that means.

"The fog is getting worse," Ellis said evenly. "I can't see five feet in front of the car. I'm using a back road to avoid traffic. That means occasional stop signs. In fact, there's one coming up and I just passed a police cruiser. I've got to stop. Can't afford to get pulled over for a ticket."

"It's your choice, of course," she said sweetly, watching the blip on the screen halt. "But if you're late, you know the penalty."

"I won't be late." Ellis cut the connection.

She hated that he felt in a position to treat her so rudely. Nobody gave her the respect she deserved. She started to punch redial but paused when she saw that the dot was moving again, faster than it had been a moment ago. That was a good sign. Cutler was running scared. She liked that. It was very satisfying.

But not nearly as satisfying as watching Lawson go down.

* * *

Ellis parked in the trees, collected the gym bag and went the rest of the way on foot. He had thirty minutes until the deadline. There was still a little light left but the Roxanna Beach Amusement World was enclosed in an impenetrable gray fog. The only sound was the steady pounding of the unseen surf. It echoed eerily in the mist, creating a disorienting sensation. With luck it would mask any noise he was forced to make.

He approached the amusement park from a point that was farthest from the main entrance, chose a spot that was concealed by the wall of an aged restroom and went to work with the wire

Amelia checked the dot on the phone screen again and hit the redial.

"What do you want now?" Cutler asked in low tones.

"You're pushing the envelope," she said, her anger building again. "You're at least thirty minutes away from town. If I were you, I'd worry."

"I told you, the fog —"

This time she cut the connection before he did, taking a great deal of fierce pleasure in the small, savage punch of the *end* button.

She had made the right decision, she thought. They were all badly flawed. It had become obvious in the past few weeks that Scargill's basic temperament wasn't going to change. He still wanted to be a hero, another Ellis Cutler, for crying out loud. She couldn't work with such a major personality defect.

Isabel Wright was another mistake. She hadn't turned out to be a meek, dithery little dreamer who would do as she was told.

As for Cutler, well, she had known all along that he wasn't going to stop being a problem until he was dead.

The only answer was to get rid of all of them and start from scratch. With the resources of the Belvedere Center for Sleep Research, she would be able to find her own dream talent.

Meanwhile, if everything went as planned, tonight she would not only get rid of her mistakes, she would start the first smoldering embers that would eventually burn down Jack Lawson's precious empire.

At the far end of the park, Ellis dropped the phone back into the pocket of his windbreaker, making sure it was still set to vibrate, not ring, and continued working his way through the eerie landscape. The hulking shapes of the long-silent rides loomed like the ruins of an alien civilization in the mist.

He was fairly sure that Amelia had called him from somewhere near the cliff side of the park. He had heard the surf quite clearly in the background. In addition, although he had listened closely, he had not heard her voice except through the phone. That meant she was not in the immediate vicinity. He had been careful to keep his voice low and to muffle his phone with the thick canvas of the gym bag.

First things first, he thought, moving past an old bumper car platform. Amelia had probably set a guard, either Scargill or another one of her behavior modification program success stories. Whoever he was, he would be somewhere near the entrance to the park.

Yolland heard the footsteps on the pavement behind the ticket booth. A jolt of alarm went through him. Automatically, he reached for the nearest fuse. Then he realized that whoever he was, the guy was approaching openly from the interior of the park.

Scargill. The doc had sent her doped-up pal to check on him. Rage replaced alarm.

Didn't she know he was a professional? He didn't need anyone checking up on him, especially not some dope fiend.

He leaned out of the booth.

"Tell the doc I said for you to take care of your job and I'll take care of mine —" He stopped when he realized he could not see Scargill in the heavy fog. "Where are you?"

He thought he heard a slight sound behind him but by the time it registered it was too late.

There was searing pain at the back of his head and then he plummeted into a bottomless pit of night.

Ellis left the guard bound and gagged inside the ticket booth. He had twenty minutes left. He wondered if Amelia would call again. If she did, he would not be able to risk answering the phone because she or Scargill might be close enough to hear him talking and realize he was inside the park.

He made his way along the back of a row of empty arcade and concession booths, listening intently for the telltale murmur of voices. He knew Isabel. If they hadn't gagged her, she would be handing out plenty of free advice to Scargill or Amelia.

But he did not hear her as he moved

among the rows of shuttered arcades and stands. That silence scared him more than anything else that had happened so far.

He turned a corner at the end of a line of food stalls and stopped suddenly when he realized the rear door of one of the booths was partially open, sagging on its hinges. He watched for a moment and thought he saw a shifting in the shadows inside.

Someone was in the booth.

He had fifteen minutes left when he switched on the phone in the pocket of his windbreaker and kicked open the sagging door at the back of the stand.

"Freeze, Scargill."

Scargill had his back to him, keeping watch at the front of the stand. He jerked at the sound of Ellis's voice and then went very still.

Ellis stepped into the booth and took in the interior in one quick glance. Despair knifed through him. His worst nightmare had just come true. Scargill was alone. There was no sign of Isabel.

"So you managed to pull off one of your tricks after all," Scargill said in a dull, flat tone. "Why am I not surprised? But it doesn't matter. You lose, pal."

"Put the gun down and move away from it."

"Sure. Whatever." Scargill obeyed.

When the gun clattered loudly on the counter Ellis realized that Scargill was shaking badly.

"Where is she?" Ellis asked. He was in a place that was so cold and so impossibly bleak nothing else mattered. He knew he could kill without any hesitation at all from this realm. He *wanted* to kill.

Something of what he was feeling must have showed on his face because Scargill looked both ill and scared. He had to try twice before he could speak.

"Hey, hey, take it easy, Cutler."

Ellis raised the pistol two inches. "Where is she?"

"Right here," Amelia said.

She appeared outside the booth, standing on the other side of the counter. Ellis realized she must have been hiding in the stand across the way. She had Isabel. Amelia gripped her forearm in one hand. With the other she pointed a pistol at Isabel's head.

"I don't know how you did it, Cutler. According to the data from the GPS indicator, you're still ten miles away. But when I couldn't raise Yolland a few minutes ago, I realized you were probably inside the park. You always were unpredictable."

Ellis allowed himself to breathe again. Isabel was still alive. Her hands were bound behind her back but she looked amazingly calm and composed and she was still alive.

"Hello, Ellis," she said quietly. "I knew you'd get here in time."

"Shut up," Amelia ordered. She kept the pistol aimed at Isabel's temple while she smiled ferociously at Ellis. "Drop the gun."

"Better do as she says," Scargill said. With a trembling hand, he picked up the pistol he had placed on the counter and pointed it at Ellis.

Ellis looked at Amelia. "You're going to kill Isabel anyway, aren't you?" He shrugged. "I might as well take you out at the same time."

Amelia looked baffled by that logic. "Vincent will shoot you dead before you can make a move."

"No he won't," Isabel said quietly, simply, her eyes never leaving Ellis's face.

Amelia laughed. "Of course he will. He understands that he needs me, don't you, Vincent? I'm the only one who can give you the right dose of the CZ-149."

"Scargill is fast," Ellis said. "He can probably take me out. But you will be dead before that happens so it won't make much difference to you. Your only hope is to put down the gun."

Scargill gave a raw, weary, utterly humorless laugh. "Looks like we've got ourselves a three-way standoff."

"Looks like," Ellis agreed. He raised his voice slightly. "This would be a very good time."

"No." Amelia took a step back. Her face worked with fury as she struggled to come up with a way to get out of the impasse. She yanked Isabel with her. "No, you're not going to do this to me, Cutler. I'm not going to let you win, not after all I've gone through to get this far. I'm leaving now and I'm taking Isabel with me. Don't move. Do you hear me? Don't move or she dies."

Amelia-Maureen was fraying fast around the edges, Ellis thought.

Clank, clank, clank.

The muffled rumble of a heavy, rusty chain lift shuddered across the park. Simultaneously a spiraling maze of small yellow and white lights lit up the foggy twilight. The majority of the bulbs that festooned the old roller coaster had broken or burned out long ago but there were enough left to illuminate the carcass of the old thrill ride in a strange, ghostly glow.

"*What?*" Amelia's voice was shrill with rage and bewilderment. Clearly unnerved, she jerked her head around to stare over her shoulder at the strange apparition that had appeared. For an instant she seemed confused and distracted by the clanking noise and the otherworldly light.

Down, Isabel, Ellis thought. *For God's sake, get down.*

As though she had read his mind, Isabel was already in motion, seizing the opportunity. She dropped like a stone to the ground, vanishing from sight on the other side of the counter. Amelia reflexively let go of her arm rather than be pulled off balance.

"*Damn you, Cutler.*" Amelia whipped back, gun swinging toward Ellis.

He pulled the trigger at the same instant that Vincent Scargill did.

Amelia Netley collapsed without a sound.

The roar of the guns filled the night, louder than the clanking of the roller coaster.

Ellis watched Scargill.

"Take it easy," Scargill said. He put the gun down very carefully on the counter. Then he wiped his forehead. "Thanks. Wasn't sure if you believed Isabel a minute ago when she said that I wouldn't kill you."

Ellis lowered his pistol. "Amelia didn't believe her but I did."

Isabel scrambled to her feet. "Are you two okay?"

"Yes." Relying on his good shoulder, Ellis planted one hand on the counter and vaulted through the opening to get to her.

Scargill followed him, moving much more slowly and awkwardly. He went to stand looking down at the very still body on the pavement. A visible shudder went through him.

Farrell appeared from the dark, misty space between a teacup ride and the carousel.

"Everything okay?" he asked, checking faces anxiously. "I heard you give me the order to start the roller coaster but then I heard two shots."

"Farrell," Isabel whispered.

"Your timing was perfect," Ellis assured him, switching off his phone.

The *clank, clank, clanking* stopped.

Ellis listened to the silence and felt the breathless anticipation that meant the roller coaster train had reached the summit of the first, high lift hill and now hung there waiting for the irresistible force of gravity to take effect.

Isabel threw herself into his arms. He wrapped her close and hard against him.

There was a grinding, metallic screech of rusted track and ancient steel wheels as the cars went over the top. Or maybe that was his heart, Ellis thought, breaking free of the dark place deep inside where he had kept it safe all these years.

There was a dazzling, intoxicating *whoosh* and a thrilling rush of excitement as the roller coaster cars plunged into the first, glorious turn.

Isabel tightened her arms around him.

No going back now.

40

Isabel flopped back against the pillows, exhausted. "I can't believe I've got three men sleeping under my roof tonight. This is definitely a personal best for me in terms of my social life."

Ellis came out of the bathroom, a towel wrapped around his lean waist, his hair damp from the shower.

"But only one man sleeping in your bed," he reminded her.

She smiled, enjoying the sight of him standing in front of her in her bedroom; relishing the knowledge that he was safe.

"True," she said.

"Could have packed Dave and Vince off to a motel," Ellis said, untying the towel.

"Not after all they've been through. Dave is dealing with the closure that he got tonight regarding his sister's death, and poor Vincent is still ill from the effects of the CZ-149. I couldn't send them away to a lonely motel room. Besides, they both needed you."

"Me?" He pulled aside the covers and

got in next to her. "I didn't do anything except tell them what to say to the cops and give them both a couple of beers after we got them back here."

"You talked to them." She turned on her side and propped herself up on an elbow. "You let them talk. That was important. You're a role model for both of them whether you like it or not."

"Not," Ellis grumbled. He leaned back against the pillows and put one hand under his head. "Got no training as a role model and no aptitude for the job, either."

"*Au contraire.*" Smiling, she bent her head and kissed his mouth. "You're a natural. No wonder Lawson is always after you to return to Frey-Salter to do special seminars for the new recruits."

"Huh." He looked at his watch, which he still wore, and sat up again, shoving back the covers. "Speaking of Lawson, I'd better turn off my phone and yours, too. I know him. As soon as he's finished doing damage control on that end, he'll call me back, wanting to ask more questions. We won't get any sleep at all."

The official story had been put together by Ellis and Lawson via a phone call while they all waited for the emergency vehicles to respond to the scene at the amusement park. It was simple and reasonably straightforward: While employed at Frey-Salter, Inc., Dr. Amelia Netley, using the name Maureen Sage, had engaged in high-level corporate espionage. She stole some very dangerous experimental sleeping medications. She was also suspected of killing Katherine Ralston, presumably because Katherine had stumbled onto the scheme.

Following the murder, Maureen disappeared, assumed her new identity as Dr. Amelia Netley and landed a position at the Belvedere Center for Sleep Research. Ellis and Vincent Scargill, agents of the corporate security firm Mapstone Investigations, had been sent out to gather evidence. Isabel had assisted in the investigation.

Tonight, fearful that the investigation was closing in on her, Amelia kidnapped Isabel with the goal of exchanging her for an airline ticket and guaranteed safe passage out of the country. Ellis and Vincent, together with the help of Dave and Farrell, had staged a rescue operation.

"Think the local cops will buy that story you and Lawson concocted?" Isabel asked, watching Ellis turn off his phone.

"Sure. It's the easiest way to clean up the mess."

She wrinkled her nose. "So much easier to let Mapstone Investigations, with its murky connection to the feds, take responsibility."

"You got it."

"Think Lawson can keep his agency out of it?"

"Lawson has managed to keep himself and the work he does at Frey-Salter out of the public eye for over thirty years. What happened at the amusement park tonight is just a small glitch as far as he's concerned. Could have been a lot worse and he knows it."

He turned off the ringer on the phone beside the bed, hit the lights and got back under the covers.

Unable to suppress another of the little quivery sensations that had plagued her since the events in the amusement park, Isabel drew her knees up under the sheets and wrapped her arms around them.

"Ellis?"

"Yeah?" He reached for her, pulling her down against him. "What's wrong? You're shivering."

"I feel the same way I did after we found Gavin Hardy's body. Exhausted but very, very wired."

"You're not the only one."

"The excitement doesn't seem to have affected Dave and Vincent. I think they were asleep before I turned out the hall lights."

"They're young," Ellis growled. "At their age, they can sleep under any circumstances. Give 'em a few years. That'll change."

She smiled against his shoulder. "You're not that much older than they are."

"Sometimes it feels like centuries." He stroked her, his hand gliding down her side to her hip. "I have, however, discovered one thing that makes me feel about twenty-three again." He nibbled on her ear. "Hell, even better than I ever did at twenty-three."

"Really?" She curled her fingers in the crisp, curling hair on his chest. "What's that?"

"You." He tightened his hold on her. "In fact, you make me feel a lot of things I had forgotten I could feel. Things I wasn't sure I wanted to feel. I love you, Tango Dancer."

"Ellis."

Joy, as radiant and sparkling as the rarest of jewels, shimmered through her. It drove out the cold residue left behind by the violent events of the evening. She reached up to catch his hard face between her palms. "I fell in love with you months ago, soon after I started analyzing your dream reports. Couldn't you tell?"

"I hoped all that advice you tacked onto your reports meant that you felt something. Why do you think I moved out to California?"

"You moved out to the West Coast because of *me?*"

He smiled wryly. "I had a long-term plan to get to know you, see if you felt the same way about me that I felt about you. I wanted to find out if I could be part of your life."

She was delighted. "You planned to court me?"

He cleared his throat. "I never thought of my plan as a courtship. Not exactly."

"Of course not," she said, dismissing that clarification with an airy wave. "You were probably thinking in terms of an affair, right?"

"It did cross my mind," he admitted.

"You told yourself that you would have an affair with me because anything more than that involved serious risk," she said gently. "You've spent a lot of time and effort avoiding that kind of risk because you learned long ago what it's like to experience a great loss. Anyone who went through the kind of trauma that you went through when you were twelve is bound to be very, very careful."

He looked at her for a long moment. "When you love, you take risks."

"Yes," she said simply. "But we both know how to do that, don't we?"

"Yes." He seemed vaguely amazed by that simple observation. He closed his hand more snugly around her waist. "As I said, I had a plan. But I got distracted."

"Your shoulder." She traced the wound with her fingertips. "I know you went through a lot of pain —"

"The shoulder was the least of my problems," he said. Moonlight glinted on his cheekbones, casting the rest of his face into deep shadow. "The real issue was Lawson and his growing conviction that I had developed a bizarre fixation with finding a dead man. I was starting to wonder if he was right. Maybe I had gone off the deep end. Then you got fired and took off for Roxanna Beach and everything started to change."

She smiled and arched beneath his hand, loving the scent of him. "I was waiting for you, you know."

"Just like I've been waiting for you all my life."

He moved on top of her and kissed her until she stopped shivering from the aftermath of violence and trembled with passion instead.

Afterward, she felt Ellis relax as if his climax had turned off a switch somewhere inside him. She was glad the heated lovemaking had proved to be the tonic he needed to allow him to sleep. Unfortunately it did not have the same effect on her.

She closed her eyes, willing herself to sink into oblivion.

Nothing happened.

She opened her eyes.

"Mmmph?" Ellis tightened his arms around her to stop her wriggling. "What's wrong?"

"I can't sleep. I know he's out there. I can feel him breathing."

"Who? Scargill? Dave? Forget 'em. They're fine."

"No, not them. Better let me up. He's not going to go away. I can't stand the thought of him just sitting there and he knows it."

Reluctantly, Ellis released her. She pushed the covers aside, got to her feet, went to the door and opened it.

Sphinx was on the other side. He rose,

stalked past her into the room, heaved himself up onto the bed, settled at Ellis's feet and went to sleep.

Isabel got back into bed.

"Everything okay now?" Ellis asked.

She smiled into the darkness, loving the feel of his arm wrapped around her and the heat of his body enveloping hers.

"Like a dream come true," she said.

41

"I found Maureen Sage, aka Amelia Netley's personal dream log in her car last night." Ellis lounged on one of the stools in front of the kitchen counter, one hand curled around a mug of freshly brewed green tea. "Got a chance to read some of it this morning. Turns out she was a Level Five herself, but she kept it a secret because she thought it would give her an edge."

"That was the doc, all right," Vincent muttered. "She was always looking for an angle."

Ellis nodded. "Amelia-Maureen was fascinated with what she saw as the potential power of extreme dreaming. She was obsessed with her plan to get control of Lawson's government funded dream research program. She went to work for him and saw her opportunity when he was at a bad point in his relationship with Beth. She dazzled him for a while with her expertise in psychopharmaceuticals, and seduced him. But in the end he canceled her experiments with CZ-149 and then he canceled their affair."

The kitchen was crowded this morning. Isabel listened to the debriefing with only a small part of her attention. Mostly she was focused on the task of fixing scrambled eggs, toast and soy sausages for three large human males and one big feline of the same gender.

It had seemed so easy at the start, she reflected, cracking the last of a full dozen eggs into a bowl. *I'll just whip up some breakfast. You all just drink your orange juice and tea while I get this on the table. No problem. Be ready in fifteen minutes. Hah.*

It wasn't until she realized that between them, Dave, Ellis and Vincent were going to go through a full jug of orange juice that she knew she might be in for more than she had bargained for when she volunteered to cook breakfast. Good thing she had bought an extra carton of eggs and a large loaf of sourdough bread in anticipation of feeding Ellis.

The men took up a lot of space. They did not simply sit or stand, rather they lounged, leaned or sprawled around the counter. The fourth male, Sphinx, watched the proceedings from his perch atop the wide windowsill. He did not seem perturbed by the commotion. Isabel knew that was because he had decided to tolerate the new arrivals.

She was relieved to see that Vincent looked a little healthier this morning. He was still very wan and washed-out from the effects of the CZ-149 withdrawal but he was no longer shivering uncontrollably. Dave was quiet and a little sad but he seemed calmer, as if he had begun to come to terms with his grief

"According to the dream log," Ellis continued, "Amelia-Maureen couldn't understand why Lawson ended the affair. After all, she was several years younger and a lot prettier than Beth. In addition, she was very, very smart and she and Lawson were both dedicated to the same kind of research. They made a perfect team in her view. She just could not deal with the fact that he did not want her."

"It was right after the affair with Lawson ended that she went to work on me," Vincent muttered. "She set up those special kidnap cases and used her knowledge of Lawson's and Beth's operations to make sure they got to me. At the same time, she approached me secretly and started giving me the injections of CZ-149."

Ellis's brows rose. "That stuff had the effect of making you believe your own press, I take it?"

Vincent grimaced. "Along with anything else she told me. But she understood real quick that you were standing in her way, Cutler. Not only were you suspicious about the string of kidnappings I was busily solving so brilliantly, you had Lawson's ear."

Dave downed what had to be half a pint of orange juice and looked at Vincent. "She convinced you that Ellis had gone rogue and that only you could stop him because Lawson refused to see the truth?"

"Like I don't have better things to do with my time than go rogue," Ellis said.

"Don't forget she was giving me regular fixes of that damned dream drug," Vincent said, sounding pained. "She told me I tolerated it well and that it would make me —" He stopped suddenly, flushing.

"An even better dreamer than me?" Ellis drank some tea and lowered the mug. "The only thing that's going to make you as good as me is experience."

"Yeah, well, it sounded like a great idea at the time," Vincent muttered.

"Don't worry, Vincent," Isabel said bracingly. "Ellis told me you are very, very good. Someday you are going to be a legend back at Frey-Salter, too."

Vincent appeared somewhat cheered by that prospect. Ellis looked amused.

Isabel tossed a handful of fresh chopped parsley into the huge mound of creamy scrambled eggs she was preparing. "Sounds like Amelia-Maureen craved what every serious researcher craves, namely unlimited funding and the freedom to conduct her work without interference. And she was prepared to go to any lengths to reach her goals."

"Her notes in the dream log imply that she was, in part, inspired by her work at Brackleton," Ellis said. "She did a lot of her early experiments on the inmates with a primitive version of CZ-149. She discovered that she could control her subjects to a certain extent if she gave them hypnotic suggestions while they were under the influence of the drug. She also found out that the stuff worked best on people who were inclined toward lucid dreaming. She never got any Level Five subjects at the prison, but she got a couple of Threes and a Four. Those experiences made her aware of the potential of the drug."

"How did she learn about Lawson's agency?" Isabel asked.

"She didn't, not at first. But she was well

connected in the world of dream research and she certainly knew about Frey-Salter. She applied for a job after the Brackleton project was shut down, and Lawson grabbed her. After she got her security clearance and found out just what went on at the agency, she was ecstatic."

"Must have looked like a dream job for a while," Isabel said dryly.

"Yeah, but it all came apart after the affair with Lawson ended," Ellis said. "When he transferred her out of the agency, she set out to gain control of the Belvedere Center for Sleep Research. That's when she realized just how useful her old Brackleton subjects would be."

"Those poor men." Isabel sighed. "None of them were very stable. They never stood a chance against her."

"Why was she so determined to keep her identity hidden while she was at the Belvedere Center for Sleep Research?" Dave asked softly.

"Two reasons," Isabel said. "The first was Ellis. She realized that he was going to persist in his investigation of Vincent. She knew that if he turned over enough rocks, he might figure out the connection to one Maureen Sage."

"So she made Maureen disappear and

created a new identity for herself." Vincent grimaced. "She was really good with computers."

"Certainly good enough to get past the rather shallow employment background checks that were the norm at the Belvedere Center for Sleep Research." Isabel poured more tea. "The only people who had to go through serious background checks there were the ones who worked on Lawson's secret projects. Namely me and Dr. B."

Dave wrapped both hands around his mug of tea and studied her. "You said there were two reasons why Amelia took a new identity. What was the second?"

"The second reason she wanted to keep a low profile, at least at the beginning, was because she knew the center depended on Lawson's funding," Isabel explained. "She was afraid that if he discovered she intended to go into competition with him, he would cut off the money."

"Which is exactly what he would have done," Ellis said knowingly. "Lawson doesn't take kindly to rivals and competitors, inside or outside the government bureaucracy."

Isabel nodded. "Yes, well, just imagine Amelia-Maureen's surprise when, after she went to all the trouble to seduce Randolph and get rid of his father, one of Randolph's first official acts was to fire me. She knew that without me, Lawson would quickly lose interest in funding the institute."

"But she had to be careful about how much she told Randolph," Ellis said. "She didn't want him to understand the real connection between the institute and Lawson's operation any more than Lawson did. She wanted to stay in the shadows. She certainly did not want Lawson to discover that his ex-lover had changed her name and was about to become the person who would be manipulating one of his most vital assets: Isabel."

"Hah." Isabel was incensed. "What made her think I could be so easily manipulated?"

"It was a big mistake on her part," Ellis assured her. "In fact, it was the one that led to her downfall. Because after you took off for Roxanna Beach, everything went wrong for her again."

"Very true," Vincent agreed. "Before she could figure out how to get you back, Gavin Hardy disappeared. She knew he must have found something interesting on Belvedere's computer. She reasoned that it probably had to do with the anonymous clients."

Isabel made a face. "She must have freaked when she realized that you were one of them."

"She sure did." Vincent swallowed more orange juice. "I made the mistake of telling her I had contacted Dr. Belvedere personally. I probably blabbed about the meetings with him after one of those extra-heavy doses of CZ-149. At any rate, not only was she really angry, she was afraid that if you and Cutler discovered that there were *three* anonymous clients, Cutler would start asking even more questions and maybe conclude that I was Number Three." He looked at Ellis. "As you just said, Cutler, it's a small world when it comes to extreme dreamers."

"She had good cause to be worried," Isabel said. "Ellis did jump to the conclusion that you were the third client."

Vincent exhaled wearily and picked up his tea. "I didn't realize that she murdered Hardy. She never told me that part."

"Of course not," Isabel said soothingly. She moved another tall stack of toast onto the tray at the bottom of the oven to keep warm. "She didn't want you to find out she was killing people because she knew that you were, at heart, still one of the good guys."

Vincent's hungover expression eased a little. He looked at Ellis. "I take it there is no next-generation version of CZ-149?"

"No," Ellis said. "Lawson killed the program."

"Yeah, well, what can I say?" Vincent shrugged. "I believed the doc. I was pretty damn desperate by then."

"Desperate enough to contact Dr. B. secretly," Isabel said, setting plates of scrambled eggs, soy sausages and toast in front of each man. "I take it he couldn't help you, though."

"Useless." Vincent perked up at the sight of the massive quantity of food. He grabbed his fork. "Like I said last night, all he could tell me was that the red tsunami was a blocking image of some kind. I had already figured out that much for myself."

Dave tried a bite of eggs. "What was last night all about? I mean, aside from getting rid of the three of you?"

"It's obvious from her dream log that Amelia-Maureen was nothing if not adaptable." Ellis ate some toast. "She changed her plans to fit the changing circumstances. Her goal last night was to set the stage at the amusement park to make it look like Scargill and I had both gone mad. She picked the Roxanna Beach Amusement World because she knew that my gateway dream involves a roller coaster. It was no big secret back at Frey-Salter. She assumed that using that backdrop would help convince Lawson that I really had fallen victim to a weird obsession of some kind."

"She intended for everyone, including Lawson and his rivals, to believe that you two killed each other and burned down the old park, taking me and an innocent bystander, Yolland, with us," Isabel concluded.

"Even if that plan didn't have the effect of destroying Lawson's personal empire, it would certainly have created enormous problems for him," Vincent pointed out. "She would have, in effect, cost Lawson three of his best dreamers — Ellis, me, and you, Isabel."

"Make that four dreamers," Dave said in a flat voice. "She also killed my sister, remember. Katherine was a Level Five, too."

There was a short, heavy silence.

Vincent looked at him. "I'm sorry about Katherine," he said quietly. "I really liked her. I swear I had no idea that Amelia had contacted her using my game-playing identity, convinced her to bug Lawson's phone and then murdered her in cold blood."

"Katherine left a clue," Dave said quietly. "Ellis and I assumed initially that it was a message telling us that you were the killer. But we misinterpreted it."

"That was the one murder we know of that Amelia-Maureen handled personally," Ellis said. "According to her dream log, she couldn't locate an ex-con from the Brackleton program in the Raleigh-Durham area and she didn't want to waste any time importing one."

"So she shot Katherine in cold blood, herself," Dave whispered.

Ellis looked at him. "In those last moments of her life, Katherine was thinking very fast and very clearly, like the trained agent she was." His words were rough with genuine admiration. "She couldn't find a way to tell us the name of her killer but she knew that if we kept looking for you, Vincent, we'd find Amelia-Maureen. So she pointed us toward you."

"She was right," Isabel said quietly.

Ellis kept his attention centered on Dave. "Katherine is the one who will become a legend back at Frey-Salter."

Dave blinked quickly several times. Moisture glinted in his eyes. Then he nodded, not speaking.

Isabel poured more tea into his mug.

Thoughtfully, she set the pot down. "Did she ever suggest that you apply for a job at Frey-Salter, Dave?"

Everyone looked at her. Dave was the only one who understood. He smiled wryly.

"Sure." He ate some toast. "She thought I might like the work. She was probably right. But I'm not a huge fan of rules and regulations and all the rest of the hassle that goes along with a job in government."

Ellis lowered his fork, frowning. "Are you telling us that you're a Level Five?"

"Uh-huh." Dave cautiously cut a slice of soy sausage with his fork and examined it with a wary expression.

Ellis looked at Isabel. "How did you know?"

"When Dave mentioned that he and Katherine were twins, I assumed there was a very high probability," she said modestly.

Ellis laughed. "Lawson is going to fall all over himself trying to convince you to work for him, Dave."

"Maybe I'll think about it," Dave said slowly, thoughtfully.

Vincent reached for another slice of toast. "I know I'm not exactly a poster boy for Frey-Salter at the moment, but the truth is, I really liked the work and there weren't many rules and regs because

Lawson pretty much runs the place his way." He hesitated in mid-bite and exhaled heavily. "Guess I'll be job hunting now, though."

"Nope," Isabel said with great assurance. "Lawson will take you back in a heartbeat."

"Why would he do that?" Vincent picked up the bottle of anti-inflammatories Isabel had placed beside his plate and shook out two tablets. "He probably thinks I was an idiot to fall for Amelia's pitch."

"You were not an idiot," Isabel said firmly. "You were just very eager to prove yourself against the older, alpha male of the group."

Vincent and Dave looked at Ellis.

"Yeah, him," Isabel said. "It's a common syndrome among young men who are moving up fast."

"That so?" Vincent asked, popping the pills into his mouth. "I'm glad to hear that because I gotta tell you, in hindsight, it sure looks like maybe I was an idiot."

"You were an idiot," Ellis agreed. "But don't worry, you'll get past it."

Vincent did not appear convinced. "Lawson's gotta be pissed at me."

"Sure," Ellis said. "He'll chew you out some. But here's a tip from an old pro on how to deal with Jack Lawson: Always know when you are holding an ace and never hesitate to play it when necessary."

Vincent frowned. "I've got an ace?"

"Lawson was an even bigger idiot than you were when it came to Maureen Sage, alias Amelia," Ellis reminded him softly. "And he didn't have any excuses. He was old enough to know better than to sleep with a member of his own research staff."

"Oh, right." Vincent brightened. "Thanks."

"No problem," Ellis said. "Now you owe me. That's how it works."

Vincent grinned weakly. "Got it."

"I have a few more questions," Isabel said. "The first is for Ellis." She looked at him. "I understand that you and Dave traded cars somewhere along the way last night. How did that work?"

"Dave got into his rented Chevy and drove like a bat out of hell until we rendezvoused," Ellis said. "I told Amelia that I had to stop for a stop sign. That's when Dave and I made the switch. He kept driving the Maserati at a nice, sedate speed. I got into his rental."

"And drove like a bat out of hell for Roxanna Beach," Dave concluded. "He had the phone so every time Amelia called him to check up on him he could give her an answer. To be honest, I'm amazed he could get that kind of speed out of that Chevy."

"On those roads and with that fog, I didn't need a hundred and seventy-six miles an hour," Ellis said.

Dave and Vincent watched him expectantly.

"So how much did you need?" Vincent prompted.

Ellis shrugged. "A hundred, hundred and ten on the straight stretches was good enough."

"But the fog," Isabel gasped, horrified. "How could you see?"

"I drove that route once before," Ellis said soothingly. "I told you that when I drive, I pay attention. Besides, there was no traffic last night."

She winced. "Because of the *fog*."

"Yeah, that helped," he admitted.

"You know, there's something really scary about a guy who actually doesn't have to stop and ask for directions. Okay, what about the wire cutters? How did you get those?"

"Farrell brought them with him. I called him right after I got off the phone with Dave. He met me a short distance from the amusement park. I took the cutters and told him to come in through the front gate when I gave the all clear. He's also the one who found out that there was still electricity running into the park. That was when we came up with the idea of starting up one of the rides as a distraction."

"Brilliant," Isabel said. "Any idea why Amelia-Maureen arranged to have my furniture torched?"

"According to her dream log, someone at the institute mentioned how much you loved it and how you kept it in a self-storage locker," Ellis said. "She also heard that you had moved it to Roxanna Beach. She realized how expensive it was and how strapped for cash you were. She decided that if you took a major financial hit, you'd be a lot more amenable to the offer of a big pay raise and your old office at the center."

Isabel groaned and told herself to let that go, too. She bent to scrape some scrambled egg off her plate into Sphinx's bowl. "Question number two is for Vincent." She glanced at him. "Last night when you and I were alone inside the concession stand, talking about your tsunami dream, what was it I said that convinced you to trust me instead of Amelia-Maureen? I mean, I know I have an honest face and I can talk pretty fast when necessary, but I got the feeling it wasn't just my logic and sweet smile that made you believe me."

Vincent watched Sphinx jump down from the windowsill and pad across the kitchen to check out the eggs.

"I think it was the cat," he said quietly.

"Sphinx?" Isabel straightened. "What did he have to do with anything?"

Everyone watched Sphinx settle down to enjoy his breakfast.

"The doc told me how you rescued Martin Belvedere's old cat after Randolph ordered it to be taken to the pound and destroyed. She thought it was a really stupid thing for you to do. It was one of the things that made her think you would be easy to manipulate."

"Nice to know I made such a great professional impression," Isabel grumbled.

"Last night, while you and I were talking and I was fighting off the effects of the last dose of CZ-149, for some reason I kept thinking about how you saved the cat," Vincent said. He stopped, as if he had explained everything, and went back to his food.

"I still don't get it," Isabel said. "Why did that make you decide to trust me instead of her?"

"I may have been doped up most of the time that I spent around the doc," Vincent said softly, "but that doesn't mean I didn't figure out a few things about her. I knew that if she had been in your shoes, she would have let Sphinx go to the pound."

Ellis looked at him. "I take it you like cats?"

"Yeah," Vincent said. "I like cats."

42

"The good news is that Ellis is okay." Jack Lawson relaxed into the squeaky government-issue chair and propped his ankles on the corner of his old, battered desk. "He wasn't obsessing on some twisted Level Five dream, after all."

"He was right about Vincent Scargill being alive," Beth agreed on the other end of the connection. "I'm delighted to know that. I always liked Vince. But it would have been a hell of a lot more convenient if you had picked up on the Maureen Sage –Amelia Netley link a little sooner."

"Now, honey —"

"I told you that woman was trouble."

"I know, I should have listened to you," Lawson said, going for humble because it was his only hope.

"What's the bad news?" Beth asked.

"Actually, there isn't any bad news today. There is good news and there is more good news."

"And the more good news would be?"

"Got a new recruit." Lawson looked out

his office window to where Vincent Scargill stood talking with Dave Ralston, showing him around Frey-Salter. "Katherine's brother is a Level Five and it seems he's decided to become a full-fledged agent of Frey-Salter. Ellis tells me he's a natural."

"Ellis would know. Congratulations." Beth sounded like she meant it.

"There are a couple of bits of less than terrific news."

"I knew it. Let's have 'em."

"Ellis just informed me that I'm going to have to cover the cost of a lot of high-quality furniture that got torched in the course of the investigation," he complained. "Got any idea how much furniture costs these days?"

"A lot," Beth said.

"I was afraid of that."

"What's the other not-so-good news?" she asked.

"My new Level Five dream analyst consultant insists that I keep the Belvedere Center for Sleep Research in operation. Isabel says she doesn't want to be responsible for the entire staff being thrown out of work. So I have had to come up with a plan to buy out Randolph Belvedere. It's a real pain in the ass because it means setting up another phony corporate front to make the purchase and operate the facility. Going to be expensive, too."

"Stop grumbling. It's petty cash for you. What are you going to use the center for now that Isabel isn't there?"

"I've been thinking that I can use it to run a variety of sleep research projects," he mused.

"All of which will be camouflage to cover your hunt for more Level Fives, right?"

"It's what I do, babe."

"And you do it so well."

She seemed to be in a good mood. He probably wasn't going to get a better shot. He took his feet off the desk and leaned forward a little, belly tightening.

"I was thinking, maybe we could have dinner together to celebrate all this good news," he said. "Maybe try that new Italian place? Invest in a bottle of bubbly? On me, naturally."

"You mean on your expense account."

"If it bothers you, I'll put it on my private plastic," he said quickly.

"Okay, I'm starting to be impressed."

"Well?" He held his breath.

There was a long pause on Beth's end of the line.

"Dinner sounds like a good idea," she

said eventually. "But I feel like eating at home tonight."

She was coming back to him at last.

Lawson knew he was grinning like a fool but he didn't give a damn. "I'll bring the champagne."

43

Ellis opened the door of Farrell's office, walked into the room and closed it behind him.

Farrell looked up from some papers on his desk. When he saw Ellis, he put the gold pen down with careful precision and sat back in his chair. Ellis could almost see him bracing himself for the worst.

"Well?" Farrell said.

Ellis tossed a file onto the desk. "In my professional opinion, you're in trouble but the hole isn't too deep yet. Still time to dig yourself out. You're in the classic spiral caused by rapid growth and overexpansion. You're going to have to pull back and restructure your debt but the situation is manageable."

Farrell still looked startled, as if he had been prepared for other news altogether. "It is?"

"Yes." Ellis dropped into one of the black leather chairs. "As far as the debt restructuring goes, I know some people."

Farrell cranked back in his chair. "Can I

dare to hope that these people are not sitting, nor have they ever sat, inside a federal pen?"

"They're legitimate investors." Ellis spread his hands. "Why does everyone assume I'm either a cop or that I've got criminal connections?"

"Beats me. Maybe it's the dark glasses. People who wear them indoors make other people nervous."

"Huh. Never thought of that." Ellis removed his sunglasses and tucked them into the pocket of his shirt. "That better?"

Farrell studied him for a couple of seconds. "No."

"Forget the glasses. Let's get back to your problem. The biggest decision you have to make is whether or not to return to basics. My advice is to follow the Kyler Method philosophy. Stay focused. Stop trying to be all things to all people and remember Kyler Method Rule Number Five: If you chase every trend that comes along, you end up chasing your own tail."

Farrell contemplated the file that Ellis had put on the desk. "Got any idea how it feels to have your own advice quoted back to you?"

Ellis smiled. "It's good advice."

Farrell exhaled slowly. "You really think

I can save my business?"

"Sure. You just got a little off course for a while, that's all."

"You mean like when I started offering classes such as 'Tapping into the Creative Potential of Your Dreams'?"

"Good example."

"I can't afford you." Farrell rubbed his temples. "You probably know that."

"You've got it backward," Ellis said. "I'm the one who owes you for what you did the other night at the amusement park."

"Isabel is family." Farrell's mouth quirked. "What else could I do?"

"You could have asked a lot of questions that I didn't have time to answer."

"There's a time for questions," Farrell said. "That night wasn't the time."

"No. But not everyone would have understood that."

"I trusted you because I knew that Isabel trusted you," Farrell replied.

"Thanks."

Farrell sat for a moment, his eyes on the blue expanse of the bay. "I didn't want to be just successful with the Kyler Method, you know. Every time I thought about Leila, I wanted to be incredibly successful. I wanted to outdo her father. I thought that was what she wanted. It was Isabel who finally brought me up short."

"How did she do that?"

"She reminded me of what Leila really wanted."

Ellis reflected on that. "Isabel is good at figuring out what motivates people."

Farrell studied him with a considering expression. "Which brings me to another subject."

"What's that?"

"Your motivations in connection with Isabel. Leila is still a little nervous about the fact that you might be using her in some way."

Ellis clamped his hands around the arms of his chair and shoved himself to his feet. "Tell Leila that Isabel and I will soon be making a major investment together."

"Bad idea," Farrell said dryly. "In case you haven't heard, Isabel quit her job here at Kyler. She doesn't have any money. Leila and I will try to help her out with paying off the furniture that got destroyed, but frankly, we don't have much spare cash ourselves at the moment. And I know for a fact that Isabel won't go to her parents for help."

Ellis went to the door. "She won't need any financial assistance from her family. She's got two new clients. One of them has very deep pockets."

"My tax dollars at work again?"

Ellis smiled. "We plan to buy a house and new furniture to go with it. We're thinking Spanish colonial."

"Does this mean marriage?"

Ellis opened the door. "It does."

"Fine by me." Farrell raised his brows. "But some people — the other members of Isabel's family come to mind — will feel obliged to point out that you and Isabel haven't known each other very long."

Isabel appeared in the hall. She looked past Ellis and smiled at Farrell.

"I just had this conversation with Leila and Tamsyn," she said. "I'll tell you the same thing I told them. Don't worry, Ellis and I have been meeting secretly for months."

"Yeah?" Farrell asked, skeptical. "Where?"

Isabel put her arms around Ellis and kissed him. His eyes heated and he kissed her back, taking his time about it.

She looked at Farrell and winked.

"In our dreams," she said.

44

Two months later, Ellis led Isabel out onto the floor of the Kyler Method, Inc., reception room and took her into his arms for the first dance of their married life.

A hush fell across the wedding guests. Everyone turned to look at the couple. Ellis did look terrific in a tux, Isabel thought, amused and proud. But then, she had known he would. Hadn't she dressed him just this way in some of her dreams?

"You are very beautiful, Mrs. Cutler," Ellis whispered. "I do not have the words to tell you how much I love you. But I do love you and I will for the rest of my life and beyond."

"You are the most handsome man in the world, Mr. Cutler, and I love you with all my heart." She laughed with joy and delight, happier than she had ever been in her life. "Although I must admit that I was a tad disappointed when I discovered that you had decided not to wear your dark glasses for the ceremony."

"Don't worry, I've got them handy." He

grinned, "I may need them later on tonight if you are still glowing the way you are now."

The musicians launched into a traditional waltz and Ellis swung her into the first slow, gliding turn. The skirts of her elegant satin gown flowed out behind her in gleaming waves the color of candlelight.

She caught sight of Jack Lawson and Beth standing at the edge of the crowd. They were talking to Tamsyn and Ron Chapman. Vincent and Dave stood with a group of people from the Belvedere Center for Sleep Research. Leila and Farrell smiled from the other side of the room. Leila's eyes glowed with the secret of her very new pregnancy.

"To think this all started because Jack Lawson sent you to recruit me for Frey-Salter," Isabel murmured.

"That was just an excuse, as far as I was concerned. I never thought that sending you back into a lab was a good idea."

"I got the impression that your recruitment efforts on Lawson's behalf were somewhat halfhearted, to say the least."

"You're a tango dancer," Ellis said. "You were born to be out in the world." He tightened his hold on her waist. "With me."

"Remember that day on the terrace outside the café when I had lunch with Ian Jarrow and he tried to talk me into returning to the center?"

"I'm not likely to forget it." His eyes narrowed faintly. "I was worried as hell that he might try to talk you back into his bed as well as back into your old office."

"I was never in his bed. That's what we were discussing when you showed up, in fact. Ian had just informed me that our relationship failed because of me, not because of him. He claimed I made all sorts of excuses to avoid intimacy." She tilted her head a little to the side, smiling. "He was right."

Ellis raised his brows. "Not your type?"

"No," she said. "I knew even then that I was waiting for the man of my dreams."

About the Author

Jayne Ann Krentz is the author of forty *New York Times* bestsellers. She has written contemporary romantic suspense novels under that name, as well as futuristic and historical romance novels under the pseudonyms Jayne Castle and Amanda Quick, respectively. She lives in Seattle. Visit her website at www.jayneannkrentz.com.